THIS LAND IS NO STRANGER

ISBN: 978-91-89141-16-2
Printed and distributed through Amazon KDP

Sarah Hollister
Gil Reavill

THIS
LAND
IS NO
STRANGER

A Nordic Thriller

(L(Y)S)

veronikabrand.com

I am a stranger in this land
but this land is no stranger within me

Gunnar Ekelöf

Finally there was only a last remaining flame to die. The abuse heaped upon the girl, the blows raining down on her, the pain, the gagging stench, the humiliation, the disgust—she felt it less and less. But one flickering light wouldn't leave her, a single hope that still burned when all others guttered.

A hope born of hopelessness. She had nothing left to lose. Only that tiny light, a wavering pinprick that she refused to give up.

Someone must know.

It was impossible. Cellphones were banned in the barracks in the forest. Of course. When one of the girls was caught with one, the men used a pair of bolt cutters to remove her fingers. Paper, pens, writing implements of any kind, communication of any kind, all forbidden—it was if they had stitched up her lips. She was silenced, muted, untongued.

The blind room, she named the foul, closet-sized cell where they kept her. No one could see in, no one could see out. What happened in the blind room went on out of sight, out of mind. The door opened and closed, making a crazy scraping sound. One man left, another entered. The scraping chafed upon her nerves like a dull knife.

She moved her fingers in the darkness, tracing words in the blank air. I was here, she spelled out. This happened.

Then the crippled old crone who fed the girl scraps, washed her when the men's filth coated the girl's skin, the nameless old woman, gruff and rough-handed, mostly mute herself, listened. Or not. The girl couldn't tell. She couldn't read the face of the other. Was it the girl's own hope reflected there, like the light of the moon, which has no light of its own, but only shines with radiance from elsewhere?

My family, she whispered to the old woman. Please. I need them to know.

Earning a sneer and wave of a hand, as if she were a fly buzzing.

She lied to the crone. My mother. My father. I have a sister. Please. The girl's cracked lips moved almost soundlessly.

Nothing. No glimmer of understanding, reflected or otherwise.

She would die. She stopped eating. Still the men would come. It didn't matter to her anymore. Her ordeal was almost over.

On her last day but one, a miracle. The crone, her face twisted in fear, brought her a bar of chocolate wrapped in paper and tinfoil. A hoarse whisper: "Give me the wrapper when you are done." Was there a knowing expression on the old woman's face? The girl couldn't tell. If there was one, it was lost amid the depthless wrinkles.

The girl bit off her nail, an already shredded, barely there fingernail, and used it as a pen. Melted chocolate stood for ink. Scratching out words no one would ever read.

Someone must know. I am lost. They stole me from the streets of Stockholm. A man with a black beard. This they did to me. And this. I am used up and have become useless to them. Tomorrow I will deny them the pleasure of murdering me. Someone must know what happens here.

Signing the forgotten name, the one they had torn from her.

Lel.

The crone came and took the wrapper away, crumpling it up as though it were trash. The girl never saw the old woman again.

Part one: The wandering bride

Songs are just words
For those who are bitter to sing
They sing to rid themselves of bitterness
But the bitterness does not go away

Loring M. Danforth, Death Rituals of Rural Greece

I

Scandinavian Airlines Flight SK904 approached Stockholm's Arlanda airport after an eight-hour trans-Atlantic journey from Newark. The red-eye left Veronika Brand thoroughly exhausted. She had not slept. Most of the other passengers took advantage of the long trip to check out, sleep masks in place. She felt alone in the darkened cabin. She hoped at least someone in the cockpit remained awake.

Tall, light-haired, thirty nine years old, Brand had no doubts about fitting in with the native population of Sweden. It was the land of her ancestors, at least on her mother's side of the family, the Dalgrens. She had never before visited. Whatever bits and pieces she knew of the language had come from summers spent with her Swedish immigrant grandparents, who kept a farm in upstate New York. In her own mind, the affinity with the country was more theoretical than real.

Brand had found herself on a plane to Stockholm because of a series of unconnected events that had happened within a space of a few weeks back home.

Home. New York, well, New York was part of the problem. She had to get out. Recently her career as a New York City police detective had cratered spectacularly. Due to a chain of bad choices involving politically connected figures in the NYPD, she had been suspended after fourteen years on the force.

At the same time her job troubles were happening, Brand's speed habit kicked itself up a few notches. She'd been juggling multiple Adderall scripts at once, as well as occasionally skimming off pills seized in drug busts. The medication was ubiquitous, overprescribed, used legally and illicitly. An addict always imagines other addicts are everywhere. To Brand the whole NYPD, from the brass to the file clerks, seemed jacked up on speed like a corps of Nazi blitzkriegers. Amphetamine made for a very energetic style of policing.

On a bleak afternoon on Manhattan's Upper West Side, she had experienced a stark, crossing-the-line moment with her pill habit. It was finals week for local high school students. Brand knew the little privileged brats would be well supplied with meds for their study sessions. She braced a half dozen teens on Columbus Avenue, cleaned out their backpacks for baggies of Addy, then sent them on their way with a kick in the pants.

Standing there in the weak winter sunshine, counting her confiscated beans, she spilled a few onto the sidewalk. Instantly she was on her knees scrambling to scoop them up. As her knuckles scraped the cold concrete, Brand suddenly stopped, realizing it was all too much. Tears welled in her eyes. Lately she had been reduced to three modes of being: drunk, tweaked, or weeping. Job troubles exacerbated her pill habit, and vice versa. She was spiraling down, but she couldn't stop.

One final development had sent her flying out of Newark to Sweden, hurtling over the Atlantic Ocean in the dark. As she parked her suspended ass in her lonely Murray Hill apartment, feeling shell shocked amid the smoking ruins of her life, her cell phone rang. The number displayed indicated a foreign caller. Aware of various phone scams that were proliferating, she told herself not to answer. She would never know why she did.

The voice came through in Swedish. The caller sounded older than old. The words didn't belong on a telephone, but on a wax cylinder. The voice of god, provided god was a woman. It spoke a cadence of syllables that Brand didn't understand.

"*Du måste komma hit. Jag har en hemlighet som du måste se.*"

The tone was hoarse and insistent. Foreign on the one hand and somehow naggingly familiar on the other. Brand puzzled out what she could. *Du måste komma hit.* "You have to come here." *Hemlighet?* What was that? "Something at home?"

"I'm sorry, um, I don't speak…"

The person on the other end of the line stammered in frustration. "*Kom hit!*" she rasped, then, in accented English, a command: "Come here!"

The line went dead. Brand tried to figure it out. What had just happened? The phone was still in her hand when it rang again.

Another, different voice, a little sunnier. "Hello, is this Veronika Brand?" Brand had been hearing an ancient oak tree. Now here was the breeze whistling through the leaves.

The second voice was that of her second cousin, Sanna Dalgren. Veronika knew her. The two had met briefly a single time, over coffee during a tourist visit Sanna had made to New York City. Brand had cut short the meeting, pleading work pressures, but in truth had felt unnerved by her foreign cousin's unflinching gaze. Since then she had been included in Sanna's pointless family emails, all in Swedish which Brand had little interest in translating. She left the communications mostly unanswered, and vaguely considered blocking them.

Sanna identified the person Brand had heard initially as the clan's matriarch, Elin Dalgren. The sister of Brand's grandfather, the woman would soon turn ninety-five years old. Sanna informed Brand that Elin Dalgren wanted especially to invite the American detective to her upcoming birthday celebration.

"You've never met," Sanna said.

"No," Brand responded. "I didn't quite get the Swedish. It sounded as though it were something like an emergency."

Her cousin gave a musical laugh. "Oh, no, nothing like that. *Mamma* said she had some family secrets to tell you. Probably cake recipes."

Sanna Dalgren told Brand Elin's ninety-fifth birthday would be the occasion of a family reunion. "We would love to invite you over here to meet your Swedish relatives."

Just when New York City had turned radioactive on her, the phone call from her relatives offered Brand an escape. She didn't really want to go. What she wanted to do was lock the door of her Manhattan apartment, climb into bed and pull the covers over her head. When she gazed into her immediate future, she saw disciplinary hearings, cold shoulders in the precinct house, perhaps media coverage, public disgrace.

She didn't really believe any of the powerfully connected cops she had gone up against would have the stones to move against her physically. But the possibility couldn't be discounted entirely. Walking the streets of Manhattan, she found herself checking her back. In the past few weeks a faint whiff of danger had marked her days. Her enemies were high up in the NYPD hierarchy. They could sink her.

The situation was untenable. Brand felt uncertain whether her Swedish escapade was a flying to or a fleeing from. She couldn't shake the suspicion she was attempting a geographical cure for her professional difficulties. But she also continued to hear the urgency in an old woman's voice, a summons that sounded as though it came from the edge of the grave.

So, Sweden. At 9:30 in the morning local time, on the day after she had left New York, the Scandinavian Airlines plane swung into its glide path. Brand heard somewhere that air travelers came in three types, window seats for dreamers, aisle seats for achievers, middle seats for the passive and hapless. Though she had an aisle seat for the flight, she felt misplaced. She didn't know where she fit. Out on the wing, perhaps?

Through the windows opposite appeared glimpses of the landscape below, not the expected winter wonderland but a dour countryside of sullen, February gray. Sunlight seemed to be having some difficulty punching through to the earth.

The cabin lights came on and everywhere around her the dead awakened. Brand experienced the moment of landing as a snapping back into a real-world ho-hum perspective after the magic of flight.

The plane taxied to the gate. Her fellow passengers listened for the chime and watched for the seatbelt light to go off, then jumped to their feet like a collection of jack-in-the-boxes. They began aggressively flipping open the storage spaces over their seats, hauling out their luggage and claiming a place in the line to disembark.

Slinging her carry-on over her shoulder, Brand exited the plane. The Arlanda terminal seemed almost eerily empty of people. She reunited with her duffel bag at baggage claim, then proceeded to customs. Brand was well aware her baggage contained items of contraband that could land her into trouble. That included a baggie of evidence-room Adderall she had filched in New York. She would just have to bull her way through. In the face of authority she prided herself on maintaining an absolute, dead-eyed calm. Approaching customs she could have been hooked up to a heart-rate monitor without seeing a blip.

A uniformed agent motioned Brand over. The woman had curly brown hair and to Brand's eyes looked vaguely un-Swedish.

"Could you please remove your head covering?" the agent asked in perfect English.

Brand took off her black knit watch cap. She offered the agent both her U.S. passport and her NYPD badge wallet.

"Just the passport," the agent directed. But the move had its effect. Brand thought she detected a glimmer of respect in the young woman's eyes. "You're a police officer?"

"A detective, yes," Brand said.

"How long is your stay in Sweden?" she asked.

"A week." A white lie. Her plans were open-ended. Brand didn't know how long she'd be in the country.

"The reason for your visit? You're not on a criminal case, are you?"

"No, no," Brand said. "A family reunion."

The agent broke her official manner to smile broadly. "You have relatives here? Where will you be staying?"

"Um, I don't know how to say it exactly. Härjedalen? I think it's a county or, they call it a *kommun*? Somewhere named Jämtland, I think? I can get the address."

The agent gave a negative shake of her head. "It is also called a *landskap*," she said helpfully. The agent released the strap on the duffel bag and lifted the first few items from their tightly packed home. The agent's non-committal glance inside went no further and the depths of Brand's duffel remained unsearched.

"Ask your family why in the world they scheduled a get-together in Sweden in February," the agent said, releasing the duffel back to Brand with a smile. "Enjoy your visit."

The halls of the Arlanda terminal were filled with large mirrors. Brand caught a view of herself in one of them. She winced at how much of a stereotypical New Yorker she appeared: black sweatshirt, black jeans, black boots. As if there were no other color in the universe. She had recently chopped her blonde hair short, and wondered if she made for an ominous figure. The Grim Reaper. She almost laughed. All she lacked was a scythe.

Cored out as Brand was, her journey wasn't over. She had a six-hour car trip ahead of her. Lukas Dalgren, one of Brand's countless second cousins, had arranged to pick her up at Arlanda. He and his family would immediately bring Brand to the clan's homestead in western Sweden, near the border to Norway. In the flurry of emails prior to the trip, she had pleaded to be allowed a stopover at a hotel, for a day of rest or even two, to give herself a chance to decompress. The dates wouldn't make sense if that was the plan, she was told.

"You will sleep on the drive," Sanna Dalgren informed Brand in an email message. Brand had immediately regretted agreeing to come to Elin Dalgren's birthday celebration. Her arrival became an event. A "homecoming," Sanna termed it.

Marshaled by her cousin, the extended Dalgren clan had started bustling around, organizing, planning, scheduling. Brand came to understand she was more well-known among them than they were to her. She was a New York City police detective. Like on television.

"We told her you are coming from America in honor of her birthday," Sanna wrote to Brand in an email. "We know you don't want to disappoint her. Your visit is something *mamma* lives for."

The whole concept of cousinage left Brand a bit cold. She never saw herself as much of a family type of girl. She wasn't even a Dalgren. She was a Brand. There were issues between herself and her own mother, Marta, who had been born a Dalgren, and with her maternal grandparents, Klara and Gustav. Hints of estrangement between branches of the family, unspoken but real, hovered in the background.

As directed, Brand was to meet cousin Lukas outside the terminal. They would coordinate via text exchanges. But as soon as she emerged from the terminal she realized the plan would not come off. Her phone refused to recognize the Stockholm cell networks offered to it. No signal, no texts, no calls.

Secretly she felt relieved. She would check into a hotel, get a good night's sleep, pick up her family responsibilities tomorrow. Rent a car, drive herself.

The airport's public address system had been periodically spitting out unrecognizable phrases in Swedish. She heard her own name pronounced in clear unaccented English.

"Veronika Brand, please meet your party in the passenger pick-up area. Veronika Brand, please meet your party in the passenger pick-up area."

Brand found herself standing among other milling travelers in, yes, the passenger pick-up area. But where was Lukas?

A few traffic lanes away a young male stood with a phone cocked to his ear. His head was shaved clean. The two of them caught each other's eye at the same instant. Lukas Dalgren put his cellphone in his pocket. He raised a hand in greeting.

"*Hallå*, Veronika," he called out. He wore an expensive mid-length brown cashmere overcoat and narrow, elegantly cut trousers. He stood beside a midnight silver Tesla sedan.

Brand crossed to him, slipping slightly on the frozen roadway of the air terminal. Her cousin moved forward.

"Black ice, Veronika," he said. "Be careful. Your shoes are wrong."

My shoes are wrong? Brand wore flat-soled slouch boots.

"You need some more like mine." The man's footwear featured deep, serious-looking treads. "I should ask now how was your flight? I'm taking a class in American-style small talk," he explained sheepishly.

The trunk of the Tesla magically opened without any obvious push of a button on Lukas's part. Brand hefted in her duffel bag herself. She noticed the car held no passengers. She searched her mind for the names of Lukas's wife and children. Her memory proved too fogged to function.

"Isabella and the girls went separately," he said.

The two of them experienced an awkward moment as they both approached the driver's side door of the sedan. "Okay if I drive?" Brand asked.

The request stopped Lukas Dalgren cold. He halted mid-step, like a cartoon character.

"You drive? But it is my car."

"I get terribly car-sick unless I am behind the wheel," Brand explained. "Do you mind?"

Brand could see at once that Lukas did indeed mind. "You are exhausted from the flight," he said. "You don't want to fall asleep while driving."

"I slept on the plane," Brand lied. She wondered if she looked as worn out as she felt.

"I'd rather you do not drive," Lukas said firmly. "The vehicle is brand new."

"Then you probably don't want me to vomit inside it," Brand said. They stood facing each other in front of the driver's side door.

"I did not expect this," Lukas said, exasperated.

"I can go ahead and rent my own car, if you prefer." Brand wondered if this would be possible. She didn't have an international driver's license. Was one necessary in order to get a rental car in Sweden? She didn't know. Lukas Dalgren looked as though his gleaming, polished head might explode.

"It's okay." Brand spoke softly. The technique was one she had picked up in her former life as a street cop, two simple words uttered confidently and directly but in a quiet, non-confrontational undertone. Pronounced the right way, the phrase brought everyone back to earth. She had employed the strategy often to defuse explosive situations.

"How will you know where to go?" Lukas asked. His manner resembled that of a petulant child.

"You'll tell me," Brand said.

Heaving a theatrical sigh, Lukas offered up the expensive vehicle's key fob.

2

A cold day to sit motionless on a tarmac sidewalk, thought Jonas Nordin. An absent sun, a February sky the color of wet wool.

Nordin worked as a security guard at the front entrance to Åhléns, the big Stockholm department store. Almost daily, a Romani beggar posted himself across the street from Nordin's own station. The beggar's method of eliciting coins from passersby involved planting himself on the pavement, swaddled in a heavy blanket, a dirty paper cup in front of him. He would remain unmoving like that for hours.

The poor wretch was probably dreaming of the cloudless blue heavens of his childhood in Romania. Now he found himself plopped down on freezing Drottninggatan, a busy shopping street in the heart of the Swedish capital.

Our modern world, thought Nordin. A marvel and a mess.

He attempted one of the empathy exercises suggested by the self-improvement programs to which he was addicted. Nordin focused on the unimaginable journey that had led the foreign mendicant across Europe from where his life began. The exercise failed. Other thoughts kept intruding, wicked, narrow-minded opinions.

Nordin knew he should think as a good sympathetic person would. He believed in an open and welcoming Sweden. His spiritual beliefs centered on the equality of souls. But a deep-seated impulse in his mind wished the beggar would simply vanish. A turd on the sidewalk, whispered his prejudice, which he found impossible to damp down entirely. Sweep it up and throw it in the trash.

The beggar-person was actually familiar to him. He even knew the unfortunate soul's name, Luri Kováč. Attempting to behave like an upstanding Swedish citizen toward the less privileged, Nordin had reached out. Several times he brought Luri cups of hot chocolate, or water in the hot summers. But still some part of Nordin wished him away.

A second Romani beggar posted nearby summoned up a much different response. Nordin knew her name, too. Varzha Luna held a particular fascination for him. The girl embraced a more theatrical approach than the sidewalk lump across the street. She made for an arresting sight. Varzha always wore whiteface makeup, always dressed in the same snow-white wedding gown.

Normally she stayed as motionless as the other one. Nordin saw her often in her spot on the street, bride of stone, bride of none. The girl might be beautiful if only she would remove her makeup, since otherwise her face remained lost behind an impenetrable disguise. No one would stop for her, Nordin noticed. No one paid the least attention. The pedestrians passed by, eyeless and heartless, unseeing and unfeeling, their shopping bags bouncing alongside beside their well-toned thighs.

But then, two or three times every hour, the girl roused herself. In a sweet, pure voice, she would sing the popular Romani songs of love and pain. The one Varzha Luna began now was a modern carol left over from the Christmas season.

Open the door, oh wandering bride of Christ
Long have I wearied and far have I come

She always went accompanied by a sidekick. Her feeble-minded twin brother Vago stood beside his sister Varzha. He played a child-size violin that was too small for him, scratching out the song's melody. Dressed in loose, harlequin-style pajamas, Vago also wore whiteface, a clownboy acolyte of a street-level madonna.

Nordin couldn't help but feel for Varzha. For him, the sound of the young girl's voice was like a knife to the heart, floating as it did over the oblivious buzz and hustle of the street. Here was a pure young woman offering up a priceless gift. A few passersby heard what Nordin heard and stopped in their tracks, delivering gold ten-*krona* coins into her paper cup. But many turned their faces away and kept walking, denying the miracle happening right in front of them.

Thus far, Jonas Nordin's life had not gone the way he intended. He had just turned thirty. His ambitions could not be contained by his present circumstances. Destiny intended something more for him, he was sure, perhaps a career in music or entertainment. Just because he was tone deaf didn't mean he couldn't work behind the scenes as a producer or a talent manager, a role beyond that of snagging teenage shoplifters at a department store.

Both of the nearby beggars were Romani, *zigenare*, gypsy immigrants in Sweden. Such people were socially designated as invisible human beings. Look how the stream of busy shoppers reacted now, Nordin thought, skirting Varzha Luna like water flowing around a rock. A stubborn minority of Nordin's fellow Swedes agreed with that bigoted inner demon of his. They believed such mendicants were bothersome and represented a blot on the city streets. Something really ought to be done about them.

Now I pass from door to door like the son of sinless Mary
Hand outstretched I walk, like he that was born the Christ

One day Nordin would formally reach out to Varzha Luna. He had already spoken to her several times, making up lame excuses for his approach. She would stare at him, silent and cold-eyed. Eventually, he would be able to convince Varzha to leave behind the songs of the Romani and move into something more pop. Nordin himself wrote song lyrics. As the young woman's manager he would bring the voice of an angel to the Swedish public.

Listening to her now, Nordin closed his eyes, transported.

✦

Luri Kováč purposefully always tried to post himself near Varzha Luna. There was no real word for "guardian" in Romani, so in his mind he used *beskyddare*, a word he picked up in *Schwedo*. That was how Luri saw himself, a watcher, a sentinel, a protector of his people. Recently young Romani women were vanishing, one after another, as if they were lambs in a barnyard set upon by hungry beasts. Luri vowed to act as the barnyard dog, fending off predators.

He recently came to accept that he was hopelessly in love with Varzha Luna. The exquisite young woman turned his blood to wine. He didn't know if she even knew of his existence.

Two men approached Varzha, one taller and bearded, the other younger and harder looking. They halted in front of her.

Romani? No, they were *gadje*, non-Roma, gentiles, pale-eyed, and cold.

Something seemed off or wrong about the pair. They were not shoppers, not casual passersby. They had zeroed in on the teenage Varzha as if she were their specific target.

After the girl's song faded to a close, the taller one extracted a leather wallet from his heavy canvas jacket. He flopped it open in front of the pretty gypsy beggar. Even from a distance, Luri could recognize the common red-bordered police ID.

So, *polis*. But not in uniform, perhaps undercover, or some plainclothes cowboys from a special unit in the National Operations Department.

Luri didn't know what to do. He thought of going over to Varzha and her white-faced brother, Vago. In terror of the *polis*, the boy was now turning in small, weak circles, whimpering. He would tell the brother to shut the hell up, that he, Luri, would help, that he was the *beskyddare*.

Should he do something? Should he intercede? But the *polis* would only arrest Luri himself, or anyway bother or harass him. So he decided to remain uninvolved for the moment, but he would continue to watch.

As if the song's ending had created a bell of silence into which words could flow, Luri now almost made out what one of the cops, the tall bearded one, said to Varzha. Mumble, mumble, mumble, out of which the word "hotel" emerged clearly.

Varzha bent her head and nodded in a sign of submission and acceptance. She turned and expressed a quick command to her wordless brother. Luri heard Vago give a moan of fear.

That did it. No more hesitation. Luri rumbled to his feet and crossed Drottninggatan toward Varzha and the others, concealing his interest, pretending the move was merely to restore circulation in his legs after sitting so long on the frozen sidewalk.

An odd thing happened. His approach earned a quick, knife-sharp glare from Varzha. Afterward, the moment remained etched in Luri's thoughts. Though they had never exchanged as much as a single word, he fancied that the girl knew him, and understood his role as a protector.

Her stern expression mystified him. Not pleading, not worried, and definitely not the closed Romani glare that is doled out to *gadje* like a dose of poison. There was mysterious meaning in her eyes, meaning that froze Luri in his tracks. Stay clear.

Stunned, preoccupied by his own emotions, Luri stood paralyzed as the two men stole Varzha away. She seemed to accompany them willingly, throwing a curt word over her shoulder, once more ordering her brother to remain behind. The two males and the Romani girl turned down Klarabergsgatan toward the traffic circle at Sergels Torg. Varzha looked back occasionally to make sure that her brother did not follow.

The idea that Varzha was not being forced disturbed Luri. Why didn't she struggle, call out? Do sheep go voluntarily to the slaughter?

He followed along. At first he still had eyes on the girl. Then other pedestrians swirled around her. She became blocked from his view, swallowed by the crowd. The white wedding dress disappeared amid the ocean of black and gray on the busy street. Was that to be his last glimpse of her?

The watcher had failed to watch. The guardian had dropped his guard.

He told himself not to be concerned. Varzha had only been removed briefly and would soon return. Perhaps someone from Swedish social services would interview her. He tried to erect a wall of calm within himself, but it was instantly beaten down by a sledgehammer of panic.

Chai nicabada! A young woman has been taken away!

Chai nicabada! A stolen maiden! Please help us!

There had been several teenage girls disappeared in the last year, perhaps a dozen, snatched from the Romani community in Stockholm. The phenomenon had triggered no public outcry. No one cared.

What would it accomplish now if Luri shouted out the alarm? *Chai nicabada*! Who apart from the heavenly angels would hear him?

Suddenly out of the crowd of shoppers the second cop appeared, the smaller, younger-looking one. It happened in an instant. Luri found himself shoved roughly off the sidewalk. The thug cracked him on the temple with a sharp chop of an elbow. Luri fell to his knees, stunned.

"Fuck off!" the man hissed in accented English, kicking Luri in the face for good measure. A nasty gout of blood spurted from Luri's nose. He sprawled backward in the gutter slush.

Left behind, the clown-faced Vago had turned frantic and fell apart.

He rushed up to Luri now, emitting unintelligible moans. The boy's white greasepaint makeup was streaked with tears.

Luri pulled himself upright with a blood-stained hand. "Where is she?" he demanded in Romani. "Where have they taken her?"

The brain-damaged boy couldn't speak, only mewl. His breath came in deep heaving shudders.

"Tell me!" Luri shouted.

3

During the six-hour drive north from Stockholm to the reunion, Brand was startled to see a sign for a turn-off that read "Oslo." Could that be Oslo, Norway? She realized she had no real grasp of the geography.

The seemingly endless journey wore on. The Tesla did not motor—it purred along soundlessly. Brand felt herself losing the battle against sleep. Next to her Lukas leaned his head against the passenger side window. His eyes were closed but she couldn't tell if he was awake or asleep. She quickly slipped a tablet of Adderall into her mouth. She had come to like the bitter taste of the drug.

The sun hovered no more than a finger's width above the horizon. The oblique angle beamed its feeble rays directly into Brand's tired eyes. But by two-thirty dear old *Sol* appeared ready to give up the ghost. Sunset came with a spectacular slash of orange, set off by a purple belt of cumulus cloud.

Pretty, yes, but disconcerting. It was still the middle of the day! She had the whole night to look forward to. Her panicked interior clock struggled to adjust. She looked at her watch. Eight-thirty in New York City, time to start the day. Brand had been awake for twenty-two hours. And quite literally, miles to go before she slept.

Darkness rose to engulf the countryside. The lakes lost the light last. Brand still caught indistinct glimmers of their icy surfaces, dull silver coins scattered over the landscape. The air became black and impenetrable. Everyone spoke of the Land of the Midnight Sun. They failed to mention the other side of the equation, the midnight dark that arrived too early in the afternoon.

Four hours in, the terrain changed. The highway climbed into a range of foothills. Occasionally they passed through a village. She saw houses but no people.

"In America we have ghost towns," Brand commented. "Here you have a ghost district." Lukas didn't answer. He was asleep. She had spoken to no one.

A heavy snow began to fall. Visibility narrowed to the twin tunnels of the Tesla's headlights. There was no longer traffic. The sense of an all-encompassing stillness made Brand slow the car, pull over, and stop. She powered down the driver's side window. An out-of-time feel took over the moment. She wondered if the Swedes had a word for the sound that falling snow makes during a blizzard.

The storm dropped a veil over the whole scene. They seemed to be nowhere. It was peaceful, death-like. Snow-laden branches drooped over the roadway. She switched off the headlights. The white-out of the blizzard instantly turned black. The surrounding darkness was as complete as any Brand had ever experienced. She hurriedly turned the headlights back on.

Attempting to raise her window again, Brand mistakenly gave a short blip to the one on the passenger side. The glass moved against Lukas's resting head. He was rocked awake.

"Sorry," Brand said.

Sleepily the man peered out at the blizzard and smiled.

"Welcome to Härjedalen, Veronika," he said. "Do you want me to take over the driving?"

"No," she replied quickly.

"Just keep a watch for any stray moose that might come our way."

"Moose…?"

"The big creatures will be out in this. They look to avoid deep snow with those long wobbly legs. That's what brings them out of the woods. They look for paths, plowed roads. You don't want to meet one head on. In Sweden, all vehicle models are road-tested to see if they will withstand a direct collision with a moose."

"Are you serious?"

"Yes, it's true."

"They don't use a real moose in these tests, do they?"

Lukas looked at her. Brand wondered if he could read drug use in the clench of her jaw. "No, Veronika, no live animals are harmed. This is Sweden, after all. Though rare, such collisions do happen. They say if you don't die from the impact, then the harsh acids exploding from the stomach of the moose will kill you all the same."

Now it was Brand's turn to stare over at Lukas. She put the Tesla in gear. The car sped up as one ghost moose after another emerged from the surrounding forests.

Gradually they drove out of the storm. Lukas directed her off the highway onto smaller secondary roads.

A half hour later he pointed out the driveway to the Dalgren homestead. As she turned into the lane, an unexpected wave of emotion crashed down on Brand. She almost let out a sob.

The ancestral home of her Swedish grandfather. Brand had never been there before, but somehow the house and its surrounding outbuildings felt disturbingly familiar. Could she be nostalgic for a place she never visited?

Memory drew her back to her childhood. She knelt on a plush green sofa in the New York farmhouse parlor of her grandparents, gazing at the black and white photograph that hung on the wall above. The scene in the photo, at once homey and foreign, exerted a power on her young self that Brand had wholly forgotten. Eight-year-old Veronika Brand imagined an entire fantasy world around the photograph, a cozy place out of one of her favorite childhood books, Laura Ingalls Wilder's *Little House in the Big Woods*. She recalled the intensity of the fantasy, how it dominated her youth.

"I haven't thought about this place for years," she murmured.

She was entering into the photo for real. Brand saw a large, two-storied house, painted with the traditional *falu* red sealant. Its corner moldings were trimmed with white, carrying over the white of the wood-framed peaked windows, the attic roofline. Beyond the main house stood another smaller but nearly identical residence. Further back were several barns, also painted *falu* red. Small square windows ran along their exterior walls.

The haze of wind-blown snow appeared pink in the headlights of the Tesla. A dozen vehicles parked alongside the lane in front of the house. "Pull in there," Lukas told her, directing Brand to an open spot. His eyes brightened with anticipation. She herself experienced speed jitters. The drug rode on top of her exhaustion, not quite canceling it out. She suddenly wished to be elsewhere.

They emerged from the warm, well-lit interior of the car into the frozen dark. Early evening. As she stepped out, the snow crunched beneath Brand's boots. The passing storm had scattered the clouds overhead. Numberless stars spangled the sky. She stood staring upward. Her breath formed frosty clouds in the night air. When they approached the front door, it swung open as if on its own, throwing out a rectangular spill of yellow light.

"*Hej*, hello, hello!"

A chorus of welcome greeted Brand as she entered. She had heard of the older group of Dalgren siblings but was not prepared for the complex web of cross-generational relations that was now assembled in her honor. There was no doubt she belonged to this tribe; even to a person as pale as she, they appeared white as snow. A woman she recognized as Sanna Dalgren stepped forward from among the foreign relatives and took both Brand's hands in hers. Sanna hugged her.

"*Det här är vår berömda kusin från Amerika!*" she announced to the crowd. Lukas, entering the room behind Brand, translated. "She calls you our famous American cousin!"

The greetings were general and enthusiastic. "Here is my brother, Folke," Sanna said in accented English. She brought forward a slouch-shouldered man who wore a bashful expression on his face.

"You are tall!" Folke exclaimed. His English was likewise inflected with a Swedish lilt.

Brand remembered her grandmother's attempts to teach her the native tongue, instruction which she fiercely resisted. She had a first-generation mother and immigrant grandparents, but she herself wanted only American English, American expressions, everything American. Still she could not escape the sounds of those three, Klara, Gustav and Alice, at the kitchen table late at night, balancing saucers of coffee in their palms, sipping the tepid liquid in the most un-American way. A peculiar tradition for cooling coffee to the perfect temperature that had never translated beyond the first generation. The rise and fall of the Swedish language sounded like singing. Even the raves and shouts of Gustav were rhythmic.

"I tell her I don't recognize her without her long-flowing hair," Sanna gushed. "So striking!"

"Oh, hardly," Brand responded.

Sanna's brother Folke clumsily half knelt in front of Brand, before dropping something at her feet. Brand drew back sharply, almost losing her footing.

"*Nej, nej,*" he mumbled. No, no. Brand realized he had only been trying to give her a pair of embroidered wool slippers, to get her to remove her wet boots and put the slippers on.

"This is how we do it in Sweden," he said in English, sweeping his hands in a low gesture at the rest of the feet that stood around her.

She removed her boots and stepped into the slippers. They looked to be handmade. Sanna took charge, guiding her in among the assembled relatives. Brand confronted a room full of people, most of them sitting in a variety of chairs that looked as though they had been specially brought in for the occasion.

The word *skål* sounded like a bell. Every glass in the room rose. Brand had as yet no glass to answer with, so she simply gestured awkwardly. As a newcomer, she was expected to introduce herself. She lost herself amid a flurry of names and faces.

"*Enn-why-pee-dee Blue!*" exclaimed an older man named Jörgen, the husband of a Dalgren cousin. Brand understood him to mean *NYPD Blue*, the classic American TV program. He grabbed her hand and shook it vigorously. "I am a large fan! Large fan!"

"Everyone!" Lukas called out. "Our dear cousin Veronika is not familiar with our customs. And she knows not any Swedish, so we will have a good opportunity to try out our language skills."

"I apologize," Brand said. "With my grandparents, I should have …" She trailed off, uncertain what she meant to say.

"When I finish loading the luggage at Arlanda," Lukas announced, "lo and behold Veronika climbs directly into the driver's seat of my Tesla!"

Murmurs rose from his audience.

"Naturally, I objected," Lukas continued. "But 'I have to drive,' she says. 'I make it a practice never to ride as a passenger.'"

"I'm sorry," the star of the anecdote interjected. "It's simply that I tend to get carsick if I am not behind the wheel."

"Oh, she is an American!" a voice exclaimed. "They must always be in the driver's seat."

Eventually, Brand managed to edge away from Sanna and duck the seemingly endless introductions. She took a moment for herself, leaning against the warm brick of the expansive fireplace. The heat emanating from an invisible source had no means of escape, turning the old family homestead into a shield against the wind howling on the other side of the walls.

Once more Brand felt herself transported back in time. She recalled the chill on certain childhood mornings, when she would wake under a mountain of blankets in the farmhouse in upstate New York. She loved the cozy sense of lying in bed, watching her exhalations turn to cloudy vapors. Her austere grandmother, Klara Dalgren, would try and extract her from the warmth and security of her sleep cave.

"*Följ med, Veronika,*" the old woman would say. But Brand resisted, anticipating the shock of that first bare foot against the cold floor. Her protests about leaving the warmth of her bed went unheeded.

Across the crowd Brand now spotted a hunched, ancient soul—Elin Dalgren, the youngest sister of Brand's grandfather Gustav, and the sister-in-law of her grandmother, Klara. The last living sibling of the 12 or 13 that had once dominated the area. Hers had been the unintelligible scratch of a voice on the trans-Atlantic telephone call that had summoned Brand to Sweden. A shrunken, Yoda-like presence, Elin held herself apart from the hub-bub of the reunion.

Brand had the odd sense of being pinned by the old woman's gaze. Elin's eyes were rheumy and cloudy with cataracts, but they fixed upon the American visitor with a spooky fierceness. Brand looked around. No one stood nearby, no one else who could be the possible target of Elin's stare. She raised her hand against her chest. Me? she wanted to ask. The primordial eyes still bore down on her. Brand waved tentatively, and got no response.

It was an illusion, she decided, a product of her exhaustion. Elin Dalgren was not looking at her at all. The woman seemed to exist, her grand-niece thought, as a totem, a reminder, a last living witness of events that had occurred long ago. The large easy chair in which she sat threatened to swallow her up. One gnarled hand rested atop an artfully carved wooden cane.

Amid the gusts of party chatter, Brand noticed a figure who appeared as much of an outsider as herself, a man about her age, maybe a little younger. He stood apart, narrow-shouldered and composed. A gentle, ironic expression played across his face. She hadn't caught his name. An odd thing, but she noticed that he would appear sitting in one of the cane chairs lined against the wall, but when Brand glanced over again a few moments later he had disappeared. Then he would reappear elsewhere, on the other side of the room. Like the innocent childhood game of musical chairs, she thought.

The formal atmosphere loosened. The dozen children present buzzed around the room. The younger ones seemed unimpressed by the visitor from America. Many of the adults wished to share drinks with Brand, pushing tiny glasses of clear liquid upon her, toasting her with red-faced enthusiasm.

"*Skål!*" The theme of the evening. She could not refuse. The fiery liquor ploughed into her exhaustion like a landslide in progress. She felt obliged to speak at least a few polite words to Elin Dalgren, but then she would have to find a place to sleep.

At that moment the old woman surprised everyone by rapping her cane loudly on the wooden floor. Despite how frail Elin looked, there was obvious strength in her. Though the children paid little mind, much of the adult chatter in the room stopped.

Brand took a few steps toward Elin, but Sanna formally guided the New York detective to the older woman. Brand had the annoying sense that her busy-body cousin somehow wanted to control or stage-manage the interaction. Before Sanna could say a word Elin reached out and captured one of Brand's hands, gripping it hard.

"*Klara,*" she muttered.

"*Nej, Elin, inte Klara,*" Sanna said. "*Klaras dotterdotter!*"

Relatives gathered around them, eager to hear the exchange.

"*Jag vet varför hon är här,*" the old woman declared.

Sanna translated. "She says she knows why you are here."

"She spoke to me on the phone," Brand said. Summoning her.

"She's very old," Sanna said. She turned back to Elin and spoke a quick sentence in Swedish. "I say to her that you are here for the reunion."

"*Nej, nej,*" Elin said, shaking her head slowly, still staring up at Brand. "*Hon är här för att döda djävulen.*"

The whole company erupted into laughter. Sanna broke in among the general merriment. "My *mamma* says you are here in Sweden to arrest the bad men," she told Brand.

"Watch out! Watch out," exclaimed Jörgen, the gent who had proclaimed himself a fan of *NYPD Blue*. He cocked his finger and made an explosive shooting sound with his mouth.

Elin Dalgren looked as if she very much wanted to say more. Her wrinkled, age-puckered mouth moved spasmodically, attempting to form words. It was painful to watch. She fretted and turned anxious.

Sanna intervened, made a shooing motion to the family before helping the old woman to her feet. The two slowly made their way out of the room. Before they disappeared Elin Dalgren stopped and turned, sending one more look in Brand's direction.

Her expression disturbed Brand. The old woman is afraid of something, she thought.

4

Later in the evening, Brand escaped the crush. She wandered the low-ceilinged second floor of the old house. The alcohol-and-Adderall mix foxed her brain. She thought that if someone didn't put her to bed soon she would drop where she stood. The hangover from the speed darkened her mood. I should not have come, she told herself.

Seeking to clear her head, she stepped out onto a small balcony, warding off the cold with a shawl fashioned from a blanket taken from one of the upstairs bedrooms. She wanted to see the stars again.

There was no moon, and no aurora. The Milky Way swept from horizon to horizon in a celestial wake of blue-white starlight. In the yard below, deep snow sparkled like piled diamonds. The red-painted outbuildings showed dark against the white landscape.

The man she had noticed earlier, her fellow outsider, emerged onto the little balcony. "Ah, here you are," he said.

"Here I am," she responded. They both took a moment to gaze up at the extravagant night sky.

He broke the silence. "Barns are painted red because of the chemistry of exploded stars."

She glanced over at him. "Is that right?"

"No, really, it's true," he said. "When stars collapse, they leave behind dust, what we call ferrous oxide. There's a lot of iron in the earth. This ferrous oxide colors the paint red. And red paint is cheap. You know, farmers like cheap."

"That's right," Brand said, laughing. "That's true all over the world. My Dalgren grandparents were farmers."

"That was Jamestown, New York, right?"

Her smile faded. "Everyone here knows so much more about me than I do about them."

"Krister Hammar," the man said, giving a curt bow. "You and I are not blood-related. My wife was a Dalgren, my connection to the family is by choice."

"Was? Is she here?"

"She is…she died five years ago now. Her name was Tove."

Brand gave a brief consoling nod. They both went inside. Leaning against the wall was a framed, colored print, a highly stylized portrait of a man holding aloft a book and wearing a narrow-brimmed cap. The print had a throwback air of Soviet realism.

"Is this who I think it is?"

"If you are thinking it's Vladimir Lenin, then yes."

Brand nodded. "So, the barns are painted red because of ferrous oxide, is it? Not 'red,' as in political reds?"

"I believe our hosts might have hidden away Comrade Lenin so as not to offend a visiting American. That piece used to hang proudly out in the hall."

"Have I fallen in among communists? I am shocked, shocked."

"I don't know if you were aware of it back then, but you had fallen in among Soviet-style communists when you spent time with your grandparents. Gustav and Klara were not just painted red, they were red through and through."

"In my childhood, they kept their beliefs to themselves," Brand said.

"Yes, the political atmosphere was dangerous for communists when they emigrated to America—to speak out was dangerous. I read where J. Edgar Hoover, your FBI director, used to pronounce the word 'common-ism.'"

"You know a lot about America."

"I went to school there. Boston College, international relations. I came back here to study law. Immigrant rights."

"You must be overwhelmed with all the immigration action here lately. And what, are you barn-red yourself?"

"Well, I guess I'm left, liberal, like most of the Dalgren family is now. Though if you dig deeper, you'll find some of the old guard. Didn't Gustav and Klara speak to you about anything?"

Brand gazed out the window. "Grandma Klara used to talk about this, the night sky in Sweden," she said quietly.

The two of them gazed up at the starry night for a long beat. "Most of us live in cities," he said. "We don't often stop to look up at the stars, too busy looking down at phones. They say this type of situation breeds atheism."

"So that's what causes it!" Brand said, laughing again.

"How could you not believe in something bigger than yourself, looking up at this every night?"

Brand turned to face him directly. "Where are you from?" she asked. "What part of Sweden?"

"As far north as you can go. At least, that's where I was born. You call it Lapland."

"Reindeer," Brand said. "Santa Claus."

"Yes, although nowadays the Sami people—my people, my mother was Sami— herd reindeer with motocross bikes, and the tourists jet in on package tours, cramming in the obligatory culture stop before skipping over to Finland's more coveted Santa's workshop. There are two of them, competing with each other to attract customers."

Brand appraised the man openly. "I felt there was something about you. I've never fit in anywhere either. I don't think I'm doing so well with this crowd."

"Give them a chance," Hammar said.

They stood in uncomfortable silence. Brand had the sense the man had something to get off his chest. She tried to wait him out.

"I'm tired" she said finally. "I think I need to go to bed."

"Listen, just now I have a case," Hammar said abruptly. "A young girl, a Romani teenager named Varzha who has disappeared. Because she is an immigrant, no one cares to look for her."

"Romani?"

"Gypsy, as you say. Her disappearance may be part of a pattern. I thought since you've worked against traffickers in America…" He trailed off.

Brand stared. "Oh, hell no," she said. "You want me to look into this disappearance of yours?"

"Your knowledge, as a New York City detective, here among us, such expertise could be invaluable."

"You have police in this country, am I correct?"

"Yes, of course."

"And I assume they investigate disappearances?"

"Well, yes. But—"

Brand cut him off. "Then that's the best course of action. I'm a big fan of letting people do their jobs."

"Okay, of course, of course," Hammar said quickly. "And you must have your own thing while you are in Sweden."

"That's right, I have my own thing."

"Americans are never without their own thing," Krister said. "Yes, right. This gypsy girl, she is of no importance."

"Oh, for pity's sake," Veronika exclaimed, mildly irritated at last. "I think we ought to leave Comrade Lenin and the gypsies and head back downstairs."

"All right." Hammar sighed. "We don't want your people to think we're conspiring up here."

They turned towards the stairs. The largest room on the second floor was more like a hallway, long and narrow and running half the length of the house. Brand noticed the wooden floorboards were over three feet wide. That had to mean they had been milled a very long time ago, from timber taken out of old-growth forest. Everything was painted white, walls and floor both.

The rise and fall of Dalgren voices still sounded from downstairs. Brand wondered where she was going to sleep. Maybe right where she stood would do just fine. She felt so tired she was dizzy.

Hammar headed toward the stairway. He turned back around. "They didn't translate what she said exactly right."

Brand couldn't summon the effort to understand what Hammar was talking about. She was worn out. Fatigue, she knew from long nights spent on police casework, could develop into an almost hallucinatory state.

"The old woman," Hammar explained. He stood poised at the top of the stairs. "They told you that Elin said you're here to catch the bad guys. But she didn't say exactly that."

He wanted Brand to ask him what Elin Dalgren had really meant. She remained standing in place. She felt unsteady on her feet, as though the room was swaying slightly.

"She said you were here to kill the devil."

Brand didn't understand. In the far corner of the room stood a children's bed, more of a divan really, piled with pillows and a stuffed toy gorilla. She crossed to it and impulsively laid down. Her mind shut off as she listened to Hammar's footsteps receding down the stairs.

5

Varzha Luna remained motionless and expressionless, as if she were still standing poised on the cold tarmac of Drottninggatan. She listened to her captors talk and tried to identify who they were. The bearded one went off on a rant about money.

Their plan was to auction Varzha as a virgin. The men who kidnapped her seemed to believe she would bring in an astronomical sum. The bearded one, Liam, groused about their paltry cut of the proceeds. He pronounced himself ready to have Varzha immediately.

The one called Mattias responded. "This gypsy girl, I don't feel one way or another about her. But JV has placed her in my care, and told me that anyone who messes with her will answer to him."

"This is a lousy business," Liam stated, his tone bloated with self-importance. "We could sell her now, five or ten times a day! Add up the numbers!"

Varzha thought of the other victims, the ones who had disappeared. Her friend, Lel. Another kidnapped girl had been cut badly on the face when she spat at a man trying to force her. Afterward dead by her own hand.

The shades were drawn on all the windows in the room where Varzha sat. It was the first stopover after the journey out of Stockholm. The fading sun threw snow-reflected silhouettes against the blinds, making eerie, troll-like shadow figures.

She looks pretty enough," Liam said, "even with the white face."

"Yes, Mattias said," turning to look at Varzha. "Pretty now—but later, no. She is the best age. Untouched. Soon she'll get old and dry up like all women. Then I wouldn't touch her with your dick, much less mine."

Varzha knew the face that stared back at her when she looked in the mirror, the dark eyes of a *kalderás* Romani, the thick braided jet black hair. She had long understood that most *gadje* barely recognized brown-skinned Romani as fellow humans. We are "others," she thought, something apart, not deserving of respect.

Exceptions existed, a few *gadje* who had shown kindness to Varzha and her brother. The fashionable woman who befriended them, with the palest white skin, so thin she looked like a boy. She brought gifts with her, candy, warm sweaters, blankets. The gifts were really small bribes, Varzha recognized, in exchange for the numberless photographs the woman took.

Even so, kind as the woman was, Varzha fell back on the ancient Romani attitudes toward gentiles. How far could she trust them? What might they want in return?

Varzha held herself apart, showing herself only when she sang.

In her youth the villagers called Varzha "*chirola chei*," bird girl. She flew like lightning through the muddy lanes of her Romanian village, commandeered horses, and rode on the back of goats. From early on she was able to whisper the language of animals, gathering them around and coaxing their love.

Family and clan wrapped her in a protective cocoon. Her stern father, a well-respected musician, her beautiful mother—they were always there, shielding her from harm. No cousin, no uncle, no neighbor had ever dared to bother or molest Varzha as she grew up. Plus there was Vago by her side, happy-go-lucky Vago. They were inseparable.

Always, Varzha sang. For the family, for the clan, for herself. From the earliest days of childhood she sang the *mirologi*, the graveside laments of her people.

Then came the horrific attack when Varzha was ten, the murders, the catastrophe that changed everything forever. Her parents dead, Vago beaten senseless, the cocoon stripped away. She learned the terrors of life all too well. In the aftermath, a man wearing small spectacles and a long brown overcoat arrived, a kindly man, who had taken them on the long journey to Sweden.

These other men who held her captive now, or thought they held her, who would seek to sell her as if she were a cow, they were simply stupid believers in their own lies. They didn't know her, didn't realize what Varzha was capable of. Not a bird girl anymore, but more an eagle intent on vengeance.

She knew Mattias would never touch her—he had too much to lose—but she was unsure of the bearded one. His gaze rested hungrily on her, then always darted guiltily away.

Since she couldn't do anything about it until the time came, Varzha sat motionless.

The two men who had approached Varzha while she sang for coins outside of Åhléns believed they were taking control of the situation. Varzha didn't resist. She played her role well. This was the whole idea, this was the plan. She intended for the *gadje* traffickers to take her. She made no protest. Leaving her brother Vago behind was the difficult part.

After Mattias and Liam made off with Varzha, a third man had been waiting a few blocks away, in a van with the engine running. He drove, maneuvering them out of the congested city center. Varzha had tried to keep an exact track of the route they took, but became disoriented almost immediately. She was lost.

The van had no windows and no seats in the back. She was shielded from the front driver's compartment by a curtain of heavy plastic. They had driven through halting traffic to the highway, then out of town by either the E4 or the E18, Varzha thought—to the north, anyway. She feared the coast the most, afraid that they would leave Sweden on a ferry in Kapellskär and her life would become immediately much more difficult.

"Nobody touches her," Varzha had heard Mattias tell the other two more than once. She learned their names. Liam, the bearded one, and Nils, the young driver.

The repetitive scrape of the plastic curtain against the van's interior wore on Varzha's nerves. After what she estimated was a half hour's drive, the van passed through a short period of start and stop traffic and then halted altogether.

Mattias opened the back doors of the vehicle and gestured her out. Varzha discovered that they had pulled into a darkened garage. She didn't have much time to survey the surroundings. They hustled her inside, up a flight of stairs, and into a long narrow room. A child's bike rested against a wall of white brick, next to a rickety dining table. An improvised couch made out of a collection of throw pillows sat opposite.

Liam sat her down on the couch. He left the room, then returned and provided her with a can of warm Coke and a chocolate bar.

A country house of some kind, or at least somewhere suburban. Varzha didn't know why she thought this, perhaps from the faint sound of wind passing through trees outside. Two small chairs sat upended in a corner of the long room, their fabric seats covered in a kid-friendly pattern of ducks and frogs. Could there be children here? Varzha wondered. Did the *gadje* import evil into their own homes?

She had always been impressed with stories of *gadje* greed. They accused the Romani of stealing, while their own thefts were comprised not of pennies but of nations, of petroleum, of whole swaths of the earth. Compared to her own people with their pathetic paper cups lifted for alms, members of the master race displayed a bottomless thirst, for gold, for power, for blood.

And sex.

Most people consider money to be the most powerful factor in life. But Varzha's motivation was purer still.

Revenge.

She would take revenge on the traffickers, for Lel and every other girl stolen from the Romani community in Stockholm. She would immerse herself in the filth of the world and drown that filth with blood. She would then seal her fate by her own doing, a choice brutally taken away from her eleven lost sisters.

Her captors didn't notice there was anything different about Varzha. Here was just one more piece of human flesh to use and discard, to bleed dry, to sacrifice. She had long kept a blank, passive expression when dealing with *gadje*. No one saw through her mask. If they had, they would know her fierceness.

Varzha let her hand trail down beneath the couch cushions. She turned up nothing useful, although she did retrieve a colorful candy wrapper, the same brand as the chocolate she was eating, Marabou, Sweden's favorite and hers as well. She took her own wrapper and snuck it back under the cushion along with the other, thinking of it as a sign of solidarity with the girls who had been here before her. I am here just like you.

An image of Lel hovered in her mind. Her dear sweet best friend Lel Pankov, alternately raped and beaten, raped and beaten, until she was no more than a bloody rag of a human, then discarded as if she were garbage. Had Lel come through this same room on the way to her death?

"Let's get the girl out of that damned wedding dress, at least," Liam suggested to Mattias. He spoke directly to Varzha. "Strip it off, darling, let's have a look at you."

She ignored him, staring straight ahead, stone faced. Varzha concluded that Mattias and the others believed she could not understand Swedish.

"The word on the street," Mattias said, excitement in his voice, "is that a virgin, a true virgin, could bring over eighty thousand kronor, ten thousand U.S. dollars, maybe more."

Street? Varzha wondered. What street was that? And what did it mean, this phrase "true virgin?" She'd been watched closely all her life, first by her parents, then by her caretaker. She was, she supposed, what they meant by true virgin, and they were going to sell her. Varzha could not understand how any woman or man could be sold. What if the plan devised by Moro Part, the Romani godfather, didn't work? What if her captors took her far away, like Lel—beyond help, beyond hope? She would suffer the same fate as her friend.

She steeled herself, thrusting the bad thoughts away. The plan would work because…it had to.

They waited for what felt to Varzha a very long time. Then the third member of the trio, the young one they called Nils, stuck his head into the room and announced that someone called "JV" had arrived.

Mattias, who had been slouched at the rickety dining table, rose to his feet. "*Toaletă*," he said to her in Romanian. Toilet. He directed her to a little powder-room lavatory along a hallway that dead-ended at a locked door.

"Someone should watch her," Liam said, getting to his feet also.

"Leave the girl be," Mattias said. "She's not going anywhere."

He stationed himself in the corridor, allowing Varzha to use the facilities and change into the clothing he had provided.

Closing the door behind her, Varzha worked quickly to remove the wedding gown. She searched in the waistband for the small sewn pocket. She ripped it open. Hidden inside was a tiny device made of plastic and metal. She examined herself in the mirror, white makeup still covering her face.

A shiver suddenly passed through her, a memory of being a child. Her mother gently folded and wove her thick hair into long braids. Oh mother, where are you now? Can you see me? Hear my prayer. Watch over me in my darkness.

Varzha undid her dark tortoiseshell barrette. She concealed the small plastic device within the shell of the hair clip, then locked it with a snap. She drew up the braids and fastened them to the crown of her head.

Mattias banged on the door. Varzha ignored him. Her dress, her whiteface mask, her whole outfit was her shield, her defense, a barrier created against an alien and heartless world. Now she wiped off her makeup roughly, letting the tissues fall where they would. The new clothing disgusted her: a low-necked white blouse, a miniskirt, and a pair of black leather boots. A gentile's idea of sexy. She saw that the skirt was not something she could possibly wear and discarded it.

Another pounding on the door. "What? Come along!"

Varzha understood who she was, a *Kalderaš* Romani. The long flower-print skirts, loose tunic tops, multiple scarves in colored patterns that contrasted with the pattern of the skirt—these were the uniform of her people. Breasts were not emphasized because they were considered unimportant, mere tools for feeding children. But below the waist, between the legs—there both men and women had to observe cleanliness and modesty at all times.

A quick minute passed before Mattias again pounded on the door. "Women," Varzha heard him comment. "I never understand why they need so bloody long to get ready."

Varzha separated the top layer of the skirt of the wedding dress. She pulled on the longer satin underskirt, tying it at the waist with a piece of torn lace. The leather of the boots they gave her was soft. They fit well. Varzha emerged from the bathroom ready to face Mattias' anger that she had refused the skirt he had given her.

"*Va fan*," Liam exclaimed when she emerged. What the hell?

He moved automatically to embrace her. Varzha reacted quickly. Forming her right hand into a flat blade, she gave a quick chop at the man's windpipe. Gagging, Liam staggered backward. He recovered and charged at Varzha. Mattias grabbed him by the jacket collar and wrenched him backward.

"Liam!" Mattias snapped.

"What the hell is going on?" said another voice.

Coming in with Nils, a fourth man stood at the head of the hallway, a tall, modern-looking guy in a black leather jacket, his short-cropped hair gelled up. Young, in his twenties.

Mattias and Liam instantly became deferential. "She hit me!" Liam cried.

"She hit me," the newcomer mimicked. "What are you, a child? Get the fuck away from her."

He summoned them back into the main room. Varzha knew who the man was, or at least had been expecting to meet him at some point in her journey as a captive. She recognized him from a photo she had studied. One of the big bosses. She was a little surprised that he had shown himself so early. The others yielded to him, addressing the man as "JV."

"This is the one?" he said, assessing Varzha. JV addressed her directly, talking loudly the way stupid people do to someone who might not know their language. "Are you okay? Have they treated you well?"

"She don't talk," Mattias said briskly. "Let's go."

JV stood Nils and Liam up in front of him, side by side like a pair of soldiers. "Stay here," he commanded, using a crisp, no-nonsense tone. "No communication whatsoever, do you hear? You don't call us, we call you."

"Yes, JV," Nils said.

"Shut up!" JV screamed. "Don't say my name!"

The flunkies stared at the floor. "Stay here," JV ordered. "You don't speak to anyone, you don't go outside, no phone, no calls, stay put until we contact you, *capiche*?"

"Right, *Ja*—I mean, right, Boss."

Such was the first rule of the stolen-girl pipeline. JV always insisted that the principle was unchallengeable and fundamental. Each step along the trail had to be severed as soon as it was taken. The path for smuggling young women to service the North Sea oil towns of Norway changed often. With this protective strategy it always became instantly untraceable.

"They going to be all right?" JV questioned Mattias, referring to Liam and Nils.

"They'll do what they're told," Mattias said. "Come on, we've got a long drive ahead of us."

He handed Varzha a pair of mittens and a down coat with a hood, which she dutifully put on. She was grateful for the warmth. She tried not to let the words "a long drive ahead" bother her. The idea of spending time with JV filled her with distaste. He resembled the ads she had seen for bodybuilding, an idiot fad so popular with Swedes. These were the type of men who collected guns and kept big-jawed dogs. For hunting, they always said. But the thought of dogs threw her sideways. Perhaps they could be used against humans.

Mattias led Varzha out of the room behind the big boss. A great sadness rose in her when she thought of Vago, abandoned and alone. She wondered if the guardian angel Luri was protecting him. She asked herself how long it would be before she saw her brother again. Or if she would ever see him again.

6

Brand woke to a silent house. She felt a queasy sense of dislocation. The washed-out quality of the light made her unsure of the time. She had a headache. Her mouth tasted vile. In the night some unknown person had covered her with a goose-down quilt. They had removed her footwear. The knitted slippers presented to her now sat on the floor next to the narrow bed.

She sat up. The deadness of the Dalgren residence puzzled her. The evening before it had been lively and crammed with people. Not for the first time, Brand cursed the evils of amphetamine. The drug was a godsend, until it wasn't. She paid for the energy its alkaloids gave her. The crash of the aftermath left her feeling ugly and hopeless.

Speed sleep was rarely restful. The dreaming mind drew a blank, but half-remembered waking dreams surfaced in her mind like breaching sea creatures. Had she really stirred in her sleep to hear voices, thuds and commotion in the night? Had she gotten up, gone to the stairwell and witnessed a shadowy form at the bottom of the stairs, something that appeared to be half human, half animal?

Brand also felt certain—almost certain—that at some point during the night she had stood at the door to the balcony. Through its small glass windowpane she witnessed a ghost-like figure cross the snowy yard toward one of the barns. Krister Hammar. He startled her by turning to look back at the house. His gaze seemed to bore directly into Brand. He disappeared through a door into the barn.

Real or imagined? At any rate the Dalgren household had appeared to be very lively through the wee hours. Now it was quiet as a tomb.

The world—reality as it presented itself—struck her as distant and false. She also felt an urgent need to pee. She stood up and pulled on the slippers. They were still damp. An attack of nausea and dizziness gripped her. She allowed it to pass. Brand took the narrow steps of the old staircase one at a time, holding onto a polished wooden rail.

The rooms downstairs were silent and empty. No evidence from the reunion party remained. The entire house appeared tidied up and swept clean. Wooden chairs that had been set out for guests were now stacked neatly along the walls. Where was everybody? She glanced outside. The front lane and side yards, parked thick with vehicles the evening before, were deserted.

A green antique *mora* clock in the big front room indicated the time was 12:17. Brand had a difficult time believing she had slept so long. The clock had to be simply decorative. Feeling like an idiot she watched the clock face to make sure the hands were indeed moving. Then it hit her. With the six hour time difference, it was six a.m. in New York, her normal waking hour when she was on the job. It still seemed impossible that it was already past noon. The mid-day light came in through the windows feeble and diminished.

She gazed out on the property. In daylight, she saw that the house stood among its outbuildings on the slope of a fairly high hill, not quite a mountain. The view was of a long sweep of snow-covered forest. In the distance was a lake, flat and white.

She dimly remembered the location of a downstairs bathroom. Her duffel had been thoughtfully placed there, parked against a wall. Next to it were her boots. She relieved herself and splashed water on her face, rubbing her skin vigorously with a rough towel. Her eyes were rimmed with red, her eyeballs, marbled with red veins. There was no shower or bathtub. Brand desperately needed to wash the stench of travel off herself. Her own pores accused her of abuse. The aquavit or slivovitz or whatever the hell the clear liquid was that the Dalgrens drank the previous night turned poisonous in her bloodstream.

A sense of shame settled in. Had she said things or done things the previous evening that were mawkish or offensive? She drank far too much. By the end of the night she was so inebriated it was as if her eyes were looking at each other. She had been guilty of patronizing her relatives, privately considering them a collection of yokels. The phrase in English was "bull in a china shop." "A New Yorker among Swedes" would amount to the same thing.

After a single day in the country, she had already botched her Swedish visit. She addressed her haggard image in the bathroom mirror. "You have wasted your life."

Brand made a solemn, silent promise to lay off the booze. She rooted in her duffel, fished out a baggie, and popped a couple of light yellow twenty-milligram pills into her mouth. Adderall—one of the most popular drugs in America, prescribed for both child and adult ADHD. Adderall—"attention deficit disorder for all." Brand had tried alternatives, Modafinil and Vyvanse, among others, but there was nothing like the real thing.

She felt restless. She had come thousands of miles, only to want immediately to escape the stifling confines of the Dalgren homestead. Delving into her family's past had been the vague goal of her visit. She recalled the previous evening, Elin Dalgren banging imperatively with her cane, the woman grasping her hand as if afraid to let go.

She wandered the empty house alone. She hesitated at the door of Elin Dalgren's apartment. The scent of an invalid hung faintly in the air, fusty and dense. Heavy curtains blocked out the already winter-weakened exterior light. Feeling like a thief, Brand ventured in. Even though the room was gloomy, she refrained from turning on the lamps.

Where was the old woman? Where was everybody? The whole house threw off a post-apocalypse vibe. A ninety-five-year-old matriarch disappeared. The previous evening she didn't appear to be able to move a single step on her own, much less vanish into thin air.

Unless the strain of the reunion was too much, and the guest of honor took sick.

The quarters felt close and crowded where the more modern upstairs spaces had been spare and empty. Stacks of books and papers covered most of the surfaces. A vintage breakfront with glass doors showed off Elin's treasures: several carved, colorfully painted wooden horses of different sizes, an elegant set of silverware inside an open leather box, a pocket watch suspended in a small bell jar.

Amid the clutter on top of an old wooden desk, Brand was surprised to discover an envelope with her own name written on the outside. "Veronika," spelled out in shaky-handed script. The flap had been left unsealed. Inside was a single, age-faded photograph.

The snapshot showed five teenagers, four of them grinning and goofing for the camera. Two boys, three girls, grouped side by side in light summer clothes. The wardrobes, the haircuts, and the yellowed age of the photograph indicated an earlier time. The 1930s, Brand guessed. She recognized the two Dalgren sisters, her grandmother and great aunt, Klara and Alice. She thought the third figure had to be Elin.

The trio of girls leaned into each other, eyes sparkling, mid-laughter. Klara wore an improvised wreath of spring flowers in her hair and a white mid-length dress, with a slightly-scooped neckline and loosely gathered at the waist. Alice had on an even more modest version of her sister's dress. Elin stood stiff and shy, her shoulders hunched.

In the center of the tableau stood Gustav Dalgren, arms akimbo, staring into the lens with such a look of youthful exuberance that his aura dominated the group. Of the five, he was the one you would bet on to do great things in the world. In the picture of a bare-chested, vigorously healthy boy, Brand could discover no trace of the brooding, bitter grandfather she knew. At the Jamestown farm a half century after the snapshot, the smell of whiskey had always been on Gustav Dalgren's breath. A violent outburst was always only a random hair trigger away.

There was another youngster in the photo, standing separate, the image blurred and darker, as if the boy hid in the shade. His scowling face contrasted with the happiness of the others. He looked to his right and seemed to be beckoning to Klara. Brand could hardly make out his features.

The old photograph represented a perfect portrait of carefree adolescence, a sweet moment adrift in time. Death had no dominion. In a few short years, the Second World War would descend on Europe, but at this moment, the darkness to come was only a bare whisper on the wind. One might extract the ink from the photo, distill it, and thereby create a tiny sip from the fountain of eternal youth. Flipping the fragile photograph over, Brand saw writing. The light was bad. She could barely make out the faded handwriting of her great aunt Alice.

Five names: Elin, Alice, Klara, Gustav, Loke.

She stared into the unsmiling eyes of the boy in the shadow to the right of the others. Yes, here was the scion of the celebrated Voss family, one of Sweden's wealthiest, Loke Voss. He had grown up friendly with her grandparents.

Brand heard a sound behind her. She turned to see Krister Hammar standing in the doorway of Elin's apartment.

"Doing some snooping, Detective?"

"Um, no, not at all," Brand said hurriedly. She slipped the old photograph into her pocket. "I was just…"

She let the words trail off.

"I have some bad news," Krister said. "I'm afraid we've had a death."

7

Elin Dalgren, Hammar informed her solemnly, had taken a fall during the night. She suffered a "cerebral event" and passed away quietly in the early morning. They sat together in the kitchen of the homestead, at a long kitchen table made of varnished yellow wood.

"She was gone before the ambulance arrived," Hammar said.

The news hit Brand like a heavily cushioned blow. Through the fog of her hangover and her overall feelings of depression and dislocation, she struggled to latch onto a sense of grieving and loss. She had not known the old woman, not really. Just that odd phone trans-Atlantic phone call that had summoned her to Sweden.

"*Kom hit.*"

Come here. The fierce insistence in Elin's voice rendered the words more than a sweet and sunny invitation to a family get-together. Or at least that's the way Brand had come to think of it.

Sanna had told her that Elin had family secrets to tell, "probably cake recipes," she had said, laughing. But cake recipes did not require the level of urgency Brand heard in the old woman's voice.

"I should have spoken to her," she said, half talking to herself and not Hammar.

"It's okay," he said.

"I tried, and then she was whisked off. And why was that? The woman was afraid. You saw that!"

The words spilled out of her mouth before she could catch them. She was aware she sounded suspicious, even paranoid.

"Elin was old, Veronika," Hammar said gently. "Old people die."

All right, Elin, Brand thought. You ordered me to come, and I am here. But now you are gone. A brief meeting, and that was all the two of them had managed. How had Hammar translated the old woman's words? You are here to kill the devil.

Hammar explained that Sanna and Folke sent her their apologies. They would be staying in town with relatives for several days, making arrangements for the memorial service.

"So you must extend your visit," he said. "The ceremony and burial will be in a few weeks."

"Weeks? Really?"

"Here the cremation takes place first, then some weeks after we gather to celebrate the life. Often only the closest relatives attend the final burial at a later date. Your presence is not expected at the burial, our grieving is a far more private affair."

"Nice and controlled then," Brand said.

"Yes, that way might sound indifferent, but eventually, goes the reasoning, the loss will become real."

He hesitated. "You will have all this time, Veronika, so you can occupy yourself with the other thing I spoke about."

The disappearing Romani girls. Mulling over her own concerns, Brand mentally dismissed the suggestion.

What do I do now? She posed the question without asking it aloud to Hammar. Skip the funeral? That didn't seem right. Go back to Stockholm? For what purpose? Fly home? No, that would be like jumping back into the frying pan from out of the fire. Hammar sensed her uncertainty.

"I'm very sorry such a bad event happened during your visit."

A death on her watch. The loss deepened Brand's mood of gloom. "I thought Swedes were silent and moody," she said. "Last night everyone was pretty chatty."

"Alcohol," Hammar said.

He got up and crossed the kitchen to the huge cast iron stove. "But you want coffee." A statement, not a question.

"Yes, please."

The man brought her a ceramic mug and a steaming glass carafe. He pushed a small pitcher of cream toward her.

"Black," she said. The brew was strong and scalding. "Now the rumors of this country having excellent coffee are confirmed."

Hammar nodded. He returned to the stove. A steel pot simmered above a low flame on a front burner. He shut off the heat. Using a wooden spoon, he dished warm rolled oats into a bowl. He added a splash of milk and set the bowl down in front of Brand.

Brand's gut churned. She didn't think she could stomach food. At the first spoonful, though, she realized she was ravenous. She helped herself to one of the half-dozen cheese *smörgåsar* that Hammar had arranged on a platter. As she ate she felt herself slowly coming back to life.

Cheese sandwiches for breakfast. Another of the sharp, intoxicating memories came to her, like the ones that had hit her before on the approach to the homestead. She was sitting at a kitchen table, not here in Sweden but in Klara and Gustav's farmhouse in upstate New York.

As a child, she ate the sandwiches greedily, even though she understood that they were not really breakfast food. No one in Queens, where she grew up and spent much of the year, ate this way. Cheese sandwiches for breakfast was not an American thing. But to her they meant summer mornings, the farm, the sound of Swedish being spoken by two people whose blood ran through her veins.

She and Hammar ate in silence, the creak and tick of the walls around them sounding like old bones settling.

"There's another issue." Hammar winced, as if afraid to tell her. "Lukas Dalgren returned home this morning."

Brand received the news with a stab of dismay. "He said he'd be here for several days. He was supposed to drive me back to Stockholm."

"I think it was the other way around," Hammar said. "You would drive him, no?"

He smiled wanly. She didn't respond. A sense rose in her that was almost claustrophobic. "Marooned here in Härjedalen then," she murmured.

"Well, Lukas is a very busy man," Hammar said. "Places to go, things to do."

"You have the American idiom down very well."

Hammar bent his head slightly to acknowledge the observation. "I'm sure Sanna and Folke will be happy to host you longer, despite the circumstances. After all, you're the first to return home in more than seventy years, ever since Gustav and Klara left for America."

Brand didn't know how to respond. Her family's past had clutched at her with icy hands, and now she had no obvious way to struggle from its grip, not with Elin gone. Brand had counted on the old woman to make clear certain things she had never been able to understand, such as why her grandparents had abruptly fled their home country during the war.

"There are buses?" she asked. "Trains?"

"I return to Stockholm today myself," Hammar said. "You could go with me."

"Oh, I couldn't possibly impose. I can't believe Lukas left me here."

"In Stockholm, I would be glad to take you around. I'm off work this month, and free as a bird. You can benefit from someone like me. Have you thought of that? Someone who knows the country and the culture, the angles and sharp edges that aren't shown in the tourist brochures and slick international marketing."

Brand's guard went up. As far as she was concerned, all men's motives were suspect. Hammar was older than she was, but not by much. She had a fine-tuned sense of whether a male might be hitting on her. Here was a new, "free as a bird" acquaintance, proposing an alliance. If Brand took Hammar up on it, it would have to be without any implications about "the boy and girl thing," as New York cops always referred to romance.

"Let me think about it," she said.

"I propose the healing powers of a hot shower to clear the head," Hammar said. He led Brand to a bathroom in the back reaches of the house, this one a modern, eye-blindingly-white tiled room with a large footed bathtub and a heated floor.

The food and the shower rendered Brand almost human. She returned to Hammar in the kitchen. He had cleared and washed the dishes. Almost startled by her reappearance, Hammar turned to face Veronika surreptitiously slipping his phone into his pocket. She hesitated only for a moment, feeling she had interrupted a call she shouldn't overhear.

"I'll be glad to drive with you back to the Swedish capital," she told him. She couldn't imagine the pleasant, soft-spoken man she saw before her giving her any trouble. With pen and paper retrieved from a side counter, Brand composed a quick note of condolence to Sanna and Folke Dalgren. The New York Yankees ball caps she brought along as gifts now seemed pathetic.

"They will be happy with them," Hammar assured her. She left the hats and the note on the kitchen table.

He announced he would go out and "take care of the car," which Brand understood to mean scraping off ice that had frozen on the windshield the night before. His puppy-like enthusiasm to be out into the blistering cold sat in opposition to her resistance to re-enter the harsh reality of her turbulent adult life beyond the farmhouse door.

Hammar returned, stamping snow from his feet, his face red with the outdoor chill. Carrying her own bag with the weight of her worldly possessions, Brand followed him out the front door. On the front porch she halted. Of all the vehicles that crowded the place the night before, only a lone ancient blue Saab remained.

"That's you?" she asked.

"Yes," Hammar answered. He sounded defensive.

"Will she make it?"

"This machine represents a high point in Swedish manufac—" he began, but Brand held up a hand to cut him off.

"I would love to drive such a magnificent vehicle," she said.

Hammar glanced at her. "I detect sarcasm," he said. "But I know from Lukas that this is your way, always to take your place behind the wheel."

"Wait a sec," Brand said. She opened her bag and extracted a black down vest that she had packed atop all her other clothes.

"Yes, the temperature drops tonight," Hammar said approvingly.

"Drops?" Brand said, amused. "Hasn't it already dropped?"

"However, my car does come equipped with a serviceable heater."

"Wood-fired, I'm guessing," Brand said, eyeing the antique vehicle.

Hammar laughed. The two of them trailed out to the car in the stinging air of a mid February day. Scalloped clouds marked the sky. The sun was not much in evidence.

"The border to Norway, that way," Hammar said. He gestured to the west.

Brand moved to the driver's side of the car. She opened the door and stashed her duffel in the car's back seat.

"It's a manual transmission," Hammar warned her. "I don't think you have many of those in New York City, with the bad traffic. Perhaps I ought to drive."

"I was born with a manual gear shift in my hand," Brand replied.

"Really?"

"Well, no, not really, Hammar. But I learned to drive a John Deere on my grandparents' farm."

"A tractor is not the same," Hammar said mildly. But he allowed Brand to have her way.

The ancient Saab sedan had rolled off the assembly line way back in 1970. Brand thought the fifty-year-old Model 96 looked comical. It was bulbous in all the wrong places, like a car designed by clowns for use in a circus routine. But inside and out the vehicle had the appearance of being lovingly maintained.

Hammar had updated it with all the latest bells and whistles. When Brand opened the door, the key was already in the ignition. An alarm dinged just as it would in a modern vehicle. With the engine already running, the car was warm inside.

Brand immediately stalled out on her first two tries at getting the vehicle moving. On the journey back to the highway, she rode the clutch mercilessly.

The Saab's owner wore a pained expression for the entire trip.

They headed southeast, toward Stockholm and the coast. A dense cloud cover settled in.

8

A half hour after departing the Dalgren homestead, Brand glided onto the empty E45. Thick stands of Scots pine and Norway spruce braced both sides of the roadway. The trees looked scrawny and struggling. The asphalt ran arrow straight. Ugly, dirty brownish-gray snow lay packed hard on both sides of the road.

The Saab proved woefully underpowered. Hammar informed her it was the rare production vehicle that boasted three cylinders—not four, not six, not eight. Such limited capacity did not allow Brand to drive at her usual breakneck pace. The car did not sail. It chugged.

They drove in silence for a few kilometers. Then out of nowhere Hammar asked, "What is the retirement age for the NYPD?"

She gave him a sideways look. "You want to know why I left the force."

"It's strange," Hammar said. "In America you say 'police force' and here we say 'police service'."

"*Allt är bättre här*," Brand pronounced in halting Swedish. "'Everything is better here.' That's your national motto, isn't it?"

Hammar smiled dutifully. "And yes, I would like to know," he said after a pause. "Why did you quit your job with the New York City police? You are in your late thirties? That's young to retire."

"Twenty and out, as they say," Brand answered the question. "Full pension after twenty years."

"Oh." Hammar looked not entirely convinced. The idea that Brand had already logged twenty years of experience in the NYPD would have meant she would have had to join out of high school. So her reference to twenty years rang false. She saw Hammar doing the math in his head.

"The decision to part ways was something of a mutual thing between me and the department, okay?" Brand said. "Are we done with me? Can we change the subject now?"

Traffic slowly increased as they proceeded toward Stockholm and the coast. Double tractor-trailers roared by the little car. A few of them were emblazoned with the word "VOSS." The red letters were outlined in black.

The shadowy figure in the photo that Elin had left for her loomed in her mind. Brand tried to summon up a comment that Lukas Dalgren had made on the drive to the reunion, which was now not even twenty-four hours in the past. There had been semis on the road then, too.

Lukas had briefly pointed out a Voss truck. "Voss Transport is the largest trucking company in Sweden, third largest in the EU. They are Dalgren neighbors. Our family does not enjoy good relations with the Voss clan. It is a long feud even from back to the war."

Brand assumed that the war Lukas had referred to was WWII. Now, as Voss trucks rumbled past the Saab, she questioned Hammar.

"They are a very big company," he told her. "Trucking, yes, transportation, even shipping, but now they are in construction and finance, too."

"Lukas mentioned something about the Voss family living right next door. I guess he meant near the homestead in Härjedalen. Have you ever run into any of them?"

"Oh, I know the Vosses."

Brand glanced over at him. "You do?"

"Not in the sense we are friends. But it is a big, spreading clan, active in the local area and in Sweden as a whole."

"And you are familiar with them how?"

"In my capacity as an attorney, I have several times faced Vosses in court," he added. "Some in the family, perhaps the majority, like to operate in the gray area between legal and criminal."

"There's a gray area?" Brand asked. "I've always tried to keep the line pretty clear."

"You know, in Sweden, twenty families rule the whole country. We turn our face to the world as a socialist democracy, but if we look in the mirror we see Wallenberg, Kamprad, Olsson and Lumberg, big names of hereditary dynasties that hold all the wealth."

He indicated one of the big Voss trucks. "The Vosses are most definitely not in the very top tier. Not in the upper one percent, as they say in America. But they are up there. They make their money in transport, though in the past decade they have diversified aggressively. The phrase in English is 'fingers in a lot of pies', isn't it?"

"And politics, is that one of the pies?" Brand asked.

"Oh, yes. Politics, finance, power. Certain Vosses are involved in shadow operations on the extreme far right. Down through the years a few radicals in the clan have fallen into trouble with more cautious family members. This is usually because of association with these extremists. Often wealth and right-wing views go together."

She had now transferred the old snapshot to the pocket of her vest. Her grandmother used to spit out the name as though it were a curse. "Loke Voss!" she would exclaim. Her vituperation stood out because Klara Dalgren was not normally a demonstrative person. She rarely had a cruel word for anyone.

"Lukas told you right," Hammar said. "The original Voss homestead is less than a hundred kilometers from the Dalgren family farm, the place we just left. The Vosses own a small village called Västvall."

"They own a village?"

"A 'village' here can be nothing more than two abandoned houses at the end of a road," Hammar said. "The village of Västvall is certainly more than that. The family has holdings everywhere. On our way up ahead we could look at some Voss properties, if you like."

"Jesus, no—let's just get back to Stockholm, all right?"

But the Voss name nagged at her as they drove on. Blocks and gaps marked her memory of childhood. There were shadows in the past of her Swedish grandparents. Could one of those shadows have the name "Voss" attached to it? She had an uncomfortable hunch that it might be true. Heavy drinking fueled bitter, screaming arguments between Klara and Gustav. Brand as a young girl overheard them fight while huddled in bed, frightened.

She and Hammar were still trailing behind one of the company's semi-trailers. The name "Voss" hovered in the fading light of afternoon.

"All right," Brand said. She wondered if he would pick up the thread and realize she was agreeing to visit one of the Voss clan's holdings.

Hammar understood. "There is Sofieborg Manor House, not far up ahead. The Vosses own it now. Mid-seventeenth century, built by a Swedish count in honor of his wife. Said to be haunted. I have visited once before. The building is impressive. You will see. It tells a story of Swedish capitalists, past and present."

At Hammar's direction Brand exited off the highway. Whatever traffic there was dwindled in the rear-view. He pointed her along a route that led through several suburban towns. Dense forests covered the slopes above the frozen, snow covered surface of a lake.

Brand was getting used to the traffic roundabouts, the foreign signage, the polite ways of other drivers. Along a stretch of suburban road a small flock of school children stepped onto the pavement in front of the car. Prattling among themselves, they seemed oblivious to the fact that a vehicle bore down on them.

Brand braked abruptly. The Saab stalled. Before Hammar could stop her she leaped out of the car to confront the young jaywalkers.

"What are you doing?" she yelled in English. "Do you want to get yourselves run over? Watch out where you're going!"

The half-dozen preteens stared at the madwoman. They didn't seem overly concerned, just puzzled. One of them, a tall girl, echoed Brand's words. She sounded as though she was puzzling out a phrase from a classroom lesson.

"Watch out where you're going," she calmly repeated in accented English.

"We have the right! Not you!" one of the others shouted.

The kids moved on, laughing and talking, not even bothering to look back. Still upset, Brand climbed back into the car.

"Very un-Swedish," Hammar said. "Here we do not attack our children."

"I don't care," Brand said, starting the car again, jamming it into gear, and pulling away from the intersection.

"You know, there are pills for what you have," Hammar said.

"Yes? What do I have?"

"Anger issues. I would say Xanor, or some other sort of mild tranquilizer."

"And now you're a doctor." Privately she wondered if Hammar had somehow discovered her habitual use of amphetamines.

Hammar adopted what sounded like his lawyer's voice: "About twenty years past the law was changed giving pedestrians the right of way over cars. Though I admit it has resulted in more accidents."

"I neglected to run them over, then, as a favor," Brand tried to keep a note of annoyance from her voice. She did not appreciate the reference to her anger issues. Even if it were true. Who did the man think he was?

Hammar directed her, turn by turn, through a sparsely built expanse of countryside. Among their many holdings, he told her, the Vosses owned the large country estate that surrounded the historic manor house.

"All this is family property," he said, gesturing around to the forested terrain.

"How do you know?" Brand asked.

"I know," Hammar answered simply.

"So do we just drive up to the front door and knock? I mean, what's our plan here?"

Hammar indicated a private road that slanted off from the public one.

"There's the driveway," he said. "Let's go do some investigating, Detective."

"Whoa, really?" Brand pulled the Saab over to examine the turn-off.

"We can go in and have a look, take direction from what we see," Hammar said. "As I told you, I have visited here before, and it is often uninhabited. During the summer, tours are sometimes offered."

The ungated drive featured no identifying signage, simply a wide, well-plowed lane that led through a snowy grove of poplars and birch. Brand ventured forward. A few hundred meters in, the house came into view. It's symmetrical design and façade of cold, yellow render stood it apart from the neighboring traditional red farmhouses. A newly tacked on extension to accommodate multiple cars jutted out from the side, disrupting the original balance of the house. The whole structure was a ostentatious attempt to indicate wealth and power.

Brand slowed the Saab as they approached. Graceful stands of birches suffused the yard with a pale light, which reflected off the residence's façade of glazed stone. Closer in, the trees gave way to an expansive snow-covered lawn. No one was around, either on the grounds or near the structure. Untracked snow piled up on the walkway at the front entrance. A feeling of limbo emanated from the place, a sense of adjournment and suspended time. Nothing about it looked lived in.

"I don't think we're going to have to knock," Brand said.

"No?" Hammar asked.

Brand gestured to a side door of the building, which hung open. Next to it were the closed bays of the garage. The situation didn't look right to her. There, a muddle of fresh footprints smashed in the overnight snow. She braked ten meters back from the house. The open door triggered an uneasy feeling. Her cop sense bristled. The deserted manor house offered a perfectly serene tableau, except for the single disturbing flaw of a wide open door.

She had not reset her watch. Eight forty-two a.m., New York time. Adding six hours brought her almost to three o'clock. The dense light of a winter afternoon made it feel much later. Enveloping darkness threatened to swallow the whole scene. She climbed out of the Saab onto the snowy gravel drive.

"Remain where you are," she told Hammar, employing her best control-and-command voice. Hammar did not move from the Saab's front passenger seat.

Only Brand's footfalls broke the oppressive silence. She approached the house slowly. Elsewhere in the yard, the surface of the snow was clean and unbroken. Not here, in front of the open door, where the snow was heavily tracked.

As soon as she crossed the threshold, Brand stepped in blood.

9

The open door gave out into a wood-paneled vestibule. This looked to be the less formal entrance to the manor house, perhaps for the help. The gloom of the fading afternoon reached inside the premises.

Brand saw there were bloody footprints everywhere inside. The markings crisscrossed the entryway. She followed the tracks with her eyes. They showed heavily on the stairway that led to the second story. Something about footprints struck her as odd. Brand could not have immediately said what the strange quality was.

She retreated. Returning to the car, she grabbed the handle of the driver's side door. She swung it open, flipped back the seat and accessed her bag.

"What?" Hammar asked. "Who's in there?" Brand heard the undertone of fear in the man's voice. She reached inside the bag. Pulling out half the contents, she piled her clothing on the back seat. Among the scattered garments she fished out a small leather pouch that was tucked within a rolled-up hand towel.

"What did you see?" Hammar asked. "If something is not right here, we should call the police."

"I am the police," Brand replied. She zipped the pouch open. Its metallic lining was specifically designed to thwart X-ray machines. Concealed inside the pouch was her duty pistol. The Glock's frame was fabricated from high impact plastic. The weapon's metal works were limited only to its barrel and firing mechanism. The composite construction rendered it less detectable during security screenings.

Through being instructed in the detection of smuggled weapons, Brand had learned how to conceal one effectively. From her cop training she understood it wasn't all that difficult to slip a handgun past an airport checkpoint. Not in carry-on, but in baggage. Blind tests indicated that security personnel missed ninety-five percent of all weapons.

She knew the methods. She had lately developed a stubborn unwillingness to venture anywhere "naked," as the jargon had it, meaning unarmed. Her recent issues with several more aggressive members of the NYPD made her paranoid. After almost fifteen years on the force, the Glock 17 she carried was as much a part of her as her eyes, her hands. Leaving it behind was out of the question.

When he saw the pistol, Hammar reacted as if struck. "What's that? Where did you get that?" An expression of sick fascination crossed his face.

Brand didn't answer him. She held up her hand, gesturing Hammar to remain where he was.

"Stay." She sounded as though she were speaking to a pet. Hammar began to object. He went quiet when Brand racked the pistol. It was a sound, she had noticed, that gave a lot of people pause.

Brand ducked back out of the Saab. She felt herself entering into crime scene mode, when a certain kind of hyper-vision took over. She needed a cool head. The comforting weight of the Glock helped anchor her.

She moved forward, once again approaching the wide-open side door of the manor house. She stepped gingerly to avoid walking over the tracks that were already there. The odd aspect she had noticed on her first approach to the premises became clear. Mixed in with human footprints were prints of an animal. A large dog, it looked like. The paw-prints were huge. Or a bear, Brand guessed, as unlikely as the possibility was.

As she crossed to the stairway, her heart rose further into her throat. Blood was everywhere. Penetrating the scene, stepping carefully to avoid contamination, actually felt a little thrilling, like tightrope walking. For the first time in a long while, Brand felt wholly alive. There were any number of customary police procedures she was violating just by being there. Her best move would be to call it in. She ventured forward anyway. The bloody tracks led upward to the second floor overlooking the garage.

At the landing at the top of the stairs she turned right. A doorway opened into a long, narrow space. This was, what? Some kind of children's playroom? The surroundings featured pint-size furniture, puppy decals decorating the walls, stuffed toys. Drawings of cute puppies, yes—and a foul, unholy stink that rose strong and sharp.

Waves of disgust engulfed her. She steeled herself to discover the source of the spilled blood. Several times in the past, her work had led her to encounter hurt or murdered children. She choked back nausea.

A bank of windows ran along one side of the room. Because they were all shaded, the light remained dim. Brand clasped her sidearm tightly. The blood was fresh red, and she could no longer avoid stepping in it. Her fear threatened to rise to the level of panic.

The first body lay tucked beside a couch-like collection of pillows, a stocky, bearded male of about thirty. Brand didn't need more than a glance to understand the man was dead, but she bent to check for an aortic pulse anyway.

Around the crotch area, the flesh displayed an extreme degree of evisceration. Brand had never before seen that level of ferocity. Someone—or something—had been hard at work on the body. Ripped apart clothing and skin revealed a bloody mass of torn flesh. Judging from the appearance of the wounds, the damage had not all been post-mortem. The victim's voided bowels raised a stench.

The body was cool to the touch. But rigor seemed not to have yet set in. That indicated the bearded man's life had been cut short only within the past few hours. In his out-flung hand he clutched a palm-size leather wallet. Brand gingerly flipped it open and saw it contained some sort of identification. She could puzzle out Swedish enough to understand the word "*POLIS*" in large, blocky red type.

Could she really have a dead cop on her hands? The discovery transformed the whole situation. The alarm bells going off in her head tripled in volume. Reaching in cautiously, she quickly searched the body for a weapon. There was none. The man didn't look like police. The beard and the clothing seemed wrong to her. But what did a Swedish plainclothes look like, anyway?

Brand stood. Recoiling from what she had seen, she crossed the room. She raised a single window shade. Weak, cloud-filtered sunlight helped illuminate the ghastly scene. A second victim sprawled a short distance from the first. The body, also male, lay blood-covered and motionless.

As she knelt to feel for a pulse, the corpse abruptly came alive. Rearing up, the man grabbed Brand in a bloody hug. She tried to escape. One forearm gripped her around the neck. Her face came inches away from the wounded man's. Something was wrong with his eyes. They stared blankly as Brand struggled to free herself.

With a jolt of fear she saw the blade coming at her.

IO

Brand parried the stab of the knife. She quickly realized that the last-gasp attack had exhausted her opponent. His thrusts now resembled the feeble movements of an infant. She was able to relieve him of the weapon. She tossed the knife away. It clattered to rest beneath the bank of windows.

The man collapsed heavily back down to the floor. He sighed out a long, rattling wheeze, then lay still. When Brand put two fingers to his neck, she felt an uncertain pulse fade and disappear.

Silence returned to the scene. Brand had a momentary sense that her presence was intrusive. She had experienced the feeling before. In the company of the dead, the living are an insult. She rose to her feet. Blood now marked the front of the down vest she wore. She left the knife where it lay and moved to search the premises. To her relief she discovered no more torn apart bodies.

She tried to parse out the footprints. Full and partials patterned the floor. Someone had evidently allowed a large animal into the room. A bear? A panther? A wolf? Were there big cats in the Swedish wilds?

Brand thought that an attack dog employed as a weapon of violence was more likely. The size of the paw-prints indicated a bullmastiff or a boerboel, perhaps a Great Dane. She tried to remember what the fearsome red-eyed beast in "The Hound of Baskervilles" had finally turned out to be. A large dog of some sort. A wolfhound?

On the job in New York City, Brand had encountered intentional, human-directed canine attacks. It happened only a few times, but those were memorable. In some neighborhoods pit bulls were virtually the only breed around. Naturally there were incidents. But what Brand saw in front of her rose to a whole different level.

At the rear of the main room she entered an adjacent hallway. The polished wood flooring along the whole corridor remained clean and unbloodied. Brand gingerly opened a closed door. She expected the worst. It was only a small, empty, powder-room style bathroom.

She stepped inside. The conventional white porcelain facilities appeared modern and ordinary. Several discarded tissues were piled beneath the mirror of the vanity, caked with some sort of heavy white paste. The doors to a small cabinet below the sink were open. The cabinet itself was empty. There was no blood in evidence anywhere.

Brand moved forward and pulled aside the white plastic shower curtain. In the stall lay several items of discarded clothing. She took a pen from her pocket. Using it as a probe, she fished out a miniskirt, then another dress. Brand was surprised to see it was a wedding gown.

Whoever had worn the garment had to have been in some kind of distress. There were tears and rips everywhere. Brand slid her finger into a small, specially made pocket torn open in the waistband. A place to hide a bride's mad money? She understood nothing of what she was seeing.

Witnessing the scene had worked a transformation in her. She hesitated before returning to the main room. She was no longer a suspended police detective visiting from NYC. All her on-the-job expertise prompted a new urgency. She became a detective again. An insistent, familiar urge kicked in, a determination to discover what had happened. It was the only way to quell the fear the killings had triggered in her. Somehow she felt this was the true, fundamental role of the police: to help beat back the natural terror that extreme violence triggers in the hearts of ordinary citizens. Cops worked to tease order from chaos.

She stuffed both the discarded gown and the white-smeared tissues into the side pocket of her down vest. As she emerged from the bathroom hallway, Brand realized her breath had a ragged, uneven rhythm to it. She needed to clear her head. She crossed to the single unshaded window. She gazed out for a moment at the deserted, darkening yard. Something bothered her about the whole set-up, something beyond the deadly hurt which humans inflict on one another.

Hammar had brought them here. He insisted on immediately heading up the driveway to the house. Why?

Beyond the grounds, at the edge of the birch woods that skirted the property, Brand detected movement. A hallucination bloomed in the faded afternoon, a sight she could hardly credit. The light was becoming increasingly unreliable.

A dark silhouette passed among the trees. Some sort of animal moved there. She caught a glimpse of a mottled coat of fur, a flash of sesame color. Brand had only a quick look. The form vanished among the trees so quickly she questioned if she had seen it at all.

Perhaps, she thought, what had happened here was no human crime. The two victims had been upstairs, lounging around, perhaps asleep. Somehow a wild predator of some sort had crept in through an open door. A bear or wolf. Do such beasts climb stairs? Brand was uncertain on the subject of Swedish fauna. At any rate, the attack went down quickly. The bloody human footprints in evidence everywhere were simply the result of the terrified victims attempting to elude their fates.

None of that seemed likely, but the prospect served to inflame her mind. The animal she had seen—if she had seen one—was fearsomely large. She imagined it bounding back over the snowy yard. Having tasted human flesh, perhaps it would be hungry for more. Her police partner in New York had once been forced to fire his service weapon in order to halt the charge of an attacking pit bull. The dog went down in a heap. The memory had plagued Brand ever since.

She heard the scuff of footsteps crossing the landing. Brand wheeled around and automatically took up a shooting stance, training her sidearm at the doorway.

Hammar.

Seeing Brand standing with an automatic, posed to blast off his head, the man threw up his hands in surrender.

"*Stanna*, Veronika!" Stop.

"I told you to stay in the car," Brand said, carefully lowering the pistol.

They stood for a moment amidst the desecrated room, decorated for a child but yielding adult horror. Brand noticed Krister had rigged two plastic shopping bags like booties around his shoes. Both bags were stained red. The dying afternoon heightened the atmosphere of spent violence.

Moving robotically, Hammar did the obvious thing, what anyone would do in this situation—he retrieved a cell phone from his pocket. Punching in numbers on the keypad, he raised the device to his ear.

"Don't do that," Brand said. She crossed the distance between them quickly and snatched the phone away. She still held the Glock.

"What are you about?" the man cried. "We must summon the authorities!"

Brand's private emergencies eclipsed all other concerns. She needed time to think. "Did you get connected? Krister! Did you reach 9-1-1?"

He stared at her. "It's not 9-1-1 here, it's 1-1-2."

"Were you put through?"

"No," Hammar admitted. "But we must call the police, Veronika!"

"Not yet," Brand said. Hammar was right. Every element of Brand's professional training told her to notify the authorities immediately. Simple humanity and respect for the dead demanded that they report the situation.

But Brand was a fraught stranger in a strange land. She was badly frightened. A wrong move could prove disastrous. In the face of her determination, Hammar backed off. He followed her out of the room, down the stairs and out to the gravel driveway.

Moving away from the manor house, they stopped in front of the Saab. Brand looked off toward the shadowy woods. No sign of her vision of a dog-like creature remained. The fog of darkness closed in on the property.

Mentally, she tried to reverse roles, and think how she would react to the situation as a detective. She listed the elements. A deserted, isolated home. Wealthy owners. A gruesome scene of violence. A dead cop. A second victim. And a pair of strangers, one of them a foreign national, who had blundered into it all.

None of it was good. How would Veronika Brand and Krister Hammar appear to responding officers? Witnesses? Persons of interest? Suspects?

Brand couldn't shake the feeling that her presence at the scene had somehow been orchestrated. She possessed the natural suspicious reflexes of a cop. Her paranoia usually served her well during investigations. Distrustful of appearances, skeptical of the facts, she questioned everything.

She tried to swallow a rising surge of anger. Somehow this Swedish immigration lawyer had led her into deep trouble. That she was a police herself might smooth things out. Professional courtesy demanded a certain soft touch. But she was not a cop. She was an ex-cop, Brand reminded herself. Still under investigation, on charges false and otherwise. A simple call to the States would open a whole can of worms. A can of snakes was more like it.

Brand spoke without looking at Hammar. "Why'd you bring me here, Krister?"

"I'm asking myself."

"You knew," she said.

Hammar sounded puzzled. "What? What did I know?"

"You bring me here to see the Voss family setup, and somehow we encounter something else. I don't know what it is yet, but I'm going to find out. I'm thinking, wow, what a coincidence. But I'm a police, and I don't much believe in coincidences. I always have to unpack them, check into what's really happening."

"I had no idea…" Hammar began. Brand cut him off with a glare. His protest sounded weak.

Fury rose in her. She paced, trying to fight it off. She had to think clearly. The sight of a subdued Hammar worked to enrage her further.

"It was you," she said. "I wanted to go slow, but oh, no, you pushed. You played me."

"No, Brand, no," he said carefully, as if placating a lunatic.

She waved the pistol. Hammar shrank from her. "Now you're scaring me."

"Shut up! Is this even a Voss house?" Brand gave a sweep of her arm. "What is this set up? What did you want me to see?"

"I don't know what to say!"

Brand paced some more, storming back and forth in front of him. She felt that her responses weren't entirely logical. For one thing, her brain was in the midst of amphetamine withdrawal. Angry outbursts tended to come with the territory.

"Okay, okay," she muttered. She took a deep breath. Visions of the bloody room assailed her. Glock in hand, she tapped herself absently on the forehead a few times, hoping to dislodge a few fresh thoughts. Then she stopped, standing stock still.

"It's a— it's a pipeline, isn't it?" Brand said. "Some sort of transfer point.

You were going to lure me up here—"

"I didn't lure you! You wanted to come. You asked!"

She ignored Hammar's objection. "You were going to get me up here, and you were going to draw me a picture. They're running human flesh through this house, aren't they? So you were going to be like, 'Hey, Ms. Big City Dick, it's so awful, won't you help the poor exploited victims?' Am I right?"

"Yes. No!"

"But it ran off the rails. You didn't expect blood, did you, Counselor? Come on. We've got a few minutes. I don't know response times around here, but Swedish police are said to be kind of slow on the uptake. Am I right? You knew!"

Hammar's face took on a gray tint, its color drained. "I didn't know...all this." He waved in the direction of the house. "How could I?"

"I can't believe I was so damned stupid." Brand was talking to herself now. "Let's head up the drive and find out, he says. What do I do? I do exactly like he says, like some—like a tool. I must be off my game. I've been in trouble ever since I pulled my duffel off the carousel at Arlanda. You played me. And I don't like to be played."

"Veronika!" he wailed. "*Vad gör du?*" What are you doing?

It was her fault, a fact which did not help with her feelings of betrayal. She had entered the manor house, acting like a cop instead of what she was, a tourist. Plus she had foolishly tampered with the scene. She extracted the torn dress and the wad of discarded tissues from the pocket of her down vest.

She turned back to Hammar. "Have you any contacts in the local constabulary?"

He shook his head.

"Well, our presence here is a little problematic," she said. "You do realize that, don't you? What are we up to? Why were we even here in the first place? Just taking a little tour of the great manor houses of Sweden? We need to decide what's what. Then we make the call. "

She didn't even mention one of the dead was police. Glancing at Hammar, she realized the man wasn't even listening to her. Brand reacted with a flare of anger. She wanted to give him a shake. Hadn't he heard her?

He was staring at the balled-up wedding dress that Brand still held in her hand. "What's that? Where did you get that?"

"Jesus, what's the matter with you?"

Hammar reached out slowly, as if moving in a dream. He took the dress from Brand. The movement was so odd that she gave it up willingly.

"Don't tell me you recognize it?"

"I need to—need to check—I'm not sure," Hammar stammered. "I think

I know whose it is."

"Come on," Brand said, skeptical. "Out of all the wedding gowns on the planet, you're telling me you can identify this one? They all look pretty similar, don't they?"

"No, no," Hammar protested. He clutched at the fabric. "It is…very recognizable. I've seen it often. I know who wore it."

Part two: The blond beast

At the center of all these noble races we cannot fail to see the beast of prey, the magnificent blond beast avidly prowling round for spoil and victory…

Nietzsche

I I

Brand sat alone at the local police station in the town of Ljusdal. For once she found herself on the other side of an interrogation table.

There had been some preliminary questioning at the manor house. The responding officers had quickly established that the bearded man was not, in fact, a member of the police force. The ID was an obvious fake. The real police had responded out of a Gävleborg County headquarters in Ljusdal. They directed Brand and Hammar to follow along behind them as they drove the ten-kilometer distance to the station.

The former market town was located on a single lane carriageway, and featured a mix of non-descript 1960's detached housing with an eclectic collection of shops and cafes that wouldn't know a latte from a milkshake. A welcome change to the endless flat fields of snow and farmhouses that dotted the landscape of the journey so far. In the station, the officers separated the two of them. She recognized the time-honored police practice of cooling out subjects and keeping them apart.

The interrogation room where she sat reflected the Swedish preference for no-nonsense functionalism. The room was in stark contrast to the windowless, strip-light illuminated boxes she felt at home in. The setting almost felt like a new office; soft ceiling lights complemented the sun's feeble rays which snuck in through a small window high up on the wall to her left. The light cast a warm glow on the clean white walls and the sleek wood table, glinting off the tell tale two-way mirror which took up most of the wall directly in front of her. Brand couldn't help but feel slightly impressed that the stylish wooden chairs matched the table, an achievement she hadn't managed in her own misshapen apartment. Brand sat on the side usually occupied by the assumed guilty, her hands clasped in front of her on the bare tabletop, gazing out of the window at a small spruce offering a shield from prying outside eyes.

A cop often thinks along the lines of a criminal. Put the right type of prisoner in this snug room, Brand considered, leave them alone, and they'd have a weapon fashioned in five minutes. Her own weapon was safely hidden in the Saab. Brand stashing the pistol in his vehicle sparked another anxiety attack in Hammar. He demanded that she turn the Glock in.

Held in limbo in separate rooms in the station house, they waited, each alone. The police hadn't taken away their cell phones. Brand looked at hers, and realized that for once she had a signal. She stood as if to stretch her legs, turning her back to the mirror, cradling the phone in both hands in front of her mouth in an attempt to conceal the call she was making to Hammar.

"Veronika." He sounded subdued.

"It's okay," she said in a placating tone, the one she always employed to chill out tense situations.

"We're suspects, not witnesses," Hammar said into the phone. "I mean, the other way around, not witnesses but suspects. No, no—"

She interrupted. "I get the point. We're witnesses."

Hammar had clearly been deeply shaken by the events of the afternoon. The bizarre crime scene collided with the image of a peaceful, safe Sweden. Brand realized she had shown lack of control in her treatment of Hammar earlier. Looking back, she thought the man had carried himself rather well. He had actually managed to stay steady in spite of, or maybe because of, the carnage around them.

"I admire the way you kept cool out there, Krister," she said. "That business was bad, real bad. I had a partner in New York, Willie Urrico. Great guy. He came out of a bloody crime scene one time and made a comment that afterwards turned famous. 'I nearly shit my socks,' he said, and we all laughed. Cut the tension perfectly, you know? Pretty soon everybody on the force was saying it whenever things went sideways. And I'll tell you honestly right now, entering that room in the manor house, I nearly shit my socks."

"How do you do it?" Hammar asked. "How do you walk into scenes like that, day after day?"

"I'm not sure," Brand said. "All the good cops who I know, they cope. Cops cope. That's what they do. Of course police also eat the gun at higher rates than any other profession apart from shrinks. So maybe coping will only get you so far."

They listened to each other breathe for a while. It had been only a few minutes since a low-ranking uniform had put Brand in the office, but the wait to be questioned felt overlong.

Hammar finally broke the silence. "I'm sitting in a room without windows, alone."

"Me, too. Talk to me if anything happens." They hung up.

Eleven minutes later by the clock on her cellphone, a Ljusdal Detective

Inspector named Sven Bok entered. He took his place across the table from Brand. The man struck her as impossibly green. His spiky haircut and boyish features made him appear too young to be a cop.

"So, Detective Brand," he began. Then he stopped. He fixed his eyes on a sheaf of papers he had brought in with him. She waited him out. Brand realized the guy was disturbed by the case.

Bok swallowed hard and continued. "Could we go again through your actions earlier this afternoon?"

"I've already told the responding officers," she said, playing for time.

"Well, yes, of course." Bok was deferential. "As you know yourself from your police work, going through an experience repeatedly can bring up new facts you hadn't thought of before."

She was impressed by the man's easy command of English. The younger the person was in Sweden, she thought, the better they were with foreign languages.

"Sure, okay," she said. "As soon as I realized the side door to the garage hung open—"

"I have to interrupt," Bok said, holding up his hand. "Why were you at Sofieborg Manor House in the first place?"

"My attorney—would it be possible to have my attorney present here? I don't know the protocols."

"I'm sorry, just for now, if you could simply answer my questions."

"Yes, of course," Brand said.

"I realize you've been through this already. But as we said, perhaps some additional details will become clear."

Brand liked the detective. She didn't want to give him a hard time. "We visited the manor house because Mr Hammar believed it would be good for me to see an example of fine old Swedish architecture."

"Your visit was…tourism?"

She felt a need to dodge the whole "reason for your visit" line of questioning. "I realized something was wrong as soon as I saw that a door had been left open. No one was around. The place was deserted. So naturally the wide open door concerned me. You have an issue around here with burglaries in unoccupied summer homes?"

"Well, yes, it is a problem."

"I directed Mr Hammar to remain in the car. I approached the house. I saw blood. A great deal of it. I entered the ground floor and proceeded upstairs following the trail of blood."

"I'm sorry, I have to ask, why not call the police right away? Why enter? Couldn't that have been a dangerous decision?"

"I felt I had to address the safety of anyone inside. I did tell Mr Hammar to call emergency."

"So you discovered the two victims. What did you do?"

"I checked for signs of life. Then I immediately exited and waited for your responding officers."

"Yes, okay," Bok said. "Did you disturb anything at the scene?"

"No. The scene disturbed me, not the other way around."

"Remove anything from the scene?"

"No," Brand lied. "Oh wait, I had maybe a little bit of blood on the bottom of my boots."

Brand thought of the wedding dress. Along with her Glock, she had left the vest, the dress and the clump of soiled tissues in the Saab. "I pulled up a window shade. I thought what little light there was left outside might make it easier to see. I wanted to make sure there were no additional victims."

"Raised a window shade," Bok repeated.

"There were five windows on the right side as you enter the main room on the second floor. I unshaded a single window in the middle."

Bok stared at her for a long beat, then looked away. "I'm sorry you had to see this on your first visit to our country," he said briskly, gathering his papers together. "Very upsetting."

"Yes," Brand said, trying to sound noncommittal. "One of those scenes, you know, we've all encountered them—they make it hard to believe that there's a hell below this."

"We've all seen them, we've all seen them…" the Swedish detective repeated. "Of course you may have encountered worse during your time in New York City. You see, here we are a small town. We don't all see such scenes. Not often. Never, in truth. Some crime comes out of big cities. Mostly for extreme injuries or deaths such as this, it's traffic accidents. But here…"

Bok closed the file folder in front of him with an air of finality. "We'll have to ask you to stay in the country until this incident is sorted out."

"That's it?"

"For now," Bok said.

Before Brand could rise, a knock came at the door. It swung part way open. A uniformed woman summoned Detective Bok. He rose immediately and went to her. Brand remained where she was.

The two of them conferred in whispers outside in the corridor. She heard a third party join in, too. Out of nowhere she picked up a single sentence in murmured Swedish.

Det är den där bitchen Dalgren.

Brand could hardly believe her ears. Even with her limited grasp of the native tongue, it was not hard to work out what the words meant. As a child she had understood some due to her experience at her grandparents farm. Even when speaking with her, Gustav and Klara used Swedish more often than their newly acquired second language, English. Gradually Brand gained an understanding as children do, simply by the process of osmosis. Now it seemed the longer she remained in Sweden, the more the language came back to her.

She had just heard herself insulted, characterized by a slur. The offensive word had been invoked by an unseen third person. She was too stunned to do what she should have, which was to leave the station immediately.

Det är den där bitchen Dalgren. That's the Dalgren bitch.

Brand couldn't be sure she understood. Who in the world would say such a thing? She had been listening to lowered voices through a half-closed door. Her hearing—or maybe her mind—was playing tricks.

She didn't object to the slur. She had often been called much worse on the job. But she could not understand how anyone in a little crossroads town in the middle of nowhere would be able to link her to the Dalgren family. It didn't make sense.

The uniformed woman returned alone from the hall. She stepped inside and shut the door behind her. Forcing a smile, she took Sven Bok's place across the table from Brand.

"Hello, Detective," she said. "My name is Naima Lindblad, and I'm District Police Commissioner here in Ljusdal."

Brand realized she had just been handed up the chain of command. Lindblad looked about her own age, late 30s. Her neatly coiffed, light-colored hair prompted Brand to question whether every woman in the country was blond.

"I know this will be frustrating for you," Lindblad said. "But I must inform you that your interrogation is suspended. Since you have a great deal of police experience, you will understand. This incident involves an ongoing investigation which we cannot compromise."

"What does that mean?" Brand asked.

"I'll have to ask you to say nothing about it to anyone. You're free to go."

Brand shook her head in puzzlement. "I'm a little confused," she said. "So you're the national police, am I right? Maybe more like our FBI?"

"We really need to terminate this interview," Lindblad said. "I'm not at liberty to explain right now."

12

Commissioner Lindblad stood and motioned to the door, gesturing the way out. "I also request that you refrain from sharing any details about what you've seen. No contact with the media."

Brand was doubly mystified. She shook her head. "All right. Okay. But no."

"I'm sorry?"

Remaining stubbornly seated, Brand stared evenly at the police commissioner. "I need you to tell me what is going on."

"I can't say anything more. You must understand."

"What I understand is that I just stepped out of a slaughterhouse," Brand said. "That room ranks up there with anything I've ever seen, and I've seen my share. In fact, I've probably seen your share, too. Now you're telling me goodbye, farewell, don't let the door hit your butt on the way out?"

"I'm sorry it has to be that way."

"I'm a cop. You're a cop. A little professional courtesy would be nice."

Lindblad turned back to the table. She spoke in a low, even voice. "But you're not a police officer, are you? Not anymore."

"Oh, I see. You've just learned of my situation in New York, and now you're shutting me out. Sorry, that's not good enough. Shouldn't the press know about something like this?"

Brand saw the hit land. The police commissioner hesitated. Having mentioned Brand's uncertain status as a police, Lindblad seemed to relent.

"I'm telling you this only with the understanding that it's in strict confidence," she said. "We've been seeing the practice of dog fighting spread in certain immigrant communities. There's no indigenous tradition of it here in Sweden. We have reason to believe some employees at the Sofieborg Manor House are involved."

"Dog fighting? Really? That's your theory of the crime? Have you seen the size of those bloody paw prints?"

The door opened abruptly. A man walked in who Brand immediately pegged as an American. He wore a parka and, underneath that, a business suit.

Detective Inspector Bok followed him in. "Here is a countryman of yours," he said to Brand. Bok then addressed his superior. "Naima, this is

Charles Joyner, an attaché at the US Embassy."

"Charlie Joyner," the man said, holding out a hand for the commissioner to shake. He smiled broadly and, as far as Brand could tell, falsely. "May I have a private moment with this fine upstanding American citizen here?"

It was almost comical, Brand considered. Her situation kept getting kicked upstairs. Next, the prime minister of Sweden was going to walk in. Maybe the King.

Bok and Lindblad shuffled out. They appeared dazed and chastened by the consulate man's brimming energy.

"Hello, Detective Brand," Joyner said briskly. He moved to sit in the chair Lindblad had vacated. He decided against it. "The Japanese have a word for the uncomfortable sensation of warmth experienced sitting in a seat another person has just left. I mean, ugh, you know?"

He perched on the edge of the table instead. "How are you? Well, you don't have to answer that. I understand you've encountered some pretty gruesome stuff. An NYPD detective comes all the way to Sweden, what does she run into? More blood and guts."

"I'm sorry," Brand said. "Who are you?"

"No, I'm sorry!" Joyner clapped his hands. He spoke in clipped sentences. "Deputy consul. Your man in Sweden. You caught me at home, Uppsala. A real special city, if you haven't been. College town. All it needs is a little more sunlight, like everywhere else around here this time of year."

Charles Joyner pronounced the name of the town as "Oopsala." Brand had him categorized as some sort of flunky assistant. Somebody's junior's junior. Sent out to clean up the Ljusdal mess.

The deputy consul leaned in. Brand could smell his breath, tobacco overlaid with a heavy mint smell.

"What I would recommend to you, right now? Return home. I know you've got a heap of trouble back there. Just between you and me and these four walls, I've been on the phone with New York. Things are happening. The situation might develop in your favor. The deputy commissioner indicated she needs you back in the fold. Your testimony would be crucial, she said. Well, I didn't hear her say that personally. I only talked to her subordinate. I don't recall the name. But that's good news, right?"

He practically bellowed out his last sentence. Brand imagined the man's superior at the consulate giving Joyner his marching orders. For chrissakes, Charlie, get the woman detective out of there. Have her airlifted if needs be. For the second time in half an hour she witnessed someone make a gesture indicating that she should exit the room.

"Sure, sure, good news," Brand agreed. She stood. "It's just that, the local constables, sir, they say, please don't leave the country for now. Then you tell me to get the hell out of town. I'm sorry, I'm feeling jerked around here. It's ping-pong city in this place."

"Don't worry about those guys!" Charlie Joyner crowed. "I'll take care of them. You just have a good flight back to NYC. Sweden in February, brrrr! Am I right?"

Brand let him guide her out of the little office and along a corridor to the station lobby. He had a limousine waiting at the curb. A car from the consulate, he said. The trip to Arlanda would be all taken care of, he said.

"Arlanda?"

"Back home!" Joyner said brightly.

Brand was half stunned and half amused by the man's presumption. Like she was a mere chess piece he could move around the board at will.

Joyner stood poised holding the station door open, waiting for Brand to head outside and dive directly into the limo.

Through the lobby's glass windows she saw the ancient blue Saab. The owner sat inside, head lowered with only the light from his phone illuminating the interior of the car against the dark afternoon sky. Even from a distance, his hunched profile gave away the fear of someone who had never been on the wrong side of the law. Brand was surprised at the sense of relief she felt upon seeing Hammar. She stepped through the door.

"My ride's here," Brand said. She pushed past Joyner.

"You're making a mistake, Detective," Joyner called after her. "No one wants you here."

Brand turned. "That never stopped me before." She strode on.

"From now on, you're on your own," Joyner said. "You get into trouble, we can't pull you out." Then he climbed into the car from the consulate and left.

Brand crossed to Hammar. She stood beside the car, waiting outside the Saab's driver's side door. Shaking his head, Hammar yielded his place to her.

"You're impossible," he said.

When she entered, she simply sat at the wheel without making a move to start the engine. Something didn't add up.

"They knew I was a Dalgren," she said. "Someone did, anyhow."

"What?"

"Someone in the cop shop, I didn't see who—someone said I was a Dalgren."

"Okay, yes," Hammar said. "Well, we must have told them. Or maybe I told them, back at the manor house, that we had just come from a family reunion. You said that, too, maybe? So the police already heard the name Dalgren, isn't that right? What's so wrong about that?"

That's the Dalgren bitch.

Had she heard the words, or just imagined them?

She turned the ignition key, engaged the Saab's clutch, slipped the transmission into gear, and performed a U-turn in the police station driveway in order to head back toward the highway.

Except for occasional navigating instructions from Hammar, they rode in silence. Brand was thinking about a dog, or bear, or bear-dog. A beast, anyway. A blond beast that moved in the underbrush like a ghost.

The vision was already fading from her mind. The light had been bad. At the time when she thought she saw the beast, her body's physical chemistry was understandably disrupted by encountering a horrific crime scene. Her respiration had been heightened. Fight-or-flight biochemicals were flooding her system. She was probably mistaken about the whole thing.

Hammar broke the silence. "You think I've tricked you, that I played you, as you say. But I've actually done you a favor."

"Oh, yeah," Brand said. "A huge favor, introducing me to that scene back there."

"You've got the Voss family on your mind, right? You're a detective. You want to find out all about them."

She glanced over at him. "Yes."

"What was in that house tells a basic truth. The Vosses are capable of violent extremes. Maybe the two dead men betrayed them somehow, or had to be silenced."

"You admit that you suspected the Voss name was somehow connected to human trafficking. That's why you brought me out there. Under false pretenses."

"What could be a better front for human trafficking than a trucking company?" he asked. "I don't think you realize who the Vosses are."

"You don't have the faintest idea what I realize," Brand said irritably.

"You know, in Sweden, you and I are equal," Hammar said. "You are not a police detective, are you? Not here. Just an ordinary person on a visit to the homeland."

"Your point is? I know you must have one."

"A bit of humility might be good."

"So everyone tells me," Brand said.

I3

Within the NYPD, the line on Detective Lieutenant Veronika Brand was simple and direct. She was a good cop saddled with serious personality flaws. Certain characterizations followed her during her ascent to Detective Lieutenant, opinions ranging from "blunt and stubborn," "arrogant and harsh," to "not a people person." Brand heard the whispers, dismissing them as male takes on an forceful woman. She kept her head down, aced the sergeant's exam, saw herself steadily promoted out of uniform and into plainclothes. After Brand gained her lieutenancy, the brass saw fit to assign her to one prestigious criminal task force after another.

No one in the department ever described Brand as easygoing. So much in life consists of looking the other way, and this was especially true in the day-to-day grind of a police detective in New York City. In her rise through the ranks from patrol to anti-crime to work on a dedicated sex crimes unit, Brand balked at the code of silence. She refused to wear the blinders that were as much standard issue for cops as a duty belt and a countdown calendar to retirement.

Over the recent winter holidays came a series of actions that wound up effectively derailing Detective Brand's career after a decade and a half on the force. In retrospect she at least partially blamed her devotion to amphetamine. She was just coming off a twelve-hour watch, crashing from a speed high. Maybe her judgment was a little off. Maybe she rushed a very delicate and explosive rape investigation.

Brand caught the case by chance, interviewing young Bristol Chambers at the Six-Oh precinct house in Coney Island. The duty sergeant tossed her the complainant who had come in the night before. Brand sat across from the teenage victim, just the two of them in the windowless interview room.

She recited the date, time, and place. "On camera is Bristol Chambers," Brand intoned for the record. "Am I correct, Bristol, in saying that you are eighteen years old?"

"I'm nineteen next month," said the kid.

"You told Patrol Officer Padilla that last night two men assaulted you in Vaux Park."

"They took me out of Tina's car and put me in their van," the girl said.

Bristol wore an extravagant fade haircut shaved down almost to the skin on both temples. Not for the first time, Brand thought the style didn't work. However much teenagers tarted themselves up to look like gangstas, their kid innocence usually shone through.

"Did anyone use force or intimidation to get you into the other vehicle?" Brand asked.

"I was with my girlfriend Tina, sitting in her Toyota. We were in the park and we wasn't doing anything wrong. They drove up on us in a white van, all of a sudden like."

"I see," Brand said.

"I got the license plate number," the girl added.

Brand concluded that Bristol Chambers was not as stupid as her haircut made her look. She had the girl write down the information. Leaving the room briefly, she requested a plate search from a police clerk. Brand returned with the cop's traditional interview offering, a can of soda and a bag of potato chips.

"Could you tell me what happened?" she asked Bristol, pushing the snack across the table to the girl. "Take your time and put it into your own words."

"They made a lot of comments about why I was with a girl that night and was I a lesbian. They were going to show me the right path, not the gay path, and all that. They told me they were 'freaks,' like real sex freaks, is what they said."

According to Bristol, the male in the driver's seat addressed the one in the front passenger seat as "Richie," and suggested he join "our little rug-muncher friend," in the back of the van.

"So this Richie climbed over from the front and made me do oral on him," she continued. "I was crying all the time and telling him to stop, but he didn't. Then he turned me over and raped me."

Bristol Chambers remained dry-eyed throughout her account, though Brand judged the young woman to be just on the edge of losing it.

In Veronika's mind the incident sounded like a prostitution encounter gone wrong. In her early years on the force, she had been enlisted as a decoy in prostitution busts. She knew the scene well.

"Bristol, why would you get into a vehicle with a couple of strange men?"

"Well, they flashed their headlights at us, and came up to the window and said they were po-po."

Brand felt a jolt pass through her. The fact of alleged police involvement had somehow previously been left unmentioned in the girl's account. "The men told you they were police officers?"

"Yeah, but I didn't think so," Bristol answered. "They were nasty looking, didn't have no badges or nothing. I smelled, like, alcohol on their breaths. I mean, around the block and everything, there's always some chud or another trying to pass himself off as undercover, you know? I thought these guys were fake. They chased Tina off, saying she was too fat, and just took me into their van."

Brand interrupted the proceedings to answer a knock on the door of the interview room.

A clerk handed a piece of paper to her, whispering, "one of ours." The registration of the white 2013 Dodge van turned out to be linked to a police confiscation case. The vehicle had recently been transferred to the anti-crime motor pool for use by plainclothes. The previous night, undercover officers Richie Miles and Devane Berline signed it out for a narcotics operation in the Coney Island neighborhood of Brooklyn.

Then came a series of decisions that Brand might have wanted to take back later, knowing beforehand what she was getting herself into. Even while she was caught up in her actions, she understood there were formal procedures that she ought to have been abiding by, boxes to check off, a chain of command to follow.

Brand didn't know Berline, but Richie Miles was a very familiar name to her, a living embodiment of everything she hated about the NYPD's bro culture. They had been in the same Police Academy class together. Early on in Brand's career, Miles had hit on her, coarsely, and in front of others. Outrageous stories of misbehavior, cut corners, and multiple citizen complaints had dogged Richie Miles every step of his career, but he had always turned up Teflon.

Even with snapping on her lights at every intersection, it still took Brand forty-five minutes in midday traffic to slog across the entire borough of Brooklyn and arrive in Williamsburg. She showed up at the Nine-Four precinct house to arrest Richie Miles on suspicion of rape, kidnapping and official misconduct.

A cop arresting another cop is always problematic. No matter that Brand was just doing her duty. The tribe interpreted any challenge as a betrayal. But at first it looked as if things might go her way. Nothing of any serious weight fell on her. Miles and Berline were suspended. The NYPD brass convened a departmental hearing.

Slowly, though, the tables turned. Bad things started to happen. Her cell phone would go off in the middle of the night. The caller would hang up when she answered. An incident with a dead rat served as a sign the situation was escalating. She swung open her locker one morning to find the stiffened fat rodent staring all blank-eyed at her.

Her standing in the department slid headlong downhill from there. A chill settled in among her fellow cops. Her duty log shrank. She felt herself marked as a traitor to the department. She called her original partner in the NYPD, Willie Urrico. He had retired to New Jersey, working security for Teeterboro Airport.

"How'd you think they were going to react?" Urrico asked. "You came after a couple of their own."

"Pointing out the obvious, Miles and Berline were bad cops."

"I don't know about Berline, but I do know Richie Miles is seriously connected. You know how it is. There's the department, then there's the cliques and factions within the department. It's like a shadow government. And he's the pope of that church."

Over the next weeks Brand watched the case against Miles and Berline fall apart. Cell tower pings turned up discrepancies in the testimony of Bristol Chambers. The phone records indicated the victim wasn't where she said she was at the time of the assault.

Ever since she had been promoted to anti-crime, Brand had worked solo. She drove a seven-year old Chrysler sedan, a motor pool reject. The vehicle was dinged and dented from its years on the mean streets. Despite that, Brand had a great deal of affection for it. The car was her refuge, her sanctuary, her private office.

In heavy traffic on the Bruckner Expressway, Brand felt her brakes go mushy. She pumped them frantically. The pedal went to the floor. All stopping power totally vanished. The situation was brutal, with cars and trucks racing past on both sides. In panic she considered jamming the transmission into reverse.

Careening wildly at top speed, she managed to steer the runaway vehicle across two lanes and onto a grassy slope at the side of the highway. The Chrysler ploughed straight up the hillside. It rumbled and bucked and finally stalled to a stop.

Brand sat stunned in the driver's seat. They're trying to kill me, she thought. Tears of frustration threatened to pour out. She fought back her emotions.

The next day the prosecutor's office dropped all charges against Miles and Berline. The victim's testimony was judged unreliable.

Brand, the cop who initiated the arrest, felt herself exposed, vulnerable.

She knew that victims simply did not manufacture claims of sexual assault. It didn't happen. No one in their right mind would voluntarily enter into such a shitstorm unless the accusation had the weight of truth behind it.

Bristol Chambers might have stumbled when recounting the details. She was a young woman caught in a nightmare. The charge itself, Brand believed, was warranted.

None of that mattered in how the case shook out. Miles was free. Brand remained in the cross-hairs. She was guilty, not Richie Miles.

You are not a police detective, are you? Was that how Hammar said it? Not anymore.

Ah, but my dear counselor Hammar, attorney at law, advocate for the weak and helpless against the strong and powerful, I've got news for you. The Catholics say that once a priest always a priest. The same is true for cops. Veronika Brand knew she could be suspended, retired, shot in a rocket to the moon—or show up halfway around the world, in Sweden—and she would still remain what she was.

She'd still bleed blue.

14

Dollar Boy worked mostly at the Härjedalen faux hunting lodge, but occasionally elsewhere. He was allowed use of an old Scania-Vabis truck to transport farm animals to the veterinarian, though usually the vets traveled to the lodge and not the other way around.

The rattle-trap vehicle dated from the 1970s. Dollar Boy's boss, the owner of the lodge, kept the thing alive out of pure stubbornness. Gösta Kron often avowed reverence for Sweden's manufacturing past. From trucks to human beings, everything had been superior way back when.

Gösta Kron. More formally, *Friherre* Gösta Benedict Leijonhufvud Kron. Known familiarly as Gösta, though Dollar Boy could expect a stinging rebuke if he ever ventured to be in any way familiar. With the help, the boss was always "Baron," capital "B," an attempt to create superiority and prestige in the absence of any royal lineage. Years ago, in his early days at the estate, Dollar Boy endured a routine of willow stick canings. The punishment came for small mistakes and youthful misbehavior. Baron Kron himself, or his steward, Hugo Magnusson, conducted the whippings.

Although they stung like the scourging of Jesus, Dollar Boy counted the punishments as minor annoyances. He dismissed flogging of staff as another of the baron's conservative idiosyncrasies. The man had great allegiance to tradition and bygone days and ways. After a few months, as Dollar Boy gained his employer's trust, the practice tapered off and ended altogether.

Now eighteen years old, the young boy was a hard worker. He fit in well at the lodge, to the degree he could indulge in personal quirks such as dying his hair bright pink. Hugo Magnusson had snarled at the outlandish 'do, but the baron had merely laughed. Dollar Boy suspected that Baron Kron actually liked him. The man was a local worthy, powerful and god-like, an absolute ruler in his world. His good opinion mattered a great deal. Which was why Dollar Boy was astonished that morning in the barn. Baron Kron came up from behind and gave him a good stroke with a leather riding crop. The blow came out of nowhere.

"*Nej*!" Dollar Boy managed to shout. He staggered backward. He was offended more than injured.

"You took the truck out while I was gone." Baron Kron made the fact sound like an accusation.

"Yes, yes! To the vet in Uppsala! I'm sorry!"

"All the way to Uppsala, boy? And without consulting Hugo?" Baron Kron again raised the crop. Dollar Boy rushed to answer before the whip fell once more.

"The specialist! Dr. Ek!"

When Baron Kron held his hand, Dollar Boy went on, a little more calmly. "Fenrir needed the specialist. And Hugo was gone, to Västvall, I think, to the neighbors, the Vosses, maybe."

As sometimes happened with the baron, the storm blew over quickly. The labor situation at the lodge struck some outsiders as odd. Members of the Kron family had always been vocal defenders of what they thought of as national purity. The current baron remembered the days in the 1940s. His father had followed right-wing firebrand Per Engdahl and *Nysvenska rörelsen*, the New Swedish Movement.

The names of the rightist groups might have changed over the intervening years, but the slant of the rhetoric remained pretty much the same. Of late a ferocious anti-immigrant feeling had reinvigorated the right, making the WWII-era fury of Per Engdahl appear remote and quaint. But anyone paying attention recognized the connection.

So a visit to the Härjedalen lodge sometimes upset the political allies of Baron Kron. For a supposed supporter of radical xenophobia, the baron seemed to employ an awful lot of foreign faces around the farm, even a few Africans.

Dollar Boy's real name was Lash Mirga. He was pure Romani, *chache Roma*, as they said. He looked outlandish, his pink hair shaved into an American-style mohawk. He was a mild and tender soul, but the mohawk gave him an intimidating look. Such was Dollar Boy's wish, to frighten away anyone who sought to hurt him or anyone close to him. He loved to witness the reaction of the baron's stiff-necked acquaintances when they beheld him in all his glory.

The estate employed several Romani "travelers." Their presence had more than once bothered the political extremists who visited. The contradiction seemed to bother the baron not at all. In fact, he appeared to enjoy the discomfort of his purist friends. He possessed an absolute faith that anything he did was correct. If he wanted to bring in Martians, robots or gangs of pink-haired warlocks to do his work for him, by his lights that would be just fine, too.

Meanwhile Dollar Boy was playing a very dangerous game right under the baron's nose. He had gained his nickname from a Yankee dollar bill he used to carry around when he was a kid, telling everyone that he would spend it in New York City one day. But Dollar Boy's present scheme involved not money but love, real English romantic love, the type featured in plays and movies. And Dollar Boy's was the most powerful kind of all, lost love.

Lel was his betrothed. The two of them were from the same village in Romania. They had come to Sweden together under the guidance of Moro Part. Dollar Boy went to work for the baron. Lel began her life as a mendicant, occupying different street corners in Stockholm. At times she worked the commuter trains, shaking paper cups at seated passengers who more often than not turned away from her.

At the end of each day Lel, Varzha Luna, and the rest of the rag-tag crew of beggars returned to Moro Part's apartment, where a half dozen of them stayed. Dollar Boy sometimes visited them. The atmosphere at the apartment was warm and communal, part schoolyard, part sweatshop, part family. They created a simulacrum of Romania as best they could. They were Moro's kids. He treated them with kindness. Mostly.

Lel was not the first to disappear. That was a girl named Ariadne.

Moro usually stationed her in front of one of the large grocery store near Medborgarplatsen, the Citizen's Square. The area was known for social justice demonstrations. Dollar Boy and Lel had wandered among the demonstrators on the big day last May. Large groups of people marched through the city shouting and singing. He liked these new compatriots of his, so earnest and courageous, standing up for the rights of others, generous with their donations.

Then, later in the summer, Lel was taken. Everything changed for Dollar Boy. He put away childish things. The peaceful ways of the Swedes no longer struck him so forcefully. He perceived dark undercurrents and secret dangers lurking beneath the surface of his adopted country. His old byword, "opportunity," fell by the wayside. His new byword was also an old one, ancient as the mountains of Romania.

Revenge.

Leaving the barn with the red welt of the baron's knout across the back of his neck, Dollar Boy crossed the yard to what workers called "the barracks." The quarters for the help shared a building with a granary and thus with the granary's rats. Some of the laborers kept slingshots around for entertainment.

Dollar Boy went to his closet-sized room, closing and latching the flimsy plywood door. Reaching into a locker beneath his cot, he retrieved his treasured iPhone. He worked in secret, checking in with the location tracker app he had installed. Consulting a worn paper map of Sweden, he found the place where the phone displayed a pulsing icon of a pinging cell tower. Somehow distances seemed more real and manageable on his IRL map than on the cell phone screen. Only a finger's breadth separated his own location from the pulsing icon.

"I am only centimeters away from you, Varzha," he whispered to the empty air. "I'm watching. I'll keep you safe."

With the baron in residence, use of the truck would be out of the question. If he left the estate that night Dollar Boy would have to take the motocross.

Actually, that wasn't really a problem. He loved the Husqvarna TC 125 motocross more than life itself. Workers at the lodge jury-rigged the motorbike with a trailer. The unit would serve Dollar Boy's purpose almost as well as the truck. Its use on a winter night would freeze a rider's body solid, but such was the life of a lovelorn teenager.

He settled in on his cot to wait, letting his mind play over the possibilities for the evening.

He knew what the *gadje* always said. Roma were knife people. But Dollar Boy saw himself as cut from a different, more modern mold. He wasn't drawn to the violence, or the weapons, but they offered him protection from his real fear. Dreams unfulfilled by a blow from a foreign hand. Some day he would step out from his people's shadow. He would go to America, where dreams come true under the lights of the Hollywood stars. There he would arm himself the way all American citizens did, with a lethal pistol. Until that golden time in the impossible future, he would just have to protect himself with a blade.

15

Brand boarded Stockholm's *tunnelbana* at the Ropsten station. Each day she woke a bit later, remediating her jet lag, adjusting to the time difference. She'd heard it said that in crossing time zones, you leave your soul behind and it takes a while for it to catch up.

After the bloody horrors at the Sofieborg Manor House, Brand felt the need to go to ground. She isolated herself in the guest house of Lukas Dalgren. Her cousin lived east of Stockholm in the suburb of Lidingö. She didn't see much of him or his family. He carefully located his prized Tesla elsewhere. He didn't inform Brand where the vehicle was, lest she think to borrow it. Brand concluded the man was somewhat afraid of her.

Lukas and Isabella endured a strained home life. They still lived together even though, as Isabella told her—giving the words a frosty air of permanence—"We're apart."

Leaving the guest house, Brand took the *Lidingöbanan* light-rail to reach Ropsten and changed to the commuter *tunnelbana*. The train immediately dove underground. The gleaming car glided along in almost ghostly silence. Its rubber-treaded wheels made all the difference in comparison with the screeching steel of the New York City subway.

In the reflection of the heavy plate glass of the car's window, Brand saw a woman still youthful, startling gray-blue eyes still prominent, her Scandinavian bone structure a legacy of her grandparents. Gray also appeared in her hair, just a few streaks here and there. She'd always remembered the scene in *Moonstruck*, when Cher went from plain to dazzling via the magic of hair coloring. She knew she was expected to aspire to the enduring lure of youthful beauty, but it was redemption that Brand was contemplating, not transformation. She must change her life. Past failures confronted her in the shadow image flashing in the *tunnelbana* window. She saw forty approaching. The smoky stench of all her burned bridges at the NYPD still hung about her person. Unsure if she could ever return to the department, she found herself a stranger on two turfs, both in the States and in Sweden.

She felt a gust of nausea, and smiled to herself, at herself. Perhaps she would feel less sick if they allowed her to steer the train. Never a passenger, always a driver. Her motto. She had left the Glock behind at the guest house, hidden in her duffel. Naked and vulnerable, she took herself and her bundle of nerves into central Stockholm.

Krister Hammar had returned again and again to the multiple disappearances that plagued the gypsy community in Stockholm. Work at the *Klara kyrka* in central Stockholm immersed him in the chaotic, unsettled plight of recent refugees, immigrants from Africa, the multiple diasporas and the displaced, and the Romani community in particular. The church fed a hundred people every day and gave shelter at night, a bed to those in need.

Hammar evidently considered Brand as some sort of investigative resource who might help untangle the mystery of the stolen girls. Her first reaction had been to put him off. As a result of the manor house experience, she changed her mind.

"Listen," Hammar had told her. "I have a friend in Stockholm who might be of use to you. Aino Lehtonen, a photographer. She used to work with my wife. And she has been shooting the Romani in Sweden for years. Lately her photos begin to reveal the missing."

"And this woman would help me how?" Brand asked.

"Let's call it for identification purposes," Hammar said. "Lehtonen's a visual detective. You will like her—she is part-American."

Brand smiled inwardly at the assumption she would like someone because they have American pedigree. She agreed to meet Hammar and Aino Lehtonen at the Gamla Stan *tunnelbanestation* in the heart of Stockholm.

She was headed there now. At a stop the train doors opened to a fresh glut of passengers. They were suited up for winter yet still elegant, many on cell phones. Pushing in with the crowd came a weather-beaten man. He carried a blue Ikea bag of reinforced polypropylene slung over his shoulder, bulging with plastic bottles.

The *tunnelbana* car lurched forward. It'd been years since Brand worked the New York subways, a rookie transit cop on the night shift, jittered up, a sweaty hand on her sidearm, scanning the cars and station platforms for anything that blipped the radar. Those were definitely not the days. The bright Swedish metro car, with its colorful fabric-covered seats and gleaming interior of ungraffitied steel, was miles away from the rank and unreliable subways she used to patrol.

Music moved toward her up the train's central aisle, from an accordionist who played with one hand and panhandled with the other. Suitably, but annoyingly, the song was "New York, New York." Brand searched her pockets and found a mass of mostly American coins, sorting among them for something in Swedish crowns while the busker waited on her.

Finally, she did what she would do in any foreign country where she didn't know how to read the coinage, simply holding out her hand with the money displayed, thinking the busker would choose one. Brand realized too late that a twenty dollar bill lay folded up amongst the quarters, nickels, and gold ten-kronor coins. The accordionist, who kept up his one-handed playing, deftly swept up the coins along with the bill, pocketed it all, and fled down the car before he could be confronted.

"American," another passenger now said, slurring the word dismissively. *Mur-ken.* Brand glanced up at him. The guy stood swaying over her, sporting a nearly clean-shaven scalp, looking as unpleasant as any skinhead she'd ever encountered in the bowels of New York City transit.

Brand averted her gaze, not wanting to get into it with the guy. She wondered about how quickly the Swedes typed her as an American. Her background must be written on her face.

"*Du,*" the skinhead said, then continued on in English. "You people come here on a seven-day tour and think you know. But you know nothing."

What have I done to deserve this? Brand wondered. She looked up. White flecks of saliva frothed in the side creases of the beefy man's mouth.

"*Jävla bitch,*" he said under his breath.

"How about you back off?" Brand said.

"Back the fuck off!" Brand demanded. The anger that had grown in her lately, usually kept at a simmer, now rose to a boil. She didn't like the guy crowding her, so she rose up, her own Swedish tall gene on full display. Her intimidating six feet had always served her well as a cop.

The skinhead tried to block her back down into the seat. She dodged the move. He and Brand wound up nose to nose. The train slowed for a station.

"What are you doing here, bitch?" the guy snarled, chest-bumping her again. "Go home!"

The New York nut lock was a move Willie Urrico had originally taught her, when she first moved out of transit and joined patrol. Skells of every flavor saw a blue uniform as something of a challenge. The savvy street cop's response to actual physical contact was to place a lateral forearm across the subject's upper chest, for stabilization purposes, then make a quick clutch at the groin.

With a deft movement, Brand did exactly that. Urrico's New York nut lock avoided whatever plumbing got in the way and aimed directly for the more vulnerable tea bags.

The skinhead wheezed out a cough of pain, his foul, fish-scented breath hitting Brand full on. She pushed the guy away. Brand was not afraid of him, but more fearful of herself, of her furious desire to inflict real damage. She turned and crossed to the exit doors.

Brand's fellow riders remained buried in cell phones, books, or whatever distraction they carried with them. She read their reaction not as indifference but as a careful observance of privacy, a sort of studied, collective froideur. Not that there was much to see. The guy stood swaying, his body cocked at half mast, still wheezing when the doors slid open.

Brand stepped off the train. She tried to quiet her inner trembling, standing on the platform as the train pulled out. She mentally pictured her actions being caught by a cell phone camera.

"Shit." She was now glad that she had left her sidearm behind that day. A weapon would have surely complicated matters, had authorities entered into the picture.

The twisted face of the skinhead on the train moved past Brand in slow motion. He slammed his fist against the window glass and glared, throwing her the horned fuck-you hand gesture.

She aimed a kick at his face and connected with the train as it gained speed. It continued on, and he was gone.

"Shit," Brand said again. She tried to summon up one of the calming techniques learned from her NYPD-ordained anger management training. But such measures seemed to be in lock-up somewhere, while the blond beast had been allowed to roam free.

16

T-centralen, the Central Station of Stockholm. Brand emerged from the underground platform on an escalator, joining the steady stream of workaday subway riders. She passed through an exit barrier and became part of the random flow of foot traffic, everyone busy getting somewhere, swarming out of an anthill.

Temporarily disoriented by numerous options to reach street level, she encountered a bizarre tableau. A community of homeless set up a crude encampment against a concrete wall that curved backward into a dark tunnel. Brand realized she was staring blankly at a young girl-child of eight or nine, her braids being fussed over by a trio of older women stood out from the group. Bulging, tarp-covered bundles were heaped high around them. The camp spilled over to an underground tunnel that led back toward the *t-bana* entrance.

Yes, the homeless, an immediately familiar sight from Brand's time on transit patrol, yet subtly different from the residents living on the streets of New York City. The same pathetic collections of possessions, sure, desperately held fragments of a disordered life, and always the jury-rigged sections of cloud-colored plastic and stuffed-full shopping bags. These common elements were probably similar all over the world, from Rio, Mumbai, and Cape Town to the shifting jungles below the Queensboro Bridge.

But the differences became clear as Brand passed among them. She saw colorfully dressed women in long skirts and scarves folding up bedding. Men in dark clothing, loose pants and shabby jackets stood by, speaking on cell phones. Other women moved aside the plastic-covered bundles of possessions, sorting, re-packing. The sense of a community hiding in plain sight was uncanny. A scattering of early morning commuters hustled past in one lane of the walkway, while the homeless encampment held the other. The twain didn't seem to meet.

Gypsies. These were the folks Krister Hammar obsessed over. The word conjured images of colorfully dressed women in skirts and scarves and men who wore small fedora-style hats. The Brits called them "travelers," or, a more loaded term, "pikeys." Brand had a vague sense that they moved communally in horse drawn carts and sang folk songs. But she recognized she possessed only a general, second-hand and undoubtedly stereotyped idea of gypsy identity.

There were a few gypsy communities in New York City, Brand recalled, mostly centered in the borough of Queens. But as a group gypsies didn't have that much of a visible presence in the States, nor the long history of being shat upon that they enjoyed in Europe. Their low profile in the US proved a blessing. Had there been a greater percentage on the streets, Brand was confident her fellow Americans would be able to summon up proper levels of prejudice, fear, and distrust.

She watched them now, fascinated. Like birds leaving the nest, a few of the younger members of the encampment floated lazily away, male and female both, dispersing into the general population. They all held the same kind of paper cup, the emblem of their trade.

Brand trailed after a stylish woman she had just met a few minutes before. The two of them entered into a maze of cobblestone alleys in central Stockholm. She immediately lost all sense of where she was.

A thin layer of ice glazed the narrow streets. Footing turned treacherous. Brand's smooth-soled black leather boots proved all wrong for the conditions. Meanwhile her young female guide, Aino Lehtonen, bounded ahead. She wore sleek, high-heeled, over-the-knee Loboutins, stilt-like, impossible boots that probably cost more than Brand's whole wardrobe.

She tried to keep up, but Lehtonen moved as nimbly as a reindeer, powering on despite the ice and despite the heels. They had entered Gamla Stan, Stockholm's old town. The thirteenth century collided into the twenty-first to spectacular effect, but with a decided lack of logic. Tiny lanes that seemed to dead end suddenly revealed escape routes. One crinkum-crankum alleyway twisted into another.

Earlier, when Brand arrived at the agreed upon meeting-place, there had been no Hammar, only Lehtonen.

"Krister called to say he'll meet up with us soon," Lehtonen had said, explaining the man's absence. "Come along."

Then it was off to the races, the leaping reindeer leading the stumbling sheep through the maze. The twenty-eight year old native had no pity on the older American newcomer.

"Keep up," Lehtonen called over her shoulder, after Brand slid around a blind corner.

They broke out of the labyrinth into an open space.

"Stortorget, the Great Square," Lehtonen explained hurriedly. "Terrible massacre here back when, one beheading after another, blood ankle deep."

As a guide, Lehtonen wasn't exactly a Virgil. But Brand's idea of herself as a commonplace tourist, present in the country to meet relatives and take in the sights, no longer had any meaning for her. Two dead men in a room where a blood bomb had gone off had blown away all sense of a casual visit.

"The Nobel Museum, the former Bourse." Pronouncing the clipped travelogue, Lehtonen sounded bored. "Beyond is *Storkyrkan*, Saint Nicholas Cathedral, where all the royals and nobles get baptized and married."

Brand took in the ancient, flat-fronted buildings rising up around the square. Many of them were richly colored in hues that seemed to defy the Swedish preference for somber earth tones. A deep red raspberry building rose next to another of Marrakesh ocher, while a façade of dusty moss stood next door to one of burnt orange.

"Pastels, really?" she commented to Lehtonen.

The woman either didn't hear or wasn't interested in Brand's reaction. She was already leading them out of the square down yet another narrow, ice-strewn passageway. They arrived in front of a heavy, old-style double portal embedded in one of the flamboyantly colored old buildings. This one was done up in carmine, with the door painted a deep Mediterranean blue.

"Here," Lehtonen said abruptly. She punched a code on a keypad set into a small, square metal box, heard a click, then pushed open the door. Clattering up a flight of stairs in her outlandish boots, she unlocked another heavy wooden door. The two of them entered an immense, loft-like space.

"My photography studio." Lehtonen assumed an off-hand tone contradicted by the splendor of the surroundings.

Large ornate deep set windows took up one whole wall. Lehtonen's studio was the real estate equivalent of her Loboutins, intimidatingly fashionable and triumphantly over the top. The view from the strategically placed windows encompassed the waterways of central Stockholm. Everything inside was white, even the floors and ceiling. The wide floorboards had been evenly sanded and painted a chalky white, same as the walls.

"White to reflect the light," Lehtonen explained. "Crucial in winter."

"You call this your studio?" Brand said. "I call it a penthouse. You could hold political rallies."

"It belongs to my wife," Lehtonen said. "Ebba's got a bit of money, mostly from media and retail companies she operates. No one's renting the place now, so it's mine."

As big as the studio was, Lehtonen had kept it fashionably spare, ascetic, and raw. There was something almost industrial about the atmosphere. Brand was reminded of the artist's lofts of Soho in New York. Several areas displayed the common features of a working photography studio. Backdrops and screens cluttered one corner. A lighting setup had been left in place, looking expensive and ready for use. An unlit light table still had strips of photographic negatives splayed negligently across it.

Brand expected a bevy of assistants in black turtlenecks to come bustling up offering espresso, but there were none. She and Lehtonen were alone together.

Or, not quite alone. The wall facing the windows featured a collection of human portraits, unframed oversize prints the size of movie posters. The edges of the enormous photographs were left ragged and uncropped. The subjects were varied. There were business people posed in expensive suits, a trio of what looked like members of a farm family, an extravagantly dressed and accessorized young artist in front of a sculpture.

A few of the photographs portrayed the Romani mendicants of Stockholm. Brand abruptly came face to face with a teenage girl wearing white makeup and a wedding dress.

Varzha Luna. The vanished young soul whom Hammar was so worried about. A disturbing memory came back to Brand, a torn shred of wedding gown, discarded in the blood-soaked manor house of the Vosses. The same dress appeared in the photograph.

In the portrait, the girl displayed a fierce beauty, proud and unyielding behind her odd theatrical makeup. A slender boy of around the same age knelt beside her, sporting a neon green Statue of Liberty crown of foam rubber. His olive makeup rendered him into an emaciated version of the Incredible Hulk. In another of the big prints, the two were together again. This time they walked alongside a hapless bourgeois woman. She gripped her shopping bags and stared straight ahead. One foot was extended, the other lifted off the ground as if ready to bolt.

"Brother and sister," Lehtonen commented. "Vago and Varzha."

Lehtonen proceeded along the gallery of her startling, gigantic photographs. Brand followed a step behind, taking in the artist's lean, straight body, more soft boy than woman. The whole package impressed her, the short spiky haircut, the tight jeans, the ivory blouse of wild silk that came off as expensively simple. Lehtonen's violent red lipstick looked as though it had been tattooed on.

"Why gypsies?" Brand asked. "Why focus on them?"

"Oh, I'm interested in interesting people," Lehtonen responded. "And by the way, the word is 'Roma' or 'Romani'. 'Gypsy' is now heard here as an insult. There are a good number of legitimate names besides Roma, different groups in different parts of the world, like *Dom, Sinti, Manus*.

She moved on to another Romani portrait, the only one in color, showing a thickset male on the street. He wore a brown overcoat, wire-rimmed spectacles and a fur hat.

"Moro Part," Lehtonen said. "The big man. He sees himself as a godfather figure. It's a very hierarchical community. Some of my sources say he may be a people trafficker, or at least a smuggler of some kind. His money comes from somewhere. I've followed him for a while now, and he's very hard to pin down."

Aino turned back to the photos of the white-faced wedding girl and the comical clownboy. "These two I've spent time with," she said. "Moro Part treats them very well. There seems to be a special relationship between them. I don't know, maybe he rescues these kids. I've heard that as well, that he's a Robin Hood character, stealing from the rich and giving to the poor."

Brand examined the portrait. She felt the challenge in Varzha Luna's gaze, as though it were fixed upon her personally. "I don't know about him, but her I'd be afraid to meet in a dark alley."

"I know what you mean. I had to work for ages just to get a single word out of her. Krister knows more."

"Her eyes look much older than the rest of her," Brand said.

"She's sixteen, if you can imagine that. It took a while for me to earn her trust, paying them for taking a photo. I know a church that works with refugees, the Roma, the homeless. My friends and I collect second-hand sweaters and coats, blankets, something warm for the night. We're not alone in this kind of thing. A lot of Swedes donate."

"What are the Roma doing living in the subway?" Brand asked. "I saw a whole encampment at the station."

"Look to Eastern Europe if you want to understand why the Roma come. The mud they slog through, the suspicion and abuse they get from non-Roma. Many times they have no shelter at all, other than tents and makeshift shacks in the woods."

Aino rapped her knuckles on the wall next to Varzha Luna's portrait. "Here is the stereotype—a street beggar singing folk songs. But in Sweden and elsewhere many Romani are academics, entrepreneurs, members of parliament. We are everything, teachers and writers and artists."

Brand pulled up short. We? Had she heard right?

Lehtonen read the expression on her face. She gave a short laugh. "Oh, yes, I am *Kaale Roma*, Finnish, through my father's side."

"I apologize," Brand said. "I shouldn't have assumed anything."

"The Romani you see on the streets, like Varzha and Vago, are mostly from Romania or Bulgaria, in social systems that keep them mired in poverty. As you understand from your work with sex crimes and trafficking in New York City, poverty renders the young vulnerable."

"Why is it everyone here knows so much about me?" She found it mystifying. This woman she had just met referred knowledgeably to her experiences on the job in New York City.

"Sweden is a small country with a small population," Aino explained, laughing apologetically. "Nothing remains secret for very long."

"What about shelters for these people? And where are the fucking police? I feel for the homeless, believe me I do, but having them camped in a train station can't be the answer. Or maybe I should speak more politely, like 'where in the bloody hell are the po-po?'"

"Oh, it's perfectly okay to drop the f-bomb around here. I sometimes teach photography to teenagers. These kids nowadays watch so many Hollywood films, they believe every American family sits down at the table and says, 'what the fuck's for dinner?' I try to disabuse them of the idea."

"Krister Hammar is very much involved with the Roma, isn't he? In his work as an immigration lawyer. What happened to him today? Where is he?"

They heard the door of the studio open. Without looking around, Lehtonen said, "Speak of the devil and he appears."

"Hello?" Hammar's voice called out from the front entrance of the loft.

He emerged into the studio space, his face red with the outside cold. He and Lehtonen gave each other a quick, polite hug. He glanced over at the huge photographic portraits of Varzha and Vago.

"I've found them," Hammar said. "Let's go."

17

A half dark had come on by the time Aino, Krister and Veronika left Lehtonen's studio. A mist covered the city and winter rain fell, making the cobblestones of Stockholm's Old Town more difficult to navigate. They crossed a bridge from one island to another, passed through an enormous stone arch and entered a commercial neighborhood on the other side.

Brand allowed Lehtonen and Hammar to take the lead. She knew only that the three of them were on their way to keep an appointment with the Romani boss-man who starred in one of Lehtonen's massive photographs.

As they walked together the photographer and the immigration lawyer would lean toward one another, exchanging soft-spoken words apparently not intended for Veronika Brand's ears. Like a brother and sister, thought Brand. Occasionally Hammar turned to make sure Brand still followed.

The commercial street was in sharp contrast to the charm of Gamla Stan. The guts had been ripped out of this part of the city to make way for retail progress. The anonymous, neutered and bland buildings stood in stark contrast to the medieval precinct they had just left. Storefronts offered racks of cute-faced fuzzy moose-head key rings, tiny blue and yellow Swedish flags, baskets of smooth wooden spoons, and an abundance of postcards, all a bit tacky looking.

Hammar and Lehtonen halted at an intersection. An H&M occupied one corner, and a modern department store, long, low-built, and brownish red, stood opposite.

"Åhléns," Lehtonen said. A long row of large display windows glowed with a warm, inviting light. Shoppers rushed past, carrying their precious goods through the foggy dark of the fading afternoon.

"This is where Varzha Luna's kidnapping happened," Hammar said quietly.

Two men waited at the store's entrance, older and younger, one stocky and the other rail thin. They were the photographs in Lehtonen's studio come to life. The young beanpole Brand recognized as Varzha Luna's twin brother Vago. The older, more impressive gent wore the same brown overcoat as in Lehtonen's full-color photographic portrait.

Moro Part, the Romani godfather. He glared sullenly as they drew near. Vago pestered his handler with repeated cries of "Zsa-Zsa." Finally Moro seemed to lose patience, arm-locking the kid briefly to shut him up.

"Your sister is gone, but she will be back," Moro assured the boy.

In a quavering voice Vago sang, *Open the door, oh wandering bride…* He put his undersized violin to his chin and drew a bow over the squealing strings. Moro gently but firmly took the instrument away.

"Sounds like a cat being strangled," he said, not unkindly. He pushed the kid back into a begging posture, seated on a tattered blanket on the cold sidewalk.

When they left the studio, Brand had slipped a pill into her mouth. Now she felt Adderall alert, amphetamine focused. She noticed everything. Vago had tucked and folded his begging blanket to form a compact pad, like a mediation prayer pillow, upon which he bounced nervously up and down. She saw that the blanket's wool fabric was brightly patterned with teddy bears scattered through, a child's coverlet. Brand's mind jerked back and forth like the head of a bird.

Aino tapped Vago on the shoulder.

"Aino!" he said happily.

"That's me," she said. "Aino."

"I know you know but what do I know?" the kid responded, laughing delightedly.

Aino turned to Hammar and Brand. "This is an old joke between us," she explained. She gave the kid a bag of pink and white *skumkantareller* as a small token gift.

"Here is Krister Hammar," Aino announced to Moro. "And this is Veronika Brand, from New York City."

Moro didn't appear interested in introductions. He gave Brand a veiled, suspicious look. "You bring the *polis* along?" he muttered to Lehtonen. "Relax," Aino said. "She's an American." As if that explained everything.

"Have you found her?" Hammar asked. "Does anyone know where she is?"

Moro shrugged in the negative.

"My head hurts," Vago said, pressing his hands on his temples. "Now more than always."

The others ignored him, caught up in tension between Brand and Moro Part.

"We only want to help," Hammar said.

"I need everyone to back off," Moro responded.

"We heard that Luri Kováč was there at Åhléns, begging at the same time, and he saw Varzha being taken," Aino said. "Maybe it would help if we speak with him."

"No," Moro said, biting off the word.

"I want Zsa-Zsa," the twin said. Aino shushed him.

"You're not my boss," Vago told her. "Moro is my boss."

"Luri Kováč is a fool," Moro said dismissively.

The comment caused Vago to laugh and clap his hands together. "Luri is a foo-foo-fool!" he crowed.

"For the love of God, Vago!" Moro exclaimed, quieting the boy. "Luri sits there on the street like a big frozen turd. He never has more than a single krona in his cup. He didn't see anything. The man is half-blind."

"In the country of the blind," Brand murmured.

"What?" Moro asked, bristling again.

"Panhandlers always have the best eyes on the street," Brand said.

Moro stared at her. Brand met his gaze. They were two dogs facing off.

"One of them had a police wallet," Moro finally said.

"One of them?" Krister asked. "Does that mean there was more than one?"

"He was in uniform?" Aino asked.

"Two men," Vago said, rising to his feet. "A beard and one no beard."

Everyone stopped and looked at the kid.

"One had a beard and the other didn't?" Krister asked him.

"Two cops?" Aino wanted to make sure. "Plainclothes? Maybe *SÄPO*?"

"I think they were pretending to be cops," Brand said.

"Enough!" Moro shouted. "I'm not going to tell you again to back off. We are *Kalderaš Romani*. We take care of our own."

Vago began turning in circles, talking to himself. "My grandfather has many grandsons. When Zsa-Zsa was a bird, I was a deer. I took care of my own. In the sky blue village. Our home, Zsa calls it. There was a stolen goat that spoke real words and gave kid's milk. We are *Kalderaš Romani*, we are travelers, we have no home, the road is our home."

His words sounded like an oft-repeated catechism. Aino took him by the shoulders to stop his spinning. "Vago," she said. "What were the men? Tall? Short?"

"Yes," Vago said.

"Roma?" Aino asked.

"Schwedo," the boy said.

Aino gave him a can of soda.

His mouth full, Vago tossed off a bit of intel that pulled them all up short. "The bearded one says to Zsa-Zsa, 'I am Officer Liam'. The other one says 'I am Officer Mattias.'"

"What?" asked Krister.

"What?" echoed Aino.

"Not *parale*!" Vago said. "Not police. Fake news, fake news!" He chortled as if laughing at his own joke.

"The kid doesn't know up from down," Moro said. "Don't listen to him."

"Don't listen to him," Vago said, repeating the words mindlessly. "I don't like going out without being white."

Brand felt for the boy. She remembered his whiteface makeup in Lehtonen's photos.

"It's okay," she told him quietly. Surprisingly, Vago quieted. She smiled at him. He smiled back.

Moro removed a small, smooth stone from his pocket and held it out to Brand. The offering took her by surprise.

"A token for a newcomer to this country," he said. "For good luck, and to ward off the evil eye."

Brand didn't want the gift, didn't trust it. But she didn't see any way to avoid taking it, either. The little gray talisman felt warm to the touch.

"If you promise to lay off," Moro said to the three gentiles confronting him, "I'll pledge to make sure you know everything."

"He won't," Vago stage whispered.

Moro laughed and gave the boy a playful cuff.

"You've told us exactly nothing so far," Hammar said. "Is that going to change?"

Brand pulled a piece of white fabric from the pocket of her vest. The move caused a small explosion. As soon as Vago caught sight of it, he emitted a loud cry and fell sobbing to his knees. He took a swipe at Brand and missed. Then he continued with his full-throated grieving.

"Made a slave to the wicked!" the boy shrieked. He wept tear rivers.

"Quiet down, Vago!" Aino said. The commotion attracted the attention of passersby.

Moro bear-hugged the kid, though it was difficult to tell if it was a consoling hug or a suffocating one.

"I can't think," Vago babbled. "My head hurts."

Moro Part pushed the tiny violin into the boy's hands. Possession of the instrument instantly quieted the boy.

"Play 'Blue Eyes,' Vago," he said. "What does Varzha always say? She says, 'Play Blue Eyes, Vago, because it gets them every time.'"

The boy took his bow and scraped out a song, "Blue Eyes Crying In the Rain." Sounding faint and tremulous in the new night, the tune hit Brand in the heart.

18

Brand steered Hammar's Saab northwest on the E18, back towards Härjedalen. They left the suburbs and outlying towns around Stockholm to enter a countryside still locked in winter. Straw-colored stubble showed above the snow in the fields. The land looked empty. Most people with money had fled the winter cold to parts south, Thailand, the Canaries, or Andalusia.

She and Hammar did not talk. The only sound in the car was the vague rush of wind and the rumble of vulcanized tires on pavement, punctuated by a volley of text messages that Hammar persistently ignored. Brand wondered if he had a place to be, someone to answer to that didn't know about his foray into the criminal underworld.

The two of them were headed toward a church in the north for old Elin's memorial service. During the long stretches of silence on the drive, Brand wondered if Hammar might be making a polite gesture toward mourning. Eventually, though, she understood his silence was based more on an innate kind of serenity. His wordlessness, Brand realized, was simply one of the man's virtues. She couldn't judge whether it was a common Swedish trait or one peculiar to Hammar. All she knew was that her companion didn't give in to the modern urge to chatter.

It would be her second visit to the province of her ancestors. Brand again brought along the Glock. A few of her fellow police referred to a sidearm as an 'Amex', as in, "don't leave home without it." The weapon was in the car's back seat, concealed in a clunky backpack she took from her cousin Lukas's guest house. Brand thought of the photo she had filched from Elin's room. The images bled into the present day, her own family's murky past somehow connecting with the bloody crimes of the Voss family.

Hammar directed her along a specific route. It differed from the one they had traveled just two days before, on their way back to Stockholm after the Härjedalen reunion. This way they would not pass by the Sofieborg Manor House. The site threw out an evil aura. It probably glowed in the dark. Brand might have liked to visit in full daylight, if there was such a thing in the Swedish winter. She would prefer the company of a forensic investigator, but that opportunity was not open to her. She was not in good odor with the local *polis*.

The scene at the Ljusdal station played over in her mind. In retrospect it gave her a case of investigatory whiplash. Bok the local cop had handed her off to the district commissioner woman. Then came the big cheese from the American embassy. Brand had been involved with high-profile cases in New York. She knew what political weight felt like when it fell on top of her.

The whole business seemed cock-eyed somehow. The deaths were horrific. The crime scene was practically apocalyptic. But really, such a grand fuss over a suspected dog-fighting case? Something didn't add up.

Varzha Luna, the striking Romani figure in Lehtonen's portrait, had been present at the scene. That much was clear. They had shown the wedding dress to Lehtonen. She had identified it as the young woman's. And Vago went agro upon seeing it. Had Varzha been murdered? Was it her blood at the manor house, mixed with that of the traffickers? But then why remove one body from the scene and leave two others?

Sofieborg Manor House was a Voss property. Two paths crossed there, the Vosses and Varzha. The explanation hovered in the darkness at the edge of a stand of birches, where a big ghost dog moved. Brand could not grasp the meaning of it all.

Vago gave them the names of the two men who had taken his sister, Liam and Mattias. Through back channels, Hammar determined the identities of the two dead men discovered at the manor house. Liam Blom, yes, and then someone called Nils Hansen. So at least one of the men who kidnapped the girl met his death almost immediately after. A falling out among the traffickers? A bloody spat over money? Impossible to figure.

The Saab snaked into hillier terrain. Slabs of granite tilted up along one side of the highway. In the distance, snow-capped mountains rose through a scrim of clouds. Hammar's presence had a calming influence on Brand. He was the type of man, she considered, whom you might overlook in a crowd. Then, coming back to him, you'd realize he was the one you wanted to be around. He had a distinctive look, his hair cut short, a close-muscled body, eyes as dark as the northern winter sky, and a mouth that somehow seemed to match his face despite being almost cartoonishly large.

Hammar looked over at Brand now, giving her a silent smile. She smiled back.

As the car swung up a hill, the road took a sharp turn. Revealed below was a lake, only identifiable by the snow laden evergreens that marked the missing shoreline. The sun sparkled on the frozen snow. "Siljan," Hammar said. "One of the largest lakes in Sweden. It's not as big as your American Great Lakes. But we have two that are almost as large, lakes like oceans."

It was as many words as she had heard him speak in the previous hour.

Relaxed now, Hammar reached for his phone, returning to the messages he had ignored. Brand played the obvious card for a lark, "Is there a mystery woman wanting to know where you are?" Hammar held back, for just a moment before replying, "No, just Sanna checking our progress."

"Good she's checked in with you. The mastermind behind luring me over here to hear out great aunt Elin's ravings, it seems I am now surplus to requirement."

"Sanna's not malicious, I don't know, she's just, she isn't what you think perhaps…" The explanation seemed to turn sour in his mouth, trailing off and killing Brand's interest in the small time worries of Sanna Dalgren.

They joined the E45 heading north. An hour later Hammar directed her onto a narrow asphalt road. They drove along a stream course, passed over a bridge, and entered a small town. Hammar gestured toward an enormous roadside statue that stood at a traffic circle.

"Some say hero, some tyrant," he said. "Gustav Vasa, the first Gustav in a long line of Gustavs. Hounded by Danes and Catholic priests, he was a bit of a Christ figure himself, as a matter of fact. He escaped the Stockholm bloodbath, lived to defeat the Danes, and essentially invented Sweden."

The sculpted figure had been stained green by time. Snow flocked the hard-lined royal visage of the monarch. He appeared to be facing down danger, ready for the wolf packs that were sure to come. The statue spoke to Brand of ancient worlds, as though the earth had gone through an infinite number of epochs before our own.

"These days Gustav Vasa is on the level of national myth," Hammar said. "You should see his statue in the National Museum. It's many times larger than this one."

They sped through the roundabout and left the village behind. Brand glanced into the rearview as the statue receded into the distance.

"My grandfather was named Gustav," Brand said.

"Yes, Gustav Dalgren, Klara's husband. It's a favorite Swedish name."

"He died when I was a teenager."

"In a barn fire in New York."

Brand glanced over at him. "You seem to know a lot of Dalgren family history."

"Everyone marked your grandfather as a great man, Veronika, and not just within the family," Hammar said. "All Sweden knew of him as a crusader for justice. His death notice ran in newspapers here. But he was ill-used by his countrymen. He and his wife Klara and her sister Alice were chased out of their home under threat of death by Nazi sympathizers."

A half hour later they swung into a churchyard. Hammar had timed the trip to arrive for Elin Dalgren's memorial service. There seemed to be no one around. Several vehicles were parked in the lot. A walkway led through a grove of misshapen skeleton trees, their branches heavy with snow.

Hammar and Brand approached the old church built of white stone, visible through the trees. The crunch of their shoes on the icy walk managed to sound forlorn. The bell tower stood beside the church as a separate structure. Both proved empty.

"Is this right?" Brand asked as they stood inside the ancient sanctuary.

"I can't understand it," Hammar said. "I know this is the Dalgren's church. I've been here a few times before."

"There's no one here."

Brand took in the small, spare interior. The church was freezing cold. Even inside, their breath clouded in the air.

"I find the films of Ingmar Bergman overly bleak," Hammar said. "And one of his most depressing works was filmed in this church. I can't remember the name. I think I've blanked it out."

Finally a woman in a white surplice emerged from the sacristy. Hammar strode forward and spoke to her. He returned to Brand.

"They're at the gravesite." He led her back outside.

Clearly someone maintained the old cemetery. Grave markers poked out neatly from the snow. Small, humpbacked drifts on their windward sides obscured the stones. Here the most ancient of the Dalgren ancestors were buried. There remained a feeling of emptiness and loss. The cemetery dated to the 16th century, which meant that the dead had been lying there for a very long time. The snow's icy, unbroken surface displayed no human footprints, although tracks of small animals appeared here and there.

"Come," Hammar said. "The Dalgrens will have gathered themselves on the opposite side." He guided her by the arm along a narrow, snow-cleared walk that ran between the graves, no more than a few feet wide. Around the side of the church, they passed a series of wooden hutches, roofed in slate.

"Those are the old church stalls," Hammar explained. "People would make the weekly pilgrimage to church, starting their walk on Saturday, taking shelter in stalls by the church overnight and returning to the slog of the farm after their souls had been cleansed. No doubt your Dalgren ancestors sheltered there."

He stopped in front of a modest and very ancient-looking gravestone, its lettering half-erased by time. "This is one of the oldest recorded in the province, Hjalmar Dalgren."

Raucous calls broke the silence. Black shapes showed against the colorless sky, passing quickly overhead.

"Crows," Hammar said, glancing up. "There's a storm coming in, snow is on the way."

Darker clouds piled up on the horizon to the west, an advancing front. There had been no new snow since Brand's first day in Sweden arrived in Sweden.

In the far corner of the cemetery stood a small collection of mourners. Brand was dismayed at how few people were there. She counted ten. One for every decade of Elin Dalgren's life, she thought morosely. Brand hesitated, feeling as though she was intruding. She imagined herself dropping into old Hjalmar Dalgren's grave, cozying up in the cramped space with the dust and bones of her distant ancestor.

"We should join them," Hammar said briskly. As they approached the grave he lowered his voice. "When the ground is frozen like this they build an overnight bonfire to thaw it out. Relatives gather around and tend the fire through the night. Reminisces. Alcohol. Toasts to the departed."

Sanna and Folke Dalgren saw them and nodded solemnly. Brand followed Hammar as they took their place beside the other mourners. A clergyman intoned the liturgy, wearing a parka over his vestments. The crows passed over again. The flock appeared in frantic, random flight to avoid the coming storm.

19

On the outside of a yellowed and cracked envelope, Brand saw words in a spidery script.

Till Veronika, min brors dotterdotter, från Elin Dalgren, Veronikas gammelfaster. Written helpfully in another hand was a translation: "To Veronika, my grand-niece, from Elin Dalgren, your grandfather's sister."

Sanna Dalgren presented the packet to Brand after Elin's burial service. "I think you should read this, dear," Sanna said.

"What is it?" Brand asked.

"Our family…" Sanna said, then didn't finish the sentence. Her normally sunny face displayed a sadness. "My *mamma* carried the burden of many secrets. Your grandmother thought you needed to understand what happened, what brought your grandparents to emigrate to America. But Klara took her truth to the grave, leaving Elin to be the messenger." The monologue seemed rehearsed, with Sanna's sadness slowly turning venomous as she spat out the final sentence.

Brand sat in the Saab, in the passenger seat for once. The car remained parked in the churchyard lot. Hammar was elsewhere, inside the old church, speaking with the relatives, she guessed. She took the packet Sanna had given her. She wanted to be alone while reading it.

Inside the envelope, a sheaf of close-written pages, first in Swedish, then, in different handwriting, a translation into English.

Dearest Veronika,

Now you will find out the truth. You were too young and too far away to know this. You might understand some but not all. I want to explain. We were a family, in more than just blood; Gustav, Klara, Alice, myself, and Loke Voss. Your grandfather Gustav and Loke did everything together when they were boys. Tumbling around in the green summers after berries. Swimming in the lakes and streams, in waters so cold they made you feel more alive than the day you were born.

Brand thought of the photograph she had discovered in Elin's room, marked with her own name, as if it was an heirloom to be passed on. Loke Voss, the mysterious fifth figure in the shot, looked pale-eyed and dark while all the Dalgrens appeared sunny and carefree. He hovered on the edges of her family like a far-off storm cloud in a blue sky.

Loke and Gustav grew into their young teens and their friendship turned to war, the innocent kind, village raids between the Högvålen boys and those from Västvall, where all the Vosses were. "I broke Loke's hand with my face once," Gustav told me, and I laughed so hard because that was exactly how he phrased it.

I did not participate in the wild fun. Klara, Alice and I kept ourselves apart. Klara knew Loke had feelings for her but she only had eyes for Gustav. Maybe Loke's sourness grew out of that, with jealousy being the beginning of hatred.

Soon for Gustav the revolution became everything. He dreamed so hard, he was so inspired! This was when he and Klara fell in love. Their courting was done to the tune of Marx and Engels.

I too believed in the hope of social justice. I could see class war happening right in front of my eyes, the capitalists squeezing us like they wanted blood from a stone. Poverty was pitiless in those days. Then of course came the Thirties, with the rise of the Nazis in Germany, and everything went dark and then went darker still. Not only Loke Voss but many others, in Sweden and Britain as well, studied hate under the tutelage of the Germans.

I admired his convictions, dear, dear Gustav. What turns one man one way and another man another way? Why did Gustav turn left while his old friend Loke turned right?

Gustav was merciless with his ridicule of Adolf Hitler, whom he always called "the house painter." The man is lower than a cannibal, he said.

The Vosses, though, they were weaned on the housepainter's poison. Loke Voss fell in with Baron Kron and the concept of the master race. He cast his lot with the Brownshirt bullyboys, becoming one of their leaders.

As Brand read on, the picture of the past slowly came into focus. Two friends, brothers almost, buffeted in the tides of history and turned against each other. It was the old story of Cain and Abel. "Loke Voss," a name she heard as a child hissed out as a curse, became less a bogeyman and more of a real flesh-and-blood figure. Still alive, Hammar had told her, and still haunting Brand's life. Another faintly remembered name from the past appeared, not a person but a newspaper. *Nordic Light.*

Here was the core group who founded Nordic Light *newspaper: Gustav, of course, our older brother Anders, his wife Stella, our old friend Per, a man named Karl Gustavsson, Klara, and her sister Alice.*

Oh, those were heady times. We were intent on saving the world. The newspaper offices served as our communal home. I still remember the ugly old building, three stories high with a roof that leaked. I always went to sleep to the clatter of the big printing press rolling out copies of the truth. Asleep or awake I would often have one of the children with me, not my own (not yet) but those of Anders, Per or Karl, it didn't matter, all kids in that community were everybody's.

One I loved more than others, sweet little Hanna. She was our niece, the youngest of Anders and Stella. I spoiled her most awfully, always taking her hand in mine, playing silly games. She is what we call lillgammal*, a kind of spirit inside of someone young, who is older, wiser, beyond her years. Even as a baby Hanna had to wear eyeglasses, and she would stare up at me, so serious and solemn that I had to forgive myself for finding it comical.*

I felt that in her child's heart there was the future, that she would live to see a better world. I had this idea we were shielding the little ones from all that was horrible in the outside world, injustice, ignorance, and cruelty. We had our little enclave at the Nordic Light *offices, a refuge, a sanctuary where I could protect*

Hanna and the other children from harm.

I was wrong.

Brand foresaw the tragedy that was coming. She wanted to stop reading but couldn't help herself. Maybe after all this story was why she had come to Sweden. To perform an exorcism on the past.

She didn't want to believe it. What possible impact could events that happened long before she was born have on her reality now? It seemed an unlikely notion. But something had twisted Brand's life. She had struggled and thrashed, trying to understand what it was. Elin's letter served to point the way.

On 3 March, 1940, began one of the most terrible nights of my life, when the terrorists came to attack our offices.

How the Nordic Light *building was laid out had the kitchen and living quarters on the third floor, and what we called the Red Room meeting hall on the second floor, the printing press, telegraph, and distribution and paper supply rooms on the first. Corridors and stairwells ran up the whole center of the building.*

The attackers knew right where to go. They knew our paper supply would burn easily, setting the whole building on fire. They were using newsprint, our own weapon, against us.

Gustav, Alice and Klara were in the distribution office *on the first floor. Karl and Per were on the second floor, the babies were already asleep on the third, with Stella watching over them. When the arson hit in the paper supply room on the opposite side of the building from us, the central stairwell acted as a chimney. We all rushed out of the distribution offices to find this huge yellow beast of a fire already stalking up the stairs.*

Gustav dashed forward but an explosion blew him straight off his feet, and he came flying back into my arms. Solid smoke, so thick that it was like hot black cotton, burst at us. We crawled close to the floor, trying for escape.

I could hear them. I hear them still. I have heard them every day of my life from that moment on. Hanna crying, screaming, oh, oh, oh, mamma, mamma! *Auntie! Auntie! Gustav, Alice, Klara and I threw ourselves toward the stairs, but again we were thrown back, our clothes and hair smoking and half on fire.*

Now no voices came from the third floor. Only the roar of the beast. It was so hot that our tears sizzled and instantly turned to steam as they streamed down our faces. We staggered outside and collapsed on the street in front of the building, staring back in horror at our beloved home that had turned into a death trap.

Karl did not make it out. Per, neither. Stella died huddled together with Hanna, and Karl's child Peter.

Just by fate, we had the twins with us that night. Sanna and Folke were colicky newborns and had to be kept separate to keep from waking everyone in the shared upstairs. I remember holding them, watching the burning building collapse, two squalling babies, their parents dead, all of us survivors made orphans of the fire. I raised them myself so the memory of evil was kept fresh in their souls.

Brand remained lost in a tangle of black thoughts. Lives destroyed. Brutality, fire and death had burned through three generations. She had received hints of the truth before, but now it appeared confirmed. A ghost had sunk its teeth into her family, a still-living ghost named Loke Voss.

The pain the man inflicted had even crossed oceans, dooming Gustav to a life half-lived, then brutalized her mother. In adulthood, alcohol served as Marta's painkiller. Her marriage to Brand's father broke apart. The woman's life became a series of bad choices and failed attempts at reform.

Like some virus, her mother bestowed the dark gift upon Brand next. Her life turned into the same sort of mess as her mother's. So it goes, Brand mused, on and on forever. Until someone breaks the chain.

How much did her own grandmother know about poor Elin's doomed fate? Did Sanna and Folke know their true lineage or had they been spared from the ghosts of the past? An unimaginable fantasy broke into her thoughts then. Brand pictured herself consumed with fury, wielding her Glock automatic as a sword. She would be the one to right the wrong. She would transform into a vengeful angel screaming down on Loke Voss. It was a strange, alien vision, but a pleasurable one. She tried to reject it, but it found a home in her exhausted, disordered brain.

A flash of paranoia hit her. Could this be why the Dalgrens summoned her to Sweden in the first place? Sanna and the others, making up a cabal, using her as their cat's paw. No, no, she reasoned. But the concept had such power, such vividness…

Hammar returned to the Saab. Preoccupied, Brand didn't notice his coming. She was surprised when he opened the car door. He took one look at her face and knelt down beside her.

"Are you all right? Jesus, you look…" He left the sentence unfinished.

Brand remained seated, staring out toward the desolate churchyard. "I want to go to Västvall," she said.

20

"Is that the town?" Brand gazed down at a farm village at the bottom of a deep valley.

"Yes, that's Västvall," Hammar said.

Earlier that afternoon at the churchyard, Brand had told Hammar about her great-aunt's account of the *Nordic Light* arson. She had tried to be matter-of-fact, but her throat had a catch in it during the telling of the tale. They stood together, leaning against the Saab in the church parking lot. A cold wind blew. Advancing storm clouds piled in the west.

Hammar responded readily to Brand's account. "You know, you could fly home and forget about this whole business. It's not up to one person to right the wrongs of history."

"They don't want me in New York, either," Brand had reminded him. "Right now I'm without a country."

"Evidently, from your reception at the Ljusdal *polisstation,* the authorities here would like to be shut of you. There might even be fireworks at your departure."

Brand smiled ruefully. "And signs reading 'Yankee go home'."

"Well, you disturb the Swedish peace. It's always a celebration when an American busybody takes her leave."

"They won't be rid of me easily."

"No, I didn't think so. But listen, I'm serious. You should leave off, pack your bags, return home. It wouldn't be a failure, only a reasonable decision. I see deep waters ahead for you."

"Being reasonable isn't my strong suit," Brand said. "I feel as though I've got to follow this thing through. But I certainly wouldn't blame you for deciding it's not your battle to fight."

At that, Hammar had placed his hand on Brand's arm. "The evidence is in," he said. "It's clear you need someone to look after you."

Brand felt a twinge of irritation over the comment, perhaps because of the truth of it. A typical male sentiment, after all. Hammar's soft smile managed to disarm her. With elaborate politeness he had opened the driver's side door of the Saab.

"Unless you'd consider the strange idea of the owner driving his own car?"

"I'll drive," Brand said, climbing in. "You navigate."

"To Västvall, then," Hammar said. "Voss country."

They had left the church behind and drove west on empty highways, climbing into a wild upland region Hammar referred to as the *fjäll*.

"'Fell', is how you would say it in English," he said.

A half hour later, on their approach to Västvall, the road ran fairly straight, a gradual incline with snow-laden pines on either side. All patches of blue sky had disappeared. A few random snowflakes floated suspended in midair, pretty portents of more to come. The turn-off to the village allowed for a good view from the top of a hill.

Brand counted four farmhouses scattered on the downside of the slope, with good spreads of land in between each of them. They were built in the same style she had seen at the Dalgren homestead, two-storied and homely looking, with square windows set in their small peaked gables. Everything was painted *falu* red. Stock pens, loading ramps, and gnarled wooden sheds clustered around the structures, everything looking sad and deserted.

Hammar pointed towards the hillside behind them. "There's more farmland up there, meadows for grazing. In the summer the cows were herded further up the mountainside. A young girl, a *fäbodjänta*, stayed with the cows, a cow tender, you could say. *Fäbod* is the word for the houses up there."

"Fah-bawd," Veronika tried.

Hammar smiled. "There were small compounds built of logs. The cow tenders lived in them for the summer. You'd hear their songs echoing up and down the mountains. Something like a Swiss yodel, but more romantic, poetic. She called the cows home."

"Sounds like a great summer job," Brand said. "Where do I apply?"

"Heavy work," Hammar said with a sideward glance. "Milking those cows, churning butter."

"I'm familiar with all that," Brand answered.

"There are probably more houses on the property," Hammar continued. "Down below, a few grand lodges exist, homes for the modern-day family members, hidden off in the woods. And that makes up the entirety of Västvall."

There was something moody about the look of the village, sunk in the darkened upland valley. It was as if the sun never penetrated and the mighty Scandinavian light finally had to retreat in defeat.

"Even today, the locals around here honor the old traditions," Hammar said. "On Saturday nights the young fools in these little villages get drunk and make raids on each other. The town in the next valley over is always enemy territory. They get into brawls or race their cars. Everyone laughs it off as simple country innocence. What else is there to do during the long winters?"

"From my experience as a cop, I'd say innocence is more a matter of luck rather than virtue."

"Luck and a good lawyer," Hammar agreed, laughing. He indicated the village below them. "Shall we go amongst them, Detective Brand?"

The faded, storm-filtered light on the mountainside turned to murk as they descended into the valley. Brand was distracted for a moment by the stark reality of the surroundings. She realized they were about to enter the home territory of people that had, directly or indirectly, figured into her family's destiny in tragic ways.

Just as that thought occurred to her, the ancient woods closed in on both sides of the little two-lane road. They entered a tree-lined vault that felt almost subterranean. Huge pines soared upward to become an overhead tangle of interlocking branches. Downed tree trunks the size of tanker trucks studded the dense undergrowth.

The forest would have blocked all sunlight, had there been any left. The winter storm they had first noticed back in the churchyard had now moved in. A heavy sky lowered on this part of Sweden, stone-black and impenetrable. The looming clouds above mirrored the dark of the woods below.

Brand peered out the side window of the Saab. She had heard about such a landscape but had never really encountered it. Here was the great, deep, enduring Swedish forest, a sacred realm that supposedly lodged itself near to the heart of the national soul.

"The forest primeval," she murmured.

"What was that?" Hammar asked.

"Nothing," Brand said. "I was just noticing that this is all old-growth woodland around here."

"*Urskog*," Hammar said. "What you call virgin forest. Never logged."

"Beautiful," Brand said, but she didn't mean it. What she meant instead was terrible, alien, suffocating.

Without thinking, Brand moved her foot off the Saab's accelerator to ease on the brakes. Encountering the arboreal landscape slowed them as surely as if they had driven into a patch of mud. Even the air inside the car seemed to have gone dense.

Turning to examine the brushy understory on the passenger side, she noticed the snow was marked by what looked like human footprints. Either that, or clumps of snow falling from the immense trees had dotted the forest floor below.

Brand thought later that her brief turn of head made all the difference. Had she been looking forward, she probably would not have hit the young child.

21

The boy sprang from the woods on the driver's side of the Saab. He ran slantwise into the road. Brand glimpsed him out of the corner of her eye. She thought at first that it might be some woodland animal. She didn't have time to react.

The hollow thud of the child's body hitting the Saab's front quarter-panel felt like a punch to Brand's gut. He rolled onto the sloped hood and slammed against the windshield with a dull crack. Instinctively, Brand jammed on the brakes. Her body lurched forward and her chin grazed the steering wheel.

For an instant the boy's face and Brand's were inches from each other. He had entered into an odd crouch, like an Olympic gymnast, his arms out as if searching for balance. But the force of impact broke his precarious pose. The little body seemed to bounce upward into the sky and disappear.

The Saab's brakes dragged to the left. Beneath its snow-glazed surface, the roadway was scattered with fine gravel. The car entered into a greasy five-meter skid. It wound up skewed toward the opposite, uphill shoulder of the road.

Hammar had also been thrust forward by the abrupt stop. His nose clipped the unpadded dashboard, not sharply, but hard enough. When he rocked backwards blood spurted from both nostrils.

Brand found herself caught in a tangled seat belt. She couldn't get her breath. She wanted to cry out. She wanted to ask Hammar if he was all right, wanted to sit still for a moment and gather her wits. Her thoughts were overwhelmed by the unreality of what had just happened.

"Oh, fucking hell," she said.

Having trouble operating the unfamiliar door handle of the Saab, finally freeing herself from the stubborn seat belt, Brand staggered out onto the snowy surface of the road. Hammar had already managed to emerge from the car.

"What was that?" Brand said. Hammar exclaimed, "*Var är han?*" at the same time.

The broken boy had vanished. He was a phantasm. A vague imprint of his head left behind a spider-web crack in the ancient Saab's windshield. That seemed to be the only sign he really existed. Then Brand saw a single cheap plastic boot lying in front of the car.

"*Vilket jävla sätt,*" Hammar hissed. In the crisis he had unconsciously switched over to Swedish. He had said either "where is it?" or "what happened?" Brand didn't know which.

She and Hammar had both left their car doors completely open. The modern, retrofitted key alarm Hammar had installed in the Saab dinged solemnly. Other than that, all was silent.

To the left, the road sloped away into a shallow, snow-filled gully. Brand first saw a thin brown arm. She had a terrible thought that the boy's body had somehow come apart. The arm lay twenty feet away. Could he really have been thrown that far?

"He's here," Brand said. To her ears, her own voice sounded cold, emotionless.

Hammar and Brand moved across the road to the ditch. Beneath the Saab's annoying robotic ding-ding-ding something else sounded, the voice of a bird, a small animal.

"Oh, oh, oh," it said.

In the knee-deep snow by the roadside sprawled a young boy. He wore not enough clothes for the weather, a pair of flimsy pants and a hoodie. He looked twelve years old. The body landed in a crumpled, abnormal posture, a single thin arm extended backward. The match to the boot on the road hung off the boy's right foot.

"*Följ med!*" Hammar spoke with panicked urgency. Come along!

They both stepped off the road to reach the child. He's not dead, Brand thought. If he's moaning that means he's alive.

"Oh, oh, oh."

Brand's police training kicked in. "We shouldn't move him," she said to Hammar. "There might be...damage to the spine."

"*Skitsnack,*" Hammar said. Nonsense. He kneeled to take the boy in his arms.

Blood blossomed on the child's face. For a sick second Brand thought of a hemorrhage, but she realized Hammar's nose was dripping bright vermilion drops whenever he moved.

"*Lilla vän,*" Hammar said, still favoring Swedish. "*Säg något!*" Can you say something?

Brand looked over at Hammar. His face was smeared with blood. "Are you okay?" she asked.

"It's nothing," Hammar said. "*Näsblod.*"

The child in his arms would not quit moaning. "We need a…" Hammar said.

"A blanket?" Brand said.

"A phone," Hammar said. Brand felt like an idiot. She could only conclude her cop competence had been left behind when she had flown across the Atlantic. She wondered about the effects of shock, for the child as well as for her and Hammar.

She dug into her pocket for her cell phone.

Hammar began delicately probing the limbs of the whimpering child. "I'm not sure, but I can't find anything broken."

"No coverage," Brand said, staring dumbly at the cell phone screen. Her phone had been failing to connect ever since she arrived in Sweden.

"I've got a phone in my—" Hammar began to say, then he cut himself off. His face expressed alarm.

Brand followed the direction of his look. A sneaking clutch of children had crept around the Saab, ten meters back along the road. They displayed the same unseasonably skimpy clothes as the injured boy. There were four or five of the waifs. Brand couldn't tell exactly how many. One halted at the open passenger door. Another ducked inside. A third was already dashing away from the car, dragging a leather satchel belonging to Hammar.

Brand couldn't think straight. Evidently the Saab had been set upon by a gang of thieving street urchins who for some reason chose to inhabit the woods. Forest urchins.

"Hey!" she called. From her kneeling position she pulled herself upright.

The key-alarm dinging abruptly ceased. The child who was reaching inside the car had snatched the ignition keys.

"Fuck!" Hammar exclaimed. "*Era små djävlar!*" You little devils! He lurched forward, causing the boy in his arms to moan afresh.

The looting of the Saab went along like lightning. Before Brand could step back onto the roadway, she saw the children gather up Hammar's camera and cell phone.

Seeing Brand emerge from the ditch back onto the road, one of the gang of lost boys, an older, taller one, emitted a sentinel-like alarm, a quick, chirp-like whistle.

The children scattered. Dragging their treasure—Brand's sweater, a bag of potato chips, Hammar's leather satchel—they disappeared, crowing, into the shelter of the woods. Brand realized that they weren't all lost boys. One was a tiny girl in a ragged black dress and tattered leggings. She had crawled out from somewhere, seemingly from beneath the car.

Behind Brand, Hammar had straightened up also. He still dripped blood and still cradled the injured boy in his arms.

With a violent animal-like twist of his body, the child slipped out of Hammar's grasp. He ducked away and ran again out onto the roadway. He displayed no apparent injury from his recent impact with the Saab. Scooping up his wayward boot, he hopped along while slipping it onto his bare foot. Then he staggered off on the trail of his partners in crime.

The boy flung a middle finger behind him as he fled.

Cursing volubly, holding up the sleeve of his jacket to his streaming nose, Hammar lurched after the boy at a run.

"Wait," Brand called to him. Then she stopped. My pistol, she thought.

"There's a loaded weapon in there," she murmured aloud to no one. The awful truth served to stun her as sure as if she had just received a sharp blow to the head.

Had she really seen what she thought she had seen? The girl in the shabby black dress had grabbed Brand's backpack. Now the child scampered down the slope with it, thirty meters away and disappearing fast.

With her went Brand's smuggled firearm.

22

The blizzard hit full force while Brand struggled through the deep drifts in the forest outside Västvall village. She had left the disabled Saab behind to follow the tracks of the fleeing kid thieves. Once she stumbled across the blood-spattered trail of Hammar and his quarry. She almost instantly lost that track, too, becoming increasingly disoriented.

"Hammar," she called out, only to hear her words swallowed by storm winds that had risen quite suddenly to a howl. Soon the human footprints on the forest floor became obscured by blowing snow. The air around Brand filled with swarms of glistening crystals, sharp and stinging. Darkness dropped with a velocity that astonished her. Any leftover daylight became eclipsed by the blizzard.

Brand's only possible choice was to follow the sloping ground downward. She assumed that eventually she would come to the floor of the low-land and the village.

If I don't freeze to death first, she thought morosely.

She knew the Swedes believed or pretended to believe in spirits loose in the forest. The *urskog*, as Hammar had called the woods she found herself in. On the night of the Dalgren family reunion, Lukas had told ghost stories about the forest spirits, entertaining the numberless nephews, nieces and grandchildren that had gathered.

"*Huldror*, pretty ladies of the forest who will lead you to your doom," he had said, using a dramatic, woo-woo voice. "From the front, they appear to be beautiful maidens. From behind they're hideous, and sometimes they have a tail!"

The children screamed with frightened delight.

Now Brand was in pursuit of a *huldra* of her own, a tiny girl in a black dress, dragging a backpack with a loaded weapon in it.

She felt enveloped in a dream. The larcenous children certainly hadn't seemed real to her. They were wood imps summoned forth by the trespass of a citified foreigner, an intruder who had dared to enter the depths of the *urskog*. They were here to bedevil her.

Such mythical creatures never came unaccompanied. Not only *huldror* haunted the forests, but evil dwarves, trickster sprites, as well as *nattmaror*, or nightmares, a species of enormous she-wolves that tormented victims in their sleep.

"And trolls," Brand muttered to herself, staggering along. "Don't forget trolls."

No doubt she would soon be meeting up with trolls and whatever other varieties of folkloric horror the Swedes cooked up to scare children and American detectives. The whole pantheon would emerge by nightfall, which was being hurried briskly along by the storm.

Frostbite was probably a more concrete danger, but in the current environment Brand's mind tended toward spooks. She thrust an ungloved hand into the pocket of her vest for warmth, and found the small stone charm that Moro Part gave her. Whatever positive vibe the dingus supposedly had wasn't helping much.

As she plunged forward, her feet froze slowly upward from the toes. The snow infiltrated her clothing and then melted, making everything wet and miserable. Deep drifts alternated with treacherous stretches of bare, wind-swept ground, strewn with trip-hazard roots and rocks. She soon felt as if she were stumping along on twin blocks of ice.

Climbing a four-meter ridge of hardened snow, Brand abruptly realized she was out of the woods. The big drift had been piled high along the side of a roadway by a snowplow.

The Swedish *urskog* had released its American victim. Visibility still sucked. Brand followed the road to the right instead of the left, toward the little village instead of who-knew-where. Her breath came hard. She thought of tragic anecdotes told by her Dalgren relatives at the reunion, who seemed to relish the idea of a cold so vicious that it froze a victim's lungs.

"Hammar!" she shouted again. She was wary of attracting the attention of the pint size gangbangers-in-the-making. They might descend and strip her naked as they had the Saab. But she had no choice. To lose a handgun represented a cop's cardinal sin. To lose a handgun to a child? That had to be a capital offense.

Then the blizzard howled her name.

"Vuh-raahhh-nee-kah."

Was she hearing things? Quite possibly, considering the shape of her mind in the wake of the assault. The fifteen-minute slog through the *urskog* had taken its toll.

"Hammar!"

"Vuh-raahhh-nee-kah." The sound was eerie, directionless.

The icy tick of sleet became constant. There was a strange quality to the weather's brutality. Occasionally the air would teasingly clear, only to be quickly obliterated again in a swirl of snow. It was as if the storm had multiple eyes, pockets of calm that opened and then just as suddenly, closed.

During one of these brief lulls, Brand witnessed two children tugging on a pair of chains that were fastened to opposite sides of a huge she-wolf's neck. The *nattmara* bent toward a clump of rolled-up carpet that was lying in the snow. The hulking creature's snout showed blood red. Brand realized the carpet was actually a human form.

The *nattmara* was…feeding on…tearing at…wolfing…human flesh. Its pair of kiddie handlers tugged gaily on the chain leashes as if they were leading the family dog on its afternoon walk.

In the instant before the pocket of calm slammed shut, Brand saw something else, too. Unaware or unconcerned about the sight of a giant beast devouring a corpse, a second pair of children knelt together a few meters away from the spectacle. The girl whom Brand had been pursuing, the little one in the black dress, held open the stolen backpack for an older boy.

The bigger kid pulled out Brand's Glock. He stared as if the piece was the Holy Grail. Emitting a cry of triumph, he then banged off two shots, aiming downward at the well-bloodied body lying on the ground. The explosions barely sounded over the roar of the storm. Brand saw the supine form jolt with the impact of the rounds. Then the blizzard closed again. The shooter became merely a dark, shapeless silhouette lost in the white-out.

The *nattmara* had been spooked by the gunshots. It tried to tear itself away from its kiddie handlers, dragging them helplessly along as it bounded away from the dead body it had just been feasting upon.

In only a few strides of its long loping body, the beast was there. It came at Brand like a hellhound, like its name, like a nightmare.

23

Cape Coast, Ghana, April 1957.

Gösta Kron took a table at a local chop bar's terrace, kicking out one of the chairs for Loke Voss. His companion suffered from a tropical illness to a severe degree. He could barely do anything for himself. A case of dysentery was the ostensible cause. Kron judged the man's true malady to be simple homesickness.

The chop bar's terrace featured expansive views of the Bay of Guinea. Back over Kron's left shoulder loomed the white-washed hulk of Cape Coast Castle. Loke saw none of it. He settled heavily into the cane chair offered to him.

Loke Voss was, what? Approaching forty? Kron had just turned twenty and was seemingly impervious to dysentery, malaria, guinea worm, camp fever and whatever else the tropics could throw at him. His only prophylactic measure was always to drink beer, never the local water, parasite-infested and lethal. He now motioned the boy waiter with two fingers now, ordering imported bottles of Guinness stout, a beverage which possessed the advantage of being okay to drink warm. The hometown brew was pure piss.

The two of them had just returned from the Ashanti gold fields, a hundred miles to the northwest. The place was in chaos. The British were pulling out. Only a month previous, on 6 March 1957, Kwame Nkrumah, now president-for-life, had declared independence for the British colony formerly known as Gold Coast.

Such an enticing name, Kron thought. Gold Coast. The new one,

"Ghana," meant something like "warrior kingdom." That was great, too, but didn't exactly have the same ring as Gold Coast. There was a hole in every human soul, Kron believed, an emptiness that could only be properly filled by gold. Gold was good, gold was great, gold was…everything.

With independence, Ghana was in transition. The gold fields were in chaos, yes, but the whole country was in chaos, too. Chaos was good, chaos was great, chaos was…everything—for the purposes of the Kron family, at least. Gösta Kron's father, Baron Henrik Kron, saw the British tucking tail as a golden opportunity. According to the old man's way of thinking, the current upheavals in Ghana represented a chance to right a historical wrong over three hundred years in the making.

In the middle of the seventeenth century, Sweden controlled every hectare of land that Kron could see from the chop bar terrace. Back then his countrymen had built or at least rebuilt the huge castle that stood up the shoreline a quarter mile away. The Swedish Gold Coast was planned to be the first of many colonies, placing Sweden on the level of the Danish, Dutch and British imperial empires. The Swedes set themselves up as slavers in Cape Coast, using the castle's dungeon baracoon to hold their human product.

Young Baron Kron couldn't care less about history. His father's tales of Sweden's colonial past left him cold. What his twenty-year-old mind did like was adventure. His mission to the newly independent warrior kingdom on the Gold Coast of Africa suited Kron to a T. The old baron made him take along Loke Voss, an ally and business associate, to keep his son in line.

Backed by the old baron, the Voss family was in the midst of building a transportation empire in Sweden, tactics that included extortion, hijacking, and—yes—murder. All perfectly legitimate business strategies, according to Loke Voss. Ghana might have defeated his digestive tract, but the man would no doubt return to fighting form as soon as they got back north.

Conquering heroes they would be, flush with lucrative contracts for mining rights. Perhaps they'd be loaded down with a few kilogram bars of gold bullion to pass around as well.

But who knew? Kron gazed over the dirty sand beach parked thick with fishing skiffs, the blue expanse of the Gulf of Guinea, the white man's big bleached castle throwing its long shadow of slavery—and he had a brief thought of remaining in the Warrior Kingdom. He could access his own inner warrior, carve out a name for himself in Africa. In a few years, a decade at the most, when the native Africans got tired of self-rule and became nostalgic for their former masters, the young baron might position his own fine self to become Ghana's new president-for-life.

Gösta Kron had stumbled across something at the sprawling central market in Kumasi that he could not get out of his mind. While strolling among the mounds of plantains, cassava root and other strange foodstuffs—oranges were green here—he encountered an ancient bearded Ashanti male dressed in a spotless white robe and an embroidered yellow skull cap. For some reason the man had a red megaphone in his lap, which Kron didn't immediately notice. He barely saw the African himself, so stunned was he to see what lay at the man's feet.

A huge spotted hyena dozed peacefully in the middle of the busy market, its evil, heavy-lidded eyes at half mast, a red-blond ruff running down its back, a crotchet muzzle fastened firmly in place on its snout. The Ashanti man, who in faltering English told Kron his name was "Kumi the Strong," casually held a chain leash attached to the beast's woven leather collar. The smell of the hyena was dead-meat terrible, which somehow only contributed to its allure.

Fascinated, Kron edged a hand near the animal's flank. The beast lazily swiveled its head and stared at the encroaching foreigner. At that moment something deep and moving occurred. Kron saw the ancient African savannah in those eyes, baboon prey, rotting carcasses under a pitiless sun, an era long before homo sapiens, before the taming of fire, before God. It was though Kron had embarked on a blazing trip in a time machine.

What Kron felt most was kinship. Perhaps he was truly an African after all, mistakenly born among the pale Swedes, a warrior king with a destiny he had heretofore not suspected.

"Jesus," Kron whispered, addressing not the Savior but himself.

He started haggling with the beast's handler right then and there. "How much if I hire you to bring the animal to Sweden?"

Owning a hyena had instantly become mandatory in his mind. He had already considered shipping home a curated selection of live African wildlife. At the market here in Cape Coast, a lion cub attracted his interest as well as a baby ape. He had eaten bush meat with the best of them on his trip to the gold fields, some from species he would stock in the private menagerie that he planned for the lodge.

The hyena would be the centerpiece. Fly it to Sweden by plane. Kron could imagine the fulsome odor of the animal filling the cargo hold of a DC-3. Headed home soon, he knew he'd eventually return to Ghana, maybe in a few months, maybe in a few years. If he didn't grab this particular creature, another blond beast of the same species would do just as well. His possession would represent what surely would be the only pet hyena in Scandinavia.

Maybe he'd pick up a wild dog, a jackal, or an aardwolf while he was at it, too. Plus hyenas ran in packs, didn't they? He'd have to have more than two or three. He would present the whole crazy menagerie as a gift to *pappa*, to wow visitors at the Kron family hunting lodge. The African specimens would also provide a comforting reminder to the young baron himself of his status as never-crowned president-for-life of the Warrior Kingdom.

24

As it galloped down on her, Brand recognized the animal. The beast was the same spotted, sandy-colored, big-shouldered dog she had seen disappearing into the woods at the Voss manor house outside of Ljusdal.

With its pair of giggling minders in pursuit, the creature blew past Brand in a cloud of the foulest stench that had ever assaulted her nostrils. The smell triggered sense memories of decomposed bodies she had encountered on the job. Somehow the rot managed to contaminate even the clean-smelling freeze of the blizzard. Brand rocked backward and stood helpless as the animal passed within a few feet of her. Stunned, she watched it go, staring as it became merely an indistinct blond blur disappearing into the wind-blown snow.

But she broke out of her paralysis as the older boy who had fired off her pistol came dashing along after the big dog. He emitted shrill whistles and called out a word in Swedish that Brand did not understand.

"Fenrir! Fenrir!"

The kid paid as little attention to Brand as the monster dog had, just seconds before. But he was running with her Glock in his right hand, so she stepped directly into his path.

"No!" she shouted. Then she thought she'd better try Swedish. "*Nej!*"

The young boy performed a slapstick slide on the roadway ice. He slammed into her, knocking Brand to the ground. She managed to kick his feet out from under him as she went down. He wound up falling backward against the bank of plow-hardened snow. They sprawled almost side by side. The hallucinatory quality of the moment embellished itself effortlessly. The kid's leather bomber cap slipped half-way off his head, revealing what looked like pink hair shaved into the style of a punk mohawk.

"*Nej!*" Brand shouted again.

She watched it happen. First the pink-haired kid took a moment to straighten out his bomber hat. Then with his other hand he raised the Glock and pointed it at her.

Several times in the course of her police career, Brand had faced off weapons on the mean streets of New York City—and in the mean subway tunnels beneath the streets, too. Knives, nunchuks, once a hatchet, once a sword, several times golf clubs and, more often, handguns, both revolvers and automatics. She had also confronted a homemade zip gun, constructed of wood, metal pipe, and rubber bands, with a threepenny nail for a firing pin. The jury-rigged weapon exploded in the face of the attacker, sending him cuffed to a cot in the ER but leaving Brand unscathed.

The clichéd time-slowing-to-a-crawl effect had never happened for her. The lesson from the potentially fatal experiences on the job was always the split-second nature of the threats.

Don't think. React.

A rock-hard chunk of plowed snow lay near her right hand, so she grabbed that and threw it at the punk. At the same instant he pulled the trigger. The bang sounded huge. The chunk shattered in a huge cloud of ice. The shot seemed to fly harmlessly past Brand to embed itself in the snowbank.

She kicked out again and connected with the hand that held her pistol. It spun out of the punk's grip and hit the ice of the road. Brand realized that whichever one of them got upright first would likely be the one to survive, so she tried to rise.

The little girl in the black dress scampered forward out of the storm. She flung Brand's borrowed, half-empty backpack at her. The child's aim was true. The clumsy pack hit her straight on. Brand's feet slipped out from under her once again. She collapsed into the snow.

Her mohawked opponent was already on his feet. He grabbed the Glock. Sweeping up the little girl under one arm, he began blasting shots at Brand as he fled back down the road.

Brand could do nothing but curl into a ball and count the rounds. They totalled six—which meant, counting the two slugs put into the corpse when the perp first got his hands on her sidearm—there were eleven left in the 9x19 magazine. Unarmed as she was, seething with fury, Brand still had the good sense not to pursue the punk while he had that many rounds left to throw at her.

The hallucination stuttered to an end. The pink-haired, kid-slinging gunsel vanished into the blizzard. His piercing whistles and his calls to Fenrir faded into the screaming wind.

She sat upright. She was not killed. She would live to fight another day.

Brand swore to herself that she would track down her sidearm if it took everything she had. An image floated into her mind of a pink mohawk scalp, bloody, defeated, and nailed to a trophy wall.

A couple of things happened at once. She heard the far-off buzz of a snowmobile. Then the chug of another engine sounded close by. Hammar's Saab loomed out of the blizzard-blown snow, skidding to a stop a few meters from where Brand sat.

Hammar swung open the driver's side door, leaning halfway out. His blood-spattered face made him appear as a vision out of the Grand Guignol. The minor crack in the Saab's windshield, dented by an imprint of a child's head, completed the package.

"Brand." Hammar's voice was oddly cool. "I say we get the hell out of here."

Leaving the scene of a crime while the incident remained in progress was another cardinal sin of law enforcement. Secure the scene, call in the cavalry, attempt to stabilize whatever confrontation was occurring. Fleeing went against every bit of Brand's police instinct. She thought of heading out in pursuit of the mohawked Johnny Rotten and his demon-imp sidekick. She realized she didn't have the heart for it.

She ran toward the driver's side of the Saab.

"I'll drive!" Hammar barked back at her, his composure finally rattled.

But Brand simply remained standing next to the half open door.

"Oh, for fuck's sake," Hammar said, finally moving over and allowing her to climb behind the wheel.

Before she got in, Brand scooped up one of the hardened chunks of snow. She offered it to Hammar. He stared, but finally accepted it and held it up against his still-streaming nose. Everything inside the car was bloodstained. She noticed his leather satchel on the floor at his feet. She engaged the shift and drove off, feeling an immense sense of relief to leave Västvall behind.

"You got it back," Brand said, indicating the satchel. "And the ignition keys, too? Did you take them off those kids?"

"No." Hammar gave her a rueful smile. His teeth were stained with blood. "I had another set of keys in my bag."

"Be prepared, that's the motto of a good Boy Scout." Brand felt lightheaded and vaguely high. The Winston Churchill line that police always liked to quote occurred to her, something about how there was nothing more exhilarating than to be shot at without result.

"You're bleeding," Hammar said. His voice came out as a nasal honk.

She glanced over at him. "No, that's just your blood."

"Your shoulder," he said, indicating her upper right arm.

There was a crease in the fabric of her jacket, a rip that showed fresh blood.

"It's just a scratch." It was a sentence that she had always wanted to say but never had the chance before. Elation flooded her.

"Jesus Christ!" she shouted. "What the hell was that?"

"Those children were Romani," Hammar said calmly, his equanimity returning.

"Did you see it?"

"See what?"

"If you have to ask 'what?' that means you didn't see it. The hound of the fucking Baskervilles back there."

She hadn't mentioned the vision of the dog vanishing into the woods at the Ljusdal manor house, not trusting that her own eyes had seen what they had seen.

Hammar said, "The Swedes around here love to interbreed dogs with the native wolves."

"Nuh-uh, pal, that beast was a wolf like King Kong was an ape." Brand second guessed herself even now, remembering how difficult it was to see anything during the blizzard of the century. She could barely see ten feet in front of her as it was.

"All that did happen, didn't it?" she asked, hoping for a reality check from Hammar. "What on earth are a collection of gypsy street urchins doing way out here?"

"You'd be surprised," Hammar responded. "A few of the more progressive villages in the area attract Romani from Stockholm with generous social services and welcoming townspeople. Much of the area has become depopulated, so they encourage any influx of outsiders."

"And how do the newcomers get along with the locals, some of whom are, so I hear, rabidly anti-immigrant?"

"There've been incidents," Hammar said.

"I'll bet."

Brand felt great, even though she realized she should be furious. She had fallen prey to the oddest ambush known to man. She had been deprived of her sidearm by a midget in a black dress, who had turned the pistol over to a teenage madman with pink hair, who in turn tried to kill her with her own gun. Plus there was the big dog.

And another thing, for which she should blame her bloody-nosed traveling companion. Everywhere she went, looking for Vosses, she ran into Roma. It was too much of a coincidence to pass unnoticed. If her hallucination had been correct, now there were three bodies to account for, two at the Ljusdal manor house and one lying on the ground in the middle of Västvall village.

"Are we in trouble?" The words came out almost before she thought of them. They hung in the air. Then both she and Hammar started to laugh, struck by the ridiculousness of the question, the answer to which seemed so blindingly obvious. Their laughter had an edge of crazy to it.

She drove up the hill to where the Västvall road met the highway. As she turned off and began to speed away, a pair of snowmobilers roared out of the blizzard. Both riders wore all-white snowsuits. They had goggles and balaclavas covering their faces. On both their machines, hunting rifles rested in gun scabbards of chocolate brown leather.

In the rear-view, Brand kept her eyes on the two. They raced briefly after the Saab. One of the riders actually unslung a rifle. He (or she, Brand was careful to qualify, since the snowsuits made the riders appear unisex) didn't manage to aim it. The other appeared to hold up a cell phone camera to take a shot of the fast-disappearing car.

With the swirling snow and the distance, Brand doubted if the picture would turn out. But her laughter over the "are we in trouble?" question died in her mouth.

25

The family gathered at Vilgot Voss's imposing residence, tucked away deep in a forest glade outside of Västvall village. Vilgot, a prim and well-groomed accountant, had modeled the place on El Tovar, the log cabin-style lodge at the Grand Canyon in the American West. He once stayed at the inn as a youth and the elaborate Western style of the architecture impressed him almost as much as the magnificent Arizona landscape.

The storm of the previous day piled snow on the branches of the big jackpines and flocked the timbers used to construct the house. Masses of ice and clumps of snow slid from the roof of the house, forming brief shadows as they thudded past the windows.

A virtual pope's conclave gathered inside the big main room of the lodge, cardinals, bishops and minor clerics from the holy order of the Vosses. The host was Vilgot Voss himself, the designated cooker of the family books. In attendance were Gabriel Voss, the military man Frans Voss, Lovisa Voss Klint, and Karl Voss. All were from what was known in the family (in spite of Lovisa) as the "brother's generation." Also present were a few of the brothers' children from the so-called "cousin's generation": Elias, Hans, Ylva, and Malte.

Not visibly present but there in overbearing spirit was the ninety-eight year old pope of the family, Loke Voss, senior.

His son, Loke Voss II, chief among the brothers, steered the conversation. Even at age seventy-nine he was usually referred to as "Junior." He despised the nickname. Abundantly supplied with coffee and brandy, the assembled Vosses sat around a wood fire, massive logs blazing in a hearth that was large enough for a person to stand upright.

"What do we know about our visitors?" Frans asked, addressing Junior.

One of Junior's children answered. "I tried for a cell phone shot of the car, but the snow was coming so hard that I failed," twenty-seven-year-old Ylva said. She was a sturdy outdoors-woman. Her wind-burned cheeks came from being exposed in the blizzard the afternoon before.

"Malte was with Ylva, and he tells me the vehicle was an old Saab," Gabriel said.

"Yes, from the Sixties, I think, really ancient, if I know my classic cars," Malte said.

"You are speaking to some people from the Sixties, so be careful what you call ancient," Lovisa said, laughing.

"I saw it too, although from far away," Hans said.

"Was it blue, the Saab?" Karl Voss asked. "An old sedan?"

"Yes," answered Ylva. "Quite a stupid-looking car."

"I think I know who that could be," Karl said quietly. "If I'm right, we may be in trouble."

"Who?" demanded Junior.

"You know the Sami lawyer we faced in the Västerbotten County *landrättighet* case a few years ago?"

"Yes!" Gabriel exclaimed. "Sami land rights, somewhere north of Umeå. Name of Hall, or Hansson, or something. A real 'pain in the ass.'"

He employed the English expression.

"Krister Hammar," Karl said, nodding. "He drives an old blue Saab. A troublemaker through and through. During the trial I learned to wish the man dead many times over."

"We lost that case, didn't we?" Junior asked.

Malte spoke up: "We're pretty sure the Saab was driven by a woman."

"A male sat as a passenger, but there was definitely a female driving," Ylva said.

"You could tell it was a woman because of the way she was swerving all over the road," Vilgot said, making a weak joke about female drivers.

"That's from a man who has totaled two Mercedes in his life," Lovisa countered mildly.

"Okay, okay, both of you," Junior said. "Frans, perhaps some of your former Karlsborg people can find out what the Lapp lawyer is up to these days."

"Karlsborg" was a shorthand term for a member of the *Särskilda operationsgruppen,* the special forces unit of the Swedish army, which was based in Karlsborg Fortress, on Lake Vättern in south central Sweden.

Frans Voss held the rank of colonel in the armed forces. "I'll put a man on it," he said.

"Two or three men," Junior suggested crisply. "Since we may find ourselves in a bind on this one. Now, moving on, the dead man."

"Yes," said Gabriel. "Mattias Rapp. One of Jarl's people, I'm afraid."

The whole room turned to Jarl Voss's father, Elias.

"Don't ask me," Elias said hastily. "I have no idea where my son is at the moment."

"God damn it!" Junior cried. "Doesn't he answer his damned phone?"

"When I call, he sees my number on the cell and doesn't pick up," Elias said. He tried to defend Jarl. "Please, *pappa*, please, Gabe, we don't know enough to judge."

"Well, things are not looking good, Elias," Gabriel said. "We hear about the Ljusdal manor house. We know Jarl has been using it. Now comes urgent news of this Hammar fellow being on the scene. Something has happened. For Jarl's sake, I hope he was not involved. I'm still trying to get information on it."

"Wherever that child goes, there's some kind of mess to clean up," Junior said.

"*Pappa*, really, no," Elias objected. "My Jarl is a good kid."

"A good kid who we've had to extricate from jams several times already," Karl said.

"He styles himself an old-style Voss smuggler from the past," Gabriel said.

"No, no, no," Elias said weakly.

"I understand we've retrieved two bullets from Mattias Rapp's corpse," Junior said. "I wonder if a ballistics analysis would yield anything of interest."

Gabriel nodded. "Yes, perhaps, but so far we've handled this whole business through back channels. A ballistics test means increased police involvement."

"I think we have sufficient pull with *SÄPO* to ask for a sub rosa forensics test of some sort, nothing public," Junior responded. "Don't you know someone at the SÄPO lab, Karl?"

"Yes, I do," Karl said.

"Malte, please pass along the spent slugs you retrieved to Karl."

Ylva raised her hand. "The body was ravaged quite badly. Has anyone encountered wolves in the area lately?"

No one answered. "I have photographs, if you wish to see them," Ylva said.

No one volunteered.

"Something went on," Ylva insisted. "We don't even know if it was the bullet wounds that killed him. Do we have a pathologist who could do a private autopsy?"

"Oh, I don't know if that's necessary," Junior said quickly. "The man is dead, after all. What would a postmortem accomplish?"

"I'd like to know what kind of thing gnawed at him that way," Ylva said.

"Wolves sometimes like to venture out under the cover of a storm," Karl suggested. "But the bear population has been active lately, or maybe it was some local dogs."

"How about you and I head out on a bear hunt if the weather stays clear?" Gabriel said to his brother. "Open their stomachs, see what we'd turn up."

"You wouldn't say 'bear' if you'd seen the body," Malte said. "Only Ylva and I have actually laid eyes on it, is that right?"

"And we thank you for taking care of things so discreetly," Junior said. "The corpse is in the deep freeze, now, no? The game locker in the other residence? So it will keep, with no immediate action required."

Ylva nodded her assent, a little too sullenly for Junior's taste. He chose not to rebuke her.

"So, summing up," he said, "no autopsy on the body for the present. We must find out from Jarl—if we can ever locate Jarl—if this man Mattias Rapp has a family. There might be some sort of payment necessary. Karl will handle the request for a secret ballistics test. And Frans will instigate a thorough probe of the Lapp lawyer's activities. I don't care for interference from his type, not at all. "

"I've got some operatives who'll crawl so far up the man's behind he'll feel a scratching in his throat," Frans said.

"What else?" Junior asked. "I think I'll place a call to the baron, just to apprise him of developments."

"I'd like to find out who was with this Krister Hammar yesterday," young

Ylva said. "The woman driver. It's very possible that these two were the killers of Mattias Rapp, and if so they both need to be schooled. This happened in our own backyard."

"Frans's people will check for known associates, specifically females," Junior said.

"You know, let me make a call on that," Karl said, getting up and leaving the room, phone in hand. As he went out, an attendant brought a man in a wheelchair into the room.

"Look who's here," Lovisa Voss said, rising to her feet.

In the chair sat an elderly individual, a slack-jawed and fumbling figure whose body had totally broken down with age. Only the eyes of the senior Loke Voss, sharp and burning, showed the man he had been in youth.

"Hello, *pappa*," Junior called out.

The rest of the clan rose to their feet along with Junior, welcoming the old man to the gathering.

"We were just settling some business," Junior said. "But we're finished now. Would you like to join us here by the fire?"

His children and grandchildren gathered in a line, dutifully shaking the hand the Voss clan patriarch kept extended. Junior ordered up a cup of hot water brought to his father, then fussed with his blankets. Someone moved him closer to the warmth of the fire.

"Business," the elder Loke mumbled, his voice reduced to a hoarse whisper. "What business?"

Karl came back into the room and topped the old man's bony head with a kiss. Then he turned to the others.

"I have some bad news," he said. "Krister Hammar has lately been seen in the company of a woman named Veronika Brand, in the country from America, from New York City. They were both on the scene at the Ljusdal manor house. I'm afraid she's a detective in the NYPD."

"So?" Vilgot commented. "Could mean nothing. I doubt if she's here in an official capacity, or we would have heard something."

"Well, now we have heard something," Junior said. "I'd say their presence here in Västvall was a message."

"Whatever could the woman want?" Lovisa asked.

The old man in the wheelchair struggled to rise. He shrugged off his attendant and ignored Karl's efforts to stop him. There was a fire in his pale eyes that impressed everyone in the room.

"They come to our village?" Loke Voss exclaimed. "Here? To our home?"

"Settle down, settle down," Karl said.

"I won't settle down! You allow them to trespass on our turf?"

"*Pappa…*" Junior said, trying to soothe him.

"Don't '*pappa*' me!" The old man's spittle flew. "I want them stopped! Stopped! Stopped dead if you have to!"

"Please, *pappa*," Junior said. "This woman may be a policewoman from America, a detective."

Loke swept his arm wide as if clearing away all arguments. "I don't care! Did I raise you for nothing? Are you a Voss? Are you a man?"

As if his own words had choked him, he stopped, haggard and breathing hard.

"Here's the real kicker, and *pappa*, you'll want to hear this," Karl said, laying his hand on the elder Loke Voss's shoulder. "I'm not certain, but I believe that Veronika Brand is the granddaughter of your old *Nordic Light* nemesis, Gustav Dalgren."

"What? What?" Karl's words immediately deflated the old man's anger. He appeared confused and elderly again.

As suddenly as he had risen out of it, Loke slumped back into his wheelchair, drained and helpless. It was one of the younger generation who spoke up, and a female one at that, the fierce grandchild whose name meant "wolf."

"We'll take care of her, *farfar*," Ylva assured her grandfather. "Please don't trouble yourself any further."

26

"So here's what I imagine police detective work is like," began a woman named Rakel, one of a dozen people gathered at Aino Lehtonen's home in Stockholm. The dinner party supposedly honored the presence of Veronika Brand in Sweden.

"The detective resembles a person in a room with one of the most complicated Ikea projects ever…" Rakel continued.

"The *Hemnes* day bed!" called out her companion, Arvid. "Our man put one of those together, and it took him three days."

"No, the *Besta*!" someone else put in. "That's wall mounted storage, famously fiendish."

After escaping the harrowing events in the blizzard at Västvall, Brand and Hammar still felt shell-shocked. It was as if they had been abruptly transported light years away from the *urskog* and its terrors. The table of polished birch at which they sat was almost as long as a bowling alley. The guests were gregarious and well-spoken. Lehtonen and her wife Ebba hosted the evening. The young photographer's spouse appeared a little older and even more chillingly fashionable than Lehtonen was.

There was general chatter. The guests spoke over each other, laughing and slapping the table in enthusiasm. Their Swedish mixed easily with English, which was impeccable. The wine had been flowing generously all evening, mostly red, which turned everyone's teeth purple.

Brand's post-traumatic stress, a hangover from the visit to Västvall, rendered the elegant evening more than a little unreal. It was hard for her to read the tone of people's talk. Were those present serious or poking fun at themselves?

Rakel spoke again. She was a formidable woman who wore over-large eyeglass frames, orange to match the color of her lipstick. "Detective work must be like assembling an Ikea project, but the parts are all mixed up together. There's no instruction sheet and no tools provided."

"And the room is totally dark," someone else at the table put in.

"Then, when you are finished," Rakel said, "you must present your work to be judged by a jury, with a defense lawyer standing by all the while trying to kick apart your pieces."

Some laughter from the assembled guests, and a smattering of half-hearted applause.

"Perhaps Detective Brand sees her job as not quite so frivolous as furniture assembly," Hammar suggested gently.

"No, no," Brand said. "The comparison is very clever."

Arvid produced yet another bottle of French Bordeaux. "I've heard it said that the prevalence of Ikea products has increased the worldwide average IQ by a few fractional percentage points, as when the Rubik's Cube came out."

"Chimpanzees in captivity must be given puzzles to solve in order to stay mentally healthy," Rakel said.

The conversation became languid and less focused. After the dinner of magnificent wild salmon poached in Riesling wine, fresh haricot verts with sliced almonds, and some sort of couscous-apricot dish, the guests adjourned to the living room. The well-windowed space ran the whole length of the house. Crossbeams of naked wood sectioned off the ceiling, alternating with skylights. The interior accents were all off white, cream white, or some other variation of white. Outside a stone terrace gave out to a generous yard. A thick border of junipers shielded the house and grounds from prying eyes.

Aino Lehtonen appeared subdued that evening. Or perhaps, Brand thought, it was the absence of the covering mask of make-up that gave her a more thoughtful look, truer to herself. Brand imagined that the whole gathering could be airlifted over the Atlantic and dropped down into a loft in New York City's Soho neighborhood. No one would bat an eye.

"Sophisticated, wealthy, socially bulletproof," Hammar murmured to Brand. "'Hipsters,' might be the English word, or 'yuppies.' To make a pun on your surname I'd tell you they are very 'brand-conscious.'"

"Please never say that kind of thing again," Brand responded with mock seriousness. She wandered about the room to observe the fashionable group. Seated on a couch nearby, a man named Boris held forth to several guests.

"Mauritania," Lehtonen said in a low voice, moving close to Brand and following her gaze. "A refugee success story. Boris has become a rather well-known male model in Scandinavia. We like to think Ebba had something to do with that, since she first put him on the cover of her store's magazine."

"I'm ashamed to say I have only a weak grasp of where Mauritania is," Brand said.

"You know, you're a good candidate for an article in my magazine," Ebba said, breaking into their conversation. "People would be very interested in you."

"I doubt that," Brand said.

"There's a buzz about the New York City detective in our midst. About you and Krister Hammar. We all think you are up to something. Are you?"

Brand gave what she hoped was a noncommittal smile. "America is finished," she heard someone say, the phrase cutting through the general conversation. She didn't see who spoke.

She tried to make herself relax and slip into the evening's warm bath of wealth and good company. Aperitifs came out, cognac, and more champagne. Glazed as she was with Adderall, the alcohol didn't immediately appeal to her. That would come later, when she wanted to wind down. Espresso appeared, served black and strong in tiny cups, with lemon peels. The cultured atmosphere was almost enough to make her believe that life should be no more than this, breaking bread with such smooth, well-presented people.

She again heard the same voice, muttering the same phrase. "America is finished." This time Brand located the speaker, a muscular man of about thirty years old, wearing a sport jacket with an Olympic patch on it. His bleached blond hair was slicked back above hawkish eyes. He focused his gaze directly on Brand, as if waiting for her acknowledgment.

"Hans," another guest said in a cautionary tone.

Brand rose to the challenge. "I don't know about America, but all my life I've heard people say, 'New York is over, New York is over,'" she said. "But somehow the city keeps reinventing itself. You should see the sidewalks of Brooklyn now, absolutely thick with eager twenty year olds."

"Yes, detective, I've seen your Brooklyn," the Hans fellow returned. "Many times."

"Sometimes I wish New York really were over. Maybe then planes wouldn't be dropping out of the sky on us."

"Oh, oh," exclaimed a few of the guests.

Hans gave a trivializing puff of his lips. "Always 9-11 with you people."

The youngest person in the room, a thirteen year old girl somehow related to Ebba, spoke up. "Maybe everyone should stop blaming America for all that's wrong in the world."

"Against youth, there is no argument," Hans said, holding up his hands in a gesture of mock surrender.

27

At the first chance, Brand fled the party atmosphere. She retrieved her boots and stepped out from a pair of sliding glass doors onto the stone terrace, yielding herself to the frigid embrace of the winter night.

Something bothered her. Somewhere in the bowels of the NYPD warehouse in Red Hook, Brooklyn, stood a large steel cabinet. Stored within that cabinet were spent bullet samples from every duty gun ever issued to city police.

Running a forensic ballistics test on a Glock was notoriously tricky. The barrels of the mass-manufactured pistols featured polygonal rifling rather than traditional lands-and-grooves.

But such tests could be done. And somewhere in Sweden, probably in the neighborhood of the tiny village of Västvall, there were spent bullets from Detective Lieutenant Veronika Brand's Glock that had lodged in a bloody, snow-bitten corpse. She didn't even fire the gun. The pink mohawk dude had.

It was difficult enough to pair ballistics from two bullets fired from the same Glock. The likelihood of a cross-Atlantic match being made was so faint it wasn't even worth considering. Yet Brand could not stop herself from considering it. An investigation would tie her to the scene in the blizzard. A loose end had been left untied.

After a few moments gazing upon the star-spangled black of the sky, Brand noticed Lehtonen. The woman stood in the shadows off to the side of the terrace, smoking a cigarette. Brand crossed over to her.

"Nasty habit," Lehtonen said. "Lately I have to hide to indulge it."

"The villagers will come with torches and pitchforks and hunt all you tobacco fiends down," Brand said.

"My wife will," Lehtonen said. "Ebba believes in rooting out all weakness in whatever guise it assumes."

"Well, I have a weakness for weaknesses," Brand said, moving closer to Lehtonen, who surprised her by slipping an arm through hers.

"You?" the woman said, offering a puff on the lit cigarette.

"Jesus, no thanks, one hit would get me started all over again. Quitting nearly killed me the last time."

"Yes, I can quit, too—in fact, it's so easy that I've done it countless times, isn't that what they say?" Smiling, Lehtonen looked sideways at Brand.

The two women stood silently for as long as the cold would allow, tuned to the stillness. Above them, the bright slash of the Milky Way ended abruptly, its full length obscured by a bank of clouds backlit by a half-starved crescent moon.

"Who is this arrogant creature who dislikes America so much?" Brand asked.

"Hans something-or-other. He's no one, just a wealthy friend of Arvid's. He heard you were the guest of honor and asked to tag along. To tell you the truth, Veronika, a lot of us have a love-hate relationship with the States, me included."

"I'd guess lately more hate than love."

"Well, the view from over here is pretty grim. But you might be surprised how many Swedes approve of a rightward swing."

Lehtonen carefully stubbed out her smoke, then rose to her feet and pocketed the butt. She extracted a tiny breath mint spray bottle and dosed her mouth with it. "I must maintain my deception," she said in a dramatic tone.

Lehtonen went back inside, but Brand didn't want to return to the fray just yet. The night sky was so stingingly fine, as was the brief taste of loneliness after the claustrophobia of being among people. She wanted to savor the mood for a moment more. She stood with her face upturned, as if the faint starlight would lend her some of its ethereal glow. The celestial fires emanated from millions of years in the past. They were too remote to do anyone any good.

Brand wondered if the Swedish waters ran too deep for her to understand. It all flowed together: the Vosses, the Romani, the terrible feeling that her detective skills might be abandoning her. She couldn't begin to figure the puzzle out, and what's more, was tired of trying.

What did she have? Fragments, mostly connected to Elin Dalgren. She remembered the look of determination on the old woman's face, the hard grip of her hand on Veronika's own. The letter and its revelations about the Dalgren's secrets, with Elin's voice crying out to be heard. The uncomfortable feeling that Sanna Dalgren had not wanted her to talk to the old woman. The timing of Elin's death. A fatal incident in the night, then death in a hospital administered by the Voss family.

Finally, there had come a gradual, uncertain awakening in herself, a growing sense of familial love. The feeling swirled in amid the ancestral demands made by blood and the dogged persistence of the past—all the burdensome things that Brand had spent years trying to escape.

The words of the skinhead on the train echoed in her mind: What are you doing here, bitch?

It's not too late, she thought. I could turn this visit into a real vacation. Take one of those cheap ferry boats into the Baltic. Go on a tour of Helsinki. Head to Copenhagen. Afterwards, fly home to New York City, tired and happy and all touristed out.

Her spider-sense tingled as she realized she wasn't alone. A figure stood nearby in the shadow of a juniper. How long had someone been lurking there?

"Hello?"

The figure didn't move. Brand felt foolish. She thought she might have just greeted a piece of statuary.

The outline animated and stepped with unsettling quickness toward the terrace. A man, Brand thought. A trespasser. His shock of white hair caught the light from the interior of the house. She saw it was the America-basher, Hans.

He mounted the steps of the terrace. His fashionable boots made ringing sounds on the cold stone. He proceeded past Brand without acknowledging her. It was odd. Brand concluded that he had been caught out eavesdropping and didn't want to be confronted.

A few steps past her, he pulled up short, as if remembering something.

"Oh, yeah," he said, employing the same ironic tone he had used inside among the party guests. He turned back to Brand. "You know when Dorothy and Toto and Scarecrow and the others are in the Haunted Forest, just before the girl and the dog are kidnapped by a gang of flying monkeys?"

He waited as though he actually expected an answer to what was clearly a nonsensical question.

"You do know what I'm talking about." A tone of impatience showed in his voice. "All Americans know the fucking Wizard of fucking Oz by heart. It's in their pop culture hall of fame or something."

His accent combined qualities that Brand could not place. Swedish, yes, but British, too? Or American? German?

"Okay, Detective Brand, who expects immediate answers in all her police interrogations but will not respond to a simple civil question of mine, I will assume you are familiar with the Wizard of Oz."

He paused as if to let her get a word in. She stared at him. Hans appeared irritated that Brand wasn't playing along.

"What do they see in the Haunted Forest? What do Dorothy and Toto and Scarecrow and Tinman and the Cowardly Lion see? Well, not Toto, since he's a dog and can't read. They see a sign. What does that sign say?"

He leaned toward Brand and extended his hand. At first she thought he was offering to shake hands, but instead he stuck out his forefinger and formed his hand into a pistol shape, pointing at her.

Brand answered reluctantly. "It points the way and says, 'Witches Castle, one mile.'"

Hans simulated pulling the trigger on his hand. "Right on the money, Detective," he said. "Or maybe I should say 'right on the monkey.'"

"Hans, is it?" Brand asked.

"Did you know the actors performing as the flying monkeys were the same ones that played the Munchkins in Munchkinland? There's a lesson in there about good and evil, if one cares to learn it."

Brand strung the man along, feeling puzzled by his sardonic aggression. "But the 'Haunted Forest' business," she said, "that's not the part of the sign you want me to remember, is it?"

"No, Detective, it is not."

"There's something else written down below."

"Yes, indeed, there is." He again cocked his hand, aimed it at Brand's head and fired off a mimed gunshot. His insolent tone offended her more than the gesture.

"Take the message to heart, Detective, and stay out of my family's business," Hans said, moving as if to return inside.

"Wait, what? What did you say?"

He halted. "I said, and I will not repeat it, don't come near the Voss family again or you will regret it."

Brand let the truth sink in. "You're Hans Voss?"

But the man disappeared into the house without answering.

The sign in the Haunted Forest, Brand knew, represented a warning. *I'd turn back if I were you*, it read.

Ebba stepped out of the house onto the terrace. "Detective Brand?" she called.

"Yes?" Brand answered, rising to her feet.

"It's the oddest thing, but the police are here, some of our own Stockholm police officers. They say they wish to speak to you."

Ebba gave a thin smile, displaying her wine-stained teeth. "What's this about, Veronika?"

28

They let her cool for forty-two minutes, sitting alone in the interview room at the local *polisstation*. Except for the Judas slot in the door with a Plexiglas pane behind it, the space was windowless.

Earlier, two uniforms and a *kriminalinspektör* named Linnéa Beck had marched her out of the dinner party. Ebba's guests lined up and stared with unconcealed delight, as if they thought the whole thing might be a show put on for their entertainment.

In front of Lehtonen's luxurious home a pair of police vehicles had pulled up, a van and a smaller sedan. In the back seat of the sedan sat a white-faced Krister Hammar, peering out of the side window. Brand tried to give him what she thought was a reassuring look but which probably read as a grimace of commiseration. The officers placed Brand in the van and Beck climbed into the front beside the driver.

Kriminalinspektör Beck treated Brand with pro forma officiousness. No, she was certainly not under arrest. They would simply like to ask a few questions of her down at the station house.

"Look," Brand informed her. "I'm an NYPD detective lieutenant with fifteen years on the job."

"Yes, Detective Brand," Beck said. "By now I have often been informed of this fact."

"I mean, of course I'll cooperate," Brand pleaded. "I can vouch for Mr Hammar, too. Do we really have to be put through this whole business?"

But they had brought her to the *polisstation* and held her there. The pace of the process felt agonizingly slow. She recognized the technique. The solitary waiting period represented a way to increase her tension. It was designed to break her resistance.

Something bothered Brand beyond the obvious awkwardness of the immediate situation. Once again she felt a nagging sense of hidden forces at work. A dynamic existed that she urgently needed to understand. It eluded her, always just out of reach. Some sort of puppet-master worked behind the scenes. When Brand tried to follow the attached strings to see who was manipulating her, the marionette apparatus melted into darkness.

Finally, a pair of Swedish cops entered the interrogation room. Both were male, both were in plainclothes, and neither one of them was Linnea Beck. The two introduced themselves as Detective Inspectors Edvin Larsson and Vincent Hult. They sat across the table from Brand. Larsson looked too young to carry much weight. They both came off as friendly and spoke perfect English. At first, they seemed not at all interested in the strong arm.

"Detective Brand," Hult began.

"Oh, it's Veronika, please."

"Yes, Veronika," Hult nodded.

"I mean, we're all friends here, right?" Brand attempted a bright smile.

Hult gave a forced one. Larsson stayed silent and fiddled with note-taking. Brand wondered how differently the interview might have gone down had her duty pistol been somehow involved. She took back her curse of the pink-haired punk for stealing the Glock.

"What's this about?" she asked.

"You indicated to Linnea that you have primarily stayed in the immediate Stockholm area during your visit to Sweden, is that correct?" Hult asked.

"I made a visit to my family's homestead in Härjedalen."

Hult nodded. His sidekick Larsson scribbled in his notes.

"So, Härjedalen," Hult said. "Anywhere else?"

"No, not really," Brand fibbed.

"On your journey to Härjedalen, did you take a detour to a village called Västvall?"

"No." The business of police, Brand reminded herself, was to sit around and listen to people lie.

"You also visited a historical manor house near the small town of Ljusdal, is that right? The incident that occurred there is quite concerning."

Brand stayed mute.

"Where do you stay while here in Sweden, Veronika?"

"Well, right now I have use of a guest house in a Stockholm suburb," Brand said. "It's Täby or Djursholm. As the crow flies, I guess my cousin Lukas Dalgren's place is fairly near to Stockholm."

"*Fågelvägen*," Hult murmured to Larsson, which Brand figured was how Swedes said, "as the crow flies."

Hult turned back to Brand. "What I want you to help us understand is why you are in Sweden in the first place."

"Well, it's a free country, as we say back home." Brand didn't like the guy, and was giving him back a little sand. "You've seen my U.S. passport and my NYPD ID. I'm here legally. I didn't have to swim the Mediterranean or anything."

"Please, Veronika," Hult said, impatient with her.

"Okay, so the boring truth is, my grandparents emigrated from here," Brand said. "I have many relatives in the country."

"You come to Sweden in the middle of February," Hult said. "You tell the customs inspectors on entry into the country that your visit is personal, that you are attending a reunion of family. But we know that what you call 'the boring truth' is not the entire truth—not the truth, the whole truth, and nothing but the truth. Isn't that right?"

Brand was impressed. The Swedish police definitely did their homework, up to and including reaching out to customs inspectors. "I attended a reunion with my family," she said. "Many of whom I've never met before. This is my first time in Sweden. As I said, many of my ancestors came from here."

"But the reunion business seems to be some sort of cover story," Hult said.

"Why would you say that?"

The younger cop, Larsson, came to life. "You've been poking around, haven't you, Veronika? I'm not sure how far your NYPD credentials will carry you in this country. Those credentials are fugazi, anyway."

Brand almost laughed out loud. The reach of American cop slang had spread from countless crime procedurals on television, even unto the interrogation rooms of the Stockholm police.

Larsson continued. "We've been in touch with our police liaison in New York City, and we understand you've been suspended from the department. And of course there are many police officers in the NYPD who are corrupt."

At that, Brand flared up. "Hey, I'm the cop who puts dirty cops in jail, okay?"

Hult made a downward motion with his hands, trying to calm the situation. "Everyone realizes you've done good work in New York, Veronika. Your many awards speak for you. But here in Sweden you seem intent on digging up dirt on a crime that happened in the far distant past. This incident you have linked to a prominent Swedish family, the Vosses. Am I getting this right? Or do you have something to add?"

"Well, I'd object to 'digging up dirt,' and I know how it looks, Inspector—" Brand began, but the younger cop cut her off.

"In America," Larson said, "I think we would ask, 'What's up with that'?"

The phrase sounded comical, pronounced in a Swedish accent. She had come to the happy conclusion that the two cops had nothing concrete, no real evidence linking her and Hammar to the scene at Västvall village. The situation actually offered Brand an opportunity, the chance to discover what—or who—had initiated the process of bringing her in for questioning.

"My relative, Krister Hammar—" Brand began, but Hult interrupted.

"—Related to you only by marriage, no? Not a blood relative? Wife deceased?"

"—Related to me by marriage," Brand nodded. "He agreed to accompany me on a tour of locations relevant to my interest."

"And this guided tour, what was the purpose?"

"Oh, just to get my bearings, I guess," Brand said. "One thing I want to understand is what happened in 1940, with the *Nordic Light* arson."

It was a shade surreal, because she had taken on the other role so many times, interrogating suspects. Now her own "I can explain" theme had a very familiar ring.

The frustration Brand felt, as an innocent person whose circumstances might paint as guilty, that too was familiar, although she knew such impatience could be easily faked. Sorting the sheep from the goats, the innocent from the guilty, that was a part of the job, an occupation that she shared with Hult and Larsson.

"You present yourself as a tourist," Hult said. "A visitor seeking out ancestors, researching the history of your family. And yet the Vosses figure somehow into this."

"Yes."

"How?"

"How? You mean, how am I researching?"

"I mean, Veronika, how do the Vosses connect to the Brands? Or it's really not the Brands, is it? That's your father's family—it's the Dalgrens of your mother's side who interest you. Why is that? It's important for us to know, because of the recent discovery of two dead bodies in a residence owned by the Vosses."

"Local police questioned you about this matter." Larsson managed to sound accusatory.

"Perhaps you should ask the Vosses about the whole business. I'd like to speak to Loke Voss myself. I just had a brief run-in with one of his grandsons."

Her words seemed to anger the younger cop in particular. "Loke Voss is a prominent and well-respected citizen of Sweden. His reputation is unchallengeable."

"Yet you say two murders occurred in one of his homes."

"I don't think we used the word 'murder,'" Hult put in quickly. "Did we, Edvin?"

Larsson shook his head vigorously. He seemed gleeful to have caught Brand in a mistake. "No, indeed, we did not mention murder, but Veronika here did. How did you know it was murder, Detective?"

"Come on, you guys, you'd never have hauled me in if there were two dead from carbon monoxide poisoning."

Brand silently gave herself the same advice she often considered offering to her own interrogation suspects.

Shut up.

"Do you think we Swedes are stupid, Detective?" Hult asked. "You're the super-cop from the greatest city in the world, as Americans always shout about New York, New York? And Edvin and I, we're slow-witted idiots right off the farm, is that it? That's Sweden to you, just simple folk and socialism and furniture you have to assemble yourself?"

"I've been to New York City once," Larsson put it. "I didn't like it."

Hult bore down on her. "Did you think we wouldn't know, Veronika? That we aren't aware of our national history? We're all taught the story of the arson fire at the *Nordic Light* newspaper. What did you think? That you could come over here and somehow put things right? Correct an old wrong? Avenge your family?"

Shut up. She definitely did not want to say the words, "I would like to have a lawyer present" or "may I speak to a representative from the U.S. embassy?" But she thought that it might come to that, given the way the interview was going.

"Now she remains silent." Larsson's sneering tone annoyed Brand.

"I'm not speaking because I don't know what to say," she responded. "There is family history involved, certainly, and, yes, I am interested in finding out about it."

"A coincidence, then," Hult said, clearly unconvinced. "Your presence in

Sweden and suddenly two murders."

"Look, damn it," Brand exclaimed. "I've been on your side of the table, okay? I know what's going on. You're on a fishing expedition here. You aren't going to detain a fellow cop. I want to cooperate. I am cooperating."

"It doesn't look like that to me," Larsson said. "It looks like you have something to hide."

"I'm seeing the same with you," Brand returned. "You aren't exactly coming clean, either. There's absolutely nothing to link me or Krister Hammar to whatever it was that happened at the manor house. So you've got nothing. Yet we get jerked out of a dinner party at midnight for some sort of bogus q and a. I'm the one who should be asking, 'what's up with that?' Yes, I'm here in Sweden doing a little historical research. So what?"

"Two men lie dead—" Larsson said, but Brand cut him off.

"Gentlemen, please, I understand how things work, okay? First this Hans Voss person baits me, then suddenly the *polis* are at the door. I sense the hand of the brass here. Tell me who set this bullshit move in motion. I'd love to know whose feathers I've ruffled."

And it's actually three dead, Brand thought, maybe more. But she didn't say it. No one had mentioned a dead body turning up at Västvall. Perhaps the corpse had been snowed over by the blizzard, waiting for the spring melt to be discovered. But she didn't think so, and suspected a different kind of cover up.

After over an hour of back-and-forth, middle-of-the-night grilling, Hult finally released Brand, allowing her to walk free. Well, not entirely free.

"I'm going to have to retain your passport," Hult said to her. "We might not be through with you just yet."

She gave it up, not without regret. A persistent voice within—the voice of logic, of sanity—urged her to bail out immediately and return to life in New York. A double murder investigation, counseled Brand's inner voice, might well serve as a roadblock to the success of her oh-so-vital mission in Sweden, to investigate her family's past.

Hult also said he'd prefer if she remained in the immediate area of the Swedish capital, within easy reach if he needed to speak with her further.

"And keep away from members of the Voss family," he added as a final caution.

"Well, they somehow keep turning up," Brand said.

That was the message she was getting from the authorities. Yes to staying put in Stockholm, no to bothering the Vosses. Immediately after Detective Inspector Hult laid down those rules, Brand moved to violate both.

29

They fled, the two of them. As soon as she emerged from the *polisstation*, she found Hammar waiting for her. He had already managed to retrieve the Saab from where it had been left at Lehtonen's. Without a word he allowed her to climb into the driver's seat.

"We have to get a goddamned different car," Brand said. "This one sticks out like a pink mohawk."

They bickered about that for a while, sounding like an old married couple. Hammar claimed there were plenty of old Saabs on the road, because the vehicle was such a miracle of durability. Brand doubted his argument. All the while they spoke, she guided the Saab through empty pre-dawn streets heading out of town. Her paranoia was such that she repeatedly checked the rear-view for a tail. She had no idea where she was going, other than away from the eyes of the Stockholm police.

"North on the E4," Hammar advised her. "Then swing northwest at Tönnebro, taking road 83." He promptly fell asleep in the passenger seat.

Daylight dawned with ice black skies. From the trials of the previous night, Brand should have been just as exhausted as Hammar. But she felt alive and awake, perhaps to a fault. She drove like a hellion, pushing the little three-cylinder Shrike engine in the Saab to its limits. Her mind raced. She wondered if she was in the midst of a manic episode. Multiple trains of thought coursed through her mind, crashing into and derailing each other. The skinhead's sneer had by now become a sour sort of mantra.

What are you doing here, bitch? Go home!

The face of the sleeping Hammar brought out feelings of gentleness and hope in Brand. Here was a man who had thrown himself into the search for missing young women, vulnerable souls from a vulnerable immigrant community. As much as she was a lone wolf, Brand realized she depended upon Hammar's presence for her mission. Over the years Brand had her difficulties with men. Serial relationships never seemed to settle into long-lasting ones. Being a police officer was notoriously hard on the "boy and girl thing." But it was more than that. Brand suspected there was something broken inside her. She wondered what it was, where it came from. Why hadn't she married? Why hadn't she had children? Could the difficulty be due to her brooding Scandinavian roots?

Or was this idea too simple? After all, there were plenty of good times. Warm summer days with trips to a pond in the woods with Grandma Klara and Alice, her great aunt. Along the way the two women taught Veronika the names of plants and trees, berries. Following the seasons, they'd take along tin pails and spend hours picking plump blueberries off bushes, Veronika, as an adolescent, often eating more than she picked. Cherry season came, and fresh peaches at almost the same time. Everything was canned or frozen for use during the winters.

There were apple trees everywhere, the best fruit she would ever eat. Klara and Alice told her the appleseeds were brought over from early pioneering Swedes. Veronika believed most of what they told her in those early years. She absorbed their ways, but during her teenage years deliberately set aside much of what she had learned.

She watched the gradual destruction of the household. The consumption of alcohol, the on again off again emotions, the unexpected angry face. Gustav drank, and Brand's mother Marta inherited the gene. Marta broke it off with Nick Brand, just as Veronika hit puberty. Later on came a second divorce, an unhappy home life, more and more erratic behavior.

The farm of her maternal grandparents at times represented an idyllic haven of peace for the young girl. But a sadness seemed to permeate the relationship of Klara and Gustav Dalgren. Brand fully realized their unhappiness only in retrospect. Some killing flaw lay at the heart of the marriage. Eventually, that flaw led to disaster. Brand stood witness to the arguments and shouting, making up her mind she would never travel the same route. Her pursuit of police work grew out of her childhood determination. Becoming a cop saved her life and at the same time damaged her chances of having a normal one.

As she slowed for a petrol stop, Hammar came awake and caught Brand looking at him.

"What?" he asked. "Was I drooling or something?"

"Not drooling, and not snoring too loudly, either," she said. "In sleep, you're perfect company."

Hammar laughed. "Only when I'm asleep, huh?"

"Where are we going?" Brand asked. "I was thinking an AirBnB or something, up in the mountains, somewhere way off the grid. I want to see reindeer out my window."

"You pretend not to know where we are headed?"

Brand realized that she did know. She had always known.

Västvall.

They had to get back on the horse that had thrown them. Her missing

Glock still weighed on Brand's mind. Even though good sense, simple reason, and Detective Inspector Hult had all warned her away from the Voss family, she knew that was precisely where her mission was leading her.

"I'd give odds there's not an AirBnb rental in all of Västvall," she said. "If there is, it would probably be infested by them that shall not be named."

"I've got a place in mind," Hammar said.

"You do?"

"Though I'm considering taking a little detour first."

"I am in your hands," Brand said.

They approached the town of Sveg. On the outskirts stood a large orange brick building that seemed totally out of place for the remote surroundings. Brand's first impression was of an old warehouse of some sort, made new with modern architectural touches. Then she saw the signage.

"Oh, you've got to be kidding me," she muttered.

"Yes," Hammar said. "The Voss Medical Center. Founded seven years ago with family money. Very controversial here. People considered it a horrible example of American-style philanthropy. There was a big outcry, protests. This style of private investment goes against our way. Sweden has one of the best public health systems in the world. No one puts their names on buildings like wealthy families do in the States. It is not done."

The renovated building dominated its surroundings. One of the signs further identified the place as "Kristina Voss Memorial Medical Center."

"Kristina was an eleven year old child of the family," Hammar explained. "She went into toxic shock and died while being airlifted by helicopter to a central hospital facility. This is the approach to medical care here. The system is very centralized and efficient."

The Saab chugged toward a traffic circle. Voss Hospital loomed in the rear-view. It allowed Brand a sense of the family's reach and power. Hammar glanced backward.

"The place is said to be often virtually empty. Under-utilized. Unneeded."

"A white elephant," Brand said. "It gives me the willies."

In the center of town stood an enormous wooden sculpture of a bear, thirty feet tall. The elaborately carved statue served as a local landmark. In her present mood it, too, struck Brand as ominous. Visions of the beast in the blizzard came back to her. Had she been mistaken? Could the creature really have been a bear?

The day remained bright, sunlight streaming through the blue sky from the west. Brand drove along squinting against the sun, as if snow blindness might be a concern. They passed through Sveg and arrived at a nearby village in the mountains. Hammar directed her to pull over in the center of town. The outside air cut surprisingly sharp when they stepped from the car.

Hammar had brought her to the site of the *Nordic Light* arson. Nothing was left of the original building, of course. Brand harbored a ludicrous thought that she might somehow see the charred, still-smoking remnants of her grandfather's newspaper offices. The town authorities had erected a silver plaque marking the location. A metal memorial sculpture represented newspaper pages, flared open and arrested mid-flutter.

"Freedom. Thought. Life." The creators of the shrine chiseled inscription into a plaque of brushed aluminum. "In memory of the five victims of the attack on the newspaper, *Nordic Light*, 3 March, 1940."

"Should be six," Brand said.

Hammar knew the poignant history of Gustav Dalgren's time in America. The man had descended into bitterness and alcoholism. His death, whispered to be by his own hand, came in a barn fire on the farm outside of Jamestown, New York.

Brand privately wondered about linking the tragedy so firmly to the *Nordic Light* attack. Gustav's death had happened long after the arson incident, almost forty years later.

"What's he like?" she asked, looking at the memorial, musing.

"What's who like?"

"Loke Voss."

"Well, I've mostly dealt with the younger one, the one they call Junior. A man without a conscience. They all are."

"How about senior?"

"I've seen the elder Loke Voss in court a few times—let's see, three times, I guess, back when he could still get around. He has the kind of face you could imagine carved on a brazil nut, have it for a keychain. That lean and hungry look, like Cassius. The worst laugh in Christendom."

"Very nice Shakespeare reference, but you haven't answered me. I wasn't asking about his appearance. Or his laugh."

"Oh, well, the man's a pirate. A wolf in wolf's clothing, with probably a murder or two in his past."

"More than these here," Brand said, indicating the memorial.

"The trucking industry is pretty vicious. Loke Voss is known for toughness."

Brand found herself curiously unmoved by the arson site. Maybe her exhaustion was telling on her. Hammar had to be wondering, if Brand wasn't in Sweden to track down the details of the arson, what was she here for? Lately, she seemed more focused on retrieving her lost sidearm than on her own family's history.

"You die in a terrorist attack, you get a victim's plaque," Brand commented as they left the memorial, a detached tone to her words. "Downtown Manhattan, where the Twin Towers stood, it's like a square-mile size plaque."

30

3 March 1940.

The pale-eyed man paced in the enveloping dark. This far north in Sweden, in Härjedalen, early March still meant bitter winter. But he didn't feel the cold.

Even though the night would represent the triumph of his young life, he steeled himself to display no excitement. But the heart beating within his chest would not quiet. He saw himself as a wolf about to be uncaged. He had chosen not to wear his beloved uniform. It didn't matter. A Browning sidearm slept cinched in its shining leather holster at his waist. That was all the uniform he needed.

Two-thirty. A waning cuticle moon. Of course, he had intentionally scheduled the mission that way. Full moonlight might destroy the advantage of a surprise attack. A half kilometer below the townspeople slept. The night was about to get many degrees hotter, the man thought. He focused on the blocky silhouette of a three-story wooden structure near the center of town. A vile left-wing daily newspaper, *Nordic Light*, was based there.

A burrow for vermin. The place was a stain on the sacred soil of Sweden. Articles, rhetoric, and rallying calls poured forth in a constant, polluted stream. The man considered the newspaper's continued existence a personal affront. *Nordic Light* journalists had in fact called him out by name several times as an enemy of the people. Their insolence filled him with fury.

He was not alone. Other men, powerful, wealthy men who knew who the real enemy was, reached out to him. The man was astonished to be summoned for a secret meeting in Stockholm. He could not believe such important individuals even knew of his existence. They spoke to him, praised him—noticed him! He took his place among those leading the charge. The communist menace from the east had to be stopped. This printing press up north was a pebble in their boot. They were pleased to request a small favor of him, they said.

"I would have *Nordic Light* silenced. Pour gasoline down its throat." Here was the greatest of the grandees at the meeting, speaking directly to him!

"This is no favor," the man replied. He did everything but click his heels and give a stiff-armed salute. "Rather it is an honor. And it is also my pleasure."

The "big shots"—he liked the English phrase—left the operational details to him. The building below now was the agreed-upon target for the night. In the weeks before he had sent in scouts. The reds were foolishly lazy about security. The printing press on the ground floor stood surrounded by rolls and rolls of newsprint. A single match would burn brighter than any *Nordic Light*. On the second floor were offices, and on the third, a dormitory.

He recruited a pair of Finns, brothers, and a Swede. The brothers had fought in the Winter War against the Russians. The other was a rather unhinged individual whom the man had long admired. During his youth they had both participated in the silly juvenile gang battles that pitted the youths of one village against those from a neighboring one. Such fights were nothing. At most they resulted in bloody noses and blackened eyes. But this fellow always went the extra distance. He cracked skulls and broke bones.

The pale-eyed man fell easily in line with the opinions of his wealthy backers. In his ultra-correct political beliefs he could not be challenged. But deep down he held to a more elemental view. The attack on *Nordic Light* was simply a heightened version of the village bully boy battles he fought almost weekly during his adolescent years. The stakes might be higher, that was all. The excitement rising in his groin was the same.

He and his men waited without speaking. The Finns smoked. The man felt the night cold reach into his bones. He consulted his pocket watch. Three a.m. He touched the butt-end of the Browning. A thought passed through his mind. Herr Himmler was fond of a wry, outlandish statement, taken from a famous play about the heroic Albert Leo Schlageter. "When I hear the word culture, I reach for my pistol."

Now the man caressing the Browning was himself Schlageter! He turned to the others. "Iväg!" he commanded curtly. Fly. His three berserkers peeled away and vanished into darkness. He would not see them again.

He stood alone. He was a dark lord, consumed with dreams of blood and fire. The sense of impending victory was palpable. His mouth had gone dry. He wondered if the same affliction affected other great warriors.

Seventeen minutes later by his watch, a soft pinpoint glow emerged from the town's darkness. Here is the real light of the North, he thought. The flames below opened like the petals of a yellow rose. Soon the fire lit the whole wooden building, even as it ate the structure alive. He could hear the alarm bells. A curious quality of frigid air: while up close sounds could seem muffled, far off they carried eerily well. Human cries came to him, shouts, pleadings. Or perhaps those occurred only in the man's imagination.

The volunteer brigade arrived too late. Against the fire's beautiful radiance the man could pick out teams of rescuers rushing forward. The tiny figures threw their ladders against the side of the building. But the ladders were made of wood, and they burned, too.

31

Leaving Sveg and the giant wooden bear sculpture behind, Brand and Hammar drove on, farther into the mountains, toward Västvall. She wondered if he was leading her straight back into trouble. The deserted, winter-bitten countryside seemed to afford no place for her. I'm lost, she thought, gazing out at the stunted pine woods.

Hammar directed her off the highway onto a smaller road, then off that onto a smaller one still. He had her pull up in front of a structure that appeared half buried in snow.

"What is this place?"

"A family summer house," Hammar said.

"Whose family?"

"Mine," he said. "Come along."

From the outside the cottage appeared to be lovely, with a deep air of the rustic and picturesque. Brand felt a stab of awe at the beauty of the Swedish countryside. The building of dark wood posted itself in the throat of a small vale. Spread out below was a frozen lake, its empty surface surrounded by snow-flattened fields and dense forests of pine, birch and aspen.

Brand now realized that Hammar had to know the Västvall area very well indeed, since his family were practically neighbors of the Vosses. Not exactly close enough to borrow a cup of sugar, say, but in the same general vicinity. Why hadn't he revealed the existence of the cottage to Brand?

"A *härbre*," Hammar called the place. Formerly a barn to store grain, now repurposed and remodeled.

The aspens in the lakeside meadows bent in the cold wind, their bark silvery in the late afternoon light. Beyond the lake, the landscape seemed to roll out in an endless succession of hills and valleys.

Hammar had accomplished a minor miracle in rehabilitating the ancient wooden structure. Brand had not expected anything like it from Krister Hammar, the urbane attorney at law. The man was an onion. There were more layers to him than Brand had yet managed to peel away.

"We brought the old structure here from its original site, my dad and I, pulling it over the ice in winter with a horse-drawn sledge," Hammar explained. "I was fourteen, it was…just before my father died. Inside the place smelled like dust, centuries of it. Back then I was contemptuous. I didn't believe such a decrepit pile of logs was worth saving. I didn't know why my father would bother. Now I feel differently."

The *härbre* dated back to the 1700s. But the interior modifications came straight out of the 21st century. Here was the Sweden of today, encapsulated: a three-hundred year old structure that represented an ancient agricultural tradition, with an ultra-modern design sensibility grafted onto it.

"This may be my new favorite place in the world," Brand said, looking around. "I never thought I'd say that about anywhere that wasn't New York City."

"Let's go in." Hammar extended his arm like a real estate agent.

Brand noticed that someone had plowed the driveway and that the heat was on inside. "I called ahead to our neighbor," Hammar explained.

The original, barn-like *härbre* represented the heart of the home, serving as the main living space. On one expanse of whitewashed wall, Hammar had hung some of the primitive-looking farm tools that had originally been stored in the building, a matching pair of wooden-toothed rakes, a lethal-looking scythe and a collection of flails. The handles on all the implements were worn from use. Brand could not help but think of the hands that had polished them smooth, calloused hands and strong arms now decades gone.

"We get water from the lake here," Hammar said. "And I'm afraid the bathroom is an outhouse, if you follow the path out back."

He knelt to start a log fire in the hearth. Moving back and forth from fireside to the kitchen area, he served a late lunch of sausage, bread and cheese. Or was it dinner? The early winter dusk suspended time. Brand felt light-headed and disoriented. She had to refer to her watch to get anchored. It had all been just one long day. A short six hours earlier, she had been facing off with Detective Hult and his juvenile sidekick Larsson.

Hammar poured them glasses of red wine, a nice cabernet sauvignon. Brand was too weary to be impressed. Her tiredness became an unstoppable force. She fell into a doze in front of the fire, thinking as she did so that now Hammar could watch her sleep, just as she had watched him on the drive up from Stockholm.

Brand woke to the sound of a dull, rhythmic pounding, coming from outside the cottage. The fire still burned. Someone—it could only have been Hammar—had covered her with a blanket of soft, patterned lambswool. The man himself was not around. A pair of felt-lined rubber boots stood on the floor near the couch where she had fallen asleep. A white hooded parka that looked as if it was thermally rated for a polar expedition lay on the empty sofa chair. She donned both the boots and the parka and stepped outside.

Once again, as on that night at the Dalgren homestead, the mad sweep of stars made her stop and stare. And there was something else, too, something Brand had never set eyes on before, outside of photographs and videos.

Teasing the horizon were the green flares of the aurora, like a minor preview of the main show to come. Tongues of lime-white flame unfurled, pulsed, and then folded back in on themselves. *Mormor*, her dear grandmother Klara, had told Brand tales of the northern lights. She created in a young girl's mind visions of a polar wonderland. Knowledge gained by experience always surpasses knowledge gained second-hand, by mere description. The reality of seeing the aurora now easily vanquished her childhood imagination. Perhaps, finally, this was the hidden reason, unknown even to herself, that Brand had come to Sweden.

Thud, thud, thud.

The sound that had awakened her might have been Hammar, down by the frozen lake, beating a dead horse. Brand headed out along the short driveway from the cottage. She discovered a path through the snow. Following the sound, she approached Hammar on the shore of the lake. He was oblivious to her presence.

Indeed he was in the midst of beating something, if not a horse. Wielding an ax with great pummeling swings, he attacked the surface ice. He had already managed to chop through a sizable rectangle near the shoreline. This was an *isvak*, a section of open water for ice bathing. The hole looked black and forbidding.

Hammar had also built a bonfire directly on the ice, a short distance from the cut-out. He had pulled up some logs near the flames to sit upon. Next to the logs, warming by the fire, were a pile of sheepskins.

The thudding sound of his effort covered the noise of Brand's approach. She stood watching him, intently engaged in physical labor. The sight formed a picture of the man far different from the one asleep in the passenger seat of the Saab.

He looked up and hailed her. Then, smiling crookedly, he slammed the ax into the ice one last time, leaving it embedded. He immediately began to remove his clothes.

Brand didn't catch on right away. She had all sorts of outlandish thoughts. But after Hammar disrobed completely, he stepped toward a small, hutch-like building at the lake's edge. Brand realized what was up.

A sauna, of course. Outside of a health club, Brand had never encountered one. At the quick glimpse of Hammar's body before he stepped into the sauna, she experienced a mild erotic charge. While he wasn't exactly ripped, and didn't have the body builder tone like a lot of her fellow New York cops, Hammar had obviously kept himself fit.

"What about boots?" she called to Hammar through the closed door of the sauna. "Can I leave my boots on?"

"Don't be a baby," came his answer from within.

Brand kicked off the felt-lined boots Hammar had provided her in the cottage. She hesitated only a moment, before throwing off her American modesty together with her clothes. She slipped into the darkened, sweltering interior of the sauna.

"*Välkommen till den tionde helveteskretsen*," Hammar said. She understood him without translation. Welcome to the tenth circle of hell.

Hell, in this incarnation, was cozy, fragrant, and hot enough to sear the skin. She sat on the small raised wooden platform next to Hammar. He ladled a scoop of water onto the pile of hot stones in one corner. A wave of steam heat came at her that the souls of Dante's inferno would have recognized.

She gasped. "Oh. My. God."

"You see?" Hammar said brightly. "I hear you call to your maker. No atheists in foxholes, and none in saunas, either."

Then he began to beat her flesh lightly, using a switch made of bundled birch twigs.

Snick, snick, snick, sounded the stroke of the bath whisk.

Brand started to lose her mind. She seemed incapable of any thought beyond heat, heat, heat. Time stretched out in an elastic way that made a minute seem like an hour. She was not aware of sitting knee-to-knee with a naked man. She didn't want to leave. She didn't want to scream. She wanted only to survive.

They had been through hell three times together now, she thought, herself and Hammar. Once at the bloody manor house, once during the blizzard at Västvall, and now here, in a more pleasurable way, in the sauna. The first two times they had survived. She couldn't predict what was going to happen this third time around.

"You know," she gasped, "a sauna is not that bad as a seduction technique. It's just a little obvious."

"You misunderstand the tradition," Hammar said carefully. "There is no seduction here. For you Americans, maybe, all nudity is sexual. In the eyes of many in the rest of the world, that viewpoint is puritanical."

"It must be my overheated blood," Brand said, aiming for irony and missing the mark.

"Let me tell you how it is here. I have been involved in a legal proceeding, held in an out of the way location. The officers of the court wound up in a sauna together after a hard day at each other's throats. Men and women both, lawyers and clerks. There was even a judge. Believe me, nothing could be further from the erotic."

He gave a derisive snort. "Then we all put our clothes back on. If the same collection of people suddenly thought to strip down in any other circumstances, it would be considered a funny social misstep. So do you understand?"

"Okay," Brand said. "I think you're all kidding yourselves, but okay."

Hammar reached out and traced a longitudinal scar that ran down the outside of Brand's right thigh. She brushed his hand away. What was it with men and their fascination with scars?

"Now what?" she asked.

"Now we..."

"Oh, no, no way."

"Of course I don't mean sex. I mean now we jump through the hole I chopped in the ice, the *isvak*. We leap into zero degree lake water."

"No way. I mean, I knew what you meant and I mean no way."

"You will be pleasantly surprised," Hammar said. "When you plunge into an *isvak* after being in the sauna, your skin feels—well, it's hard to describe. Your body feels silky, as though you've turned into a seal. Radiant. Totally alive."

"I don't want to be a radiant seal."

"It'll be good, I promise."

Hammar took her hand. He thrust open the door of the sauna hut and stepped outside.

He led Brand toward the gaping hole in the lake ice. Their bodies sent off plumes of steam. Hammar's eyes glistened with the blue-green reflection of the aurora. The haunting array of the northern lights, growing more pronounced every second, uncoiled above them.

"Don't think," he said. "Just do."

Brand didn't think. Instead, she balked. At the sight of the black water, a pool of freezing ice that just happened to be masquerading as liquid, she turned abruptly away from Hammar. Grabbing a bonfire-warmed sheepskin to wrap around herself, Brand headed back to the cottage, barefoot in the snow.

32

A few years previously, all traces of the erotic had vanished from Brand's life. She had been drinking too much, and made an attempt to dry out. Sex disappeared when alcohol did.

After a stretch of sobriety, she had to question her new reality. How had the human species managed to procreate before the discovery of fermentation made getting drunk possible? Participating in partnered sex while undrunk struck her as more and more awkward, mawkish, and unlikely. She eased off the throttle with men. She threw herself into her work.

Her attempt at sobriety was triggered by a suicide attempt, her second, at age thirty-two. Her first try was not really a serious one. She OD'd on pills and red wine when she was still a teenager, just about to turn twenty.

It was over a decade before she tried again. Her dark life had gotten a lot darker by then. She thought the NYPD might save her. But cops turned out to be as squirrely as asylum inmates.

"You know the only profession with a suicide rate higher than cops?" her partner Willie Urrico asked her. "Psychiatrists."

Everyone on the force drank. At that period in her life, the passing of her thirtieth birthday frightened Brand. The milestone had become a millstone around her neck. The idea of her own mortality suddenly occurred to her. In response, she tried to outdo everyone on the force. Out-drink, out-fuck, out-not-care them all.

Nothing helped. Urrico started offering her mouthwash and aspirin before they headed into the precinct house for roll call.

During a late-night vodkathon, a hard-drinking assistant district attorney named Jeffra Sanger gave her counsel. "If I ever want to end it, I know exactly how I'd do it."

"Yeah?" Brand's words came out slurred. But she experienced a flicker of interest.

"This place is an island, remember?" Sanger was talking about Manhattan. The Hudson River bounded the borough of Manhattan on the west. The Harlem and East Rivers cut off the eastern side.

"Really, we're on an island?" Brand responded sarcastically. "Coming down a little hard on the obvious, aren't you, Jeffra?"

The two of them were both rebounding off rancid sexual encounters with vile men. As the night wore on, commiseration descended into misery.

"Here's how you do the deed, Veronika. You take a cross-town walk, west to east." Sanger looked solemnly into Brand's eyes. With a sudden spasm of almost-sobriety, the woman bit off an additional four words. "You. Just. Keep. Going."

"Just keep going," Brand echoed.

"Uh-huh," Sanger said. "West to east."

"West to east, right."

Sanger leaned in close. "The Hudson River might not do it. But the East River, baby, nobody comes out of that alive. It's not really a river, actually. It's a tidal strait. The currents run back and forth like freight trains."

"Growing up, I was on the swim team at the Queens Aquatic Club," Brand noted.

"Don't matter, sweetheart," Sanger said. Citing an infamous confluence of the East and Harlem Rivers, she added, "You ain't doing the breaststroke in the currents of Hellgate."

A few rounds of drinks later—more than a few—Brand became separated from her fellow drunks. In search of her misplaced vehicle, she staggered alone down a sidewalk on East Twenty-Third Street. She decided to try out Jeffra Sanger's suggestion.

West to east. Just keep going.

She passed beneath an overpass of FDR Drive, crossed the frontage road, the bike path, and the thin strip of weed-choked land along the East River. No fences stopped her. No "life is worth living" anti-suicide sign turned her away.

The black water appeared half congealed, like oil or gelatin. On the opposite shore, the lights of the Queens waterfront shimmered. Queens, her home borough, just across the water. In Brand's bottle-blurred vision, the surface of the river read like an invitation. I feel like going home, she told herself. She just kept going, over the top of the rusted retaining wall, standing poised for a single instant, then, falling forward.

On the way down, a jagged piece of bulkhead metal tore a foot-long gash in her right leg. The concussive slap of the water knocked the breath out of her. The current sucked her away in the general direction of the big landmarked Pepsi-Cola sign on the far shore.

It's hard to believe that death enjoys irony, but life certainly embraces it with a vengeance. A police boat had recently been summoned to the area. The rescue squad was in search of another suicidal jumper, this one a fifteen year old male last seen in the river off nearby Corlears Hook.

The police patrol fished Brand out. One of the cops, Stan Medelino, recognized her.

"Brand? My God, you went in after that kid jumper?"

She couldn't speak. Officer Medelino took her silence for a yes. Brand passed out. Six hours later she woke in Bellevue Hospital.

She was a hero. "East River Rescue Cop," ran the tabloid headline the next morning, even though she had rescued no one, not even herself. It took a week for the lost body of the doomed fifteen-year-old to turn up.

Brand let the lie ride about her rescue attempt. She didn't have to tell anyone that she had jumped into the water to save a boy. They all just assumed. Feeling like a fraud, she accepted the departmental commendations and honors. Willie Urrico, one foot out the door into retirement by then, looked at her slantwise. But he made no move to challenge her.

For a while, in the wake of all that, Brand put the bottle down. Quitting her every-night swan dive into a river of vodka took all the strength she had left. After a few years of sobriety she was able to take a sip of alcohol now and then without slipping directly back into binge-drinking. But one result of her death plunge held on. She stopped her occasional visits to swimming pools altogether.

All her previous life she had been a fish. The dip into the East River cured her. Flashbacks to her suicide attempt made her whole body shake. Eventually she found herself shying away from open water of any sort. Even to glance at the *isvak* cut into the lake outside Hammar's cottage had made her gut roil.

If Brand had been a different person she might have gone to a behavioral therapist to get over herself. Deep down she knew some sort of shadow lay across her soul. It had been there since childhood. Maybe from birth. Parents always bequeath their miseries to their kids. The pain felt truly embedded, anyway. It was too deep to heal and too deep to reach. Like the bottom of the East River.

If she had summoned the courage to face her demons, perhaps Brand could have made a stab at a half-sane existence. Maybe that evening on the frozen lake would have turned out differently. She would have been able to take the après-sauna plunge with Krister Hammar. Her mental block had stopped her cold.

33

Brand was on a slow bell the next morning. Remaining under the covers, trying to make herself disappear, she sank further in the pillowy goose-down mattress. Sounds of Hammar moving about came from the kitchen area of the cottage. Dread arose in her at the thought of facing him.

In Sweden during winter, the sun rises late and sets early. The light now was milky and dim. The darkness outside slowly changed without Brand being able to catch it happening. Only a slight modulation in the atmosphere signaled the dawn-less beginning of a new day.

Her walk of shame that morning brought her out of bed and out in the cold to visit the outhouse. She slunk past Hammar, who crouched in front of a blazing hearthfire. He had already spread a low table with food.

"Morning," she mumbled. She was unclear about her feelings. Ambivalence had settled in during the night. In the harsh light of the morning after, Hammar appeared to be no more than a helpful guide during her Swedish visit. No romantic attachment adhered to the man. Getting naked in a sauna wasn't sexual. So, okay. She would treat the whole world as if it were a sauna. No matter how hot it got, nothing was sexual. Nothing meant anything.

Seated atop the wooden throne in the outhouse, the urgency of her sojourn in Sweden appeared to be draining away with her morning pee. She felt lost, confused, directionless. Her offhand reaction to the site of the *Nordic Light* arson fire now struck her as inhuman. The skinhead's mocking question reasserted itself.

"What are you doing here, bitch?"

Good question, she thought. What am I doing here? Brand's purpose seemed to evaporate in front of her eyes.

Then she realized she had just ventured sleepy-eyed through the snow to an outdoor toilet and hadn't thought twice about it. Oh, my God, she thought, I'm Swedish. She headed back into the cottage and settled into an oversize, comfy-looking armchair. Hammar ignored the atmosphere of awkwardness. His secret smile served to anger Brand. Say it! she wanted to shout. Say what, she didn't exactly know.

Hammar sensed her mood and didn't speak, serving her coffee silently. They were wordless for a long beat.

"What was that last night?" Hammar finally asked.

Brand realized the directness of the question left her wide open. Don't say it, she told herself. She said it anyway. "It was what it was."

They both winced at the cliché. Brand hurried to change the subject. "Surely, Hammar, you do have clients? And what, they can all go hang while you take time off to pal around with little old me?"

"You are not old," he said. He added a simple three-word statement. "You interest me."

Brand laughed. "So that's what that was last night, interest."

"Deep and abiding," he said.

"Listen, no big changes, okay?" she told him. "We go on like before. I don't want you mooning over me. None of this white knight business, like you have to protect the lady from harm. Nothing like that, okay?"

"I would never presume," Hammar said gallantly. "However, you may protect me from harm whenever you wish."

"Okay."

"Okay."

And that was that. Actually, Brand well understood that no "that" was ever really only "that," especially when it came to the boy and girl thing. Maybe her read of the situation was wrong, and she was making a total fool of herself.

The strange sense that had visited her before struck her once again. She first experienced it venturing into Elin Dalgren's deserted bedroom on the day after the family reunion. Something didn't add up. The events that had occurred since she arrived in Sweden had a logic that seemed to hover just out of her reach. Brand thought she might be able to straighten out the links in the chain, but when she went to try, everything remained stubbornly jumbled and disjointed.

Without consulting each other, Hammar and she both began to dress for the weather. The brilliant sun of the previous day only weakly broke through a tough, leathery cover of lowering cloud. A dull cold without wind. They left the cottage together. Brand automatically climbed into the driver's seat. When she attempted to start the Saab's cold engine she found she didn't have the knack.

"It's just the low temperature," Hammar commented needlessly. He exchanged places with Brand. Working the car's choke, he got the engine to turn over. Then he got out, walked around to the passenger's side, and again yielded the wheel to her.

"So, Västvall," she said. "Like a dog returns to its vomit."

They drove on deserted roads, punctuated only occasionally by signs of human habitation. Most structures appeared empty and abandoned. They saw no one.

They crested the familiar ridge and left the highway on the small approach road to the village. Plunging again into the spooky, all-enveloping old-growth forest, Brand had the sense of history recycling itself. She tensed as they passed the point where the child had dashed out of the woods in front of the Saab. But the woods remained vacant, with no footprints or other signs of the bizarre incident, which after all had happened only two days previous.

The recent blizzard had stacked drifts of snow everywhere.

"This morning, while you slept, I checked into things on the web," Hammar said. "There's still no report of a recent death or homicide in Västvall, or none that I can find from a fairly thorough search of the news feeds."

Brand made no comment. She puzzled over a pair of events that appeared linked. Sofieborg Manor House, with two dead. Then Västvall, with one more. Now the return to the little farm village triggered vivid memories. Her thoughts seemed to trip over each other, running quickly through her mind.

The nagging, elusive perception suddenly burst forward. Brand almost pulled the car over, the idea presented itself so clearly.

"They're tracking her somehow," she said.

"What? Who?"

"I don't know yet," Brand said, excited. "But think about it. We try to follow the traffickers, right? We go to the manor house, then to the Voss village. Both times we run into the big blond beast. So someone else is following the chain, too. Someone else has to be on her trail."

"Well, I have to ask again, who might that be?"

Brand didn't have an answer. "Someone."

"All right," Hammar said. "What do we do with this new understanding of yours?"

"I don't know that, either."

It wasn't much, but it was something. A couple of links in the chain had become firmly connected in Brand's mind. She steered the Saab onward, down to the floor of the little valley. Maybe they would find the truth there.

They halted the car where the small lane split to the right and left. "When you come to a fork in the road, take it," Brand muttered, recalling the Yogi Berra line favored by Willie Urrico.

"Västvall village is that way," Hammar indicated, pointing.

"The other way?"

"A right turn will bring us to a river that streams into a large lake," Hammar said. "But I think we look at a third way. There's something odd up there that you ought to see."

He gestured to a snowy track that Brand hadn't noticed, leading up a slope before curving away into the woods.

"That isn't even really a road. I'm not sure we'll be able to get back down."

"You're right," Hammar said. "Pull over. We'll leave the car and walk."

That option also struck Brand as questionable. The forest appeared dense. A *nattmara* could well be abroad. They were defenseless and unarmed.

She remembered seeing an old black-and-white movie western starring Jimmy Stewart. The hero quelled violence in an unruly frontier town without ever carrying a sixgun. He remained totally weaponless throughout the movie. Marlene Dietrich was in it.

But that was fantasy, and this was real. She was again a little disconcerted to discover how naked she felt without the Glock. It was like the common dream where the dreamer is onstage without clothes. She would be venturing out vulnerable and exposed. She found herself rubbing Moro's stone like a worry bead, but the little magic charm was no replacement for real-world firepower.

At least they were well shod and warmly encased in parkas. She and Hammar proceeded up the single-lane track. They moved into the *urskog* once more. Brand had to steel her mind against more flashbacks. Her companion stopped once, ungloved his hands, and pulled the hood on Brand's parka tighter, snapping the clasp at her neck.

"There is no bad weather in Sweden," he pronounced solemnly. "Only bad equipment."

They continued on. In the narrow, snow-covered lane lay a few frozen clumps of what looked like animal dung.

"*Nattmara,*" Brand suggested, not quite seriously.

"Horse," Hammar corrected her.

The surrounding forest began to feel dense and threatening. Brand had disturbing memories of the afternoon of the blizzard. A sense of dread overtook her. She and Hammar mounted a small rise to encounter a bizarre makeshift memorial that stopped them dead in their tracks.

34

A flat, circumscribed clearing. All the snow and underlying vegetation had been burned away. A bald patch remained in the middle, a scorched circle twenty meters wide. Coming upon it suddenly, as she did, Brand had difficulty understanding what she was looking at.

Stuck in the ground stood a collection of wooden crosses. They were not Christian-style crossed T's, but X-shaped ones. Weathered boards nailed together formed an intersecting overlap. Each cross rose a dozen feet or more from the blackened earth.

The drifts of the recent blizzard had melted off the charred section. Items of clothing draped across each cross. The empty-sleeved arms stretched out as if nailed to the wooden planks. Skirts splayed out below the shirts and sweaters. Leggings or slacks were also fastened in place. The scarecrow figures, one after another, filled the whole clearing. Some of the crosses had shoes attached to them, small handbags, a necklace of coins or a cheap ornament.

Diminutive, crucified figures. Wearing children's clothing, or that of a young person, anyway. Teens, young adults.

Placed at the necks of a few of the shirts and sweaters were round paper portraits, curled and stained by the weather, drawings or photos of the faces of young women. Several had their lips outlined in garish red. The moon-shaped heads had been fixed to the wood where the X-planks crossed. The paper rustled and flopped forward in the light breeze passing through the surrounding forest. The scarecrows seemed to be bowing their ghostly heads to Brand.

She counted eleven.

"This is what you wanted to show me?" Brand asked.

Hammar shook his head. "I don't know what this is," he said solemnly. "It certainly wasn't here last year when I visited. There was an encampment of travelers somewhere around here."

Brand wondered what she would find, if she moved forward to examine the homemade Golgotha more closely. Would the face of Varzha Luna stare out at her?

Then, oddly, she encountered herself as a child. Although, not really. On the far side of the clearing Brand saw a tiny human being.

She recognized the little figure even without the tattered black dress.

"Hey," she called out impulsively.

The imp bolted.

"It's her," she blurted out to Hammar. "The little thief who stole my backpack."

The two of them scrambled after the girl as she dashed into the woods. They came up behind a half dozen women wearing layers of sweaters over long skirts, their shoulders draped with heavy blankets against the cold. The women stopped to turn and stare at the interlopers. The child whom Brand had just seen buried herself in the skirts of one of the women.

Splashes of color, red kerchiefs and bright garments, showed against the snowy expanse of the forest. The group seemed to have just returned from gathering firewood. Retreating quickly, taking their child and their bundles of tinder with them, the women followed a foot-path beaten into the snow. Together they headed further into the forest.

One of the wood-gatherers wore an orange-yellow skirt and a gold-patterned jacket of padded silk. She proved easy to track. The woman moved unerringly on the snowy pathway. For Brand and Hammar, it was like pursuing a slash of sunlight in the midst of a stark-white polar sea. Eventually, the woman began turning from time to time to check on her pursuers. She seemed oddly unconcerned about being followed.

Brand and Hammar reached a second clearing, this one much larger than the first. They entered into another world, a sprawling encampment in the woods. Centered around an old half-collapsed wooden barn and a pair of outbuildings, the camp included several trailers and improvised lean-tos.

"Romani," Hammar said.

Amid the cluster of structures stood an old-fashioned tent made of drab, olive green canvas. This was decorated relentlessly with bits of color, plastic flowers, banners, flags, ribbons, until the tent fabric sagged beneath all the festoons. Everywhere there were stretched tarps of black plastic, held in place by ropes and thick wooden supports.

No dogs, and no *nattmara*. Brand realized they were being confronted not by animals but by the assembled women they had just followed through the forest. The female Roma stood with arms folded, forming a colorful tableau in their patterned skirts and scarves, garbed head to toe in contrasting prints, stripes, checks and dots. With sober, expressionless faces, they gazed at

Brand and Hammar. The attitudes on display seemed an example of Romani dominance, of Romani determination, as if the women knew they had strength in numbers.

No dogs, and no men, either.

From among the assembled women Brand heard the murmur of the word "*gadje*," meaning outsiders, non-Roma people. With a sudden jab of memory, she recollected the little stone talisman that Moro had presented her, a charm against the evil eye.

She searched in her pocket, located the stone, and held it out. The murmuring went silent.

The woman in the gold-patterned blouse who Brand had followed into the camp stepped forward. "American detective?"

Brand cursed inwardly. Did every single person in the country know who she was and what she did?

"Moro," she said. "I know Moro Part."

The pronouncement of the name spurred a wave of chatter in Romani.

"You come from America?" the woman in the gold-patterned jacket asked.

"Your English is very good," Hammar said, evading her question.

"*Polis*," the woman said, indicating Brand.

The effect was immediate. One of the others spat on the ground. Several more gave Brand their backs, turning away in a manner that implied ostracism or rejection.

"Please," Brand said. "We want to help."

A half dozen women stayed where they were, crowding sullenly together.

"I want to help," Brand said again. "We saw…"

She gestured back over her shoulder, in the general direction of the ritualistic crucifixion shrine. Using her forefingers she formed a cross.

"Eleven crosses," Hammar said. "Crucifixes."

"Who made the shrine?" Brand asked. "Who put the crosses there? The missing girls. In the forest, in the meadow burned by fire, who made the crosses?"

The women looked at her without speaking. One of them stepped forward. "*Vi har gjort allt själva,*" she said in very clear Swedish. We made it by ourselves.

A couple things happened at once. The crack of a rifle shot sounded, breaking the heavy silence of the *urskog*. The women scattered, instantly disappearing into the surrounding forest.

Hammar and Brand turned to see a lone male figure standing behind them. The man stationed himself where the path led into the encampment clearing, cutting off their retreat. He wore a white canvas camo suit, heavy boots, a knit cap, and snow goggles. A hunting rifle rested on his hip, held negligently so the barrel pointed skyward.

"*Kom hit,*" he commanded. Come here.

35

To visit Gammelhem, "Old Home," the not so old Härjedalen lodge of Baron Gösta Kron, Brand had to take a journey into the past. It was as if some sort of private historical reenactment was underway.

The rustic two-story hunting lodge, newly built to resemble something out of the nineteenth century, featured Beaux Arts touches, bygone relics from the Swedish upper class's obsession with Parisian culture. The numerous barns and outbuildings were constructed out of fieldstone, not *falu* red wood. The estate spoke of wealth, solidity, and a stubborn, haughty anachronism.

The help, too, struck Brand with a timeless sort of feel. Many of them appeared to be African. Given what Hammar told her of the baron's virulently anti-immigrant politics, that didn't make much sense, either. But there they were. She and Hammar could see several laborers pass in and out of the barns, all wearing calf-high rubber boots.

The expansive central yard of packed snow, only partially plowed and everywhere dirtied by the tracks of animals, displayed all the touches of a working farm. Plastic wrapped hay bales were stacked and covered with tarps, spoiling the old-time feel. White-painted wooden fences in fine repair led off toward the fields. An old Scania truck had pulled up near one of the barns, parked back-end in.

A half hour earlier at the Romani encampment, the rifleman-in-a-snowsuit had sternly informed Brand and Hammar that they were trespassing. He marched them back to the Saab. Climbing into his own vehicle, he ordered them to follow him.

"I'm Hugo," he pronounced in imperious English. "The baron's man."

"What the hell is going on?" Brand demanded of Hammar.

"We are summoned," Hammar said.

"Yes? Where?"

"To the estate of this so-called noble man whose land we have invaded," Hammar said in a mocking tone. "Baron Gösta Kron."

The "baron's man," Magnusson, drove a shiny black Volvo station wagon. Brand and Hammar humped along close behind him in the Saab. They left the Västvall area and headed a few kilometers farther into the mountains. The surrounding landscape seemed to have been tilted up on its end, given a good shake, and emptied of people. The baron's estate, as they approached, appeared as a rare center of life and activity in the area.

Brand drove up an elegant, quarter-mile alée posted with denuded birch trees, then pulled into a cobblestoned courtyard swept clean of snow. Among several vehicles parked there were a Daimler Maybach twice as ancient as the Saab, but in sparkling shape, as well as a mud-splattered Land Rover and a Volvo box truck.

Now, as Hammar and she climbed out of the Saab and glanced around at the lodge, farmyard, and grounds, Brand couldn't decide how deep in trouble they had landed. She was certainly surprised about the diversity of the laborers. Some she swore were Romani, as strange as that might be.

Then Baron Gösta Kron emerged from his residence, a vision-from-the-past example of Swedish nobility. He halted on the elevated stone porch of the hunting lodge, hands on hips.

"Krister!" he called out almost merrily.

"*Hej*," Hammar answered with a nod.

"You two know each other?" Brand muttered under her breath to Hammar. He didn't respond.

Baron Kron kept the tone light. "And you must be Veronika Brand," he said. "The New York detective who is poor Gustav Dalgren's granddaughter."

Brand felt vaguely intimidated. She reacted as she always did to intimidation, with an immediate frostiness. "Are we being detained or something?" she asked, staring up at the bony figure of the estate's owner. "Under arrest?"

"Oh, no, no," said the baron. "I merely requested Hugo here to ask if you cared to join me this afternoon."

"When a request is made by someone carrying a hunting rifle, it tends to sound more like an order," Brand said.

"An attitude of command is common in an overseer," the baron responded. "That's all, Hugo," he added, dismissing the man.

He extended an arm to motion Hammar and Brand forward. "I was just settling in with a pre-luncheon cocktail, if you'd care to join me."

The invitation, the setting, the faint air of danger proved impossible to resist, at least as far as Brand was concerned. She mounted the steps to the small terrace, examining her host. Not David Bowie's thin white duke, exactly, but a thin white baron. Trim, casually well-dressed, he wore his age well. Brand estimated the baron had to be at least seventy years. She would learn that he was actually over eighty.

The interior of Gammelhem revealed itself not as a residence but as a full-blown shrine to blood sports. Dead animals crowded every square meter of wall space. The trophies seemingly came from all seven continents, including a stuffed sea leopard from Antarctica. Rhinos and big cats surrounded a line of timber wolves mounted as if in a snarling pack. From closer to home in Sweden, elk, moose, fallow deer, and wild boar contended with full-size bear, lynx, and wolverine. All were preserved by faultless taxidermy.

Through a bank of windows giving out on the grounds, Brand saw something she could hardly credit. In a large steel cage, a pair of Bengal tigers playfully shadow boxed with each other in the snow. The enormous animals stopped tussling and turned to stare directly at the window where she and Hammar stood.

"Are those…?"

Hammar followed Brand's wide-eyed gaze. "Oh, yes. The baron keeps quite an extensive menagerie."

Penned goats and sheep foraged in a sloping paddock below the lodge. The twin tigers seemed to have an eye for them, too. Farther down the hill, near the collection of barns, a herd of exotic, shaggy-haired Highland cattle gathered in hock-deep snow drifts. The combination of predators and prey animals struck Brand as somehow perverse.

She gestured at the Bengals. "Woody Allen made an observation, 'The lion will lie down with the lamb, but the lamb won't get much sleep.' When those tigers let out their roars in the middle of the night, do the cattle stampede?"

"How typical of a Jew to misquote the Holy Bible," the baron said. "The prophet Isaiah mentions not the lion but the wolf and the lamb."

"I think the insomnia is the main point, isn't it?" Brand returned lightly.

"My dear ones are named Hillary and Bill," Baron Kron said, indicating the two tigers. "It amused me to name them so, even though they are actually mother and son. We can visit them later, perhaps to get their views on the latest Middle East crisis. But now, come, I am anxious to introduce you to Jimmy."

He led them up another set of stone steps, walls on both sides again dominated by heads of dead beasts. At the top of the stairway stood a welcoming committee of two: a Romani woman, colorfully dressed, standing with a small-statured chimpanzee got up in a traditional bellhop's uniform.

"You see, I have turned out the whole circus for you," the baron said.

36

The little ape took Brand by the hand and led her into an immense, gallery-like sitting room. The woman, evidently the ape's keeper, trailed behind. Hammar and the baron brought up the rear.

Brand had never experienced the touch of a chimpanzee before. The little guy's skin was creased and black but gave off the uncanny warmth of a human hand. He loosened his grasp when they all arrived at a small seating arrangement of couches and leather club chairs.

"Veronika." The baron took up Brand's hand that the chimpanzee had just dropped, put it to his lips, and led her to a couch. He sat down beside her. Up close, he smelled of tobacco. Underlying that was the slight scent of decay.

"I must have your permission to call you by your Christian name," he said. "I feel as though we are old friends. You must use mine, which is Gösta."

The baron gestured toward the chimp bellhop. "What might Jimmy get for you? He makes an excellent martini. And we also have a very nice bottle of French champagne just waiting to be corked. Or perhaps beer?"

Brand resisted informing the man she wasn't thirsty. The emotional hangover from the scene at the sauna the night before put her off alcohol. More to see the animal perform than because she would consume one, she chose the cocktail.

The chimp's female handler pronounced a few curt words in an unrecognizable tongue. The little ape ambled over to a wet bar set-up. He climbed with an easy movement onto a stool in order to reach the countertop. Brand watched, fascinated. Jimmy unerringly selected an emerald bottle of vermouth from a crowded shelf of liquors. He opened it, splashed a few drops into a shaker and then immediately dumped the liquid back out.

"He needs to know if you prefer gin or vodka," the baron asked.

"Um, gin, I guess," Brand said.

Again, the Romani woman directed the chimp with a brief command. From the collection of bottles, the animal fetched up a liter of Beefeater. He poured a generous portion into the shaker that had been rinsed with vermouth. Using a scoop, he added ice, then closed the shaker and gave it an agitated rattle.

"Shaken, not stirred, you see?" the baron called out.

Transferring the mixture into a glass, the chimp climbed down from the stool. He took the cocktail off the countertop. Bringing it over to Brand, he slopped only a very little liquid on the way.

"Thank you," she said, accepting the prize. She found it difficult not to applaud.

The chimp stared up at her with a teeth-baring grin that looked more like a grimace.

"Should I tip him?" Brand asked.

The baron laughed. "Oh, you must taste your martini first. Sometimes Jimmy has a heavy hand with the vermouth."

"It's excellent," Brand said, taking a sip. The taste of the gin took her back to her days as a drunk, and not in a pleasant way.

"*Gå nu*," the Count commanded. Leave now. The handler led the little chimp away. Brand was sorry to see them go.

"Do you like my little fellow primate?" Kron asked, rising to serve himself and Hammar glasses of champagne. "Chimpanzee, you know, that is a Bantu word that means 'fake man.' I find it interesting to keep such a creature around me, though he can get tiresome. The comparison between ape behavior and that of the homo sapiens is always instructive."

"Homo sapiens means 'wise human,' doesn't it?" Brand said. "Although there are times when I look around and have to conclude wisdom is not a particularly prominent feature of the species."

The baron gave a smile and nodded. "I don't wonder that you feel that way, knowing how you must have experienced the scum on the streets of New York City."

"And the woman, she is Jimmy's keeper?"

"The Roma are, as a people, excellent animal trainers," the baron said, again sitting down beside Brand. "It is one of their traditional skills. Years ago they kept bears, a practice dating from the Middle Ages, perhaps even before. Bears travel well. It was a way for their trainers to earn a few coins in whatever town or region they found themselves."

Hammar spoke. "That's the stereotype, anyway. They were enslaved in Romania for some four hundred years. The Romani had to be creative about ways of earning money. They were skilled coppersmiths, tinsmiths, accomplished when it came to working silver. But surely, Baron Kron, you know more about their history than most."

The baron laughed. "One thing I know is that the word 'money' in the Romani language is spelled 'l-o-v-e,' just like love in English. Though they pronounce it 'low-vey.'"

"I would suppose equating money with love is probably the real truth in any number of languages," Krister said.

"Might you keep wolves, Baron Kron?" Brand felt the need to cut through what sounded to her like a bit of dueling between the two men.

"Please, call me Gösta, I insist."

Brand nodded. "I have seen, twice since I've been here in Sweden, a creature I cannot identify, very large, dog-like, with light-colored fur."

"Yes, we have gray wolves in Sweden, though I'm quick to say none are captive here at Gammelhem. There is a population nearby, in *Fulufjället*, the big park on the Norwegian border. They range widely, and a few times have ventured onto my land. We are not here that much in winter. This February visit is an exception. But our caretakers say they sometimes hear the howls at night."

He cocked his head and switched accents, from Swedish to something approximating Romanian. "Listen to them—the children of the night. What music they make!"

He laughed. "Do you recognize the source? How often do you get a chance to hear an actual baron quoting a count? And Count Dracula at that, eh?"

Brand nodded, not willing to be distracted by the man's dramatics. "Perhaps the gypsies in the camp by the river, they might keep a tame wolf, maybe a wolf-dog."

"Ah, you must really guard your language, my dear. I know the word 'gypsy' is still acceptable in America, but here in this country is frowned upon by all our culturally sensitive citizens."

"The Romani, then, in the camp by the river."

"The Roma in that encampment are my guests."

"We encountered a sort of shrine."

"Yes."

"You know of it?"

"Of course. I would be a poor landowner not to know of a monstrosity such as that erected on my property."

"What does it mean?"

"I couldn't say."

"Are you aware the Romani community has lost many young women in recent months to human trafficking? The shrine seems to commemorate that fact."

"You would know more about it than I do, Veronika."

"I don't think that's true. I suspect you're a man who knows more than he lets on."

Baron Kron drained his champagne cocktail. "It is always refreshing to speak to an American, and even more bracing to speak to a New Yorker. I so rarely have the chance. You come right out and say whatever is on your mind, as contrary and impolitic it may be. Conversation with my countrymen is often indirect. It resembles more of a chess game. Whereas speaking with you, Veronika, I am reminded of a boxing match."

"Why are they there?"

"They?"

"The Roma, on your land. A few days ago we encountered a host of them, children mostly, in the forest above Västvall."

The Count sighed theatrically. "Virtue being its own reward, I normally do not like to trumpet my charity," he said. "But since you force me I must confess. To a limited degree I have sponsored some members of the Roma community."

"Sponsored?"

"Yes. We provide them with work opportunities, housing at times—although as you know they are a restless people. Perhaps you also know that this area, Härjedalen, is not my primary home. I come here to hunt. I hail from the south, near Malmö. I thought that to relocate members of the community here might relieve some of the pressure down there.

"Voluntarily?"

"Oh, yes, I do it quite voluntarily."

"No, I meant, do they 'relocate' voluntarily?"

"I know what you meant. I was just pulling your leg, to employ the American phrase."

The conversation was cut short. Three striking women entered from the opposite end of the room. They were all similar in appearance, young, Asian—Thai, perhaps, or some exotic international mix—and all impossibly elegant. This is what wealth can buy, Brand thought.

"My dears," Baron Kron said, opening his arms expansively to greet them.

37

The baron stood with Magnusson, his superintendent, watching the dumpy blue Saab leave the estate. It happened that the car followed immediately after the big Scania truck. Dollar Boy was heading out on another veterinarian run to Uppsala.

"Are you sure we should have allowed that pair to depart unhindered, Baron?" Magnusson asked. "I feel they were insufficiently disciplined."

"You put in a call to the Vosses about them?"

"Yes. With the result that Junior Voss said he would immediately dispatch the two cousins, Ylva and Malte."

The baron chuckled lowly. "That young woman, Ylva? With her on the job we'll soon see Detective Brand and the Sami lawyer field-dressed and hanging by their heels in the big oak tree at Västvall village."

Ylva and Malte Voss were famous within the family—and in the whole country, too—for being world-class biathlon competitors. Their style was a caricature of the mythological Nordic warrior.

Magnusson understood Gösta Kron preferred to have any nasty business conducted well away from the estate. Thou shall not sully thy master's hands, was forever the rule. Still, Magnusson worried that the New York detective and her Sami ally would somehow escape the net.

"They enjoyed the animals," the baron said mildly.

Before Brand and Hammar left he had conducted them on a tour of the estate's private menagerie. His ladies did not accompany him, forced by the very un-Thai Swedish weather to remain indoors. The three—two of them were twins—did not much like Gammelhem, much preferring Malmö, or the penthouse apartments in Stockholm or London.

Baron Kron accompanied his two guests around the grounds. The big aviary was closed. The birds had been transferred to his place down south. But all the other beasts were present.

Truth be told, the baron was a little bored with his zoo. The lionesses lazed about, dulled by being retired from the hunt. The big male king of the pride had died almost a year ago. Jimmy the chimp bellhop had been reduced to a party joke. The Bengals, Bill and Hillary, seemed to be rendered somehow less regal by long captivity.

The tigers dutifully allowed the baron to demonstrate his fearlessness. They padded over to him and lowered their sleek heads to be petted. A funky musk scent rose in a cloud from their pelts.

The hyenas were the baron's first and favorite of all the animals in the menagerie. The zoo had been founded around them, in fact, sixty years ago. The beasts never failed to impress visitors. Two from the pack remained in their paddock when he led the New York detective inside the barn. As they always did, they languidly turned their heads toward the humans, as if assessing the visitors as prey. The baron rattled the lid of their food locker and they came alive, trotting forward and vocalizing joyously.

Ak-ak-ak-ar-ar-ar-haroool!

Smiling proudly, the baron turned to Brand. "Your American president, Roosevelt, not the communist but the first one, Teddy, he kept a hyena as a pet. He named it Bill."

Unfortunately the big male, Fenrir, had already been loaded into the truck for his trip south. Hyenas were the rare species where the females were normally bigger than the males. Fenrir was the exception. He was large beyond measure. As the baron and the Brand woman had emerged from the barn, the noble made it a point to flip back a corner of the tarpaulin covering the Scania's cargo bed. The chained animal lay crouched in the dim interior of the truck, its eyes twin pinpoints of glowing amber.

"You know, despite appearances, they're more closely related to cats than to dogs." The baron had thoroughly enjoyed seeing the creature's effect on his guest from New York. The blood drained from Veronika Brand's face. The baron moved forward, wanting the pleasure of catching the detective as she fainted from fear. But he was forced to conclude that the streets of New York City had trained the woman well, because she stood her ground.

"He's named Fenrir," the baron said. "That's the great wolf of our mythology, son of the trickster devil god Loki. He's often quite docile, but today the poor thing is scheduled for dental surgery. I would not advise climbing in there with him."

A minor incident at the truck had marred the baron's equanimity. He caught his man Dollar Boy exchanging words with Krister Hammar. The two of them spoke in what sounded like Romani, a language Baron Kron had never bothered to learn.

As the old man passed by with his swagger of privilege, he gave the kid a stinging whack across the shoulders with the leather switch he carried. "*Prata svenska!*" he barked, telling Dollar Boy to speak only Swedish. Kron had an impulse to strike the Sami lawyer, too, but pinched it back before walking on.

Now he watched Brand and Hammar drive away from Gammelhem in their preposterous Saab. The woman drove, the baron noticed disgustedly. He had a momentary thought that he should not have allowed them such unfettered access to his lodge and grounds. A disturbing picture formed in his mind. Brand and Hammar might meet with his man Dollar Boy down the road. They would exchange intel and hatch plans. A tiny eruption of rage bubbled up within the baron.

Veronika Brand was the kind of woman whose looks you didn't notice, until suddenly you did. She hid her sexual appeal under a bushel. Commonplace minds couldn't see it, the baron thought. Sun-colored hair, yes, and piercing gray eyes, but a certain hardness to her face prevented most people from considering her pretty. His visceral recognition of the woman's beauty only added to his irritation. His own feeling of attraction offended him.

The woman Cynny, the non-twin of the threesome, approached from behind him just then, wrapping her arms around his shoulders. The scent of sandalwood perfume enveloped the baron like the breath of heaven.

"Come inside." Cynny made the simple words sparkle with multiple meanings.

The baron's upset vanished in anticipation of coming pleasure. He was never much given to second-guessing himself. He would discipline Dollar Boy upon his return. Let the Vosses take care of the two meddlers.

38

Once they dropped off Mattias Rapp in the small village of Västvall, Varzha was alone in the car with "JV," Jarl Voss. They drove toward the Norwegian border in Jarl's super-expensive cocoon of an automobile, a Volvo SUV that Varzha thought he probably prized more than his own mother.

Considering the circumstances, she had an easy time of it. He threatened no violence and Varzha felt no fear. The two of them weren't all that far apart in age. On the rare moments he wasn't talking on the phone, they listened to his idiot black metal music full blast. He acted like the king of Sweden, and forgot the real king, Karl Gustav. Technology kept his royal highness well-connected to the rest of the world. Jarl seemed childishly proud of the three newest-iteration iPhones he kept in his car.

"Cold, warm, and hot," he explained. "One for family, one for business, and one for social."

Varzha returned a blank response to whatever nonsense Jarl might spout, carefully maintaining the pretense that she did not understand Swedish. She noticed he never used the family phone and would ignore it whenever it buzzed. He did, however, answer the "warm" phone, the one for business, frequently leaving it on speakerphone so Varzha could hear both sides of the rapid-fire conversation. Mostly he described where they were and how much longer it would take to reach their destination, which he referred to as "the chalet."

In one exchange, an accented male voice asked Jarl Voss about Varzha herself. She picked out the word *agn*, bait. The idea made her sick. She imagined herself dangling from a fishing line over the heads of faceless men with money in their hands, shouting out numbers. A supposed virgin, sold to the highest bidder.

In truth, Varzha suspected that Jarl saw himself more as Sweden's queen rather than its king. She saw him as what she knew him to be, a gay boy. He liked to chatter and boast about his clothes, but would probably be horrified if forced to remove hers, the kind of man who might beat a woman but would never sleep with one. Several times on the drive he snorted white powder, either cocaine or crystal, she didn't know. The drug revved him up. He talked whether anyone was listening or not. He was constantly on the phone, speaking fast, saying nothing.

A single question burned in Varzha's mind. Had Moro Part and Dollar Boy managed to wreak vengeance on those who would prey on young Romani girls? They had vowed to do so, but the scheme was risky and open to mistakes. No word had come on the fate of her abductors, Liam and Nils. She tried to ready herself for an explosion of wrath when the news came to JV.

They followed a river valley west into the mountains. The land they drove through was like an abandoned bird's nest, where only a litter of cracked eggshells showed that any creature had ever lived there at all. They had passed long stretches of nothing but empty pine woods, full of *kasali*, forest spirits. Varzha didn't like the Swedish countryside, especially not in winter. Stockholm was better, crowded with life and opportunities.

Anxious and jittery as she was, Varzha managed to fall into an exhausted sleep. She woke abruptly to hear Jarl screaming and pounding on the steering wheel. Blocking the road ahead was a herd of snowy white animals with brown spots, nubby horns, and sly sweet eyes. Several of the reindeer stood mid-pavement, lazily gazing at the SUV with what seemed like mild interest. Some still clung to the side of the hillside slope, while others had already crossed the road and were continuing downward toward the river.

Jarl reached across Varzha to the glove box and pulled out a small pistol. A child-sized weapon, Varzha thought with disdain, a little palm-sized .22 automatic. Against a hundred-and-fifty kilo reindeer, a pea-shooter like that would do nothing. The creatures were famously thick-skulled.

It didn't matter to Jarl. Her madman captor leaped out of the SUV waving the weapon. Varzha opened the door on the opposite side of the vehicle and stepped out, too.

She had to do something. The fool was going to open fire.

She began to sing in her high, clear voice. A *manele*, a Romani folk song of love and loss.

The sound echoed eerily off the surrounding hills. Both Jarl and the beasts went stock still. The man stopped brandishing his stupid lady's gun. Moving slowly, gracefully, dreamily, as if under a spell, the herd gradually moved off the roadway. Evidently, love was a universal concept, and reindeer understood loss.

They drove on. Varzha saw Jarl occasionally turn to glance over at her, a quizzical look on his face. He had heard something in her singing that had touched his cold Voss heart. When he had tossed the pistol back into its hiding place, though, he had made sure to lock the glove box.

The revenge scheme Varzha had embarked upon depended on a frighteningly small piece of electronics, which she kept concealed in a wooden barrette clasping the thick braids of her hair. Dollar Boy found the device for them. It was supposedly the world's tiniest cell phone, designed, he said, to be smuggled into prisons. "Beat the Man," the model was called. Compared side by side, tiny keypad and all, it was only a little larger than Varzha's thumb.

It gave her people pinpoint accuracy to Varzha's physical location, her life-line. If the tiny device were ever discovered, her captors might kill her.

All of Varzha's modesty had been burned away by her anger over the kidnappings. She retained her maidenhead but lost her innocence. Varzha Luna was like no Romani girl who ever existed, proud, fierce, and without shame. When this was all over, she swore secretly, she would see Vago safe and then hang herself. Perhaps she would pour gasoline over her body and burn alive at her old post on Drottninggatan, in front of Åhlens department store.

So far no one had thought to search Varzha. The easy way she had gone with the men when they came for her on Drottninggatan should have betrayed her secret motives. She had displayed passive willingness, not fear. That alone might have alerted the men that something was off, that she did not resemble their other victims. But Mattias and the others noticed nothing. They were clearly very stupid and careless. The idea that roles could be reversed, that the predator could become the prey, never occurred to them.

Everything depended on the loyalty and fortitude of Moro and Dollar Boy. Dollar Boy had lost his true love, Lel, to a rape hotel in Norway and eventually to suicide. He had repeatedly sworn blood vengeance. But Varzha understood that the human heart was susceptible to change. Perhaps Dollar Boy had distracted himself with another girl. Perhaps the fire in his heart flared only for a little while and then had been snuffed by the passage of time.

Moro she trusted more. He was protecting the lives not only of a few girls but of his entire clan. He was also as fierce as a mongoose. Varzha had never actually seen a mongoose, but it was an animal from far back in the history of her people that killed snakes and that everyone always said was unstoppable. She herself had once witnessed Moro and two other *chache* Roma boys take on a whole gang of Schwedo Nazis and bloody them all, putting more than a few of the skinheads in the hospital.

The three of them had sworn an alliance, a *wortacha*, Moro and Dollar Boy and Varzha. The two males, who were not accustomed to see females as equals, were forced to treat her as one. Varzha's fury rendered her powerful. The others in the *wortacha* were at first dismissive, then reluctantly accepting, and finally awed.

All she could do was to follow the scheme that they had laid down—to allow herself to be taken, and to be followed by Moro and Dollar Boy, who would eliminate her abductors one by one in the most painful way possible. Varzha refused to be a victim, preferring instead the role of an avenging angel.

Lel had been her sworn sister as well as being Dollar Boy's intended. Varzha knew a few of the other stolen girls, also. She had volunteered for the dangerous duty, insisting on the path forward. Now she would pursue the plan through to the very end, adhering to the scheme even if it meant her death. It was not a prospect she relished—she especially feared for Vago if she was gone—but she would do it for Lel. She would do it for the others who had been fed into the trafficking pipeline. She would do it so future perpetrators would know that they, too, would pay for their evil with their lives.

For the high crime of driving in a car with JV now, Varzha would be disgraced in the eyes of her people. The community would turn against her simply for being alone with men, *gadje* men. They would never respect the purity of her intentions. None of that mattered.

Back in Romania, her mother had often recounted the story of Papusza, a legendary singer and poet who violated the fundamental rules of Romani society. Papusza made a foolish move, trusting a *gadjo* with her exquisite written poetry. Of course the gentile betrayed her, translating the texts into Polish and selling her words for all the world to read. Such public exposure rendered her invisible within the Romani community. She died ostracized from family, from friends, from her people. The message of her mother's story was clear to Varzha. Any dealings with *gadje* were bound to result in catastrophe.

"Tonight we see the Turkish woman doctor," Jarl said into the phone, startling Varzha out of her thoughts. He used the phrase on the warm phone, the business one.

As far as she was concerned, Turks were the villains of the world. In the hierarchy of immigrants, where every immigrant shit on the immigrant below, Turks might be among the lowest of the low, but they could always look to the Roma to slag off and beat down. A Turkish doctor? Female or male, the prospect struck fear into her heart. She realized she was in greater danger than ever.

They followed the river valley deeper into the mountains.

An hour later Jarl pulled the SUV into the driveway of a chalet of weathered wood. The A-frame structure sat on a small rise a kilometer off the road, within a pine forest, overlooking the white, snow-covered expanse of a frozen river.

A black Mercedes sedan blocked the driveway. It turned out the Turks had already arrived. Two males climbed out of the car, an older one, a heavyset bear of a man with a woolen hat pulled down over his ears, and another younger, more handsome one, evidently the driver.

A few seconds later a stylish woman emerged. She looked like no doctor Varzha had ever seen. She more resembled an actress in a Turkish video melodrama, not the star but the star's girlfriend, maybe, the one who never left his side but always got killed halfway through the movie.

Jarl played the big man, the host. Herding Varzha before him, he led the others into the chalet. The place smelled musty and unused, with a simple vacation home layout. A towering stone fireplace, its hearth cold and filled with old ashes, dominated the living space. Above was a balcony. A kitchen opened to one side, a hallway to the other. Outside, expansive wooden decks surrounded the structure.

The Turkish arrivals took their places in an arrangement of chairs and couches. Varzha noticed that Jarl and the handsome driver kept exchanging smiles and glances. The other two were all business. They spoke in accented Swedish. Jarl pulled his prize offering front and center.

"She is not completely ugly," said the woman doctor, eyeing Varzha head to toe. The girl recognized the strategy. In the marketplace you must always denigrate the goods before you buy.

"She has not been touched?" asked the older man.

"Totally pure," Jarl promised. "I've been with her the whole time, since she left the protection of her family in Romania. Top quality goods."

The older man took Varzha's chin in his meaty paw, turning her head this way and that. "All the same, she must be examined to see if she is intact."

The doctor surprised Varzha by swatting the man's hand aside. "Not for you, Fevzi," she snapped. So she is the big boss, Varzha thought.

"Come," the woman said to her. She picked up a large carrying bag she had brought with her.

"I need to witness, in order to be sure," the man who was called Fevzi said.

"You stay right where you are," the woman ordered. "I do the thing." Then she added, glancing at Jarl, "Me alone."

"Use the back bedroom," Jarl said, uninterested in participating. This was part of the business that excited him least—both professionally and personally. The three men watched as the two females proceeded down the back hall.

"Time for a celebration," Jarl said brightly. He laid out a half dozen rails of cocaine on the coffee table. Fevzi sent the driver out to the Mercedes to retrieve a bottle of Johnny Walker blue label.

The woman doctor led Varzha into a small room with a single bed. She shut the door behind them.

"Lie down on the bed," she said, pantomiming her command with a gesture. "Do you speak Swedish?"

Varzha shook her head. "We will have to make do," the doctor said.

She proceeded to speak Swedish anyway. "My name is Hira Nur. I am a medical doctor. You will do as I say."

The woman retrieved a small pouch from her bag. The pouch contained some sort of metal instrument. The sight of the strange tool alarmed Varzha. She didn't know what was happening. Was this it? The first rape among many? When the doctor attempted physically to place her on the bed, she pushed back.

Escape was not possible. Varzha knew that, but she attempted to flee anyway. Bursting out of the little room, she turned down the hallway, away from the open living space in front.

"Voss!" Hira Nur shouted. But Jarl was already on her, chasing down Varzha as she ran. Catching the girl by the hair, he slammed her against the wooden paneling. She called out in pain. Her thick braids unraveled, and the barrette holding them in place clattered across the floor.

They stood facing one another, Varzha cornered, breathing hard, the doctor Hira Nur framed in the doorway of the little bedroom. Fevzi and the driver loomed behind Jarl.

"I've been so nice to you, *älskling*," her captor said. His voice had a nasty edge to it. "But I can be not so nice, too."

As Jarl advanced, his foot crushed the wooden barrette. He ignored it, reaching out and gripping Varzha roughly by the neck.

"Are you going to behave?" he yelled.

"Voss," Hira Nur said, staring down at the broken hair clasp.

"Are you?" Jarl shouted. A spray of his spittle landed on Varzha's face. He shook her like a rag doll.

"Voss," the doctor repeated. She knelt down and picked up the shattered barrette. With it came Beat the Man, the world's tiniest cell phone.

"What the fuck is this?" Hira Nur demanded in English.

39

Brand watched Dollar Boy and Moro through the binoculars Hammar provided. They had followed the boy as he left the baron's estate in the big Scania truck, watching from a distance as he rendezvoused with Moro Part. The two then had driven on, Brand careful not to be noticed on their trail. In that way, Dollar Boy unwittingly led them to an isolated A-frame vacation home located on the banks of the frozen-over Hede River.

The highway continued west toward the Norway border, a few kilometers away. Dollar Boy and Moro parked the Scania truck in a turnout along the road. Brand pulled the Saab into a snowed-over lane nearer to the chalet. She and Hammar got out to wait and watch what was happening.

Through the binoculars, she saw Moro train his own pair of field glasses toward the isolated chalet. A fancy Volvo SUV and a Mercedes sedan were parked next to the building.

"There," Brand said. She allowed Hammar a glimpse through the binoculars, not removing the strap from around her neck. "So they are tracking the pipeline after all."

She put the glasses to her eyes again. As Brand watched a tall individual emerged from the chalet. He ducked briefly into the Mercedes, and then returned to the house carrying what looked like a bottle of booze.

"What's going on?" Hammar said. "What was that?"

"Male subject, I'd say around six feet, blond, young, maybe about thirty, black leather jacket."

"Do you see anyone else?"

"Not at the chalet," Brand said. She swung the glasses around to check on Moro and Dollar Boy.

"Dollar Boy," Brand muttered. "Where'd he get that handle, I wonder?"

"I don't know," Hammar said. "I had just a quick word with him at the baron's. I didn't have time to question him about it."

"I notice he's wearing a hat. Camouflage, hiding the pink hair. It must be hard to get lost in the crowd with a hairdo like that."

Hammar examined the darkening sky. "I'd say maybe a half hour to twilight. No moon tonight, so…"

"So we work by the light of the aurora," suggested Brand facetiously.

Downslope, the river twisted around in a long curve. Between ragged sheets of ice, the water was black. Downstream, at the inner crook of the river's bend stood the chalet. A ridge above the lodge forced the highway off to the south, further isolating the property.

Held in suspension as the last daylight faded, Brand traded the field glasses back and forth with Hammar. They surveilled the two Roma males as they surveilled the chalet. Finally she saw movement around the Scania.

"Whoa, here we go," Brand said. Dollar Boy dropped the back gate on the truck and allowed the muzzled hyena to jump off onto the snow. The animal crouched low, pushing its snout upward.

"What's happening?"

She handed the binoculars to Hammar. Brand still had not totally worked out what had been going on between Varzha, Moro and Dollar Boy, or what the baron's involvement might be. Clearly, despite the danger, the three Roma principals had somehow been able to remain in communication with each other. And someone—probably Dollar Boy, along with the beast Fenrir—had been following after Varzha and brutally eliminating her abductors at every stop along the human trafficking pipeline.

Brilliant, Brand thought. Berserker crazy, for sure, but brilliant. Instead of being a victim, the girl had turned the tables and succeeded in becoming the victimizer, first at the first stop in the trafficker's pipeline, the Manor House, then at Västvall village. Brand believed Varzha might actually deserve a medal for cleaning up her little corner of the world.

Was the same bizarre business about to happen at the little chalet on the shores of the Hede River?

"Are we going down there?" Hammar asked.

"That kid's got my Glock," Brand said. "I want it back."

"He is also in possession of a very big dog, while you are unarmed, so I'd say the balance of power tips in his direction."

Brand shook her head in frustration. "Why don't Sami immigration lawyers carry firearms? Aren't you guys natural targets for extremists and nut jobs?"

"The person most likely to be shot by your own gun is yourself," Hammar said primly. "Besides I'm a lover, not a fighter."

"You're always attempting to provide evidence of that, yeah."

"My hunting rifles are secured in a gun locker in my home."

"Well, fuck," Brand said, primarily because she couldn't think of anything else to say.

She had not allowed her eyes to stray from the binoculars, still focused on the turnout where the Scania had pulled off the highway. The light had become too dim to see much of anything with the naked eye.

"They're moving," she said.

Brand had parked the Saab on a logging lane that ran up a small rise a couple of hundred meters to the east of the chalet. Without further discussion she and Hammar moved together down the slope through a snow-locked stand of graceful fir trees. They closed in on the chalet from the east. Moro and his blond beast handler, Dollar Boy, were approaching from the west.

As she slipped and slid down the slope towards the river, Brand's mind raced, doubts dunning her at an insistent pitch. They were coming at it all wrong, she was convinced. Hammar shared a priority with Moro and Dollar Boy, to extract Varzha from the clutches of the traffickers. But the two Roma men would not stop there. They were bent on revenge, employing Fenrir as their method of terror.

"Krister," she said, breathing hard from the exertion of plowing through the deep drifts. They halted beside the icy water edge, part frozen, part roiling with deathly rushing current beneath. A large crack threatened to split the river in two, a natural parting of the seas. The water looked black deep, making Brand shiver just to look at it.

"We have to split up," she said. "You head off Moro and the kid. I'll get into the chalet for the girl."

"I have to confess I'm a little hesitant about confronting demon-dogs from Norse mythology," Hammar said.

"It'll be all right," Brand responded. "Fenrir's chained and wearing his muzzle."

She pushed Hammar in an upriver direction while she turned toward the woods between the riverbank and the chalet. The strategy prompted more questions than it answered. Splitting forces in the face of the enemy was always portrayed as an ultimate mistake in warfare.

And what was the plan if she somehow managed to slip into the chalet without being detected? Scoop up the girl and run? They had been forced into one of the single worst decisions in any situation: well, we have to do something. Wouldn't it be better if they just waited for everyone else to battle it out and then step in and pick up the pieces?

Brand half turned back toward the river to call out to Hammar when what she witnessed stopped her cold.

A black-masked figure materialized in the fading light. It seemed to levitate out of the woods to land on the river ice. She could hardly believe what she was seeing. An additional actor in the drama had appeared out of nowhere, on skis, wearing snow camouflage and hefting a sleek-looking battle axe.

The action went down in dead silence, Brand's scream dying in her throat. A quick, monstrous swipe of the weapon, and the newcomer dropped Hammar where he stood. Brand felt the hit herself, falling to her knees in the snow, her breath knocked out of her. It had clearly been a death blow.

As if the first figure had magically cloned itself, a second identical one appeared, also flying through the air and landing expertly on skis.

It happened in an instant. With a single horrible, dismissive movement, the two commandos kick-shoved Hammar's crumpled body into the river, dumping him as casually as if disposing of a bag of garbage between the sheets of ice. Brand heard the faint splash and saw the body disappear. The two figures whirled around and vanished back into the woods.

40

Dr. Hira Nur examined the tiny cell phone carefully, before dropping it and smashing it with her foot. The sight of the device sent everyone's head in a spin.

"You didn't search her?" screamed the heavy-set Turkish man at Jarl Voss. He sounded panicked. "We've been set up!"

"No, Fevzi, no. It's nothing. I'll take care of this," Voss said.

"We need to leave," Hira Nur said to her partner.

The pair headed down the hallway to the chalet's front room, leaving Jarl Voss behind to deal with the captive.

"The face," Fevzi snarled back at Voss. "Mind the girl's face!"

Jarl pushed Varzha back into the tiny bedroom, shoving her roughly onto the bed. He will kill me, she thought. The idea felt curiously irrelevant. She thought of Vago, and, oddly, of Luri, the Romani beggar who always took up a post near Varzha and her brother.

Her captor retrieved a plastic zip-cuff from his pocket and bound Varzha's hands tightly behind her back. "You're still goods," Jarl hissed at her furiously. The girl's eyes seemed to show contempt, not fear, enraging him further. He tied her further and left her lying on the bed.

In the main room the Turks rushed to pack up. The handsome driver now avoided Jarl's gaze.

"It's not over," protested Jarl.

"Do you think the little bitch didn't use that fucking phone to contact the police?" Fevzi demanded. "They're on their way here right now."

"Bring out the girl," Hira Nur said briskly. "We're taking her with us. You can go to hell."

"I checked that idiotic phone," Jarl said. "There was no signal."

Hira Nur pulled a handgun from her voluminous purse.

"Okay, okay," Jarl said, raising his hands in surrender. He cursed himself for leaving his little automatic in the SUV.

As he turned down the hall to the bedroom he stopped short. A strange cackling noise erupted from some kind animal in the woods outside the chalet. All the talk among the Turks halted instantly, the call sounded so odd and so close.

"Ak-ak-ak-ak-hoo-arool!"

"What the hell!" Fevzi said.

Jarl forced a laugh. "You are unfamiliar with our local wolves?"

"Ak-ak-ak-ak-hoo-arool!"

In the bedroom, an immense sense of relief flooded through Varzha. She knew what the animal howl meant. Dollar Boy and Moro had come. They were here. She was saved.

Hearing the chalet's entry door open, Jarl turned.

"Who's that?" he asked.

"Hassan, our driver," Hiru Nu said, still clearly shaken by the bizarre baying from the woods.

What came up the stairs, however, bore no resemblance to Hassan the driver. The beast seemed to grow in size as it emerged from the stairwell, bringing a foul smell of death along with it. The animal's spotted blonde fur already showed blood from its murderous work on the Turk driver. In a single bound the hyena blew past Jarl to knock the two Turkish traffickers to the floor. Fevzi and Hiru Nur attempted to crawl out of the way, but both proved within easy reach of the hyena's tremendous jaws.

Snapping off a first bite, Fenrir ripped a gobbet from the side of the woman doctor's neck. Jarl stared in horror as her carotid artery blew a great black gout of blood across the room. The beast barely stopped to swallow. It swung around to dig into Fevzi's lap, ripping and tearing while the man bellowed. Still bleeding profusely, Hira Nu collapsed forward.

That was enough for JV. He took a running leap at the chalet's bank of thermal windows, bounced off them and fell to the floor. Behind him the big beast was still slashing and tearing at the Turks, but briefly swung its scarlet snout toward Jarl. The Voss scion scrambled back to his feet, rattled in panic at the door to the deck, and finally managed to get it open.

Dollar Boy and Moro halted at the top of the stairs, gazing at the carnage in the main room. Seeing Jarl about to flee, the younger Roma shouted and raised a handgun in his direction, blowing off a single shot that went wide. Jarl tumbled out the door and onto the deck. He crawled to the railing and leaped over, running off into the woods surrounding the chalet.

Dollar Boy cursed. "Get Varzha!" he yelled, giving a rare order to Moro, a man unaccustomed to being told what to do. But the dire nature of the situation required adjustments on everyone's part.

That included Fenrir. The hyena worked at the twin carcasses slumped on the couch, gorging and swallowing, gorging and swallowing, the blond fur of its chest soaked red. The dead still let loose with random wheezes and moans, but they were clearly gone. Dollar Boy jerked the steel chain around the beast's neck, pulling it off its victims. Fenrir snarled at him, not hyena laughter at all, but a terrible low vocalization that had Dollar Boy believing he might be next.

He managed to drag the hyena out onto the deck and show him the most tantalizing sight to any predator's eyes—a prey animal running away. Jarl struggled through the drifts piled deep in the surrounding forest. Fenrir leaped over the deck railing and took the twenty feet into the snow banks below with ease. Dollar Boy trailed behind, giving shrill whistles of encouragement, as the beast closed on the staggering, weeping figure of Jarl Voss.

It was not to be. Out of the woods came a black-masked figure on skis and in snow camo, wielding a compact crossbow. Dollar Boy didn't see the bolt fly but saw the effect of its impact. Fenrir fell mid-leap, skidding across the snow and winding up in an unnatural posture, struggling to rise but unable to do so.

Dollar Boy rushed forward. With its nasty habits and craven behavioral tics, the spotted hyena is a difficult animal to love, but the species had its fans. The pink-haired Romani teen was one of them. He knelt beside Fenrir, real grief washing over him, seeing the shaft of the bolt embedded in the creature's noble heart.

In a reflexive move Dollar Boy raised the Glock in his hand. Steadying the weapon, he shot the wielder of the crossbow who had taken down his cherished totem animal. Wild as his aim was, with his heart overcome emotionally and eyes dimmed with tears, he still managed to make a clean hit.

A kill shot to the head.

The strange ski commando fell backward into the snow.

Dollar Boy could not quite believe it, but another similar figure stepped into the place of the dead one. This one held a sleek metallic axe.

Dollar Boy had a gun. Checkmate, mate. He again aimed the pistol and pulled the trigger.

Nothing happened. The Glock merely dry-fired with a sickening click. Fetishizing the stolen weapon as he did, petting it obsessively in his cubicle bedroom at the dormitory on the baron's estate, Dollar Boy had never accurately counted the number of rounds remaining in the magazine. He labored under the delusion that he could go on firing the pistol forever.

In the last instant of his life, Dollar Boy was gifted with an uncommon vision, the sight of a battle axe arcing through air, about to deliver the blow that would split his head apart. He had not time to form the thought that he had been blessed with a warrior's way of death, and had thereby gained an automatic entry into Valhalla.

41

Ylva and Malte had formulated their mission that evening with their usual precision. The primary directive was to preserve the life of their common cousin's worthless son, Jarl. No Voss shall die, no matter how idiotic and feckless he might be. That led to an obvious choice of tactic. Surprise would be the only way to go.

Tactics determined equipment. Skis, yes, but no rifles, although Ylva and Malte were both Olympic-level athletes in the ski-and-shoot sport of the biathlon. They'd bring along their absurdly customized, deadly accurate Anschutz 1827F .22s, as well as more transportable long-guns, but would leave all the firepower behind in the SUV.

Instead, they would employ knives, crossbows, and, for flair, the battle axes that they had practiced endlessly with as teens, but never got to use in actual battle. Malte was more than proficient in every weapon imaginable, but in axe technique he yielded to Ylva, who had named her blade after a she-troll.

"Are we being childish, do you think?" She and her close-as-kissing cousin sharpened their axe blades in the motor pool workshop at the Voss family estate in Västvall.

"To me, the challenge of limiting ourselves is invigorating," Malte replied. "If you told me, 'bare hands only,' I'd go along with that, too."

Ylva felt the same way. Since childhood she and Malte had mirrored each other's looks, moods, and desires. Twin cousins, they called themselves. "Ylte and Malva," the other members of the family teased.

So.

Silence, stealth, cunning. Their bywords for the mission.

It was easy enough to pick up the trail of the blue Saab as it left the baron's estate, heading into the mountains toward the border of Norway. There was only a single main highway threading through the area, running alongside the Hede River. Malte drove the Porsche Macan turbo, hanging back from their quarry, moving up meter by meter for a visibility check before dropping off again.

Ylva agreed with Malte that the New York detective and her Sami partner would be forced to stop before the Norwegian border. They were most likely heading to where their idiot cousin Jarl was hiding out. No one in the Voss family could understand how Hammar and Brand were able to track Jarl's progress through the country so closely. Everywhere Jarl went, the two seemed to show up.

"Probably some GPS device," Gabriel Voss had said, igniting a family discussion on whether any technology existed that could track a GPS tracker. After a quick internet search Malte reported that there didn't seem to be.

"You'll have to invent one, Gabriel," he said lightly to his uncle.

"Not a bad idea," the man said. "But you two can't wait around for that."

Following Veronika Brand and Krister Hammar proved to be the next best opportunity. Jarl Voss had clearly gone rogue, embarked on one of his wild-hair adventures. Via GPS tracker or some other mysterious way, Brand and Hammar had known where he was every step of the journey.

"Find the damned idiot," Gabriel had told Ylva and Malte. "Bring Jarl back and we'll put him in a barrel, feed him through a hole. He gives us any more trouble, we plug up the hole."

On getting the call from Magnusson, the baron's man, Ylva and Malte had geared up, commando style, and moved out. While driving they liked to play opera arias at top volume. The Porsche Macan sported a bumper sticker that said, in Swedish, "How to win a biathlon—Anyone passes you on skis, shoot that fucker in the ass."

When the Saab had stopped and pulled into the woods, they did the same, posting themselves on a ridge above a cottage along the river.

"The dead man's place," Ylva whispered as they examined the chalet through field glasses. "It belonged to Mattias Rapp, Jarl's right hand."

Malte nodded. "The body in our game locker at Västvall."

"So it would make sense Jarl would set up there, waiting to cross the border," Ylva said.

From their post on the ridge they were blocked from a view of Jarl's Volvo parked on the other side of the chalet. The sighting would have sealed the deal for them. Neither could they see the big Scania truck parked farther down the highway.

As usual in such situations, they indulged in a quick back and forth over choice of ski wax, with Malte arguing for high fluoro and Ylva rolling her eyes.

"It's like minus eight and dropping, this snow is way too dry for high fluoro," she said, kicking a small flurry at him with her boot. "Gotta go blue."

They were waxing not for grip but for speed. It wasn't a debate, not really, more a pressure-valve release of nervousness and anticipation. They went with LF, blue low fluoro wax.

It turned out not to matter much. They had great good luck, schussbooming down off the ridgeline like valkyries as darkness dropped. Suddenly there was Krister Hammar, walking alone on the frozen river. Ylva dispatched the meddlesome lawyer with a battle axe blow to the head. Together she and Malte dumped his body through a jagged crevice in the ice, watching it slide into the river's abyss.

But disaster struck a few minutes later, on their approach to the chalet through the woods. Ylva worried about not knowing the exact location of the New York detective. She feared Brand might be armed. At any rate the woman might prove to be a hard case. Instead, they came upon Jarl Voss, consumed with fear, nose running with snot, fleeing panicked through the woods with a monster wolf on his tail.

She and Malte had to react purely on instinct. Malte dropped the bizarre beast with a single crossbow shot through the heart, a spectacular feat given the low-light conditions and movement of the target. Ylva gave a yell of triumph and approval.

"*Fräckt!*"

It was to be the last achievement of Ylva's hero cousin. Yet another strange apparition arrived on the scene, stranger still than the beast, a young punk with his pink hair shorn into a Mohawk style haircut.

The newcomer had a pistol in his hand. He raised a gun and fired.

Her beloved Malte fell next to the downed beast.

Ylva retaliated, killing the shooter.

She knelt and put an arm underneath Malte, cradling her twin cousin, watching the light fade from his eyes.

"Help me!" she screamed at the pathetic, fear-struck Jarl.

The stupid kid stared, paralyzed.

Feeling a rare, gut-wrenching sense of panic herself, Ylva dragged the bleeding Malte out of the woods with no help from her younger cousin. Jarl was a Voss, so she resisted the urge to end his pathetic life. He was the cause of this fiasco. His drug dealing and human trafficking had led the family down an unsavory path they had not chosen.

The two managed to lift Malte into the Porsche. While Jarl drove, Ylva tended to Malte, checking for a pulse, shining a flashlight in his eyes, monitoring for signs of life, performing what limited triage she could. It all seemed hopeless. She could see brain matter amid the clumps of clotted blood from his bullet-shattered skull. Malte was gone, or going quickly. Ylva, frantic, screamed at Jarl to hurry his sad ass.

To no avail. Malte Voss breathed his last on the pedal-to-the-metal journey to seek emergency help at the Voss Medical Center in Sveg. Feeling his pulse fade, Ylva didn't want to believe it.

"Faster, you fool!"

"It's too late," Jarl said.

"Shut the hell up!"

"Look, we should just go home."

"Home?" Ylva yelled. "Home, you ass?"

"There'll be, like, outsider eyes in Sveg," Jarl said, attempting to reason with his raging cousin. "Doctors, police. They'll want explanations. We need time. The family will have to figure out how to play Malte's death."

"He's not dead!" Ylva shrieked.

Jarl looked at her with pity in his eyes. She couldn't stand it. He was about to speak again. She silenced him with a punch alongside the head. Jarl took the abuse. He had no defense against the wrath of Ylva, none at all. Even as children, she had always terrified him.

Malte's death. The two words practically stopped Ylva's heart. Her fury collapsed into despair.

"Just get us to Sveg, Jarl," she said quietly. "Just get us to the Medical Center."

A weather front advanced from Norway, and it began to snow.

42

When she saw Hammar's crumpled form sink from sight, Brand broke out of her paralysis and sprinted toward the river. As she hit the bank her feet went out from under her. She sprawled backward. Limping upright, she staggered toward the stain of bright crimson blood, splashed around the hole where the wounded body of Krister Hammar had disappeared.

Brand's disturbing memory of seeing Hammar pushed into the icy water worked on her, but she forced it out of her mind. Instead, she recalled stories of people falling into freezing water and surviving for several minutes, fifteen even, maybe as long as a half hour. Something about the extremities shutting down and brain function slowing to a crawl, with life being maintained on oxygen already in the circulatory system.

Don't give up. Never give up. Always the driver, never the passenger.

But she couldn't bring herself to lower her body into the flowing, bone-chilling current. A paralyzing vision of the East River seized her mind. She commanded her limbs to move. They refused to obey. She yelled Hammar's name, as if that would do a damned thing.

His words at the sauna came to her. Don't think. Just do.

Fear choking her, she kneeled at the water's edge feverishly searching with her hands in the black water. Her upper limbs instantly froze in the frigid water. She flipped her body and committed to the cold, the darkness helping to pull her in deeper. She felt her feet land on the mucky bottom as the water reached to her chin. The cold pressed every bit of air from her lungs, but she compelled herself to feel around in the dark current, hoping against hope.

Nothing.

Panic-stricken, flashing on her own previous flirtations with death, she tried to scramble back onto the safe land, fell, and almost got pulled back in by the weight of her own body. Finally succeeding in heaving her body out, she lay there, helpless, unable to catch her breath, watching a black curtain fall in her mind.

She could not do it. She simply could not go back in. The darkness defeated her.

He's down there, she swore to herself. His head might be split open by a berserker's battle axe, he might be drowned and frozen, but she had to retrieve him, dead or alive.

Looking down river, Brand could perceive the vague outline of a contorted tree, half submerged, half sticking up out of the ice.

She could not think of doing what she had to do. She could not even imagine thinking it. And she most definitely could not do it.

He would do it for you, came the thought.

She rolled over, sucked air into her lungs with great freezing gulps, then flopped forward, slipping into the current, forcing her body through the chunks of ice debris haphazardly scattered along the shore.

The East River had reached out and grabbed her once again.

Darkness. Cold. The world telescoped down to those two qualities alone. She would die.

Kicking her feet, she found again the squishy bottom. Moving with the flow, she bumped along, a blind woman, a bobbing, sightless human ice cube. Her body kept pushing up against the fractured ice sheets, forcing her back with every labored step.

She counted off the seconds. Five, ten, fifteen. She thought of the exotic creatures deep in the Pacific's Mariana Trench, fish that carried their own illumination with them. Clawing at her belt, her cold-stiffened fingers found her small tactical flashlight, a little Stinger that had been with her since her subway patrol days.

The cold took over her body. Her brain began to shut down, her thoughts went foggy.

She would not find Hammar's broken body. She would die, condemned to a freezing underwater grave.

Miraculously, the Stinger worked underwater, illuminating the unforgiving pull of current forcing her forward. But it didn't matter, since the flashlight's beam penetrated only a few feet.

The ghostly shape of the submerged tree came into focus. An ethereal figure hung in the dendritic tangle, swaying slowly back and forth in the flowing water.

Brand almost floated right past Hammar. She dug her boots into the shifting sand on the bottom, found a foothold, and grabbed hold of his collar. He was impossibly snarled among the branches. She worked to dislodge him. Despite not feeling connected, her frozen hands followed instructions from her brain.

She dropped the Stinger and yanked. Branch and body moved together. With a heave she managed to break the man free, but the effort cost her. For a sick second the two of them floated free, and the current took her again.

Kicking out with one foot, Brand caught hold of a gnarled branch, using it as a lifeline to pull herself toward the shoreline. Heaving the Hammar's lifeless body forward, she clawed out of the relentless flow, dragging herself and her burden through the cold slosh of the shallows onto solid ground. The still, icy air froze them in place.

They lay side by side for a long moment, two frozen corpses, one more dead than alive, one more alive than dead. Brand faded in and out, her body shaking involuntarily in survival mode. Her companion was unnaturally still. She felt unable to move with purpose. They would perish there together.

A few snowflakes fluttered in the air. Staring upward, Brand could see clouds splinter, revealing the stars in the sky. Far off, she heard the sound of a single gunshot from the direction of the chalet. The report came to her faint and muffled, but rang out in a way that seemed familiar.

Her Glock, Brand thought, fired off inside the chalet.

After a beat, another shot from the same gun, sharper this time, echoing across the flat river to the opposite shore. She concluded that the shooter had now brought the pistol outside, emerging from Mattias Rapp's cottage.

They were coming. She had to move. Brand judged afterwards that it was the hardest thing she had ever done, hauling herself upright that night. She peeled herself off the winter ground with a slight ripping sound, because in the mere seconds she had lain there her sopping clothes had frozen to the earth.

Brand found strength she didn't know she had, humping Hammar's dead weight to the car, placing him upright in the front seat. With her cold-stiffened hands, she eventually located the ignition keys to the car. Once the engine turned over she put up the heat to full blast. With great difficulty, she began guiding the car on the twenty-minute drive to the medical center in Sveg.

When the interior warmed she pulled to the side of the road and stripped off Hammar's jacket. Shivering uncontrollably, she struggled to remove a sweater and underneath that a long sleeved undershirt, stripping him to his bare skin. She knew the cold water drill—remove wet and frozen clothing immediately. For herself, there was only time to take off her sodden jacket.

With that done, she drove on. Her lifeless passenger slumped in the seat beside her. The aurora flared green and purple off to her left.

She had no choice. The Voss Medical Center in Sveg was her only hope. She sped through the deserted downtown to the outskirts. The brick rockpile looked dark and empty. A lone blue-white sign shone like a beacon: *Akutmottagning*. Brand didn't know what that meant (acute care?), but it looked promising.

She left the Saab running with Hammar still inside. She dashed to the front door. It slid open noiselessly. Incredibly, the place seemed vacant.

"Help!" she cried. "Someone!" She attempted to put Swedish spin on the word. "*Hjälp!*"

Her call echoed through an empty hallway. She had a frantic thought that the Voss family had somehow ordered care withdrawn for their enemy clan, the Dalgrens.

Then a trio of medical personnel spilled out of an inner doorway. Rattled and pushed beyond the limits of her endurance, Brand burst into tears upon seeing them. She couldn't find words. Gesturing to the vehicle parked outside, she sank to her knees.

The night turned senseless. She later remembered only bits and pieces of the first few hours. The hospital personnel stretchered Hammar in. As he passed Brand was felt certain he was dead. His corpse-like pallor gave her little hope. The wheeled gurney disappeared into the bowels of the medical center.

Additional figures in scrubs appeared. They seemed to be concerned for her—for Brand herself, while the real worry had to be Hammar.

"No, no, not me," she mumbled, as they ushered her into a curtained cubicle and began to take her vitals. "Help Krister," she said weakly.

The doctor assigned to her care, a youngish woman with a brisk, no-nonsense manner, shocked Brand with a curt announcement.

"Your body temperature is low," she said in English. "Thirty-two-point-two degrees."

As far as Brand's brain could tell, this meant she was essentially deceased. The blood in her body had been frozen. But the doctor clarified the situation by converting the number from Celsius into Fahrenheit, a calculation that at the moment Brand herself would have found impossible.

Even so, a core body temperature of ninety degrees was in the emergency range. She had presented at the medical center with ghost-white skin and enlarged pupils.

Treatment of hypothermia the staff could handle, having had a lot of experience in that particular area. Hammar's case presented more difficulties. Apart from a head wound, where the battle axe had scalped off a section of skin, his time in the water had shut down brain function to a degree that was impossible to determine. He remained comatose and unresponsive. Brand was not allowed to see him.

As her mind swam into clearer focus, she kept anxiously asking about Hammar's condition. The doctor—her name tag read "Annika Gedin, *Läkare*"—tried to calm her. Brand kept babbling.

"He was in the water...through the river ice...he drowned..."

"Yes, yes," Annika said soothingly. "Your friend is in very serious condition. But he is still alive. I have read of such cases. All is not lost."

The woman perched alongside Brand on the hospital bed. "Do you know about something called the Mammalian Dive Response? The Diving Reflex? Parasympathetic stimulus to the cardiac pacemaker increases in response to environmental conditions."

Brand wondered if the doctor was speaking English after all.

"It happens when the human body is submerged, especially when the water is very cold. The circulatory system attempts to save itself. There's bradycardia, or extreme slowing of the heart rate. Oxygen in the blood withdraws from the extremities and concentrates in the brain and vital organs."

"So he'll be all right?"

Annika reached out to pat Brand's arm. "Krister is not out of the woods yet—is that how you say it? He's lost blood. His head wound is very serious, but the blow did not crack the skull."

The doctor smiled. "Is your friend a hard-headed individual?"

"No," Brand said. "He's a mushy-headed old softie."

Annika informed Brand that they would be airlifting Hammar to a central care center as soon as he was fully stabilized.

The next morning, before full light, Brand crept out of her own room and searched the cavernous medical center, passing like a revenant through the empty corridors.

She found Hammar, unconscious, his head wrapped in bandages so completely that it was difficult for her to be sure it was him. What little of his face that was visible displayed bruising and a harsh frostbite coloring.

But the respirator's wheeze and click reassured her. He was still breathing. Hammar would never be able to forgive Brand if she had pulled a mere vegetable out of the drink. He had better come out of his coma, she thought, and tell her how they would both live to sauna together again.

There in the darkened, eerily silent medical center, Brand climbed into bed beside Hammar. She cuddled up and slept beside him until a shocked nurse came to separate them a few hours later.

As she shook the cobwebs from her brain a single overriding conviction gripped her. The Vosses would be coming for them. The Voss Medical Center would be the first place they would look. She and Hammar had taken refuge in the lion's den.

Part three: The vengeful master

And a terrible stench rose up from the dead bodies lying in the square and that was a pitiful and everlasting sight, how the blood-soaked water and wood ran down the gutters.

Svenska Krönika, an eyewitness account
of the 1520 Stockholm Bloodbath

43

Polisinspektör Oliver Engmark, the first responding officer from the tiny village of Hede, felt himself in over his head. The scene at the Rapp chalet along the Hede River overwhelmed him.

Engmark should say the former chalet of Mattias Rapp, since the structure had already burned to the ground by the time he arrived. Fire crews could do no more than wet down the smoking ruins, standing in silence, taking only a cursory notice of the dying hisses and cracks as the blaze consumed the last of the structure.

What a fiasco. Engmark had never seen anything like it. In the drive sat a burned out Mercedes, an expensive current model sedan, and an equally upscale Volvo SUV, also destroyed. Two dead within the house, plus one male on the drive just outside of it, half cooked by the flames but still recognizable as human.

Complicating his preliminary investigation, snow had increased steadily since the previous evening. The soft, accumulating fall obliterated anything in the form of impression evidence left on the grounds. Certainly there were signs that something happened on the shores of the river, but *polisinspektör* Engmark had no idea what. He put a call into the National Forensic Centre, requesting personnel reinforcement, and stood by to bide his time.

The valley of the Hede served in former days as a haven for cross-border smuggling. Before that, in the medieval era, it was an avenue of invasion. The kind of violence he saw was more suited to those periods than to the relatively quiet times to which Engmark had become accustomed. A few domestic disturbances were the worst the district of Härjedalen could offer its law enforcement officers.

Engmark only dimly recalled the last homicide in the area, over two years ago, a stir crazy wife shooting her husband during a stretch of unrelenting winter storms. The dead man had not been careful enough where he spat his tobacco, Engmark remembered.

His trainee, *Polisaspirant* Lovisa Svärd, insisted on donning the full Tyvek hazmat suit and booties. She stepped through the charred, collapsed interior of the house. What she hoped to find that Engmark might have missed in his own inspection was a mystery. He stood in the driveway and looked on. Perhaps it was a good idea for the young trainee to get her feet wet.

"Two deceased here," she called out, which Engmark had already established. "Adult male and adult female."

Yes, yes.

He watched Svärd crouch over the bodies, only partially visible to Engmark because so much building debris stood in the way. The trainee wielded a pen or a probe of some sort and poked at the corpses. He was about to warn her off and say they must wait for forensic specialists when she called out.

"Looks as if mortality preceded the fire," Svärd said.

How could she know that? Engmark thought.

"How could you know that?" he shouted.

"Because she bothered to examine the oral cavity of the deceased," said a voice behind him.

Engmark turned to see the celebrated Stockholm Detective Inspector Vincent Hult on the scene. The overwhelmed Engmark felt the earth shift beneath his feet. The new arrival represented such an influx of political weight that the local constable experienced an impulse to grovel.

"Detective Inspector Vincent Hult!" he barked out. "I am *polisinspektör* Oliver of the Hede substation! Thank you for responding so quickly to my call!"

The response time was indeed remarkable. The cottage fire had been called in almost simultaneously at 2312, first by a passing motorist and then minutes later by the owner of a residence across the river. Engmark marked his arrival on the scene at 0207, behind the fire crew. He put a request out for aid at 0420 or thereabouts.

Now here it was a little after 0800, and Hult had made the trip from Stockholm in record time. Unless…a police helicopter?

"If our two DOA's had still been alive when the fire hit," Hult explained, "their respiratory tracts would display evidence of smoke inhalation. But I would bet Miss HazMat over there found the nasopharyngeal epidermis to be pink as cotton candy, though perhaps a little fried by ambient heat."

"Yes," said the constable.

The man informed Engmark that a simple "Hult" would do when addressing him. He took charge of the scene with breathless efficiency. Shooing Trainee Svärd out of the burned house, Hult ordered her to walk the driveway for evidence. He seemed most interested in the relatively intact corpus lying sprawled near the chalet, dead from either smoke inhalation or as a result of a smashed skull.

Engmark stuck to Hult, kneeling with him beside the corpse. Taking the initiative, the constable introduced a pen into the mouth of the deceased, hoping to find whether any fire effect was pre- or post-mortem. Hult gently batted the forensic attempt away.

"I'd say the head injury alone was enough, wouldn't you agree?" The wound gaped, brain matter clearly visible, but now collecting a light frosting of snow from the persistent flurries in the air.

"The Mercedes sedan?" Hult asked. "Any intel on that?"

"Norwegian plates, registered to an Oslo import-export concern." Engmark said, glad he could at least demonstrate his investigative prowess by offering this bit of information.

"Has anyone checked with the border control station at Västra Malmagen, to see when the car might have come across?"

Brilliant! Engmark thought. Hult deserved all his awards and accolades. A true genius of a police detective!

"I was just doing that when you arrived," Engmark lied. He wondered why the Stockholm detective had not inquired about the other burned out hulk, the Volvo SUV.

Hult took a last look at the victim, closely examining the head wound, then rose to his feet.

"Your forensic team," Engmark asked, rising with him, "is it by any chance coming to examine the torched vehicles?"

"Oh, I'm here 'all by my lonesome,'" Hult said, pronouncing the phrase in English. "I happened to be in the area and heard the call go out."

Engmark marveled. Masterful! What a man! A real bloodhound—not in from Stockholm at all—happened to be in the area!

From her position halfway up the drive, Lovisa Svärd whistled, the type of loud piercing sound for which Engmark had never developed the knack. She gestured off into the dense forest on the far side of the burned-out chalet.

"Something happening over there," she called.

They skirted the trees at the edge of the property. A faint track in broken snow ran off to the west. Svärd had a head start. Engmark followed behind Hult as they forced their way through thigh-high drifts.

"Trainee!" the constable shouted ahead. "Halt your progress!"

Odd that Engmark hadn't discovered the strange, bloody scene before, in the woods only a hundred meters from the cottage. The sound of it was certainly loud enough. When they got closer the sight proved garish.

"Oh, lord," the atheist Engmark murmured. "Another body."

Crows and ravens several dozen strong picked at something half covered in the snow, something blood-streaked and large. A pair of pine martens, perched comically on their back haunches, watched from a safe distance, but skedaddled on the approach of the humans.

The birds, however, had to be scared off by Trainee Svärd. Several swooped at their harasser before retreating. They settled on branches of the surrounding birches and pines, looking on with their blank, dark eyes.

"An animal," Svärd reported. "Dead."

"We can see that, Lovisa," Engmark said.

Hult gazed down silently at the crow-ravaged form.

"That's the biggest damned wolf I've ever seen," Engmark said.

"It's not a wolf," Hult returned. Then he did an odd thing. Hult physically and roughly herded the constable and his trainee backward, away from the scene.

He addressed Engmark and Svärd in the dry, domineering manner of a military man commanding subordinates. "Listen to me very carefully."

The two nodded, caught by his tone.

"I want an absolute embargo on this," he said. "No one, I mean nobody outside the three of us, hears about it. You keep your damned mouths shut, do you understand?"

"Yes, Detective Hult," the two uniformed cops mumbled.

After that, the mood at the crime scene changed. Hult instructed Svärd to cordon off the area where the dead animal lay. By the time an elite team of investigators showed up, Hult had already sent the constable and his trainee back to Hede village. He made them swear, as they departed, to total silence about what they had seen in the woods.

44

So many came from so far. Varzha had never seen such a gathering of travelers, hundreds of men, women, and children who appeared as if summoned to Dollar Boy's funeral by a higher authority. They crowded into the big rented dance hall in Spånga, a suburb on the far edges of Stockholm.

She was proud of her people. Some of the cars pulled up in front of the hall were beautiful and expensive, including late model Volvos, Mercedes, a Lexus, even a Rolls Royce. Sure there were battered old wrecks that blew smoke, too, and mud-splattered pickup trucks. Many of the attendees traveled by public transport, but everyone turned out in their best finery. Tradition called for white symbolizing purity, or red, which represented vitality. Some now chose to wear black, the universal color of mourning.

The beauty of the Roma was on display. In keeping with the deceased boy's nickname, American dollar bills covered Lash Mirga's casket. How had people found so many? Varzha wondered. She herself had trouble coming up with a single bill, until her brother Vago reminded her that he had kept a cache of useless foreign currency collected during their stints of street begging.

The bloody scene at the Hede River kept intruding in her mind, the shock of seeing dead bodies while Moro's strong arms lifted her above it all. The images would not relent.

She remembered something Moro Part had told her when she was barely eleven years old, recently removed from the violence she had witnessed in her village in Romania. The attack on her parents had been ugly. Vago raged forward to stop it, and he, too, was beaten savagely. She still heard the angry bellows of the crowd, still felt the heat of the fire incinerating those she loved. Since then there was a stone where her heart had been.

"We must take our destiny in our own hands, Varzha," Moro Part had told her. "The *icke-romer* will never give it up to us. We must seize it."

Moro embarked on a campaign of education and indoctrination. He instructed Varzha in the ways of the world, which in his view existed entirely in black and white. Romani or gentile. Varzha's people on one side, and on the other the "*icke-romer*," as Moro sometimes called them, the non-Romani.

Vengeance figured prominently in Moro's world-view. An eye for an eye. Accept no blow without responding two-fold, four-fold, a hundred-fold. For a long time, Varzha trusted Moro. He was a rock to which she clung. Now, feeling the sadness of Dollar Boy's passing, gazing at his coffin only a few steps away, Varzha questioned everything she heard. Was vengeance the only way forward?

Moro did all the organizing of mourners, she knew. The gathering was as much to honor Moro's reach and power as it was to mark Dollar Boy's death. The influence of Moro Part as a *Kalderaš* godfather could be measured not only by the number of mourners, but also in the speed with which they came together. A mere two days after the violent "Battle of Hede River"—as Moro was calling it, half in jest—here they all were.

Varzha wore black. No more the white-faced wedding dress girl—she was through with begging—she wore a modest silk dress for the funeral.

Gold coins draped around her neck, strung on a black ribbon. Considering her presence at Dollar Boy's death, Varzha thought she might be treated as an honored guest at the funeral. It was not so. She felt shunted aside and ignored. Lash Mirga's family sat beside the casket and greeted guests. She knew not one of them.

Varzha recalled the only image she had seen of the great poet and singer, Papuszka. In the photograph, her wise face showed its age. She still wore her hair in long braids. To Varzha, Papuszka was a vision of the past. To be honored, yes, but not imitated slavishly.

Times changed. Varzha was not the same person she had been only a few days before. The supposed changeless realities of the Romani had become transformed, whether her people admitted it or not. The rules for a *Kalderaš* "maiden" were changing—even that word sounded old-fashioned now. Varzha imagined the world opening for her like the petals of a rose. She wondered what possibilities might exist for her, beyond the lockstep inevitability of marriage and family.

Mooning around Varzha at the funeral, Luri Kováč represented another figure stubbornly holding onto the past. The tongue-tied street mendicant had often taken up a post on Drottninggatan near to where Vago and Varzha usually stood. He had cleaned himself up for the occasion of the funeral, wearing a bright red felt vest. Shaved, trimmed, and well groomed, he now less resembled a bear than a bull.

Wherever Varzha went at the gathering, there was Luri. When she approached the casket to lay down her dollar offering, just as she most wished to be most alone with her thoughts, Luri approached and hovered beside her like a bodyguard. Though she was fond of him, she did not need the protections he offered up. In particular she did not believe that Dollar Boy's *muló*, his ghost, might haunt her in the future. She was through with such superstitions.

Romani caskets were always extra large, in order to fit the possessions of the dead. For the journey into the afterlife, Dollar Boy's body was adorned with clothes, photographs, his beloved iPhone, a collection of knives, tufts of hair from the animals he took care of at the Baron's estate.

All the items had been smuggled out of the barracks at Gammelhem without the Baron knowing anything. In fact, none of the non-Romani knew the true circumstances of Dollar Boy's death, not the Baron or Magnusson, not the police, no one beyond Moro's inner circle. He merely failed to appear at the estate, failed to return from his vet run to Uppsala, failed to bring back Fenrir. Such was the absolute separateness of the Romani world from the *gadje* that a huge funeral like this could go off unremarked and unnoticed by the Swedish community at large.

Varzha meditated bitterly on the injustice that no elaborate funeral arrangements had been mounted for Lel. Her sworn sister, and Dollar Boy's intended, had perished by her own hand after enduring the physical limits of brutality at the hands of foreign beasts. Through no fault of her own, the girl had died in disgrace. The Romani community turned its back on her. Such was the way of the world, Varzha thought. Perhaps her bitterness was itself *gadje*, influenced by their ideas of equality and social justice.

Pallbearers loaded Lash Mirga's casket into a station wagon to begin its long journey across the sea, finally to arrive at a cemetery in Romania. The women's lamentations wound down and the vehicles began pulling away into the night. Varzha found Moro sitting alone in the dance hall. The man looked tired, dazed by alcohol, but supremely satisfied at the obvious success of the gathering. He did not remark upon her presence as she sat down next to him on one of the folding chairs set up for the funeral.

Varzha stayed silent. Moro sighed. She sighed. There existed a bond between them. Moro had physically removed her from the clutches of the traffickers. He had carried her past the ravaged bodies, in a place where the sharp scent of death hung like a fog. He had set fire to the Hede River cottage as they left it.

The big man had always been gentle and kind to her. She felt not a whiff of judgment from him. On the contrary, she suspected that the Romani godfather admired her. Yet Varzha had not been prepared for repercussions of that terrible, elemental, insistent word, vengeance. The two syllables could be spoken easily, tossed off, as if they meant no more than a blowing of the nose, or coughing—something done and quickly forgotten.

She did not grieve over the deaths of the traffickers. But sitting there in full view of a boy cut down before he had much time to live, Varzha was no longer certain of her own righteousness. Or of Moro Part's.

Together she and Moro had brought back the body of poor Dollar Boy and disposed of the Baron's old Scania truck. They watched the vehicle plunge into the icy waters of a lake somewhere in the *fjäll*. Varzha was unclear exactly where. The sight of the huge truck breaking through the ice was spectacular. Its destruction made the switch to the greater comfort in Moro's well-heated Mercedes sedan all the more pleasurable.

So it was over, Varzha thought. But on their drive back to Stockholm, Moro began to speak about loose ends left untied. He reminded her that Jarl Voss still walked the earth.

"The Turkish traffickers, yes, they won't bother us again," Moro said. "But Jarl Voss escapes retribution. This is not a suitable outcome. This is not our way."

Varzha wondered if such a worm of a man as Jarl Voss was worth her anger and her effort. Moro often made reference to an ancient tradition among the *Kalderaš Romani*, to destroy enemies "unto the third or fourth generation," as the Old Testament advised. He spoke about the Romans sowing the fields of Carthage with salt, in order that no phoenix would ever rise from those ashes.

For the time being, she and Moro Part sat quietly together, experiencing a pleasant air of exhaustion, grief and camaraderie. They idly watched the workers cleaning up the remnants of the gathering at the big dance hall. Finally she broke the silence.

"Why must it be unto the third or fourth generation?" she asked.

Sleepy Moro did not want to be disturbed. "Tomorrow, we talk."

But Varzha felt the need to put her mind at ease. "Jarl Voss, well, he's a gay boy, so he probably won't have kids. How do we destroy him unto his children, much less his grandchildren and great-grandchildren?"

"You are thinking wrong," Moro told her. He sat upright and stretched, then recited the Biblical passage. "For I am the Lord thy God, a jealous God, visiting the iniquity of the fathers upon their children unto the third and fourth generation, to them that hate me."

"Third or fourth? Which is it?"

"I've always thought to err on the side of making certain," Moro responded.

"So, okay, the fourth generation. But what does that mean in the case of Jarl Voss? I still don't understand."

"You have to go the other way," Moro instructed her, interrupting his lesson with an enormous yawn. "Jarl Voss, he represents the first generation. Who is his father?"

"Elias Voss," Varzha answered. Moro had schooled her in the Voss family's genealogy.

"Yes, so that is what?"

"The second generation." She marked the count on her fingers, careful to use the left hand in the way that her grandmother had taught her, then stopped—shaking her hands as if shaking off the old superstitions.

"And who is Elias Voss's father?"

"Vilgot Voss," she answered. "Vilgot Voss is the third generation."

Here was the other side of Moro Part. Not the kindly man who watched over her and Vago and petted them and brought them pizza. This was the Old Testament voice from the past. Varzha came to the sickening realization that Moro did not believe the job was done.

"Yes, all right. And Vilgot Voss's father?"

"Loke Voss, the fourth generation."

"So there you have your answer."

"Loke, the old man, he's like a hundred years."

"No one is too old to die. In fact quite the opposite. He should be dead already."

The overhead lighting abruptly went out in the dance hall, so that the only illumination was the flicker of prayer candles. The sweet strains of a sad song floated over the dim interior. It was Vago Luna, playing his child-size violin, "Blue Eyes Crying in the Rain."

Luri Kováč performed a lonely solo soft-shoe in the center of the empty, unlit floor. The few Romani women who still remained in the cavernous space began to weep again.

Moro held up the four fingers on his massive, paw-like left hand, folding them down one by one.

"Jarl Voss, Elias Voss, Vilgot Voss, Loke."

45

Human joy has many different expressions, but human grief is more single-minded.

Four hundred and fifty kilometers to the northwest of the Stockholm dance hall where the Romani memorialized Dollar Boy, another funeral gathering occurred with far different mourners in attendance. Though they were fewer and perhaps less exuberant than the Roma, the same black thread ran through the weave.

Jarl had not delivered his dead cousin to the Voss Medical Center in Sveg. Ylva kept yelling at him to go to the big hospital facility that the family had funded. Repeating the demand over and over, she was clearly off her nut. Go to the Medical Center, she kept insisting.

"Better a mortuary," Jarl told her.

Ylva struck him in the mouth again. This time he slugged her back. Vanquished, the poor girl retreated, weeping, clutching Malte's dead body in her arms. They drove like that for the rest of the way to Västvall.

Junior Voss had smoothly orchestrated the public announcement of his nephew Malte Voss's death. A tragic accident, a bitterly ironic end to the life of such a brilliant marksman—that he would die by a stray rifle shot while tramping through his beloved forest at Västvall. The local constabulary accepted the version of events presented to them. The source of the bullet was delicately left uninvestigated. There were many hunters in the woods of the Voss estate that day. A communal bear hunt had been organized, with rounds going off all the time. Lynx, red fox, many hares and even a wild boar were taken, though no bear.

And tragically, supposedly, one human.

"He died doing what he loved." What a vile formulation, thought Ylva Voss, the dead man's unconsummated soul mate. Malte didn't want to die doing what he loved. He didn't want to die doing what he hated. He was thirty years old. He didn't want to fucking die at all.

A portion of Ylva's soul had been taken. She had been halved, rendered permanently off balance as surely as if a limb had been amputated, unable to walk, talk, or think normally now that Malte was gone.

Alongside the black, cruelly vibrating thread of grief, a red hot wire of fury also ran through Ylva's soul. She had no patience for mourning. The dulled and muffled quality of the family memorial, held in Vilgot's sprawling rustic lodge, angered her. Malte's biathlon friends livened up the gathering somewhat, guzzling brandy and smoking weed around a bonfire at the back of the grounds. Ylva had little tolerance for the bro attitude, either.

Thankfully Jarl made himself scarce. Ylva had already socked him more than once. Though Jarl was the stronger of the two, when it came to Ylva he turned weak. She had bent him to her will as a child and he could not undo it. Ylva took full advantage of his inability to resist. She blackened his left eye as soon as they returned to Västvall from the catastrophe along the Hede River. Jarl was the cause of it all. He slunk around the compound, retreating to his quarters, attempting to weather the storm.

Due for a reckoning, that boy. Jarl understood that fact. He avoided Ylva like the plague.

In the region of the world around Västvall, whatever Junior Voss said went. The specific circumstances of Malte's death were kept carefully under wraps. No autopsy, no official examination of the wound. If they had been conducted, tests would have determined the fatal shot came not from a hunting rifle but a 9mm round, probably fired by a Glock pistol. Questions would have multiplied. Inconsistencies in Junior's official line might be brought to light.

None of that happened. Malte's father Vilgot made a stab at rebellion, demanding a full police investigation. He was quickly voted down by the other members of the brother's generation.

"What happened?" asked a stern Junior Voss of Ylva. She was the only Voss able to bring back a coherent account of the incident.

"What happened?" echoed Vilgot Voss.

To Ylva's ears, it was like a goddamn chorus. Brothers and wives and cousins all wanted details of what went down when Malte was killed. They were like bees buzzing around her head. All she wanted to do was remain numb.

She bit off her words when responding. "I nailed the guy who shot him," she said. "Some gypsy asshole. Split his head open to the chin. He's dead. You won't see him around anymore."

Small satisfaction. "There were others," Ylva added. "The immigration lawyer, we got him, too. And the American detective woman."

"She is no longer among the living, is that correct?" asked Junior. "You took care of her also?"

Ylva didn't want to say it, didn't want to come out with the most bitter word in her life at that moment, but she forced herself. "No."

"Then you didn't finish the job?" Junior made her say it again.

"No."

"Hmm." A bullshit non-response from Junior Voss's lips. For Ylva it contained a whole encyclopedia of comment. Are you a Voss? Did you love your cousin Malte? How could you fail him in this way?

Her cousin Hans represented Ylva's only refuge from maddening grief. They met around the bonfire in the yard, lost amid the hail-fellow fraternity of biathletes.

"As soon as this is over, you and me, right?" Ylva said to him.

"Yeah, sure," Hans said. But Ylva could tell he was wavering.

"The American detective is in this business up to her neck. Plus we need to nail a few more of those Roma fuckers."

"You know, maybe we should let things cool out for a bit," Hans said. "The Hede business is all over the news."

"Damn it, Hans!" Ylva snapped, raising her voice. "Are you saying what I think you're saying? You want to back out?"

Her outburst drew the attention of the biathlon bros around the campfire. They looked over as if Ylva was harshing their mellow.

She drew Hans aside. "If that detective goes back to New York, we've lost her."

"You think?" Hans said. "Maybe it would be even better to do her over there. I could do with a trip to New York."

Ylva felt alone. All right, she thought, if I have to pursue this solo, so be it.

Her father Gabriel Voss came out of the lodge and found the two of them. "Good news and bad news," he said.

"Always the bad first, you know that, *pappa*," Ylva said.

"The Sami lawyer didn't die. He's in a coma at the hospital in Sveg, about to be airlifted to Stockholm."

Ylva cursed. "Are you sure? It can't be the guy, *pappa*—it just can't! I broke his head open. Then Malte and I threw him into the river. That body won't be discovered until the spring."

"And yet there the man is, in a hospital bed in our own medical center, a hundred kilometers away."

"No! I refuse to believe it."

"Belief isn't necessary for truth, and exists altogether outside it."

Ylva turned to Hans. "Are you coming?"

"Hold up," Gabriel said. "According to our sources, the flight for life airlift isn't happening until tomorrow morning. So a nighttime visit to the medical center would be fine."

"We have to get geared up," Ylva said.

"Your grandfather wants to speak with you, that comes first."

"All right," Ylva responded, still impatient. "So, wait, you said, bad news, good news. What's the good?"

"The American detective is with him."

"Really?"

"That's what we hear."

Ylva smiled grimly. "'Two birds with one stone,'" she said in English.

"Yes," Gabriel said.

Ylva noticed that Hans looked a little sick. He was going to be of no use, she decided. Her mind buzzing, she returned to the lodge to seek out her grandfather, Loke Voss senior.

"Hi, *farfar*," Ylva said to the old man, kneeling next to his wheelchair.

"I'm sorry for you," he said. Loke searched his granddaughter's face with his pale, watery eyes. "I know you and Malte had a special bond."

"I'm sorry for us all," she responded automatically. Save me from age, Ylva thought. Perhaps, she considered, it was better that Malte died young. His beautiful self would never have to suffer the indignity of years.

Everyone in the family feared that Malte's death would be a shock to his grandfather's system. The tragedy would claim two Voss lives instead of one. But the old man clutched at Ylva's arm with surprising strength. His expression was odd, pleading. It was as if he would siphon some of Ylva's youth in order to somehow sustain him in life. She saw him struggle to formulate his thoughts.

"I've heard that woman detective is involved," Loke said, his hoarse voice barely rising beyond a whisper.

Ylva nodded. "The American, Veronika Brand."

"Veronika Brand," the old man repeated. He had a strange, wistful tone to his voice, as if he were about to cry. "I've never met her."

"Of course not," Ylva said.

"Must she be…removed?"

Ylva reacted with mild surprise. Ylva didn't know how to respond. What was he asking? Why was he asking it? He did indeed appear to weep, or perhaps it was only an old man's rheumy eyes leaking.

"Must she…?" Loke repeated, trailing off.

"Yes," Ylva said firmly.

"The death…has to stop!" Loke called out, afterwards abruptly sitting back and falling into brooding silence.

Old age, concluded Ylva. One gets soft. A man at death's door, of course he would wish for the death to stop. And if wishes were horses beggars would ride.

Ylva rose to her feet. "That's all right, *farfar*. I'll make it stop."

Then she went about her business.

46

"What I'm finding difficult to understand is how the animal could be taken from the estate without your knowledge."

Detective Inspector Vincent Hult had never before confronted his patron in such a direct manner. Normally the Baron expected and received deference due to his position. Even though nobility was challenged and debased in these egalitarian times, it still counted for something in Swedish society.

"Do you know how to tell when a Roma is lying?" the Baron asked. "His lips are moving. The boy responsible for this foul business, Lash Mirga, has disappeared. I've informed the constabulary of his disappearance. So far, your police investigation has turned up nothing. I will have to put my own people on it."

Hult felt that the ball he had served to the Baron had returned quickly to his side of the court.

"I understand," he said placatingly, trying to smooth the Baron's feathers. "You believed the beast had simply been taken out for veterinary procedures."

"Yes, I was lied to," the Baron said in a clipped manner. "It happens, if you deign to deal with the lesser races."

They had gathered for *fika* around a small table in one of the barns on the Gammelhem property. Hult, the Baron, his man Magnusson, and Junior Voss—the four males stood in rubber boots and matching duck jackets of heavy-duty canvas. Two of them, the Baron and Junior Voss, displayed the casual condescension of power, with the other two clearly subordinate.

Separated from them by a stout fence, a paddock spread with wood shavings featured a jumble of landscaped boulders at its opposite end. Three spotted hyenas, two pups and a nursing dam, its teats engorged and prominent, lounged lazily at the mouth of a den built into the rocks.

"What I want to know from you," the Baron said to Hult, "is if the connection of Gammelhem to this tawdry affair has been contained."

"I believe it has," Hult responded. "The knowledge of the animal's presence at the Hede River scene has been limited to two officers, and they have been directed to remain silent on the matter."

"Fenrir…" the Baron mused, gazing over at the other members of the small hyena pack he maintained at the estate's zoo. "I carried him in my arms onto the plane from Ghana. He grew into his magnificence here, in this corral."

"We buried the beast with proper ceremony," put in Magnusson, leaving Hult and Voss to wonder just what might be the suitable internment rituals for hyenas.

Junior spoke: "The Roma and your damn demon dogs from Africa are a separate matter. I have no doubt that you and Magnusson will punish your own people to everyone's satisfaction. I am much more concerned with the possible involvement of the American woman and the Sami lawyer."

"They left the lodge immediately after the truck carrying Fenrir," Magnusson said, earning a glare from the Baron.

"What were you doing hosting them?" demanded Junior. "They're very dangerous to us!"

"Gentlemen!" Hult cut in. "We are focusing too much on deciding whose mess this was. What we need to be doing is cleaning it up quickly and thoroughly. I offer a mea culpa myself. I had the two of them brought in to the central *polisstation* in Stockholm, attempting to frighten them off. Perhaps I let them go too easily."

Junior cursed. "It's ancient history, this whole *Nordic Light* thing! I wasn't even born! What does the bitch want? Does she expect my ninety-eight year old father to offer some sort of public apology?"

"Detective Brand's motives don't matter in the least," Hult said authoritatively. "She is a lonely, bitter woman who was recently fired from her post in the NYPD. It would be sad if it weren't so pathetic. But like a wounded animal, she can still bite."

"Not particularly good-looking, I hear?" Junior Voss asked.

"Ill-favored," Hult said.

"Oh, I don't know," the Baron mused. "I've often thought there's a kind of beauty that has something wrong with it. An off-kilter look can be alluring. It is not the perfect, magazine-style, prefabricated prettiness that is so commonly foisted upon us. I'm thinking of someone like Bette Davis, or maybe more of your generation, the Streep woman."

"I don't see any of that in the Brand bitch," Hult said.

"Not to my taste, of course," the Baron added quickly. "But I wouldn't deny her intelligence, however much her life is in pieces."

"Say we remove her from the scene," Junior said. "What could we expect in return?"

"Remove…?" Hult asked, letting the question dangle.

"I'm afraid my niece Ylva has formed a violent hatred of this Brand person," Junior said. "She is heartbroken over her cousin Malte's death. She was so fond of him."

"Hult?" Baron Kron asked. "What do you say?"

"It depended on how it was done, or course. To kill a visiting cop—"

"—A suspended cop, disgraced in her own jurisdiction," Junior cut in.

"Okay, but the job still requires a certain degree of care," Hult said. "In this particular case, my involvement must be masked. I'm not in any position to have it done myself."

"Of course not," Junior said hurriedly.

"If the woman could just…vanish?" Magnusson suggested.

"Turn up with the spring thaw," the Baron agreed.

"Listen, gents," Hult said, "as long as things don't get too messy, I think I can handle any repercussions on the part of the police."

"We are agreed, then," the Baron said. "Try to control Ylva, Junior, will you? Bless her black heart, I know the young woman can be a terror when she wants to be."

"What about the Sami lawyer, gentlemen?" Magnusson asked. "We have not spoken about him."

"Already dead, or soon will be," Junior said. He screwed up his face into an expression of disgust. "Damn, those animals stink like Satan's anus."

Kron gave a sweet smile. "I no longer smell it myself. The odor stems from a substance excreted from certain glands. They smear it everywhere they go."

"Ugh," coughed Junior. "I'm feeling as though they've smeared it on me."

"Would you like to hear the term for the excreta? 'Hyena butter'!" Kron laughed coarsely.

"I have to leave or I'll vomit," Junior exclaimed. "I need something to wash the stench out of my mouth."

"Shall we adjourn to the lodge, then?" Kron suggested. "There is a cuvée of Krug I've been wanting to attack."

As they left the barn, the Baron took a last glance over his shoulder at the hyena dam. She panted hungrily in the darkness of her den.

47

Brand knew she would have to leave the medical center as soon as possible. The effects of hypothermia dissipated, leaving only a maddening prickly feeling in her extremities. She was healthy enough to go, the doctors at Sveg were willing to discharge her, but still she failed to depart.

Hammar remained in a coma. It seemed less and less likely that he would regain consciousness anytime soon. In a four-hour operation that occurred while he was still under, surgeons pieced back together the pieces of his skull, inserting as a temporary fix a series of tiny stainless steel screws into the caved-in parietal bone. They would soon be flying him via helicopter to a hospital in Stockholm.

The threat of imminent discovery by the Voss family formed the pressing reason Brand had to absent herself from the hospital sooner rather than later. Not only that, but somewhere nearby, law enforcement authorities were playing a game of connect-a-dot. They would soon place her and Hammar at the chalet along the Hede River.

She had hewed as closely to the truth as possible when explaining Hammar's injuries to the hospital staff. He had broken through on the frozen river, she said. His nasty head wound occurred in the rough and tumble journey under the ice. As though there were sharpened battle axes submerged in the current, and the poor guy had bumped up against one of them.

Soon enough, the local cops would link what happened at the chalet near the Norway border with the comatose hospital patient and his hypothermic caretaker. The hospital staff would take a closer look at the slice in Hammar's scalp. Questions would arise that would be difficult to evade.

It was inevitable. Brand should depart before it all came tumbling down on top of her. "Go where?" was the natural question, with "anywhere but here" being the natural response. She had to maintain her liberty. Her Dalgren relatives would be of no use. They would be the first to be contacted by any authorities searching for her.

Brand thought of Aino Lehtonen. Then of Moro Part, the Romani godfather. Her only possible allies. At the same time she feared their involvement. It was clear that Moro was not only a man of immense power in the Romani community, but also the mastermind of the revenge plot. The godfather's tireless campaign against the traffickers felt Biblical. But we live in a world of rule of law, she reminded herself, not an Old Testament realm of eye-for-an-eye.

During the day, Brand had become something of a ghost in the medical center at Sveg. She wandered the deserted halls at all hours, slept in the lounges, ducked out for food at the village's few restaurants. The weather remained bitter and she could not stay outside for long.

Still she hesitated to leave. Perhaps immersion in the stingingly frigid waters of the river had dazed her mind more than she knew.

The sight of a police uniform in the lobby of the hospital jolted her into action. The police woman was only checking on a victim of a car accident, but Brand took the hint. She threaded her way back up through the maze of medical center hallways to the room where Hammar had lain for over twenty-four hours now, dead to the world. The staff was well familiar with the coma victim's helpmate, his assumed girlfriend, his guardian angel.

Entering Hammar's room, she saw a slim, unfamiliar doctor or nurse bent over his motionless form. A female, anyway, in the midst of administering some kind of strange treatment, pressing a pillow down onto the face of the figure lying in bed.

At Brand's entry, the woman turned her head, and despite the surgical mask Brand recognized her immediately. She had taken time to familiarize herself with as many members of the Voss family as she could. Ylva Voss was a biathlon hero who had been pictured many times in the press.

The woman reacted more quickly than Brand. She snarled what appeared to be an oddly happy greeting, as if delighted to see the American, then took up a steel bowl resting next to the patient's bed and spun it across the room like a Frisbee. The thing clocked Brand directly in the middle of her forehead, stunning her. But she staggered forward, tackling the younger, fitter and more ferocious woman in a desperate bid to save her friend.

The battle was one-sided. Ylva pummeled Brand with repeated blows, flinging her around the hospital room. They crashed against a utility column, an IV stand, and a computer monitor suspended on a heavy steel boom. Pieces of equipment fell atop the unconscious patient, ripping his IV tubes away and displacing the bed a few feet toward the wall.

And of course a blade came out. Ylva pulled a full-size Ka-Bar from her belt, the kind of seven-inch clip-pointed fighting knife employed by the US Marine Corps. The monstrous weapon seemed to grow longer the closer it came, until it filled Brand's vision.

Only by an extremely lucky kick did she manage to deny her attacker the immediate advantage of the knife. As Ylva scrambled backward to retrieve it, Brand managed to reach over and trip the room's emergency alarm.

Lights flashed and a claxon sounded. Ylva came at her again. Brand dodged. Then the biathlete turned the knife on Hammar, stabbing down at his motionless form. A terrified Brand grabbed at her, making the woman miss. She managed only a deep strike into the mattress.

The blade stuck. Ylva struggled to extract it. Brand got in her only good hit of the battle, cracking her attacker with a fist to the side of the throat.

Then the first of many hospital staffers crashed into the room, filling it with shouts and warnings. Cornered, Ylva lifted up a stainless steel supply cart that must have easily weighed eighty kilos, hurled it through a closed window, and followed it out through the shattered glass.

The medical personnel rushed to check on the patient. Brand stepped over to the broken window. In the evening darkness she saw a figure scramble across a lower-story rooftop immediately below her. Ylva Voss turned to look back once, then slipped from the edge of the roof to the ground.

The female cop who Brand had encountered in the lobby charged into the room and joined her at the window, breathing hard and half-panicked. She worked a shoulder-mounted comm unit but seemed to struggle to operate it in her fluster.

Brand left the police woman standing amid the trashed-out hospital room. She maneuvered her way through the maze of empty corridors and left the medical center without anyone stopping her.

Two minutes later she was in Hammar's Saab. Spatters of dried and frozen blood still marked the interior from its owner's grievous head wound, as well as from his previous nosebleed.

Even with the cold, the Saab started on the first try. Brand headed east, leaving Sveg via the main highway. She drove not knowing exactly where she was headed.

48

After a few hours of chugging along deserted back roads, Brand broke into an empty *fäbod*. It wasn't one of the made-over modern ones. The small, slope-roofed hut, one of several grouped together, displayed gray weathered siding of uneven timber. Bracken lay tangled in the snow piled up outside.

Inside, the place smelled of mouse shit, mildew and something vaguely familiar, human or animal rot, she couldn't tell. Stained, flower-print curtains hung limply in the downstairs windows.

She chose the place from the lack of footprints or car tracks in evidence. Abandoned, she concluded, or at least unvisited. The Saab she managed to hide behind a half-collapsed outbuilding. The car was another problem.

"Oh, there are plenty of old Saabs on the roads here in northern Sweden," Hammar had responded, when Brand complained that the vehicle stuck out like a sore thumb.

"Krister, the whole damned Saab automobile company just went tits up," she pointed out. "They're not making them anymore."

"I saw a 1969 Model 96 in tan just recently, a few months back," Hammar had responded, breezily ignoring her main point. "We always salute each other with honks of the horn."

Recalling the conversation now, Brand felt a blast of sentiment for the owner of the Saab. She knew the car could nail her. There were any number of law enforcement entities in the hunt. The American interloper was now linked to many crimes, a chalet burning, various and sundry disruptions of the peace at a medical center—not to mention a string of murders. A BOLO or APB would have likely been issued, if Swedish police had such a system as a be-on-the-lookout or an all-points bulletin.

The Vosses, too, would pounce if they encountered an ancient blue Saab anywhere on the road. Perhaps, in the immediate area, the family and the police were much the same thing.

So she was marooned, lost during winter in the *fjäll*, the fell, the marches, the Swedish uplands. Alone in one of the least populated area of Europe. The Fell could just as well be Antarctica for the frozen wilderness expanse of it.

"You've thoroughly screwed yourself now," Brand whispered, the words spelled out in cloudy vapor as they were swallowed by silence.

Exhausted, cold, and hungry, guilty of breaking and entering, she did what she could. Half-blind in the darkness, she made a thorough search of the shack, looking for food and weapons. She found neither, not even a stale cracker or a household hammer. Debris lay scattered on the floor. A discarded plank featured an array of evil-looking rusty nails, ready to impale Brand's foot. She laid it carefully aside.

A woodstove stood in the corner. After a few tries she got a fire going. She worried about the smoke giving her away. But a grove of trees shielded the place from the road. Besides, the flue didn't draw well enough to send more than a puff or two up the crumbling chimney. The major part of the smoke merely seeped into the interior.

The bed was only a wood-framed cot. The ragged foam mattress pad looked as if it would disintegrate in a cloud of toxic dust, should she lie down on it. Brand tried to make it serviceable by sweeping clean the rodent droppings as best she could. Items of clothing salvaged from the Saab served as bed linen. She left her parka on. Hunger she would have to endure.

Better to light a candle than curse the darkness, and there was a stub of one on a windowsill. Brand lit it and placed the wavering flame near the head of the bed. She climbed aboard, covering herself with Hammar's bloody parka.

Exhausted, battered by the beating she had just taken at the hands of the Voss madwoman, she still could not sleep.

The musty smell that had engulfed her now summoned up memories of another hovel, a wreck of a place in the woods of upstate New York that the family always referred to as "the deer shack," since it was only used in the fall hunting season. As a child she abhorred everything about it, the filth, the air of abandonment and disuse, the carcasses of white tails strung up on poplar trees outside.

She much preferred the farm. In memory, her childhood was forever sunlit. She spent winter holidays as well as summers there, while her mother took the opportunity for serious solitary drinking back in Queens. But in Brand's mind Jamestown was never snowy, always green and golden. She was allowed to roam free, an incredible blessing unavailable to a small child in New York City.

Brand pictured herself in a sea of waist-high grasses, harvesting daisies, black-eyed Susans, and Indian paintbrushes to bring home to the farmhouse of her grandparents. Somewhere in the background, a crew baled hay in the fields, black-and-white Holsteins lowed in the meadow, and all was right in the world.

The image was a lie. She picked flowers not out of childhood innocence but in a desperate attempt to salve the emotional wounds that afflicted Klara and Gustav Dalgren and her great-aunt Alice. Her painstakingly gathered bouquets did no good.

Even as a young child, Brand recognized that something was not right with the household. Dark currents ran under the surface. Gustav drank. There were nights when she heard him rage in the downstairs kitchen, crashing and yelling until Brand found herself sobbing with fear.

Now lying awake in a Swedish *fäbod* halfway around the world in Härjedalen, a word she could barely pronounce, she tried to sweep those memories away and replace them with more pleasant ones. She recalled a late summer day when oppressive heat lured Klara, Alice and her into the farm's woodlot. A spring pooled amid a stand of sugar maples. The older women stripped down to their linens and sank down as far as they could in the cool water. Only their heads remained visible, floating disembodied. They both wore looks of contentment.

Brand, twelve years old and shamefully shy of her body, crouched on the bank. The voices of Klara and Alice drifted on the hot summer breeze, going from Swedish to English to a confusing combination of both.

The two women never entirely got the hang of America or the English language—they would have reacted with puzzlement about what "got the hang of" meant. They used a characteristic *mmm* and *awww* to show they were paying attention, the sound like a murmur. *Walter* was 'Valter', *win* was 'vin', *wine* was 'vine', and no *z* sound existed at all, only *s*.

Why had her aunt and grandparents come to America, Brand asked her mother, if they loved Sweden so much? Marta Brand never answered directly, simply passed on to other subjects. She had put a firm distance between herself and the old country ways of her mother and aunt. Marta was a good-time American girl, too busy living it up in the present to bother with the past.

The Jamestown farm was cursed. Even an idyllic memory like that of the afternoon at the spring could turn sour. The two sisters emerged from the water and walked slowly back toward the farmhouse. Their underclothes dried only gradually in the humid August air. Their hair remained damp. They carried their dresses bundled in their arms. Twelve-year-old Brand wanted the two adults to get dressed already. She worried about them being seen.

Alice began chattering about swimming as kids in a lake in Sweden, frigid even in summer. She spoke about Gustav being with her and Klara, as well as a person called by a name that sounded to Veronika like "*Low-keh*."

"How handsome he was, wasn't he, Klara? And what an eye Loke had for the ladies!"

Brand remembered her grandmother reacting not at all, remaining stone-faced.

"And a special eye he had for you," Alice added teasingly.

Klara turned and slapped her sister hard. Brand had seen Klara chasten Alice before, sometimes with words, sometimes with a gentle cuff, but never anything as sharp as that slap.

The candle flickered in the tiny shack where Brand was squatting. She reached into the inner pocket of her parka for the photograph she had retrieved from Elin's deserted room. The group of four happy teenagers and one younger child stared out at her from Sweden at the dawn of the 1930s.

Flipping the fragile photograph over, she could barely see, in the flickering candlelight of the mildewed *fäbod*, the neat, spidery writing. The hand was not of her grandmother Klara, but of Alice.

Five names: Elin, Alice, Klara, Gustav Dalgren, Loke. Loke Voss.

Yes, here was the Voss family elder, Brand thought, the boy with the troubled expression in his face. He remained in the shadows to the right of the others, looking longingly over at Klara.

Loke. Accused of igniting the *Nordic Light* fire, he had never been held publicly accountable for the arson or deaths. Smoke from those flames drifted across the Atlantic and hung over the Jamestown farmhouse like a pall.

Brand realized she had been destined to come to Sweden all along. Her whole life fed into this moment. She was somehow meant to confront Loke Voss for the crimes of the past. But her target seemed to recede each day she spent in the country. Her ancestors loomed accusingly in her mind. What are you doing here? they demanded, the question echoing that of the skinhead on the train.

She slipped the old photo back into the chest pocket of her parka. When sleep finally settled on her, a wolf-faced *nattmara* came and sat on her chest. The evil hag whispered death and despair into Brand's dreams, until a stolen pistol materialized and scared the nightmare away.

49

The mountains and forests that rose around her were blank. She was the sole human left alive in the dead world of the Fell. That morning in the *fäbod*, she bit into her last Adderall. Fifteen minutes later, as she strode out to meet the day, the speed kicked in. She started feeling like an All-American girl.

To Brand's eyes, the fabled Nordic light—the real, actual Nordic light, not her grandfather's doomed newspaper—always had a strange feel. Now the sun, visible behind a scrim of polarizing clouds, somehow morphed and doubled itself, as if she were living on a planet illuminated by twin stars. It was a trick of atmosphere, sure, and Brand had heard of it happening, but that didn't make it any less unsettling.

A network of small, snow-covered lanes ran off the main highway, the north-south artery located a dozen kilometers to the east. She tramped on. The amphetamine salts coursing through her blood forced her jaw to tighten, which helped suppress an urge to sing a hey-ho song of the open road. Plentiful animal signs showed in the snow, both scat and tracks. But no people were around anywhere.

The whole area proved eerily empty. She passed an ancient abandoned rail locomotive, decayed and crumbling in the middle of the woods. It looked as though the operators had hopped off and left the big machine there, legging it to more promising environs. Whatever steel rails there were lay buried in snow.

At every crossroads ("if you see a fork in the road, take it" echoed the voice of Willie Uricco), Brand flipped her last ten kronor coin to decide which way to go. Her bad luck held. She lost her grip on the coin and dropped it into a snowbank. She spent a fruitless few minutes searching for it.

Her mind never stayed on any single track for long. Forks in the road led her to think of spoons, which made her think of food. Forks also made her think of knives, a lethal seven-inch blade in particular. Ylva Voss had left her monster knife embedded in the mattress of Brand's comatose partner in crime, Krister Hammar.

The police would have been all over the incident in the hospital room, just like they had to be all over the business along the Hede River. They would interview Hammar, but of course the man had the right to remain silent, notwithstanding his total inability to speak. Hee-hee, ha-ha, went Brand's mind. The Adderall failed to focus her as it usually did. She felt dizzy and dumbstruck, as though several IQ points were draining out on the road behind her.

With the morning, the sky had turned sickly blue-white, the color of skim milk. After a quarter hour there appeared what passed for a metropolis in the Fell. Three houses stood jumbled together in a row, with a barn facing them across the road. One of the houses featured a thin finger of smoke coming from its chimney. Human habitation was both a threat and opportunity for her. Houses made her think of food.

A well used black Ford truck sat parked in the driveway of the barn. Brand held back, surveilling the scene for a full fifteen minutes before deciding that there was indeed no one home at any of the houses. The smoke from the chimney merely indicated a heating system at work. She could move forward without much possibility of surprise.

Hot wiring a vehicle always looked so simple on TV crime shows. She had once been on a stakeout where she and Uricco watched a degenerate junkie try for what seemed like forever to hijack a Toyota sedan. After about ten minutes, the bungled attempt began to strike them as funny.

"The most stolen model in the frigging country, this guy can't put two wires together," Urrico said, wheezing with laughter.

At the present moment Brand possessed no slim jack lockout tool, no tools at all. She forced a passenger window on the truck, because that side was shielded from the residences across the road. She managed to gain entry without busting the pane entirely. Climbing inside, lying on her back beneath the steering column, Brand faced a nest of wires worthy of Medusa's hair. She tried every possible combination.

The truck resisted, remaining stubbornly inert. Brand finally found and connected the hot wire to the starter motor. The engine turned over, but only weakly, stunned by the cold along with everything else in the country. After that first miracle hint of success, the starter showed no life at all.

Cursing volubly, damning American manufacturing, engineering, and Henry Ford himself, Brand risked discovery by getting out and popping the hood. She worked to clean and tighten the battery cables as best she could, skinning her knuckles in the process.

"The job's not complete unless there's blood," she recalled her father Nick Brand saying about working on cars.

She got back into the truck and touched the wires together again.

Nothing.

She forced herself to stave off despair. Backtracking, she tried to trace her path to the *fäbod* where she had slept. She got lost, found her way, then lost it several times more. It took an hour to locate the abandoned house, remove the Saab's tiny battery, and haul it back with her to the Ford pickup.

The Saab operated on a six-volt electrical system. Such a limited battery would never serve to run the big Ford. But it might turn the engine over. Then the truck's generator would take up the slack. Brand jury-rigged the two batteries in series. Then she tried the hot-wire again.

Again, nothing.

Then, something. The truck rumbled and bucked to life, coughing, spitting smoke, flirting with dying again and again. If Brand's trespass wouldn't nail her, the random braap and bang of the engine would.

Complaining all the while, the vehicle took her away down the deserted, snow-packed road.

She got lost in the puzzle of lanes again, doubled back, found the highway. The accursed owner of the stolen Ford had parked it with only a quarter tank of gas. She didn't know how far that would take her. South, anyway, always south. The broken passenger window bled in cold air.

In a collection of villages huddled beside an immense frozen lake, Brand found a roadside truck-stop type restaurant that looked anonymous enough for her to venture inside. She killed the truck engine without knowing if she would ever be able to revive it. She didn't care. Her mouth watered with the scent of cooking. Hunger made her reckless.

The place proved nearly empty. No one looked up as she entered. She ordered and consumed a plate of waffles with cream and something called cloudberry jam. What a wonderful name for a sweet, Brand thought, lapping it up. She ordered another plate, and refueled with more hot coffee at the same time.

She was out of cash—possessing no love, as the Romani would say. No credit card either. She would have to beat the check somehow. Brand did not like the cashless society, not one bit. She needed the feel of money, the non-digital kind, the look of it, the exactitude of it. The restaurant had three exits, including one near the restrooms. But the whole dine-and-dash dodge was complicated by the fact that her getaway vehicle would have to be hot-wired.

She turned to a fellow diner, a woman with a young child in the next booth. First she tried in Swedish, slowly, painstakingly sounding out the words.

"*Jag undrar om jag kan...,*" she began, but the woman interrupted her almost immediately.

"I speak English," she said.

"Your cell phone, please, for a short call to Stockholm." Brand understood she looked like a total bum, what with random scrapes and bruises visible on her face from the hospital room beating. One of her eyes had turned various shades of purple and red. Her swollen upper lip resembled a half-flat tire. The formerly white parka had turned gray and looked as though she had slept in it, which she had. The topper was a watch cap that any homeless person would have rejected as beneath his dignity.

Even so, the woman gave up her cell to her.

Brand took the phone, then looked at the woman helplessly, "I don't have the number!"

The woman took the phone back and tapped in some letters. "What's her name?" she asked.

"Lehtonen, Aino Lehtonen. Stockholm."

The woman worked a bit of magic on the phone and handed it back to Brand. The line was already ringing.

"Are you calling from a secure line?" Lehtonen asked immediately when she heard Brand's voice. "I'm afraid the police might be listening in."

"What does that mean?" Brand asked. "I borrowed a cell."

"Listen, I can't be mixed up in this," Lehtonen said. "I'm seeing the whole mess all about to blow up. At least one of us has to stay clean."

She tried to ring off.

"I need help," Brand said. "I'm out of money. Please, I'm alone out here."

"We have had two visits from *snuten* recently. The detectives asked after you and Krister. You aren't in the newspapers or on the television yet, but that will come. Don't contact me again."

The line clicked dead.

Brand handed the cellphone back to its owner. The woman examined her as she did so. Was it a look of suspicion, or was Brand only imagining it? She sat and sucked down more coffee, feeling sleepy from the food but at the same time jazzed from caffeine and anxiety. Fear rose in her gut as she felt an Adderall crash coming on.

Lehtonen was right, the wretch. The Roma photographer hadn't signed on for this. But who had? Murder and mayhem, multiplying dead bodies in a country that had the lowest murder rate in the civilized world. Her allies were meeting bad ends—Lehtonen frantic with paranoia, Hammar near death in a hospital bed.

Slip out, move on, sleep in the stolen truck. Brand vividly pictured how this would all end, with her waking in the freezing cold to see a SWAT team—they called them *piketbilar* here—creeping up on her, assault rifles

220

raised, screaming about getting her hands where they could see them.

The woman at the next table fielded a call on her cell phone, listened for a moment, then signaled to Brand.

"Excuse me? It's for you."

Moro Part.

With a flood of relief Brand realized Lehtonen had come through after all, and had given the number to the Romani godfather.

By the time she finished the conversation with Moro, the woman had risen and stood next to her, ready to leave. Her child flung himself around at the end of his mom's arm as if he thought Mama might be a piece of playground equipment.

"*Tack så mycket,*" Brand said, thanking her in Swedish and returning the cell.

"American, yes?"

"Yes," Brand said.

The woman placed a two hundred krona bill—twenty bucks in U.S. terms—on Brand's table. "I keep this for emergencies," she said, smiling sympathetically before dragging her child out of the restaurant.

50

Moro Part showed at the roadside restaurant later that afternoon. Darkness had already fallen. Brand knew she should be honored that such an eminence would send not a lackey but come himself. He arrived in a shiny black Mercedes.

"I need to drive," Brand told Moro when he pushed open the passenger door. "I get carsick otherwise."

"In the back," Moro commanded, waving his hand dismissively. "There's an ice bucket back there if you need to puke."

Brand had made her request more feebly than she usually did, and was too tired to argue with a man not to be argued with. She climbed into the back seat.

"You are all right?" Moro asked. "You look like home-made shit."

"Thank you," Brand said. She lay down as the car eased out into the highway traffic. Immediately she began to feel nauseous.

"Varzha Luna?" she asked. "Is she…?"

"She is very well," Moro answered. "Though not everyone appreciates her methods. Some say she is *ruinate bunuri*, soiled goods. But you will be happy to know she has fielded a proposal of marriage."

"So she will wear a wedding gown for real."

"Yes," Moro said. "And a Roma marriage festival, well, it goes on for days, in some instances lasting longer than the marriage itself."

"*Gadje* not invited."

"Exceptions can be made," Moro said magnanimously. "In your case and in that of Krister, should he come back to us."

"He's in Stockholm by now, at some sort of a rehabilitation center."

"You are well informed, though I would not advise a visit." Moro lifted his arms from the steering wheel. He crossed them and spread the fingers of one hand and formed a circle with the other, making the "five-oh" street gang signal for police.

Throwing a sign looked comical on him. "That's backwards," Brand said.

"How does it feel to be on the other side of the law for once?" he asked.

"Uncomfortable."

"How'd you get here? I didn't see the famous blue Saab anywhere around. I hope you had enough sense to ditch that thing."

Brand stayed mute. Moro made a face. "You stole another car!" he exclaimed.

"A truck actually," Brand said.

Moro's rolling laugh filled the interior of the Mercedes. This was not the same gruff Romani godfather she had seen on the street corner in front of Åhlens. That man was an ominous presence, unpredictable, dangerous. Here was the flip side of the coin. The man could actually appear personable.

"See any *snut* along the way?" he asked. "Police always cause trouble."

"I've noticed that," Brand said gamely. "It takes a fuss to settle a fuss, is what my old partner Willie Urrico used to say."

"Such a crazy place, your hometown. Too many animals crammed into a too small zoo. I hear the crime rate is skyrocketing without you there to keep things in line."

Brand smiled. "I have to say that lately I've been missing the peace and quiet of New York."

"Forgive my manners," Moro said. "I have a Scotch whiskey with me that's worth invading Europe for."

"Sure," Brand said. The speed was fading on her. She wanted sleep more than anything. A drink would send her to dreamland. Moro handed back a flask.

"You want a Coke with it? Coca-Cola always settles the stomach."

Brand took a pass. Taken straight, the alcohol hit her stomach like a sucker punch.

She leaned forward to pass the flask back to Moro and gestured around the lavish fittings of the luxury vehicle. "All this from street begging, huh?"

Moro cocked his head. "Among other endeavors. I know what it looks like. But I take care of my people. Which is more than I can say about most governments in Europe."

"Where's my pistol?" she asked.

"Which pistol is that?"

She stared. "I was afraid you were going to say that. I want my sidearm back. I'm off my game without it."

"With or without a weapon, you are doubtless very game. Do you still have the charm I gave you?"

Brand pulled the little stone amulet from her pocket. "You know, I've always wondered why you saw fit to gift it to me, not Aino, not Krister."

"You realize it's a phallus symbol, right?"

Brand colored. Moro again laughed. "A fascinum," he said. "The Romans used them to ward off the evil eye."

"I see it now." Jesus, Brand thought, the little dingus really did vaguely resemble a penis. "Here, you can have it back."

"Oh, no, no, you still have need of it."

"My part in this is done."

"You never know," Moro said.

"You could just leave it alone, you know," Brand said, thoughtful. "Bygones be bygones, water under the bridge, let sleeping dogs and every other cliché I can't think of right now. Let it rest."

"We understand that Jarl Voss is still alive and well."

Brand hesitated, uncomfortable with the vision of revenge rolling out endlessly. "I recall Gandhi or somebody, saying an eye for an eye makes the whole world blind."

"The great man and I share the same great-great-many-greats-in-the-past grandfather," Moro said brightly.

She didn't exactly believe him. But Brand knew that the Romani people had originally migrated out of India at some distant point in pre-history. Setting themselves on the road that they traveled still.

"You know," Moro continued, "whenever I hear what my cousin the Mahatma said, I think, an eye for an eye? When someone takes an eye from me I take two from him. That leaves me with one and him blind. And you know what they say about the country of the blind."

As if, Veronika thought, as if the blood spilled on the banks of the Hede River had nothing to do with Moro.

"Well, I know what they always say about revenge. Dig two graves."

He swiveled his head around, ignoring the roadway in front of him. Just for a moment, Brand caught a dark glint in his eyes, a quick flip from the mammalian to the reptilian. Then it was gone, and he was once again the jolly man concerned about her well-being.

"You look tired, Detective. You look like Santa Claus the day after Christmas. We will have you back in Stockholm, in a safe apartment I know of, very nice, flat screen, Netflix, all yours until we see how this all shakes out."

"And is it? All going to shake out?"

"Of course. You will see. Hammar will come back and all will be well. Plus you'll be happy to know I have an invitation for you from Varzha Luna. Her engagement ceremony will take place near to Storkyrkan, the big cathedral in Gamla Stan."

"Near the church?" Brand asked. "Not inside?" Inwardly she was dismayed that a sixteen-year-old girl on the cusp of adulthood would be married off.

"We *Kalderaš Romani* aren't allowed on such occasions. Third of March, keep the day open."

A shadow stirred in Brand's mind at the mention of the date, like the reflection of a dark cloud passing over the surface of a pond. But she was tired and didn't want to think beyond the here and now. She stretched out and closed her eyes.

"I have music," Moro said. "Some nice flamenco guitar, very soothing."

The acoustic melodies lulled Brand to sleep. She dreamed of drowning, then violently of murder and mayhem. She woke once in darkness. She leaned over, upchucked into the ice bucket, and realized Moro had covered her with a rough wool blanket. Then she fell back asleep.

51

A great saucer-flowered magnolia stood on the Dalgren farm in Jamestown, New York, spreading shade on a hill overlooking the farmhouse. The tree served as Brand's refuge during her childhood, when family tensions got too intense for her. She would climb into its limbs with a book, or just lie beneath it and gaze at the sky through its generous branches.

As a child she wasn't often at the farm in spring. But once she was, and the vision of the magnolia in extravagant bloom stuck with her later in life. Beautiful, yes, but beauty in such profusion that it toppled over into excess.

"Too much of anything is never a good thing." The two sisters, her great-aunt and grandmother, had always emphasized the point. The message was largely lost on Brand. She came of age in the increasingly excessive lifestyle of American culture at the end of the millennium. She found that too much vodka, for example, could be just right.

But the vision of the magnolia stayed with her well into her adult years. The tulip-like pink-white blossoms garlanded every branch, their perfume sweet, overpowering, a little sickly. Then, in the space of less than a week, it was over. The petals sprayed down like baby pink snow, or they turned brown and died while still attached the limbs. Rotting on the ground, they formed a thick, slick mass, slippery underfoot.

"It seems a lot of effort to go through just for a couple of days of being pretty," Veronika said to her great aunt Alice. "I'm going to have to change my opinion of that tree."

Alice gave a gentle laugh. "It is trying to attract a mate."

"Really?"

"That is what flowers are for, yes. You know that."

Brand was then thirteen years old. Her mom and dad's marriage was crumbling. She thought she understood all about the birds and the bees. Not the physical act but the boy and girl thing, as she would sardonically come to refer to love and romance later on, remained a stubborn mystery.

Her mother said she was sending Veronika to the Jamestown farm every summer "to keep her out of trouble." She meant to save her daughter from the influence of the fast kids on the streets of New York City. Brand believed it was more a case of Marta parking her somewhere, anywhere. She needed to go about her business, whatever it was, unhampered by a tagalong child.

Her mom grew up on the farm herself. Evidently she didn't recall that farm kids were in a way a lot more advanced than city kids. The example of the barnyard taught them all about sex. Plus there were many more places away from prying eyes in the country than in the city.

As an adult she rarely thought of her childhood loves. But that tree near the farmhouse, flowering so extravagantly, lingered in her mind.

"There's not another magnolia anywhere around here," she commented to Aunt Alice. "I don't think there's one within fifty miles."

"No, dear, they're not that common."

"So that means all the frou-frou about putting out blossoms is for nothing."

"I guess so," Alice said. "But the tree doesn't know that."

"Poor thing." The idea struck Brand as unbearably lonely.

She was that tree. Putting out her flowers for nobody.

Her grandfather died the spring she turned thirteen. There were three barns on the property. He perished by fire in the oldest and smallest one. A few minutes past eleven o'clock one night that year, Brand woke from sleep to women screaming. A disorienting orange-yellow glow turned dark to day outside her bedroom window.

In her white cotton nightdress she rushed downstairs. She slipped on a pair of rubber boots in the mud room off the kitchen and stepped outside. Her first emotion, before she knew the full scope of the tragedy, was one of excitement.

The old barn—that's what they always called it, to distinguish the ancient structure of gray, weathered wood from the new barn and the cow barn— would not be that much of a loss. No livestock were ever housed in it. The haymow was full of moldering bales too rotted to offer much good nutrition to the cows. A lot of useless junk packed the lower floor. The structure practically pleaded to be put out of its misery.

So Brand's eyes were shining as she crossed to the spectacle in the lower yard. Divorced from the natural human concern over property loss, a fire in an unoccupied barn can be a magnificent sight. She halted to stare, shivering like a human tuning fork. A whole crayon box of tints, shades, and colors blew out of the barn roof. Deadly looking whips of yellow, orange, blue, illuminated huge billows of sooty smoke. The fire rolled upward into the night, accompanied by a hellish freight train of a roar.

"I will never forget this night," thirteen year old Brand whispered to herself.

The fat bellow of the fire at first drowned out what her grandmother was shouting. She and Great-Aunt Alice clutched each other, sinking to their knees at the very edge of the blaze, screaming and moaning. Brand saw their silhouettes framed by the flames. It took her a moment to grasp Klara's words.

"Gustav, Gustav, Gustav!"

Outlined in the square of the barn's open double doors, the fire painted the interior a bright sun yellow. Brand could see all-consuming heat turning everything inside shimmery and strange.

In the middle of the roaring tableau, a figure hung by the neck on a rope attached to a beam that crossed the roof of the barn. The black form looked Biblical twisting there in the midst of the fire. Brand had thoughts of the Book of Daniel's Shadrach, Meshach and Abednego, servants of the Most High God.

In the instant that the rope burned through and the body collapsed in a heap to the burning floor of the barn, Brand finally understood the true extent of the horror. The dead man was her grandfather, Gustav Dalgren. She powered forward and joined the weeping females, thrusting herself in between Klara and Alice as if they could shield her from grief. The three of them all huddled together while the flames still sent out waves of intense heat. Days later Brand's face was still red as if from radiant burn.

More odd than death, her first reaction was a stab of extreme guilt. The thought floated up in her mind unbidden, a shot of psychological venom.

He did it because of me.

Oh, no, Veronika, another interior voice answered, attempting to smother the crazy notion before it took another life—before it took her life.

No, no, no. Klara would certainly not want Veronika to feel guilty, Alice wouldn't, her mother wouldn't. It was just a stupid wayward brain wave brought on by the extremity of the situation. She managed to beat the idea back, but it simply retreated into her mind's darkest recesses, not exactly alive but never extinguished.

Grandpa Dalgren always ran hot and cold with his only granddaughter. In his drunkenness he'd sometimes seize Brand up, holding her squirming in his arms, slobbering and telling her he was sorry. For what, he never said.

Other times she caught Gustav staring at her from across the farmhouse kitchen, bleary-eyed from whiskey. The slack expression on his face tilted into an almost evil sneer. He was not in control of himself. The sight of him looking at her would give Brand a skin-crawling impression.

He hates me. My own grandfather hates me.

The suicide was hushed up. The roof of the old barn gave way. The whole structure fell into a charred jumble. The body of the deceased was cooked in thousand-degree heat. Neighbors came running to find Klara, Alice and Veronika still knotted together in a weeping heap.

Gustav had run into the burning barn to try to save the structure, Klara told everyone. The neighbors and the fire crew came too late. Such was Klara's story and she stuck to it. Law enforcement authorities showed up throughout the remainder of the night. No one seemed much interested in challenging the accepted version of the incident. There was no investigation, no autopsy.

"Death by misadventure," read the post-mortem medical certificate, listing heat shock as the cause. As with any burning, Gustav Dalgren's body had retracted into what is termed a boxer's pose or the pugilistic posture, elbows and knees flexed, fists clenched and raised. For a man who had began his life as a fighter for social justice, the end was somehow fitting.

"Gustav was never the same after we came here," Klara told Marta when she came up from New York City for the funeral. It was as close as either woman ever came to an explanation. "Leaving Sweden broke him. Here he is, another victim of the troubles during the war, but fifty years later."

His American neighbors called him Gus. They had always found him distant. No one knew his history. The funeral was sparsely attended, the casket, of course, closed, the mortician's art not up to the task.

Klara, Alice and Veronika remained quiet about what they had seen. The three of them never colluded, never agreed that this was what they would say, and that was the brave face they would present to the world. In fact, Brand had bitten her tongue for years, since she never spoke to Klara or Alice about the lie, and never confessed the particulars of the death to her own mother, the dead man's daughter.

But in her mind the lie grew until it achieved capitalization, the Lie. Fed on fear, grief, and memory, it became a beast that haunted her well into adulthood. She mostly kept it contained, but every once in a while it broke loose, appeared in the mirror looking like the very spit of her, and stalked abroad dressed in Brand's clothes.

52

The Voss family gathered in Stockholm for the 70th anniversary of Voss Trucks. The day marked Loke Voss' first truck purchase, a fleet which would eventually grow into a European transportation giant. Tributes, both floral and otherwise, flowed in from around the country. Everyone honored the economic and social contribution of the company and the distinguished public service of its founder, Loke Voss. The celebrations at the Stockholm Cathedral would attract luminaries from government, military and business. Since the Voss transportation empire reached well beyond Sweden, representatives from the international community attended as well. The King sent best wishes for the affair.

The unstated sentiment behind the festivities held that the founder was after all ninety-eight years old. There would not be that many more occasions to celebrate. The next opportunity for such a commemoration might well be a funeral.

Within the family, the only discordant note was sounded by Ylva Voss. "Do you think *farfar* is strong enough for this? He's been looking a little rattled lately."

Her father, Gabriel Voss, knew the real source of Ylva's feelings on the matter. She believed it would be unseemly to hold a party so soon after the death of her cousin Malte. But the huge fête had been planned long before the incident on the Hede River. It wasn't just close relatives, either. The whole family-owned trucking company was involved. A hundreds strong convoy of vehicles from Voss Transport had been organized.

"The celebration has taken on a life of its own," Junior told her. "I'm sure Malte would have wanted it to go forward."

So Ylva kept her own counsel. She had noticed that her grandfather had changed lately. His face had taken on a haunted look. Hearing the approaching footsteps of mortality, that had to be it. The paper-thin walls of the old man's heart could rupture at any moment. But was there something else? Ylva caught him pawing through mementos, photos from the past, including some from periods better left buried. He often sobbed like a child.

It was an open secret in the family that Loke had been the unseen hand behind the *Nordic Light* arson. Of course, he hadn't meant for anyone to die.

He wasn't a murderer, for pity's sake, not of children, anyway. The inflamed passions of the time were to blame. The *Nordic Light* newspaper was clearly an organ of Soviets, a treasonous outlet in a time of war and an extreme danger to the state. *Nordic Light* had to be silenced, it was that simple. No doubt if Loke could go back, he would do it all over again.

Ylva wondered that an obvious clue to her grandfather's involvement in the arson had always been ignored. It had happened on 3 March, Loke's birthday. She actually appreciated the arrogant quality of scheduling the arson attack on that exact day. It made her laugh, like hanging a sign around your neck declaring "I'm guilty!" and daring the world to do anything about it. In his youth, her grandfather had been a real pisser. He wasn't one to apologize, ever.

No, there was something else bothering him, Ylva felt sure. Amid the flurry of organizing the anniversary celebration, it often seemed she was the only one paying any real attention to the man himself. The rest of the family rushed around busily, treating the *patriark* like the still eye of the storm.

"Is something bothering you, *farfar*?" she asked, kneeling next to Loke's wheelchair. She looked into her grandfather's eyes, trying to discern the source of the shadow on his life. All the Vosses had pale blue eyes, but Loke's were extraordinary, a kind of unflecked gray that was the rarest eye coloring of all. "Goat eyes," was the insult flung at him in his youth, one for which he made his schoolmates pay in blood.

"Are you happy?" Ylva persisted. "You know, if the celebration is too much for you, you can go home after the church ceremony, we can have you watch it on TV. You could stay right here at home. Would you like that?"

They were in the Stockholm townhouse in Östermalm, the whole family filling the rooms of the luxurious and grandiose city space. Elias Voss kept his son Jarl elsewhere, monitoring the boy closely, since he always seemed to fall into some kind of trouble whenever he was in the capital, which was all the time. By hook or by crook, Elias would see to it that Jarl was present and sober for the gathering at the Cathedral.

At that moment, with Ylva staring into Loke's arresting eyes, she thought he resembled a stroke victim, trying to articulate but unable to speak.

"I've done wrong," the old man moaned.

"Oh, no, no, *farfar*, you've been good! So good! Look at the whole world lining up to honor you! Would they do that for a bad man?"

"I loved her," he said, his voice a hoarse whisper. He began to weep.

All the tears a man's man holds back in his early years, Ylva thought, all those left unwept because after all boys don't cry, well, the dam always breaks eventually and they pour forth in old age.

"She…she…she…" Loke stuttered.

"What is it? You can tell me," she said in her most comforting granddaughter's voice, the one that nearly always got her what she wanted. But she couldn't get anything more out of him. Then Junior had come in, angry at her for upsetting his father.

As the anniversary celebration approached, Ylva made her own preparations. She considered that she had come at the American detective and her Sami sidekick twice now, both times with blades. It was time to employ a proper weapon, one that she trained herself in for years, winning shooting competitions all over Sweden.

The Anschütz 1827F biathlon rifle, manufactured by a German company, looked like it was put together by a committee of the insane. At the thing's heart lay an ordinary .22 long rifle, rendered extraordinary by the demands of the sport. Add-ons, appurtenances, and modifications attached themselves to every section of the weapon, from a cheek guard fastened to the stock, to a snow cover on the front gun sight. The special biathlon magazine poked awkwardly up mid-barrel. The 1827F was a rifle in the sense that the international space station was an airplane.

The Vosses owned one of the colorful buildings off the Stortorget, the Great Square. The top story was given over to a tower arrangement. The cramped, belfry-like interior contained an apartment, now empty, that had been used over the years by this or that family member. It was a measure of the Voss wealth that such a gem located in a neighborhood of outrageously pricey real estate was left vacant. But the building's elevator did not reach to the top floor apartment. One had to climb a narrow flight of stairs. What a bother! No one wanted it.

Hours before the anniversary celebration, Ylva set herself up in the tower apartment. Her worry over the public event was not limited to concerns about her grandfather's health. She knew that the American detective was still running free somewhere, sniffing around, bound to make trouble. The combined efforts of the *polis*, the military (Frans Voss had set the *Särskilda operationsgruppen* on her trail), and the formidable security corps of Voss Transport had so far failed to locate Veronika Brand.

In the aftermath of their encounter at Voss Medical Center, Brand had either left the country or holed up somewhere. Either way, Ylva did not feel like taking chances. Something had set the madwoman against the Voss family and against Loke Voss senior. Brand was the granddaughter of Gustav Dalgren, the editor of *Nordic Light*. Ylva didn't believe anyone (apart from herself) could nurse a grudge over an event that happened that far in the past.

What was Veronika Brand's problem? Perhaps the bitch just wanted to talk over old times with Loke. Perhaps she was compiling an oral history of her family.

Uh-huh. Ylva didn't think so, and she didn't much care about motivations anyway. She liked the idea of covering her granddad's ceremony in case Detective Brand thought to crash it. Granted, taking the woman out might mar the anniversary festivities somewhat. Then again, it could also be seen as the ultimate tribute to Loke Voss. It depended how you looked at it.

The small casement window in the tower apartment had a clear view of the square. Ylva was forced to lean halfway out onto the gabled roof to position herself properly, but really, nothing could be easier. She could make a shot like that in her sleep.

The .22 long rifle bullet is not ordinarily that powerful of a load, much smaller and slower than those used in many sniper situations in the military. But Ylva did what she could to boost the speed and heft of the projectile, choosing a lead-tipped, steel jacketed magnum cartridge. With the wallop that a round like that would pack, she didn't think she would need a second shot.

As she sighted the rifle in, she had a thought that the distance and angle resembled Lee Harvey Oswald's kill shot in Dallas. Eighty meters, more or less, tower window to square, though the angle—she gauged it at twenty-two degrees—was slightly greater. And of course Oswald had to hit a moving target, the presidential limousine moving at five kilometers an hour.

As kids she and Malte had fooled around trying to duplicate Oswald's shot on the Västvall estate. They hooked a little four wheeler ATV to a flatbed wagon with a couple of pumpkins on it, then cajoled Hans Voss into driving it slowly past where the two of them had positioned themselves atop a farm silo. Of course their younger cousin had objected to the arrangement, but they extended the length of the rope between the target wagon and the four wheeler, so there was no real danger.

She and Malte took turns blasting away, hooting and hollering.

"Slower!" Ylva shouted down, laughing at poor frightened Hans. "Go slower!" The boy was driving like a bat from hell attempting to remove himself from the line of fire.

It took Malte a dozen tries, but Ylva managed a bull's-eye on her third. Not that difficult of a shot at all, despite what the conspiracy theorists might say.

53

Stockholm is a horizontal, not a vertical city, approachable on a human scale, unlike the claustrophobic soar of New York. There are no bona fide skyscrapers, The capital's tallest building tops out at thirty-two floors. But at least Brand had an upper story view from her apartment, or hotel room, or pied a terre—whatever her quarters might be called. There were streets, waterways, and parks visible from the twin west-facing windows. The mostly gravel gray landscape displayed a few surprising bits of green, pine trees that had hung on through the long winter.

The Stockholm archipelago made for a city of islands and bridges, tens of thousands of islands, skerries, sea stacks, tombolos, islets, and rocks, linked by the most amazing collection of bridges in the world, and Brand had come to believe that here was a good correlative for the Swedish people, connected by numberless strong bridges of community and cooperation, but after all separate, independent, immune.

Moro Part had assigned Brand a minder, Sandri, stationed in the long empty corridor outside her room, always there whenever she peeped out. She never seemed to catch the man coming into the room, but *kaffe* and food had always appeared as if by magic whenever she woke from sleep.

Three rooms, a small suite. Brand experienced moments when it felt like a jail. Taking full advantage of the bathroom's elaborate Jacuzzi-nozzled tub, she bathed twice within twelve hours, washing off the verminous stench of the deer shack. Black silk pajamas, her size, materialized, her filth-ridden clothes disappeared, only to show up again cleaned and neatly folded. She was a captive princess.

Even with all that, she was shocked to find a bottle of prescription Adderall in the medicine cabinet. Moro Part, she decided, knew her all too well. She slipped back into addiction as if it were a comfortable suit of clothes. Mostly, though, Brand allowed herself to be bored, a blessing in the wake of the constant drumming, recently, of excitement, violence, and event. A feeling gnawed at her, a question she was not ready to answer. Had she joined the enemy, let go of her pledge to uphold the law, disgraced herself and the work she had done for the past twenty years?

She stayed off social media, focusing instead on local news feeds and newscasts. She understood enough Swedish to figure out the reporting. Film footage helped. The media played the incident along the Hede River as drug violence, three Norwegian Turks murdered by hands unknown. The limited reporting made no mention of the Voss name or the incongruous presence of a spotted hyena at the scene.

Moro had informed her that Dollar Boy had gotten his pink-haired head fatally split open, but there seemed to be no mention of that in news reports, either. Nor of Hammar or Brand. The furious knife-fight in the hospital room at Sveg had likewise somehow been kept off the media radar. What was going on?

Twenty-nine hours into her stay, Sandri the Quiet Minder knocked and entered. The windows showed dark, with an overcast sky reflecting the city lights. Brand had just woken up, luxuriating in bed despite needing to pee. She lazily felt another nap coming on.

"Mademoiselle," Sandri said, addressing her in accented French. He handed over an iPhone, then discreetly withdrew to his post out in the hall.

A FaceTime convo was already in progress on the cell phone's screen. Some poor mook totally swaddled in gauze moved a pair of parched-looking lips in a failed attempt at speech.

Veronika couldn't speak, she was so relieved. A sob of relief rose in her throat. Finally she mastered herself. "You're awake."

"Awake but dreaming," Krister Hammar whispered, his first words to her since coming out of an eighteen-hour coma.

"Wow," Brand said. "You look terrible. You look like Santa Claus on the day after Christmas."

"My head hurts, but I'm in a lovely morphine haze," he said, twisting his mouth into a horrible approximation of a smile. "How do you feel?"

"Jesus, a lot better than you look." Brand felt an enormous tenderness toward him.

"Do you know the Arctic explorer…"

"Don't talk. Talking looks as though it hurts you."

"There was a man," Hammar told her, "a Dane named Peter Freuchen, an— an—an arctic explorer…"

He seemed to be having difficulty forming words, and Brand tried to shush him again. She didn't care about any Dane explorer, so relieved and happy was she to find Hammar living, breathing, and speaking.

He would not be shushed. "So Freuchen got buried when a snow bank collapsed on top of him. No way out. Slowly freezing to death. Know what— what—what he did?"

"No," Brand said, indulging him, tearing up. "What did Peter Freuchen do?"

"Took a crap, formed his poop into the shape of a trowel, let it freeze solid, then dug his way out with that. That's— that's— how I feel. Like I just dug my way out of a coma with a shovel of frozen shit."

Hammar and Brand both laughed, but his laughter passed into a spasm of coughing.

"Krister...I...I'm so..." Brand said, then stopped, unsure of her feelings or what words might pop out. "I'm glad, just...glad, that's all."

"How did you—?" He trailed off, his lips moving spasmodically.

"How did I...what?"

"How did you save me? Was I under— beneath— the water...?"

"Well, no poop was involved," Brand said. "Although I could well have shat myself from sheer terror."

"Where are you? No, wait, you better not say." He lowered his voice. "There are *polis* here."

"Here, too—in fact, you're looking at one. Your friend in blue, always on duty."

"No."

"Yes," she said. "Hang up and rest, okay? You need to get better. I foresee some sauna therapy in your future."

Even trying for a smile caused Hammar to wheeze. "You are trying to— to—"

"Kill you, I know."

"Varzha Luna?" he asked. "No one has told me..."

"Sleep now. She's fine, I'm fine, everything else is total crap."

A long wordless pause. She wondered if the man had fallen back asleep. "Krister?"

"Yes?"

"I can trust Moro, right?"

"No," he said.

Brand punched the red screen button to end the call, then began to cry. Exhaustion, apprehension, and sadness swirled within her. For the first time since coming to Sweden she fully gave in to tears. Sandri, her caretaker and guard, stuck his head into the room, as always arriving softly. She handed the iPhone back to him, and he wordlessly gave her a colorful embroidered linen handkerchief to dry her tears.

54

By the morning of the third day sequestered in her hotel room Brand felt the first twinges of cabin fever. What, am I a prisoner here? She would pose the question if only she had someone to ask. Sandri, her near-mute minder might only smile and shrug. Moro Part would be the one to supply the answer. The big man had promised to visit but never did. So when there came a knock Brand thought it could be him, coming to liberate her.

"Yes?"

Sandri stuck his head through the half open door. "A visitor," he said, stepping aside to allow a slight, brilliantly dressed woman to enter the room.

Varzha Luna. A wave of sentiment hit Brand that took her by surprise. Perhaps she hadn't fully recovered her emotional equilibrium after all. Here was the young woman who had somehow become the focus of Brand's sojourn in Sweden. She appeared impossibly young, impossibly vulnerable. Brand rushed to embrace the girl.

Varzha submitted to the hug. "Veronika Brand," she said softly. Her English wasn't equal to the situation, and Brand's Swedish wasn't, either. They made do.

"Hello!" Brand exclaimed. "How are you? I am so happy to finally meet!"

"I want to come thank you," Varzha said haltingly.

"Thank me? You were the brave one!"

Varzha smiled shyly. Brand took a step back to examine her.

The girl had left off her usual heavy white makeup. Clear-faced, she appeared a delicate, ethereal beauty. She wore an ankle-length skirt of many colors, a beautiful embroidered tunic, three lovely silk scarves, each setting off in complementary hues the rest of the ensemble. Over it all went a warm woolen monkey jacket with elaborate brocade, a gorgeous number that would fetch thousands of dollars in any Madison Avenue boutique. A little round Astrakhan cap topped off the outfit.

Varzha performed an odd, formal half bow. "I would to…" She stumbled over the words. Sandri lurked in the background, feeding her the English in a whisper.

"I would like to invite you…to my engagement blessing ceremony."

Brand beamed a smile. "Oh, yes, congratulations! But you are too young to marry!" she blurted out.

Varzha looked to Sandri. "No, no!" Brand said to him. "Don't translate that last part! Just tell her I am happy for her."

Drawing Varzha into the suite, Brand gestured to an arrangement of chairs pulled up next to a couch. They sat, communicating in smiles, nods, and sign language. The girl knew the words, "New York City," and two of them repeated that to each other a few times.

Sandri interposed. "She can't stay," he said.

"Get me to the church on time, right?" Brand said brightly. She felt strangely flustered, not wholly in total control of her thoughts or feelings. She wanted to tell Varzha…what?

"I have to say—" She broke off. "I am a police."

"*Polis*," Varzha repeated, nodding.

The words came out in a spill. "I have to say how much I admire you. I've done what you did, I mean, in my job as a police officer, I've served as a decoy in prostitution stings, and it was the most dangerous work I've ever done."

Sandri appeared baffled. Brand waved him off. "That's okay, that's okay—you don't have to translate all that… Just say I admire her, all right?"

Again, Varzha responded with a shy smile. She resembled a girl one minute, a ninja warrior the next, like a gem with many varied facets. She wore a string of small gold coins around her neck, the kind of adornment Brand had often seen in Lehtonen's photos of Romani women. In a graceful move, Varzha bent her head, removed the necklace and presented it to Brand, along with a beautiful multi-colored scarf.

"Oh, no, no, no, I can't accept!" Brand said. But a glance at Sandri's stern expression prompted her to take the gifts.

"Thank you!"

Varzha stood. "Moro? Moro Part?"

"Yes?" Brand rose also. "Of course I know Moro."

"You go to him now," Varzha said, managing the sentence in clear English.

"Um, okay, yes," Brand said, looking over at Sandri, who nodded.

"You must," Varzha said, showing a flash of stern authority. She floated toward the door, a Romani princess putting to shame the insipid environment of the suite, with its modern, mass-produced furnishings.

She stopped before leaving, turned, and impulsively hugged Brand. "I will see you…?"

"Oh, yes. I would be delighted to come to your engagement ceremony.

Sandri knows, right? Where it is, where I should go?"

Varzha nodded. "Sandri knows," she said.

Brand laid a hand on Varzha's arm. "This…this vendetta is over. Is it over? Someone has to say it's over. Otherwise it's just bitterness."

Varzha remained expressionless. "Go to Moro. Important."

Then she left, taking most of the magic out of the room when she did.

Sandri returned to the suite an hour later, giving Brand time to bathe. She wondered how one dressed for a Romani engagement ceremony. When she emerged from the bathroom she found Sandri had entered the suite and left behind, on a hanger hooked to the mirrored door of the suite's bedroom closet, a simple burgundy frock, quite stylish. She would have gladly worn it to a cocktail party in New York.

On a side table was a small pouch full of cosmetics. Not her particular choice of war paint, but in a pinch… When Sandri came for her she was more or less as ready as she was ever going to be. She wore the coin necklace given to her by Varzha.

"He says you should come and I will show you where you meet." Whenever Sandri said "he," it referred to his boss, Moro Part.

"Okay," Brand said. "Then we'll go to this… I don't know, what is an engagement ceremony, anyway?"

"The blessing of the union foretold," Sandri said soberly.

"Do I look all right? Presentable?"

Sandri made a motion to her hair. "You must cover."

This was the reason for Varzha's gift of the scarf. Brand hated to give in to what she considered a sour stricture on female behavior, but figured, when in Rome… She put on the headscarf and followed Sandri out the door of the suite.

He conducted Brand down the long corridor to the elevator, punched the button to take them to the basement, and led her across the cavernous parking garage to the parked Mercedes sedan. They met no one on the way.

Brand could see Sandri struggle with himself as he opened the driver's side door for her. "He said you drive." A frown of doubt showed in his face that was almost laughable. Clearly, for him, the natural order of things was being disrupted.

Never a passenger, always the driver.

"Thanks," Brand said, and slipped in behind the wheel. "You tell me where to go." Sandri went around to the other side of the vehicle and climbed into the passenger seat.

"Gamla Stan," he said. "To Stortorget, the Great Square."

He directed her out onto the busy streets of the capital. The day was 3

March. The bright, unseasonably warm pre-noon held a tantalizing hint of spring. The clear expanse of the sky shone bright blue. Everywhere on the streets and in the parks Swedes shamelessly shed their heavy clothes, faces raised to capture the copious onslaught of Vitamin D. They passed a good number of people leaning up against buildings, basking in the intense rays of old Sol pouring down on them.

Had they gone mad? But no, it was a communal coming out party, a poke in the eye of the long unending winter.

Traffic was severely restricted in the narrow streets of the Old Town. Sandri had to guide her on a circuitous route, passing the island on something like a belt highway, exiting, then approaching the central square from the south.

"Here," he said, pointing to a truck-loading space along an impossibly clogged street. Brand could feel the man itching to get back into the driver's seat. She was being kicked to the curb.

"Moro will be in the café, voila," Sandri said, indicating a coffee house a few doors away. Brand left the car, yielding the wheel to her minder. Heading toward the open square, she passed another line of flagrant sun worshipers soaking in heat reflected off a bank building's stone façade.

The café was as crowded as the sidewalks. The mood on the street and inside the restaurant was giddy with sunlight. Brand saw Moro Part before he saw her. He sat alone at a table, reading a newspaper. Examining him, she recalled the enormous portraits in Aino Lehtonen's studio. The photographer had caught a very different version of the man.

That Moro had been dressed in a shabby brown overcoat. As he trudged his collection route, visiting each member of his street cadre in turn, Lehtonen had followed along. He carried a black cloth bag and accepted money from Roma street beggars, children, men and women both. Lehtonen's camera caught a great shot of Moro's mitt-like hand, reaching out with the black bag to receive the mendicant's kronor coins and crumpled Euros.

In the café the man wore an entirely different guise, that of a sophisticated businessman, with an expensive tailored three-piece suit in pinstripe gray. There was not a hint of Fagin about him. She was surprised to see he was reading *Svenska dagbladet*, the conservative daily.

She approached. Moro's face lit up. Setting aside his newspaper, he heaved his massive body to standing.

"Magnificent," he pronounced, examining her outfit. He gave a practiced kiss on both cheeks.

"I feel pampered by you," Brand said.

"Sit, sit! I will pamper you still. I've ordered coffee and pastries." His enthusiasm felt designed to be contagious, but Brand was immune to the man's charms. She didn't feel she could cozy up to him. The civilized, well-dressed gent beside her was also the brutal strongman who engineered the violence that went down on the banks of the Hede River. And the Manor House, and the blizzard attack at Västvall. She felt like seizing his hands and examining them, see if they still had blood on them.

The server arrived, a young woman carrying a pair of porcelain cups steaming with coffee so black it looked like tar.

"Doppio espresso, fair-trade, shade-grown, French roast," Moro said in a sardonic tone.

"Yes, that's right," the server said. "So, who called this meeting?" she added, chirping out a riffy question from a popular television show.

"I did," Brand and Moro both answered simultaneously, dutifully completing the joke. But Brand got the idea that although she was familiar with the pop-culture reference, Moro might have taken the line seriously. At least, he didn't laugh along with them. She saw his eyes narrow and once again caught a glimpse of the sinister Moro, but just for a moment, before being replaced by the benign Moro. It was enough to scare the server into a quick retreat.

"Despite the rumors, I am not the King of the Roma," Moro said mournfully.

"And yet here you sit with a gentile in a Swedish café."

"Far away from the blue skies of the land where I was born." Moro drained his double-shot espresso in the European way, with one throat-searing gulp.

His whole mien was sorrowful, which was puzzling in a person about to preside over a happy occasion like a marriage engagement. Then again, Brand thought, what would be the appearance of someone who had recently set about committing a series of ruthless murders, as vicious as any she had seen?

"I honor you," Moro said, "in recognition of your efforts on the part of my people."

"Thank you, although I fear I've caused you more trouble than I'm worth," Brand said. She sat back to display the gold necklace that Varzha had given her. "Do I make for a convincing gypsy?"

"No," Moro said. "You could maybe fool the *gadje*, but never the Romani. You are only guilty of the serious crime of cultural appropriation."

Brand laughed. "Do we go now?" she asked. "Your man Sandri told me the cathedral will be busy today. Lots of different services."

"Not quite yet. I too have a gift for you. But first I must tell you a story."

Ah, yes, Brand thought. With Moro, there will always be a story.

"I wonder if you know that Gustav Dalgren was a hero among the Roma. From your puzzled look I see that you do not. But in the years before the fascists targeted our people he acted as a great supporter. He idolized Ivar Lo Johansson's novel on the Roma, *Zigenare*, and set out to follow the author's footsteps. Gustav spent 'a summer on the homeless people's hiking trails.' I never met the man myself, but his name is still pronounced among Romani. He foresaw the genocide, the slaughter of the *pharrajimos*, what you in the West label the *Holokosto*."

Brand had a vague awareness that during WWII a half million Roma perished in Nazi death camps. But she wondered where Moro was going with all this. Gustav a gypsy hero? Really? Part of her was becoming weary of the past. Events of more than a half century ago kept erupting into the present. At the moment the whole business struck her as tiresome and annoying.

"The Romani still maintain the legend of Gustav Dalgren. I will tell you a story of your grandparents during those years, Gustav and Klara, a terrible story that has come down to me."

Brand almost interrupted Moro with a "please don't." The man bulled forward.

"A gentleman named Loke Voss led the brownshirts in Härjedalen. They loved to smash Romani skulls. The only one who stood up for us was Gustav Dalgren. He would not back down. He spoke out all the time, for Roma, for the workers, for the poor and powerless. His newspaper *Nordic Light* was like a poke in Hitler's eye. Everyone knew Gustav walked around with a big fat target on his back. Voss and his troops were out to execute him."

"I know all this," Brand said. "I mean, I know about the newspaper arson."

"You know, but you do not know," Moro responded.

"I have come to suspect that I am somehow here in Sweden to confront Loke Voss," Brand said, her tone a little snappish.

"Confront. What does that mean?"

"I will expose him as the one who lit the match."

"Yes, yes, a worthy pursuit. But I wonder if all this confronting and exposing goes far enough. I was in the middle of telling you a story."

"Yes, forgive me," Brand said sarcastically. "I must have been distracted by the enthralling nature of the tale. Please continue."

Moro nodded, taking her words at face value. "In the spring of 1940, two women climb a hillside above Västvall village. The first of May. Snow still lies on the ground. As they hike they dream back over their childhoods, warmer days and better times. The village children all played up here together, racing through the forests and fields, at times lying lazily atop the cows chewing cud, the hot animal scent filling their nostrils."

How could Moro possibly know all this? Brand wondered. Snow still lies thick on the ground? It was all pure fantasy and embellishment.

"The day I speak about, the women are older and they have put aside their childish things. Two sisters on the threshold of adulthood, one 21, on 19. They go in secret, telling no one, especially not Gustav Dalgren."

"Wait," Brand said. Two sisters? This was a story of her grandmother Klara and her great-aunt Alice?

"Wait," she said again. Wait.

But the man would not stop.

55

"Loke Voss has set himself up in an old *fäbod* on top of the mountain. He is a brownshirt, a rising figure among the Swedish fascists. He makes his collection of mountain shacks over into the local Nazi headquarters. The sisters take their lives in their hands venturing up to Loke's *fäbod* hideout."

All right, Brand wanted to say. Okay. Please stop now.

"The two women approach, wearing their modest home-sewn linen dresses and clumsy farm boots, an unflattering look overall, but practical. They walk the length of the *fäbod* to the farthest building, a cabin built of peeled logs. A flag with a swastika cross inside a black circle hangs from an outstretched pole above the door. The banner snaps in the breeze, flinging its fabric upwards and reminding the women of the Heil Hitler salute.

"They stand for a moment, unwilling to knock on the door, afraid to open it. They hear voices raised in song. A band of Loke's boys come marching up the mountain from the other direction, swinging their arms in unison. Their chorus is enough to make the stomach turn."

Here Moro softly sang the Nazi marching song.

Raise the flag! The ranks tightly closed!
Brownshirts march with calm, steady step!
Clear the streets for the brown battalions!

Clear the streets for the storm division!"

"Then comes a shrill whistle, as a sentry at the opposite end of the compound wakes to women's presence.

"'Reds!' he yells. *'Vänsterfolk! Kommunister!'"*

"The marchers break ranks and charge toward the interlopers, pushing and shoving, screaming into their faces. The women find themselves trapped in a gauntlet of Nazi bullyboys, many of whom are youths they recognize from the neighborhood. The older woman especially is roughed up. The marchers tear her dress. She grips her sister's hand so tightly that she draws blood, thinking if she let go they would both die."

No, please. Stop. I don't want to know.

"Out from the cabin door steps an unlikely savior. Loke Voss appears and immediately calls off his young dogs. Obeying his commands, the tormentors back down. The older sister straightens herself and walks calmly toward Loke. The younger one tries to match her courage but trembles like a leaf."

Brand stared fixedly at Moro. She felt pinned to her chair. Her breath came with difficulty.

"Can you picture it, Veronika?" Moro asked. "Loke is courtly, smiling, inviting the older sister into his cabin lair. He wears calf-high black boots and the familiar brown uniform. He sports a captain's insignia. Even though he is still a boy, he believes he has come into his own. With his slick yellow hair and spooky pale eyes, he looks every centimeter an Aryan. Nietzsche's blond beast personified.

"From childhood the older sister always had Loke in the palm of her hand. He loved her and hated her all at once.

"'Gustav,' Klara Dalgren now says to Loke, simply and quietly.

"'Yes, yes, always Gustav,' Loke says. 'Always something with Gustav.' He laughs. But it is not a real laugh. It is more like something has gotten stuck in his throat and he is trying to get it out.

"'Come, Klara,' he says.

"'Alice, wait outside,' Klara Dalgren says.

"Alice tries to stop it. 'Sister, no—'"

"Loke silences her. 'Yes, dear sister Alice, wait here.'"

"The two of them, Loke and Klara, disappear into the cabin."

Moro leaned forward and placed the heavy meat of his hand upon Brand's. "We don't need to go inside to know what went on within, do we?"

Brand found herself unable to respond. She wanted to challenge him. You can't know! How could you possibly know? The words caught in her throat.

"The older sister appeals to Loke inside the cabin that afternoon. Spare Gustav's life, she begs. She knows the Nazis will kill Gustav if he keeps on speaking and writing against them. Loke is the man who will order the assassination done."

The picture Moro drew drilled its way into Brand's mind. Fury and disgust rose in her. Her mind buzzed with the words from Elin's letter. The older man's hypnotic voice droned on.

"We don't have to see to know what happened. We witness the older sister plead for the life of Gustav, the man she loved. We can see Loke Voss's smile crease his face. We hear their dull footsteps as the two of them climb the stairs to the cabin loft. Klara's ripped dress, torn by his bullyboys, enflames Loke's mind."

Brand had heard enough. "Stop!" she shouted. Other customers in the café turned to look. Moro lowered his voice and continued.

"Gustav never finds out. His baby daughter comes along the next November, when he and his wife have already fled America after the arson. Gustav is overjoyed to have a daughter."

"Marta…" The whisper emerged unbidden from Brand's lips. Her mother. Which meant…

"All babies are born with blue eyes. But as Marta Dalgren grows into toddlerhood, an awful understanding dawns on Gustav. Before that, he is industrious around the farm in his newly adopted country, still active in worker's rights, the same old Gustav we know and admire in Sweden. Then the truth settles on him. He changes. He breaks down. The bottle comes along and destroys everything.

"Because the darling daughter that his wife had given birth to now shows those oddly colored eyes, gray with a hint of heliotrope. A very rare color, very distinctive. Your same inherited eyes, Veronika. Poor Gustav knows exactly where he has seen them before. Staring back at him from his daughter's face are the remarkable and instantly recognizable gray eyes of Loke Voss."

Brand rose to her feet. "You're lying!" she shouted. But she knew it was the truth. Loke Voss was her mother's biological father. Which made Veronika, at least in blood, a member of the Voss clan.

She had knocked over her chair. Other people in the cafe looked over at them.

"Sit," Moro said. "I told you I have another gift for you, one you have yearned for and felt incomplete without."

He righted Brand's toppled chair. "Sit," he commanded again. "And I will tell you exactly where to go to find your missing pistol."

56

Brand stared at Moro.

"You have the Glock?"

"I don't," Moro said. "But I can tell you where it is."

"Where?"

"Take up your sword again, Veronika," Moro whispered. "Take it and use it. You know what you have to do."

"Goddammit, Moro!"

"Klara's rapist is right here," Moro said. "Loke Voss is nearby, at the cathedral for his big anniversary celebration. It will be quite easily done. Avenge Klara. See to it that poor Gustav did not kill himself in vain. An eye for an eye. A death for a death. You must murder the devil or you will never be free."

Moro's voice was insistent, almost teasing. It felt like it came from another world, another time. The strange thing was, the very strange thing, was that Moro's words seemed eminently logical. Of course Veronika Brand should assassinate Loke Voss. There was a symmetry to the act that could not be denied.

Amphetamine continued to disrupt Brand's thinking. Her thoughts stuttered and skipped. She found herself suddenly out on the street. The hordes of sun-happy citizens appeared wolfish and gross to her. She pushed along among them, shouldering happy, sun-struck Swedes out of the way.

Her mind fell into a muddle. She was having a panic attack. She was not having a panic attack. She would finally be reunited with the missing pistol. She would kill her grandfather and then shoot herself. She would do nothing of the kind.

Faces loomed up and fell away. Someone shouted. She was having a psychotic break. She was not having a psychotic break.

Brand didn't know how long she wandered, down one impossibly narrow cobblestone street in the old town and up another, buffeted by other pedestrians. She found herself in the Stortorget, the great square, busy with people. Ahead was the stock exchange and the Nobel museum, and to the north of that Brand could see the copper-green tower of the church, a brick Gothic rockpile with a stone obelisk poking up to one side of it.

"You must go to the cathedral," she heard a voice say. She stared wildly around. Was Moro Part here? No, it was just a tourist urging on another tourist. Brand's mind would not stay on track. What time was it? A thought winged in from nowhere. Moro wore an expensive watch, a Rolex. Was it a knock-off? Her thinking skittered this way and that.

Brand entered a dream. A great deal of time seemed to pass. She threaded her way through the square toward the big church. St. Nicholas Cathedral, she knew—or thought she knew—was Lutheran, once the official state religion of Sweden. The Roma were, if they were anything, Catholic, Orthodox Christian or Muslim, their beliefs mixed with folklore, stretching back as far as their Hindu origins.

What was a Romani girl like Varzha Luna doing having an engagement ceremony at a Lutheran church? Given her disordered mind, the thought was strangely cogent.

"Find the engagement party," Moro had told her. "Varzha Luna will give you your lost pistol."

Thirty meters away, she saw a small group of Romani celebrants gathered around Varzha Luna. Beside her stood her brother Vago and a man wearing a black suit, standing stiff and awkward in a way that Brand read as "groom."

As Brand moved forward her attention shifted from the engagement party. Another large group emerged from the direction of the cathedral. Specters in her nightmare, a whole clutch of Vosses posed for a group photograph with Stortorget as a backdrop. Most of the figures were recognizable from Brand's research.

Jarl Voss. Elias Voss, his father. Vilgot Voss, his father. "Junior" Voss.

And there, in the midst of them all, held up at his elbows by a pair of younger family members, stood the shuffling old man whom Brand would murder.

Loke Voss. Family patriarch. Right-wing instigator of the fire that had broken her family. Rapist. Devil.

Grandfather.

At that moment a screaming howl descended upon the whole city of Stockholm, obliterating any other noise beneath its hollow roar. Every truck in the Voss Transport fleet sounded their air horns at the same time. The awful bleating and honking, in honor of the prestigious company and its founder, echoed through the Old Town like an orchestra of air raid sirens.

Veronika Brand might have been the only creature in the whole city who didn't hear the cacophony for what it was. She thought it might be the tinnitus roar of her own blood through her veins. The screaming urged her onward. She dream-walked toward the old man posed among his children in the square.

57

Through the scope on her 1875F, Ylva tracked Veronika Brand's progress. She saw the American detective move in the direction of the church, and understood that almost every member of the Voss family would be gathered there.

Ylva had difficulty getting a clear shot in the crowded square, filled with sun-worshipers and ordinary citizens enjoying the day. But she held up for another reason, which she didn't even fully admit to herself. She wanted to drop the woman right in front of her family, at the feet of her father and uncles and nephew.

Pow! Take that, my dear idiot relations, who walk around in a daze half the time. Maybe then they would begin to take Ylva seriously. They had ignored her warnings. Now she would show them the truth.

Her target vanished briefly, obscured by a gaggle of Japanese tourists. Ylva decided as soon as she had a clear shot she would take it. She was hanging half out the window now, concentrating, the greatest short-range sniper rifle in the world held tight against her right shoulder, its scope locked in on the woman who had brought about Malte Voss's death.

The noise of the Voss Transport air horns exploded, but Ylva was in total Zen mode, centered, impossible to distract. With the sound echoing over the square, she did not hear the door of the tower apartment open behind her.

Veronika Brand came into view again. The cortex of Ylva's brain initiated a message that reached her right forefinger, directing it to squeeze-not-pull the trigger.

An old man came alive during the dual celebration, marking both his company's anniversary and final birthday of his ninetieth decade at St. Nicholas Cathedral in the heart of Stockholm. As he stood in the great square, surrounded by family, he saw a woman moving toward him.

He knew the woman, knew the way she held herself. In the careful but certain way she moved, Loke Voss saw the woman he loved more than any other, Klara Dalgren. She was Klara. She was his own blood and she was here to celebrate his life's achievements.

Voss had been waiting. He longed for the granddaughter of his heart. Watching Brand move toward him, his face lit up. As he lurched out from among his children and his children's children, he careened forward with the sure-footed movement of a man half his age.

He would finally be able to embrace his granddaughter, Veronika Brand—the child of the rape-spawn child, Marta, whom Loke had sired with the love of his life, Klara Dalgren.

"Veronika," Loke now exclaimed with an old man's desperate, sentimental despair, the last word he would utter in life.

His forward charge thrust him abruptly between Brand and a tower window eighty meters away.

When the old man's head fell forward at an awkward angle and a red bloom appeared on his right temple, Brand snapped out of her dream. Adrenaline coursed through her body. She instantly grasped she was in the midst of some sort of firefight. She felt more than heard the hollow ping of the rifle shot echo across the square. She didn't duck, but bent low to catch her grandfather's body in her arms.

The two of them stared at each other for a quick, evaporating moment. Love struggled with hate and disgust in her eyes. A plea for forgiveness showed in his. She saw the light fade, the signature gray of Loke Voss's eyes dying to a flat, lifeless transparency.

No one in the crowd or among the Voss family immediately understood what was happening. Brand had no time to process every thought that came at her, but jumped to the conclusion that somehow Moro Part had been the source of the fatal bullet. She half-turned toward the engagement party, expecting to see the Roma godfather.

Instead she saw the stolid, black-suited male standing beside Varzha step forward. The engaged husband, Luri Kováč. He raised a pistol, aiming it in the direction of the Voss family. Brand had an instant to recognize the weapon as her own Glock.

The sight of the handgun finally ignited panic among everyone standing nearby.

"Unto the third or fourth generation!" Luri Kováč yelled out, his thus-always-to-tyrants exclamation obscured by truck horns.

He fired off a reckless spray of shots—wild ones that harmed nobody but served to further panic the crowd. It turned out that human screams could cut through the sound of a thousand air horns. Bystanders flung themselves every which way, instinctively ducking as they ran.

Luri dropped the Glock and raised his arms in a gesture of surrender. The overheated pistol clattered to the cobblestone pavement of the square.

Trying for gentleness in an impossibly electrified moment, Brand laid the still form of Loke Voss on the ground, hoping it wouldn't be trampled in the crush. All was chaos. The assembled members of the Voss family scattered.

Brand watched as Varhza Luna stepped forward. Time stuttered, a movie reel sprung loose from its sprockets. As one of the fleeing Vosses stumbled past her, Varzha reached out and struck the figure once. The blow came so quickly that Brand never saw the knife.

"For Lel!" Varzha called out, though no one but Veronika heard her.

Jarl Voss. His face showed a flash of hurt surprise. Momentum carried him a few steps forward. He clutched his side, where blood blossomed along a bloody slash just beneath his ribcage. The wounded man dropped to his knees.

Varzha showed herself to him, making sure her former captor understood that it was she who had given him a mortal wound.

With a brief look over her shoulder, the Romani girl locked eyes with Brand. Varzha gave a sober nod. She then joined the general rush of fleeing pedestrians, disappearing among the crowd. Luri Ková́č just stood, dazed, as confusion erupted around him. He looked after Varzha with hurt in his eyes, as if offended that she had disarmed him, as if agonized she was leaving him behind.

A collection of impromptu heroes tackled Luri to the ground.

Brand ignored the tussle. Don't do it, her mind commanded. Do not pick up that Glock. Your fingerprints will be all over it when the *polis* come. And they will come. There's one running in your direction now. Perhaps seeing a weapon in your hand he will shoot you dead. At any rate your prints on the pistol will put you in a Swedish prison for years.

Don't do it.

Swedish prisons were notoriously cushy, she thought. No life sentences here. She'd be out in no time.

Don't do it.

Brand bent down and picked up her long-lost duty gun, reuniting with the weapon that had been stolen away by a mohawk crazy-man with pink hair.

As she straightened with the pistol in her hand, Brand gazed over the mad scramble in the square. An arresting sight caught her eye, a pair of figures in a window at the top of a building a football pitch away.

The two were clearly visible. They seemed engaged in an embrace. With a start Brand recognized both of them.

Moro Part attempted to push Ylva Voss out of the eight-story window to her death. Ylva fought to stop him from doing so.

The outlandish biathlon rifle dropped first, plummeting through the air. Again, Brand felt more than heard the impact as the weapon bounced once and settled. Then the shooter and her attacker followed, Moro and Ylva locked in a death grip, tracing an arrow-straight trajectory before also slamming onto the stone pavement.

The two bodies bounced not at all.

Part four: Coda

58

Krister Hammar stood looking out the window of his second floor office, his back to the functional ergonomic desk that was scattered with the legal documents that had consumed his life before this tawdry affair. He was waiting on his 11 o'clock appointment. Involuntarily he began counting the dead, folding his fingers over one by one, as he had once seen old Elin Dalgren do, toting up the evils done to her family amidst her plans for retribution.

A few hours earlier he had dropped Veronika Brand off at the express train to Arlanda airport. Their leave-taking had been awkward. Hammar could not decide if they should embrace, if he should kiss her cheeks, or merely bid her a fond farewell.

Brand had appeared flustered, also. In the end they settled on a stiff bow and a handshake, performed there in the antiseptic public precincts of the express station.

The swift walk back to his Vasaplan office had not given him time to process the exchange. But now, Hammar shook his head. A bow! The formality represented a denial of all the rigors they had been through. With a drop in his gut he realized—too late, since she was already on a plane back to New York City—that his feelings toward Brand were more complex than he previously understood.

What was their precise relationship? Not that of comrades in the foxhole, as he had felt during their recent travails. Alternative images flashed through his mind. Partners on a dance floor, a couple in the basket of a hot air balloon, two more-than-friends driving back roads together in an ancient blue Saab.

Ridiculous. Though his physical wounds had healed, his moods swung wildly. From elation he experienced a blast of disappointment. She was gone. He had let her go. He consoled himself with the idea that the woman had not dropped off the edge of the earth. America was within easy reach.

"Scandinavian Air has daily non-stops to New York every day," he muttered to himself out loud, then immediately realized the stupid redundancy of his words. "Daily… every day." Good lord, man, get a grip on yourself. Had her flight left yet? He should call her. Wish her a happy flight. But her phone rarely worked in Sweden.

His thoughts tumbled. With a stab of guilt he thought of his late wife,

Tove. She had warned him about the Vosses, cataloging their crimes in her work as a journalist. She died in a car crash that Hammar had always half-believed revealed the hand of the Voss family. So he harbored his own revenge, festering inside him since Tove's accident and the blurred months since. Then he discovered her files, and everything came into sharp focus, a tangled web of underhanded dealing and outright swindling of native property holders.

The Vosses. The family was deeply involved with an ongoing land grab in Norrbotten and Lappland, hijacking the birthright of the Sami, Hammar's people. Generations of the Voss clan took what they wanted with impunity, destroying anyone who got in their way. But Tove was not just anyone.

Hammar's attention was diverted by a sight in the square below his window. Two benign looking elderly people, struggling against the strong wind that had blown into the city overnight.

Sanna and Folke Dalgren.

Veronika Brand's great aunt and uncle, the hosts for the Dalgren reunion that seemed to have happened a hundred years in the past, had arrived for their scheduled debriefing.

To see them from afar made the two of them appear harmless, capable of no act of violence greater than stepping on an ant. Yet here they had arrived, a couple of prime movers—the prime movers—behind the violent events of the past weeks.

Sanna and Folke passed out of sight below. The stench of death clung to Hammar's skin. He already knew what the two elderly Dalgrens would say, how they would claim their righteousness.

Human traffickers, desecrators of the culture, figures of power and ruthlessness, didn't they all deserve the most violent ends possible?

But all the while Sanna and Folke sheltered safely at the family home in Härjedalen, Hammar himself had stepped in the blood of their victims, choked on the heavy smell of iron in his nostrils, recoiled at the sight of chopped flesh strewn throughout the death house in Djursholm. He had witnessed horrors that could never be unseen.

Hammar heard the two as they made their way down the corridor to his office, their voices light with laughter. They entered without knocking, chattering happily. Practically ebullient with their victory. Them with their clean hands.

"Sit!" Hammar welcomed them with a command, motioning to the chairs normally reserved for Hammar's clients, ready to entrust him with their darkest truths. "And yes," he said in response to the questioning looks of anticipation on their faces. "I dropped Veronika off at Arlanda Express. Her flight to New York should be taking off right about now."

"I'm a little surprised the police handed back her passport so readily," Sanna said, easing herself into one of the comfortable chairs.

"Detective Inspector Hult remains under investigation for his collusion with the Vosses," Hammar said. "An indictment is forthcoming. Which is why Veronika pretty much got off scot-free."

"Why we all did," Folke added.

"By design," Sanna said.

"Yes," the other two agreed in unison. Hammar considered he had been too easily drawn into the Dalgren's revenge scheme. His misguided belief was that it would in some way right the wrongs against Tove, born a Dalgren herself.

"We are missing someone else here, also," Folke said.

"Dear mother Elin," Sanna said. "I grieve she didn't live to see her stolen life, friends and family, avenged."

Folke nodded. "It was she who insisted we reach out to a certain American detective."

"We needed Veronika, didn't we?" Sanna asked in almost a pleading tone. "Blame me. I recruited her. I brought her to Sweden."

"Let's not talk about the woman," Hammar said.

"No, let's not," Folke said.

Sanna reached out to lay her hand on Hammar's arm. "The real mystery is how you made it off your death bed so soon."

"With enough morphine," Hammar said, "Anything is possible."

Folke smiled. "Last time we saw you, you looked like—"

"—Like Santa Claus the day after Christmas," Hammar interrupted mirthlessly. "Yes, our friend Moro Part's line."

"Now the police say Moro Part killed Loke Voss," Folke said.

"What?" Krister was surprised.

"Took the rifle away from Ylva," Sanna added, nodding. "Knocked her out and did the deed. Then she came back awake, attacked him, and they fell."

"That's ridiculous," Hammar said. "For one thing—"

Folke cut him off. "Don't you see? They want anything but a Voss killing a Voss. Anything but a granddaughter killing her grandfather, even accidentally. It's much tidier for them if the Romani godfather did it."

"In the end, revenge was dished up suitably cold," Sanna said.

"Stone cold," Folke said. "Over a half century in the deep freeze."

"The Dalgrens do not forget," Sanna said briskly. "Everyone's dead who should be. And everyone who is left alive will have a few more breaths to cherish but will die soon enough anyway."

"That's the cheerful Swedish outlook," Hammar said. He shivered inwardly.

The three again fell silent. Folke fooled with his pipe, tapping the unlit bowl in his hand. A vague sense of unease still hung in the air.

"You know, I'm sorry," Hammar said. "I know I said we shouldn't talk about her, but I can't help thinking of Veronika. I was never really comfortable keeping her in the dark."

Folke responded with a phrase in English. "What she didn't know couldn't hurt her."

"You played her like a harp," Hammar said. And me as well, he added silently to himself.

"Did we?" Sanna asked. "I was never sure. At times I believed she was playing us."

"What's done is done," Folke said. "Our Veronika left the country none the wiser."

"Which makes me challenge the idea that she really is a great detective," Sanna said. "Or even a competent one."

"Recall that I myself would not be present here if we had not involved her," Hammar said. "I'd be a frozen block of ice floating in the Hede River."

"Still, even so, I agree with Folke about the quality of her professional expertise." Sanna stared off, musing. "She didn't half know what she was doing. Pretending to hide her drug use. I feel for the poor woman. It was painful to watch her groping her way through this mess. Perhaps we should have laid out our entire strategy right from the start."

"No regrets, you two," Folke said. "We've already been through this. Our American cousin acted as an absolutely vital element in the plan, did she not? Whether she was ignorant of our strategy or not, it turned out not to matter."

"'Eyes the color of the winter sea,'" Sanna said with a bite in her tone. "I just happened across that phrase in a novel I picked up. The line made the hair on the back of my neck stand. I thought, that's her. That's Veronika. With her Voss eyes."

"Oh please, Sanna. This is not a novel. It's real, real people massacred," Hammar said.

"There's no playing the innocent now, Krister," Sanna said, her voice ice cold, her eyes hard as metal. "It's too late for that."

She was right. He was bloody whether or not he wielded the axe or pulled the trigger. He had throughout believed his motivations more pure than their second-hand hate—the dream of retribution his dead wife's family had nurtured since the dying embers of the *Nordic Light* had been extinguished.

At the sound of footfalls on the oak floor of the corridor, the three paused.

"Are you expecting anyone?" Sanna asked. She and Folke twisted around to look behind them, waiting.

For a moment, she stood in the doorway, a vision in her all-black New York clothing, hair covered by the same watch cap she had worn entering the country.

The blood drained from Hammar's face.

Veronika Brand crossed the room towards them, a set expression on her face, not giving anything away.

"I thought you put her on the express train to the airport," Sanna hissed.

"I did!" Hammar responded. He started to rise, then slumped back in his chair.

"Hello, everyone," Brand said quietly, standing over them.

They stared at her.

"Did I miss anything?" she asked.

BOOK CLUB QUESTIONS

» How are minorities like the Sami and the Roma portrayed in the book? How have the authors dealt with stereotypes and prejudice?

» How have your perceptions of the Roma changed from reading this book?

» Do you have more or less compassion for victims that are from a minority group?

» What is the role of the Sami in Swedish culture and society? How are they portrayed in this and other books?

» Aino Lehtonen has a mixed heritage but what aspect of this stands out and is this important to how she is perceived by her peers in Stockholm?

» Why does Krister care so much about the Roma?

» How does the representation of women differ from other crime thrillers? Does it reinforce or challenge gender stereotypes?

» By the end of the book, Varzha is engaged to be married. Was this an expected part of her narrative?¨

» Krister Hammar's wife, Tove, is a silent character in the book. How would her voice have influenced the storyline?

» What do Elin, Veronika and Varzha have in common?

» Loke takes out his revenge on Gustav by raping Klara. How does this objectification or ownership of women contrast to how other women are portrayed?

» What are the strategies that Varzha Luna employs to assume control of her life?

» How does the use of Swedish enhance or detract from the story telling?

» How effectively is Swedish used as a tool for reinforcing Veronika as an outsider?

» When Veronika visits her relatives in Sweden, they all speak English to her; how does that affect their relationship?

» What does Veronika's voice and her choice of words say about her character?

» Varzha captors assume she can't understand Swedish. What does this say about both her captors and migrant groups?

» Why would you take revenge for something that happened a long time ago?

» What would Elin and Klara say if they knew what happened after their deaths?

» How does Loke Voss react when he meets Veronika?

» Moro Part plays a critical role in facilitating the revenge plot, but what do you think are his true motives?

» Why are Ylva's and Malte driven to avenge perceived wrongs?

» Why does Veronika do what Krister Hammar tells her?

» Krister Hammar could tell Veronika about the cabal but doesn't. Why do you think this is?

» What do you think happened to Lel and the other trafficked girls?

» When Veronika was confronted with the crime scene in the Djursholm house, was she critical enough of Krister Hammar?

» Krister owns an old Saab that he takes care of lovingly. How do the authors use his car as a way of defining his identity?

» What role does Nordic mythology and nationalism play for the Vosses?

» When Varzha is being taken from Drottninggatan, she doesn't seem to object. Wouldn't this have made her captors suspicious?

» The book takes place mainly in two regions: the capital city of Stockholm and the desolate province of Härjedalen. How do these two regions define the characters and the story?

» What role does weather play in the book? How would the story have been different if it had been set in summer?

» Why do you think the authors chose the region of Härjedalen as the setting for their story?

» What cultural differences does Veronika encounter in Sweden?

» How are the car journeys used to understand the characters?

» Veronika expects Swedes to be tall and blond and she is surprised that the person who meets her at customs at the airport looks 'un-Swedish'. What misconceptions or stereotypes do you think the book challenges or reinforces?

» What sense do you get of Nordic culture and people from the book, in terms of looks, style, behaviour and lifestyle?

» How would Swedes describe a stereotypical American? Does Veronika live up to that idea?

» The Vosses seem to be fascinated by the holding onto a reactionary ideal of Swedish culture. Is this a trend that is relevant now or have people always thought this way?

» How do perceptions and assumptions about US culture (for example, American TV crime shows) shape the reception Veronika receives in Sweden?

» In what ways do Veronika's conflicts with Swedish police illustrate the differences in public safety officers in Sweden versus America?

Printed in Great Britain
by Amazon